Raspberry Crush

Jill Winters

NEW AMERICAN LIBRARY

New American Library
Published by New American Library, a division of
Penguin Group (USA) Inc., 375 Hudson Street,
New York, New York 10014, U.S.A.
Penguin Books Ltd, 80 Strand,
London WC2R 0RL, England
Penguin Books Australia Ltd, 250 Camberwell Road,
Camberwell, Victoria 3124, Australia
Penguin Books Canada Ltd, 10 Alcorn Avenue,
Toronto, Ontario, Canada M4V 3B2
Penguin Books (NZ), cnr Airborne and Rosedale Roads,
Albany, Auckland 1310, New Zealand

Penguin Books Ltd, Registered Offices:
80 Strand, London WC2R 0RL, England

First published by New American Library,
a division of Penguin Group (USA) Inc.

First Printing, September 2004
10 9 8 7 6 5 4 3 2 1

LIBRARY OF CONGRESS CATALOGING-IN-PUBLICATION DATA:

Winters, Jill.
Raspberry crush / Jill Winters.
p. cm.
ISBN 0-451-21214-2 (trade pbk.)

1. Triangles (Interpersonal relations)—Fiction. 2. Bakers and Bakeries—Fiction.
3. First loves—Fiction. I. Title.
PS3623.I675R37 2004
813'.6—dc22
2004009244

Set in Adobe Garamond
Designed by Erin Benach

Printed in the United States of America

To LL—a girl's best friend.

And CS—I'll always remember the sideways glance.

Acknowledgments

There are many fabulous, supportive people I would like to thank:

My editor, Laura Cifelli, who is not only sharp and intuitive, but also hysterically funny. My agents, Meg Ruley and Annelise Robey, who enthusiastically further the Plum Girl cause. My best friend, Jessica, who saved my manuscript's life—yet again. My brother, Jason, who always asks how I'm doing even though he will inevitably get a long, winding answer. My darling, mystery-savvy mom, who helped me fix the kinks in my plot. My dad, who laughs at the absurd with me and anxiously awaits *A Day in the Life of the Joneses* (but then, who *doesn't*?).

Many thanks to the former roommates of Spice Apartment, Sarah and Amy, who still crack me up, and who always read my books. Thanks to all the readers who have written me, and to *Boston College Magazine* for their wonderful feature. Thank you, Megan S., my friend of forever, a paragon of strength and sassiness, who is unfailingly genuine. And thanks to my whole family, who face my books out at the local bookstore, and who put up with me—at least half of the time.

Chapter One

Billy felt someone tug on her hair, and whipped around. "Oh, you scared me," she said on a startled breath, pressing her hand to her heart.

"Oh, sorry," Melissa said, smiling. Her cheeks were pinkish from the brisk autumn wind outside, even though her long, curly hair remained unmussed, and she already had a black coffee in hand. "What were you looking at? You looked like a zombie in headlights."

Billy grinned at her coworker, and what seemed like an exaggeration, then turned back to face Doubleday's. "Just that book," she replied, motioning through the metal gate to the new book about French Impressionism that was on display. There probably wasn't much new to say about it, but Billy was steadfastly devoted to Renoir.

She turned and fell into step with Melissa as they headed toward the escalator. "Hey, where's Des?" Billy asked, looking over her shoulder, expecting to see him trailing behind. Des was Melissa's stepbrother, who worked with them at Bella Donna Bakery. They were all expected at today's early-morning meeting, which would focus mostly on last-minute details for the jubilee the bakery was catering that weekend.

Rolling her eyes, Melissa said, "We took the train in together, but when he stopped to bond with a homeless guy, I felt it was time to ditch him." Billy grinned and thought that sounded about right. From what she could tell, Melissa and Des Aggerdeen shared a T ride to work, a last name, and an address—now that Melissa had moved home to attend law school—but that was it. There didn't seem to be much love lost between them, probably because they were vastly different people. While Melissa was a smart, ambitious law student with somewhat elitist sensibilities, Des was a pseudophilosophical student in the proverbial school of life. A self-proclaimed poet, musician, and ar*teest*, he was obsessed with reaching out to the common man (even though he was one himself—and whether or not the common man liked it).

Des and Melissa didn't interact much at work, but when they did, it seemed clear that Des viewed his stepsister as vapid and coopted, while Melissa viewed him, simply, as lame.

Now Billy stepped off the escalator and headed to the crowded enclosed bridge that stretched over Huntington Avenue. It connected the Prudential and Copley malls, and at this early hour it was clogged with professionals who were shortcutting their way to work. Billy ducked and swerved as best she could, but for the most part got squished. It was almost laughable the way men—especially those in their twenties—blatantly elbowed people to get ahead, showing no concept of even low-grade chivalry.

Just then Billy noticed that Melissa was no longer at her side. She'd flown several feet ahead, moving through the crowd with Darwinian determination. Occasionally Billy was struck by how confident and assertive Melissa had become since college.

They'd met freshman year at BC, where they'd both started out as business majors. By sophomore year, Billy had changed her major to art history, and Melissa had changed hers to poli-sci, but they'd often crossed paths on campus. Back then Melissa had been brooding, maybe a little antisocial—one of those girls who dressed in black and had a poster of Fox Mulder on her dorm room door.

Now she still wore black, but it was part of the sleek-chic look that she'd adopted during her postgraduation life in New York City.

Billy, on the other hand, figured she looked pretty much the same since college, not counting the twenty pounds she'd gained—seven of which she'd packed on since she'd started working at the bakery. She tried not to dwell on it, even though on a five-foot-two-inch body, it definitely showed.

And not counting her hair, which had gone from brown to dark cherry red. Technically it was an accident, but Billy had grown to like it. She'd used "Cinnamon Sunset," which was supposed to be subtle, but instead changed her hair to a pretty, crimsony color that never seemed to wash out.

"So did I tell you the news?" Melissa said, glancing over and abruptly realizing Billy had fallen behind. "Hey, where'd you go?"

"Wait," Billy called with a laugh, and hurried forward.

"Watch it," someone snapped when Billy accidentally stepped on his heel.

"Oh, sorry!" She ducked between two middle-aged men carrying briefcases, just as Melissa reached back to grab her hand and pull her up. A laugh slipped out of her as she was facilitated forward.

"You need better survival skills," Melissa said, smiling. "You'd never make it in New York."

Billy doubted that was true. She'd make it in New York; she just might not make it on time. "So check this out," Melissa said when they reached the other side and stepped into the airy vestibule of the Copley Mall. "Donna promoted me to assistant manager last night; it's official."

"That's awesome, congratulations!" Billy said brightly, though she wasn't the least bit surprised. Melissa had been working at the bakery for nearly a year, juggling the job with her hectic class schedule, and it was obvious that their boss, Donna, considered her quite an asset.

The deeper they walked into the mall, the more serenely peaceful it felt. Most stores didn't open for another hour, so there were only a few people milling around as soft piano music played overhead and golden October sunshine poured down through the skylights. Billy had worked at Bella Donna Bakery for only a couple of months, but she could feel herself settling into the routine already, while her life as a well-paid Web designer evaporated into memories.

It was hard to believe it had been only six months since she'd lost her job at Net Circle, a Web marketing and development company in downtown Boston. Six months since her boss had looked pointedly into her eyes and said, "The bad news is, you're fired— the good news is, it's nothing personal." The company had been going under, about to declare bankruptcy, and Billy had been naïvely shocked to discover it.

She'd been even more naïvely shocked to learn firsthand how bad the job market was. In fact, if she hadn't run into Melissa last summer, she wouldn't be working at Bella Donna now, which was turning out to be an uplifting transitional place until she found her next "real job." Not that she was in a rush; she still had money saved, and it seemed the farther away she got from corporate America, the more she put off returning to it. Plus, ever since Tia had quit, Billy had taken over as Bella Donna's cake decorator, which worked out perfectly. Although she still dealt with customers and cleanup, for the most part she worked in the back, combining two of her great passions in life—art and cake.

"When does your promotion start?" Billy asked now as she and Melissa stepped onto the escalator.

"Today," Melissa replied, leaning against the rail. "So I guess you'd better be nice to me," she added wryly as she lifted her coffee cup to her mouth. "I'm your boss now."

The escalator rolled up, taking them to the second floor.

"I'm gonna grab the paper," Melissa said, veering off toward the newsstand.

"Okay, see you in a second," Billy said, and walked into the bakery, where Katie Spiegal and her grandmother, Mrs. Tailor, were sitting at one of the square wooden tables, helping themselves to the spread of pastries that Georgette had baked for the meeting. Katie was a full-time employee at Bella Donna, while her grandma occasionally filled in and helped out at catered events.

"Hi, guys," Billy said, smiling as she shrugged off her battered, green velvet coat and walked behind the counter.

"Hey, what's up?" Katie said with her usual bubbly friendliness.

"Billy, that coat doesn't look warm enough," Mrs. Tailor said, her voice tinged with nurturing concern.

"Don't worry; I'm fine," Billy assured her, though in truth her coat probably wasn't warm enough. But she didn't wear it for practical reasons or for the look. She supposed she wore it for sentimental reasons, because she still associated it with the time in her life, over four years ago, when she'd first gotten it. Strange as it might seem, the soft, worn jacket felt imbued with the misty, insulating ambiance of those days gone by.

"Please have a cinnamon roll before I eat them all," Katie said, and flipped her head over to pull some wavy blond hair into a bun.

"Um, I think the twelve I had yesterday met my weekly quota," Billy replied as she hung her coat on the brass rack in the corner and punched in. Georgette's cinnamon rolls were one of the bakery's claims to fame. Rather than being big and soft, they were small and crunchy, exploding with brown-sugar crust and maple-syrup glaze.

Just then Georgette emerged from the kitchen. She wiped her hands on her apron, already chewing heartily on something. "Hi, Georgette," Billy said, and grabbed a clean apron off the wall. Still chewing, Georgette nodded a greeting as she crossed the room, then plopped down beside Katie and reached for a powdered cruller.

Meanwhile, Billy paused momentarily to appreciate the homey, inviting warmth of the bakery. It was a cozy, elegant little shop with soft lighting, shiny hardwood floors, and polished oak countertops. There were small square tables around the room, and an antique chandelier that hung from the ceiling.

As Billy approached the table, she tied her apron strings into a bow, careful not to cinch them too tight around her stomach—a.k.a. "the beast"—because the beast needed breathing room.

"When's Donna gettin' started with this meeting already?" Georgette asked, licking powdered sugar from her fingers, then drying them on her apron. "I've gotta lotta baking to get to." With one hand she fluffed up her white pompadour, and with the other she adjusted her clunky, old-fashioned glasses. The large, octagonal lenses were lightly tinted pink, making Georgette's blue eyes appear almost violet.

Billy had some unfinished cakes to get to herself, but she figured today's meeting would be a quick one. Donna would just be going over some last-minute details for the Dessert Jubilee that the bakery was catering that weekend. Apparently the jubilee was an annual event in the small coastal town of Churchill, Massachusetts—which, coincidentally, was the hometown of Billy's ex-boyfriend, Seth.

Seth Lannigan . . . the one that got away.

They'd dated for only a few months, four years ago, but whenever Billy thought of Churchill, she still thought back to crackling nights on the beach—of Seth hugging her, running his mouth down her neck, and whispering to her about the future. The irony of that needed little comment (yet why not give one anyway?).

Billy sat down at the table and reached for the pot of coffee in the center. After she filled a cup, she snagged a pistachio muffin off the pastry platter. "These things are killing my diet," she remarked.

"I didn't know you were on a diet," Katie said.

Billy smirked. "Yeah, I have the same problem."

"You don't need a diet, anyway; you look perfect the way you are."

Coming from Katie, Billy almost believed it, because Katie just had that effect. She was one of those sparkling girls people gravitated toward—someone who uplifted everything around her. She had a freckled face, tanned from a recent trip to Cancún, and a skinny little body that looked like a bag of bones, but was somehow adorable. Her grandmother, Mrs. Tailor, was wizened but just as tiny and cute, with watery green eyes and deep wrinkles across her face. Katie had moved in with her a couple of years ago, because she hadn't wanted to leave Boston when her parents had relocated.

Recently Katie had broken up with her boyfriend, but Billy figured her single status wouldn't last long. Unlike herself, who always took forever to find someone new. Then again . . . she could hardly complain when, after a recent bout of *forever*, she'd found Mark Warner. Handsome, charming, and—most important—interested, Mark was a distribution rep who used to come into the bakery on business, and six weeks ago he'd asked Billy out. Although they weren't officially exclusive yet, they seemed to be heading in that direction.

"Hell-*o*," Melissa sang out as she entered the store with a *Boston Globe* folded underneath her arm. Billy, Katie, and Mrs. Tailor said hi, while Georgette grumbled something under her breath and reached for another pastry.

Melissa's designer heels *click-clack*ed loudly as she walked briskly into the back, and once she was out of earshot, Georgette remarked, "Oh, goody—the *prin*cess is here."

Billy reserved comment, because the tension between Georgette and Melissa was common knowledge—and pretty hard to miss. Basically Melissa thought little of telling people what to do, and Georgette didn't take well to orders. But Billy suspected it went beyond that. She had the distinct feeling that Georgette, who'd been a high school cafeteria lady for years before becoming a baker, defensively resented Melissa's general air of superiority.

"Hey, did anyone see *The Bachelor* last night?" Katie asked.

"No, I missed it," Billy said, tearing a Sweet 'n Low over her coffee. She neglected to add that she'd missed it on purpose. *The Bachelor* was a reality-TV show in which good-looking women all vied for one man—usually a phony pretty boy with a tediously bland personality.

"I saw it," Georgette said, and snorted. "I'll tell ya, no man would ever lead me around by the nose like that." She tore off a hunk of scone with her teeth, then added bitterly, "No man'll ever treat me like dirt again."

As always, it was an effort to segue to her "asshole ex," Gary. The two had lived together for nearly twenty years. They'd had a son together, though they'd never gotten married, and obviously Georgette still harbored resentment that Gary had left her and married another woman. But on the upside, being dumped had been the impetus for a fresh start. She'd quit cafeteria work to pursue her love of baking, and even without formal training, her skills in the kitchen had dazzled Donna and landed Georgette a job.

And despite how much she hated Gary, Georgette still loved *men*. In fact, they were practically all she talked about. Unlike Billy's sister, Corryn, who'd pretty much shunned the opposite sex since her divorce, Georgette was constantly on the prowl, claiming that fifty-two was her true sexual peak, and describing in detail how much she longed for a young stud to ease the tension.

Just then Des Aggerdeen came trotting in, his shaggy hair flopped over his face and his guitar slung over his shoulder. "Hey," he said, smiling at Billy with sleepy eyes.

"Hi, what's up?"

"Man, I so don't feel like being here today." Des groaned as he folded his lanky body into the chair beside her. "The band was practicing late last night, and now I just wanna crash." Another irony about Des: He had a "Kill Your Television" sticker on his guitar case, and a vocal disdain for pop culture in general, even though his grunge-rock band, the Sophists, exemplified exactly that.

"You should come see us play sometime," he said, looking at Billy. "It would be awesome to have someone in the crowd who totally feels the struggle." She suppressed a grin; she had a feeling "crowd" might be stretching it. But it was endearing the way Des took a special liking to her. Convinced they shared some kind of artistic connection, Des often referred to Billy and himself as "creative vessels." Of course, it embarrassed her a little, too, because she wasn't in the habit of elevating herself like that—especially not out loud.

"When is this damn meeting gettin' going already," Georgette groused for the second time, and reached for a chocolate croissant.

"Bureaucratic bullshit," Des remarked, again looking at Billy. "Sometimes I just want to hop in an old 'sixty-nine Chevy—just the shirt on my back—and head for the coast. Just ride the wind, you know?"

"Oh, Des, give it up," Melissa called out as she returned from the back. She carried a fresh coffee in a pink cup with *Bella Donna* scrawled across it in black cursive, and the notebook Donna always used to conduct the morning meetings. "Okay, this will be a quick one," Melissa said as she set her stuff down.

"What do you mean?" Georgette interrupted. "Where's Donna?"

"Actually, I'm running the morning meetings now," Melissa explained. "I've been promoted to assistant manager." She paused to sip from her cup, ignoring the luscious array of pastries right below her, which she always did. In fact, Billy rarely saw her ingest anything other than black coffee.

There were varied reactions to the news of Melissa's promotion: Katie smiled and said, "Congrats"; Des nodded, his expression blank; and Georgette bugged out her eyes, flared her nostrils, and balled up her fists until her knuckles turned white.

While everyone went over last-minute details for the upcoming jubilee, Billy ate the rest of her muffin, not sure why she'd bothered to cut it in half in the first place. Then Melissa asked her how the sheet cakes were coming, and Billy exaggerated, saying that everything was right on schedule. In addition to the extensive dessert menu, Churchill's Jubilee Planning Committee, which had hired Bella Donna for the event, wanted three sixty-inch sheet cakes presented at the end of the night. Billy was decorating each with a waterfront theme, using some Churchill postcards as a guide. Unfortunately she was still behind on her work, because when it came to drawing, crippling perfectionism sometimes slowed her down.

"And, everyone, remember to wash and iron your uniform for this weekend," Melissa added, referring to the catering outfit, which was just a twist on the old penguin suit: white shirt, black pants, and a dorky pink bow tie. "Okay, does that wrap up jubilee business?"

Des raised his hand. "I just want to go on record that even though I'm working at this thing, I totally don't respect these elaborate spectacles of obscene self-indulgence. It's like nobody keeps it *honest* anymore, you know?" He slid his gaze to Billy, and did a fist pump to his chest on the word "honest."

Agreeably, Billy nodded, while Melissa rolled her eyes. "Annnyway . . . I guess the only thing left to go over are some upcoming changes to our daily menu." Georgette straightened in her chair, on alert—or maybe on attack—as Melissa explained, "Donna and I were thinking that we should make Bella Donna's menu a little hotter, a little trendier. You know, more like something you'd see in New York."

Curling her powdered-sugared lips, Georgette bared her teeth and asked why.

"Obviously it'll draw in a lot more business," Melissa explained with a shrug. "And we'll attract more of the lunchtime crowd if we add some interesting sandwiches." Georgette sighed and fidgeted loudly in her chair, until finally Melissa said, "Do you have a problem with that, Georgette?"

"Yeah," she replied haughtily. "I don't see why we gotta keep changin' stuff. Things seem fine the way they are, if ya ask me."

"Mmm-hmm, well, let's just try it my way, okay?" Melissa said, smiling almost saccharinely at her. Then she addressed everyone. "Starting today, I'm putting up a sandwich suggestion box. Customers can drop in requests for items they'd like to see on our menu, and then Donna and I will go through them and choose which ones sound good." Billy reserved comment; surely Melissa hadn't *intended* it as a power play, but that didn't mean Georgette wouldn't blow up.

After a few final points, the meeting faded to a close. Mrs. Tailor left, because she'd come in only for the meeting, and Melissa headed to the back to return Donna's notebook. As she went, Georgette muttered something under her breath—something along the lines of "Eat shit." Very luckily, Melissa didn't hear.

Billy started straightening the tables and chairs, getting ready to open the store, and Katie said, "I'll put on some music."

"Oh, damn," Des said, hitting his hand on his thigh, "I forgot to bring in my band's new demo CD."

"Yeah, *darn*," Georgette said sarcastically as she swiped up one last Danish and stuck it in her front apron pocket.

Billy suppressed a grin, and Katie asked, "Musical requests, anyone?"

Georgette grumbled, "How about 'Back on the Chain Gang,'" and stomped into the back.

Chapter Two

Seth turned the lock to his mother's house and shoved the heavy front door open with his shoulder. Once he hauled his bags inside, he dropped them on the floor, and immediately felt overwhelmed by the familiar feeling of home.

It was the spacious beach house he'd grown up in, right on the Massachusetts coast. How long had it been since he'd been home? He'd flown back for Christmas two years ago, but he'd been able to stay only the day, and then had to fly right back.

Now he was back to fix up the house and put it up for sale. It was a favor to his mom, who was staying in Dublin longer than she'd planned, taking care of her older sister, Melanie. Seth's dad had died ten years earlier, and his older brother, Ian, lived in Alaska with his wife, so Seth was the only one who could come, but honestly, he was grateful for the excuse to take a few weeks off. Owning a consulting firm took up most of his time and attention and, in fact, most of his life.

Seth walked through the foyer, feeling the emptiness of the house, but it had a different kind of quality than the emptiness of his studio apartment in Seattle. It was peaceful and calm. He could feel the golden insulation of autumn and faintly hear the shifting waves of the ocean that stretched behind the house.

He followed the hallway to the airy, Spanish-style kitchen, which was flooded with light from the bay window and the sliding glass doors that led to the back deck. Sighing, he walked closer to the window and looked past the backyard and out to the water. It didn't take long for the tranquillity to get to him, making him feel almost antsy—like he needed to do something productive. Maybe he could call Lucas, his VP, to see how things were going at the office. But he really didn't feel like doing it. He knew Lucas could handle whatever came up; he loved the company almost as much as Seth did. Besides, Seth hadn't taken a real vacation in two years, and if he called the office now, it would be like admitting defeat.

His mother had mentioned some repairs on the house that she wanted done; he supposed he could start on those, but he wasn't that motivated. Yet he couldn't just relax and do *nothing* . . . could he?

The doorbell rang.

Seth crossed back through the hall, swung the door open, and found his mom's best friend, Sally Sugarton, standing on the other side. A smile broke across his face. "Hi! How are you?" he asked, reaching out to hug her. Sally was a petite woman around sixty, with silvery blond hair, elegant gold-rimmed glasses, and a penchant for pantsuits. There was something about her that always reminded him of his mom, and right now he supposed that made her feel closer than Dublin. Because Seth was six-two, he had to bend a little as he embraced Sally's delicate frame tightly but tenderly.

"Oh, your mom told me you'd be here. It's so wonderful to see you!" she said excitedly. Pulling back, she clapped her hands, which were slim, manicured, and still weighted down by an emerald bauble that Seth could trace back to his childhood. "You know, she is so proud of you. Of course, it's nice to know you haven't forgotten little old us. Now let me look at you," she said, and gave him a quick once-over. "Clean shaven, handsome, still blond, no gray yet."

"I'm only thirty-one," he said with a laugh . . . though he supposed it wasn't inconceivable that work stress might give him gray before his time.

"So how long will you be in town?" she asked, leading the way down the hall and hooking the first right into the family room. Seth followed, but didn't bother trying to keep up with Sally, who flitted almost as fast as she talked.

"I'm not sure how long," he said. "There's some fixing up I want to do here—"

"Oh, good, the cleaning woman's been doing a good job," Sally said, inspecting the coffee table for dust. Next she crossed the room and checked the mantel of the heavy stone fireplace. "I was afraid that with the messy divorce Susannah's been going through, she might be slacking off on the job. Especially after her husband's private investigator snapped photos of her and Jay Millis carrying on behind the *fromagerie*."

Screwing up his face, Seth asked, "How do you know all this?"

"What do you mean?" Sally said, confused.

"Skip it," he said, grinning. Of course she knew; Sally had always fallen somewhere between social butterfly and prying buttinsky.

"But anyway, about your visit . . ." she said. "It's so nice how reliable you are, Seth. I mean, how many people do you know that you can truly count on when you need a favor? How many men are so solid and dependable? How many truly understand that helping others is what it's all about?"

"I take it you want something," Seth said.

"Well . . ."

"What is it?"

"I've overextended myself," she blurted, "and now I need to beg you for a favor!" That was another thing about Sally: When she wasn't getting into everyone's business, she was heading fifty different committees. Suddenly it was all coming back to him. "You know the annual Dessert Jubilee?" she asked.

"Oh, right," Seth said, recalling the founder's-day event held in the town square every October.

"Well, I'm in charge of it this year, just like the last two years in a row—but of course, you wouldn't know about that, unless your mother told you—but anyway, I scheduled a meeting with the caterer this afternoon, forgetting that I'm already committed to the Boston Ladies' Society. But unfortunately I can't move things around, because the rest of the afternoon I'm hosting a variety show at the country club."

Crossing his arms over his chest, Seth waited for the favor to drop.

"Oh, could you be a prince and meet with the caterer for me?" Sally asked finally. "You just have to go over some last-minute preferences that the planning committee voted on yesterday, and review the official invoice."

After a pause, he nodded. "Sure, okay." It sounded pretty tedious, but at least it was something to do.

"Thank you, thank you!" Sally chirped, clapping her hands together. "And we can ride into the city together. We'll take my car."

"Let me just put my stuff upstairs and we'll go," Seth said.

He took the spiral steps by the kitchen to the upstairs hall, and once he set foot inside his old bedroom, a surreal kind of nostalgia took hold of his senses. This space had been *his*, and everything looked exactly the same, only barer than he'd remembered.

The room itself was minimally decorated—a gray-and-black comforter on the bed, a desk, and a computer. Seth had moved out when he went to college then gotten an apartment in the city, but his mother had kept the room his, because he'd still visited often.

In the corner was the black leather recliner he used to sit in to read, and an end table stacked with books. He walked over, curious what he'd been reading the last time he was home, but as he picked the first book up, its title was lost as Seth's attention was immediately diverted by a photograph that slipped out from between the pages.

As he studied the picture his chest tightened, as if something were clutching his heart and slowly squeezing. Smiling wistfully, he expelled a breath and sank into the recliner. His ex-girlfriend, Billy Cabot, was hugging him right outside this very house. Jesus Christ—*Billy*.

It'd been a long time since he'd thought of her, but apparently his recollection was as sharp as ever. Passionate, sincere, pretty, and sensitive. They'd been going out only a few months when Seth had landed a job with Mackland Associates, the largest consulting firm in the Northwest. He'd sent his résumé in before he'd even met Billy, but when Mackland called, there was no way he could walk away from that opportunity. It had been his dream job. Part one of his dream, anyway. Part two was owning his own consulting firm, which he never could've done, at least not so successfully, without the vital contacts he'd made working for Mackland.

Still, as he looked at Billy's picture—at her bright, open smile, her energy, her warmth—Seth's heart sank a little. It seemed that even when life was going right, something still had to be wrong. A huge career opportunity, in exchange for this girl he'd left behind. Maybe there could've been something there; the little dating he'd had time for in the past couple years hadn't made nearly the same impression on him. (Jesus, what would his ex-girlfriend, Laura, think if she heard *that*?)

Now Seth ran his fingers lightly along the photo, taking in the image of Billy—her shiny dark hair, pale blue eyes, and the curve of her full, ripe mouth. He tried to remember the day the picture had been taken, but he couldn't. He was holding her soft, cuddly body against him, and she had her face tilted up, not even looking at the camera. It could've been any day.

He wondered what she was doing now . . . wondered if she was happy, wondered if she was still the funny little Catholic virgin she'd been back then.

What would've happened if he'd had the balls to ask her to come with him four years ago—something that would've been absolutely crazy to do? They hadn't known each other nearly enough for a step like that, and with the amount of daily hours Seth had worked at Mackland, Billy probably would've dumped him and moved home in a matter of weeks.

Still, he wondered . . .

"Seth!" Sally called from downstairs, snapping him out of his reverie. "Are you ready?"

"Coming," he replied, and set the picture back where it'd been for the past four years.

As he met Sally in the foyer, at the foot of the main stairs, she said, "Isn't it nice to be home?" *Home* . . . It sounded strange to think in those terms, since he lived on the other side of the country. But Seth supposed Massachusetts would always be an important part of him—even if he'd left an important part behind.

"Did you forget you have a mother?"

"Hey, Mom," Billy said, resting her cell phone in the crook of her neck. She leaned down to kiss her dog, Pike Bishop, good-bye, then snatched her battered green coat off the sofa. "When did you and Dad get back?"

"Last night," Adrienne replied. "We had a *wonderful* time."

"Really? That's *great*," Billy said, a little surprised her mother didn't have something to critique.

After locking up her apartment, she descended the brownstone steps two at a time. She didn't normally come home on her lunch break, but she'd wanted to check on Pike, who now lay sleepily in his dog bed. Last week there had been an *incident* with the first-floor tenant, Lady McAvit, who'd accidentally left the door to her greenhouse open. Pike Bishop had meandered inside and eaten several of her precious heirloom tomatoes, and she'd been harboring an icy grudge ever since.

The thing was, normally Pike was an excellently behaved black Labrador. Billy had gotten him about a year ago, after an unusual rash of burglaries in her upscale Brookline neighborhood. Living alone she'd felt vulnerable, and since her landlord allowed pets, she'd gone to the pound and immediately fallen in love with Pike. At the time he'd been sad-looking, shaky, and shivery—not exactly guard-dog material, but Billy had suspected that his former owner had abused him, and she just knew she had to take him home. To take care of him. If she took him home, they could take care of each other.

She could always count on Pike to use the doggie door in the kitchen that led to the back stairwell, and the second doggie door at the bottom of the back stairs. Behind the brownstone was an enclosed yard where he could play. Normally it was a very efficient system, and normally Lady McAvit's greenhouse was locked up tight.

Of course, it wasn't right for Pike to eat her tomatoes, but Billy had tried several times to apologize. She'd even sent a big basket of fruit, but to no avail. Lady McAvit was still giving her the deep freeze. They'd passed each other on the sidewalk this morning when she was picking up her paper; Billy had said hello and gotten a sneer in return.

Oh, well. Some people took longer to heal—Billy figured her sour-faced neighbor would eventually come around.

"Billy? Are you there? Belinda? *Hello?*"

"I'm here, Mom, I'm here," Billy said quickly as the front door of the brownstone thudded closed behind her, and she stepped out into the crisp October air. "Sorry, Mom, I'm just trying to catch the train. What were you saying?"

"I was telling you about the cruise."

"Oh, right. Go on," Billy said, but wasn't totally listening again because she was busy hurrying down her hill, and she rounded the bend onto Beacon Street just as a green-and-white train came clunking into view. Shoot, if she didn't catch this T, she'd have to wait five minutes for the next, and as it was, she was already going to be late getting back to the bakery.

"Well, after we boarded the ship, we found our cabin," her mother was saying. "Then we put our luggage away. Of course, your father always claims I bring too much. . . ."

Billy darted haphazardly across the street, navigating around the oncoming traffic, and hopped up onto the platform just as the T driver was closing the doors. "Wait, oh, wait, please!" she pleaded, looking desperately through the glass. She didn't honestly expect any pity, though, since T drivers almost never reopened the doors, and seemed to enjoy shutting them prematurely anyway.

But to her shock he pulled the lever and let her onto the train. "Come on, come on," he grumbled, motioning impatiently with big hair-covered hands.

"Oh, thank you!" Billy groveled, and hopped up the steps. She dropped down into the first available seat.

"Hello? Billy, are you *there*? *Belinda*?"

"Sorry, sorry, I'm here, Mom," she said with a giggle, because this one-sided conversation with her mom was getting ridiculous.

"Well, what are you doing? What's going on?" her mother asked, sounding somewhere between confounded and panicked.

She explained about the train and apologized—again.

Adrienne said a few more things about the cruise, and then said she'd fill her in more in person. "How's Friday night? You and your sister can come over for a healthy dinner."

"Sure. I don't know about Corryn, but I can come. But, um, don't cook on my account."

"Oh, it's no trouble."

"No, *really,* let's just order a pizza or something."

"A *pizza?*" Adrienne echoed, sounding horrified. "A pizza is nothing but a soggy, artery-clogging disk of saturated fat."

"Like I said, how about a pizza?"

"Don't be smart. You know I don't eat like that anymore."

True—a few months ago Billy's mom had gotten on one of those annoying health kicks in which the bettered party couldn't feel bettered unless she took everyone else with her. Apparently a persuasive segment of *Dr. Phil* had given Adrienne the motivation to change her lifestyle. Of course, Billy wanted her parents to be as healthy as possible—hey, she hoped they outlived *her*—but Adrienne seemed incapable of having any kind of epiphany without projecting it onto others, volcano style.

"Well, come on, give me updates," Adrienne said now.

"Updates on what?"

"On your life. I've been gone for two whole weeks. Surely there must be *something* new," she insisted—quite erroneously.

"There's really not much to tell," Billy said.

"Well, have you found another job yet?"

"No."

"Have you even looked?"

"I've looked," Billy said, with the implied understanding that "looked" was a fairly broad term. She was going to look; she *intended* to look. "Things have just been really busy at the bakery, especially with the Dessert Jubilee coming up this weekend—"

"Not even any good *leads?*" Adrienne persisted. "How many résumés have you sent out this week?"

"Mom, I hope you didn't call to nag me," Billy said, cutting her off at the pass.

"Fine, I won't nag. Just tell me how many résumés you've sent out since you lost your job at Net Circle, and exactly when you plan to have a new job."

What was this, a police investigation? And when had her mother become the career counselor from hell?

"Look, if something new breaks, I'll let you know," Billy said.

"Fine," Adrienne sighed, frustrated, "but you're a Phi Beta Kappa college graduate; you shouldn't be working in a bakery."

"Let's move on . . ." Billy warned, wondering exactly how many ways her mother could work "Phi Beta Kappa" into a conversation.

"Fine, fine. So has Corryn met anyone yet?"

"No, I don't think so," Billy replied nonchalantly, even though her mind was saying, *Puh-lease.* Their mother was truly in denial if she thought Corryn was over the anti-men sentiment that was the bitter remainder of her divorce. In fact, the only date she'd been on since Kane had left—compliments of her mother's astute matchmaking—was a disastrous setup with a surgeon who turned out to be gay.

"Nobody? Not one date?" Adrienne asked, sounding pained.

"Mom, she'll date when she's ready."

"Well, these are some pretty awful updates. At least tell me something about Mark. How are things going with you two?"

"Good," Billy said, leaning her head on the T window, feeling the corners of her mouth angle up, happy to have a boyfriendesque figure in her life to say was doing well.

"Why don't you bring him over to the house on Friday night? He never comes over here. Doesn't he like us?"

"He's working late on Friday, I think. I'm supposed to see him tomorrow night." Billy wished she could see Mark more often, but because of his recent promotion he had a lot more on-site visits to stores all over Massachusetts and parts of Rhode Island. That left him little time on the weeknights to plan dates with Billy—and Billy was very sorry, but she was not scheduling those dates around her mother.

"So has he talked about the future?" Adrienne asked.

"We've only been dating six weeks!" Billy said with an exasperated laugh. "If he talked about the future, I'd be suspicious." As it was, Mark Warner was almost too good to be true: He was tall, dark, and classically handsome, not to mention charming and exceptionally outgoing. In fact, the only thing that wasn't completely jelling was the passion factor, but Billy figured it would get better over time.

"Have you found out what he makes yet?"

Billy rolled her eyes. "Mom, why do you bother asking that? I keep telling you, I don't know what he makes, and I wouldn't ask him anyway, because then it looks like I care, and I don't."

"So tell him you're asking for me."

"Much better—listen, Mom, we're about to go underground," Billy said as the train jerked to a stop at St. Mary's Street. "I'm gonna lose you in a sec, but I'll call you later, okay?"

"Wait—maybe Mark has a friend for Corryn? An older brother?"

Right. Billy could just see Corryn being one of those brother-sister-duo couples. Although the friend thing was an inevitable possibility, because Mark had more friends and acquaintances than anyone Billy had ever met. *Too* many, actually, but that was neither here nor there in terms of Corryn, who refused to be set up anymore. "I don't think so," she said.

"A cousin?"

"Lay off Corryn. What's the rush in finding her someone?"

"I just don't want her to end up like Aunt Penelope," Adrienne said, descending into an all-too-familiar lament about her unmarried older sister. Luckily, the train was sloping toward the underground tunnel.

"Gotta go, Mom."

"Okay, we'll finish this conversation on Friday night."

What conversation? Billy felt like asking, but she didn't get the chance, because her phone blitzed out as soon as she hit the dark.

As she settled back in her seat, she noticed that the disheveled guy sitting in front of her had turned around and was staring. She kept her gaze fixed on the window, on blackness rushing past, hoping he would get bored and turn back around. Instead, he spoke to her: "What's your name?" She pretended not to hear. "What's your name?" he said again.

She flashed him a quick, closemouthed smile and ignored the question.

"What's your name?"

"Uh, Billy," she replied, still looking out the window, hoping that would pacify him. Hoping, but not truly believing.

"Billy, do you love me?" he asked loudly. When she didn't respond, he leaned closer, covered his ears with his hands, and burst into song: "La-la-la-*laa*!" Just then the train jerked to a stop at Copley, and Billy hopped off.

Once she hit the sidewalk, she shook her head, laughing to herself, as she pulled her hair into a ponytail and crossed the street at the same time. She could deal with crazy people on the T—she could also deal with drunk people—but she hated when they singled her out.

Chapter Three

Seth cringed as he drove down I-95 with Sally's sports car shaking and sputtering, and Sally looking oblivious in the passenger's seat. "Jesus, when's the last time you changed the oil in this thing?" he asked.

"Oil?" Sally repeated vacantly, and studied Seth's Palm Pilot. "I really need to get one of these. Then I'd be able to keep track of all my social obligations."

Seth doubted that was possible, but it definitely might help. The car jerked, and Seth gently applied pressure on the brakes until it steadied. "What is *up* with this car?"

"Oh, don't worry; it always does that," Sally said with a wave of her hand. Just then the car jittered, vaguely like a moth's body in a porch light. "See, it's just a little nothing."

Seth shot her a sideways look. "Then why are your glasses crooked?"

She brought a hand up to straighten them on her face, and moved from mundane topics like her sputtering car to more fascinating, worldly subjects like Tara Brent's upcoming wedding, the new eggless quiche at Marie's Café, and the recent acquiring of the Churchill Art Gallery by local eccentric Greg Dappaport. "And I suppose you heard about that new man in town, Ted Schneider?"

Seth said no.

"Oh, he's just terrible! He moved to Churchill a couple of

months ago. Lives on his boat—some hideous old contraption he keeps docked in the marina. Nobody even knows *why* he moved to Churchill, or what he does for a living." Scoffing, she added, "If you ask me, the man is just crusty and ill-bred."

"Well, maybe he just likes to keep to himself," Seth said with a shrug.

"No, keeping to yourself is one thing. Hostility and evasiveness about your past is another."

"Well, maybe he had a tough childhood," Seth suggested absently as he looked for his exit off the Mass Pike.

"Tough childhood? He's sixty!" Sally exclaimed, and shook her head. "Now people are worried that he's going to do something to ruin the Dessert Jubilee this weekend. Oh, and I suppose you heard about what he did to Archie Winston?"

"No, I must've missed that," Seth replied, suppressing a laugh. Christ, how would he hear? Sally seemed to think the *Churchill Gazette* was a national paper.

"Well, first let me say that nobody respects a person's right to privacy more than I do"—Seth reserved comment, because he was pretty sure laughing in Sally's face would be rude—"but really, when you come to a small town you have to expect that people will want to get to know you. From what I hear, this Ted Schneider flat-out ignores people who try to talk to him. And his rusty old boat is a complete eyesore, Seth—"

"About Archie?" Seth pressed, trying to get her back on task.

"Oh, well, one morning Archie went down to the water, innocently asked Mr. Schneider about his lineage, and the man practically took his *head* off."

"Wait, if you don't know his lineage, then how do you know he's 'ill-bred'?" Seth asked wryly, slanting his gaze to Sally's.

"Something in the eyes."

As Seth drove, the familiarity of Boston's Back Bay struck him.

It had really been too long since he'd been here. There was something innately welcoming about Boston—the old stone architec-
ture, the vibrantly green parks, the clean openness, and the quaint
historic charm of the city. He remembered how much Billy loved
the little white lights that lit up the trees on Boylston Street all
year round. But then, Billy had decorated her own apartment with
strings of lights—both white and colored—always huffily refuting
anyone who claimed they were solely for Christmastime. Seth smiled
to himself, remembering Billy and those cute bursts of huffiness
that always passed quickly.

Now he looked for a parking spot near Copley Square, doubting very much that he'd find one, while Sally moved on to an even
less enthralling topic than local gossip. "So, Seth . . . how's your love
life? Any special ladies I should know about?" He could feel her eyes
on him now, studying him, waiting intently for his response. He
supposed Sally had a surrogate mother–type of interest in seeing
him "settle down."

"No, not really," he replied. "I haven't had much time for a personal life."

"What do you mean? Oh, don't tell me you've turned into one
of those workaholic types? Seth, your mother wouldn't like that,
not that she's not proud of you, of course she is, of course we
all are, but still. Work isn't everything." Yeah, he'd begun to realize that over the last several months of work and little else. In
fact, in the back of his mind he feared that if he didn't break the
cycle, he might never find something more meaningful—something
better.

But he kept it to himself.

"What about love?" Sally pressed. "What about a wife? What
about a family, a special person who will make your life more
complete?"

"I've only been back in town for two hours," he interrupted, because he didn't want to think about the things that were missing. "Maybe you could wait a few days, and then *ease* into reevaluating my whole life."

"Well, you're a very handsome boy, Seth. Tall, blond, handsome, smart, successful, sweet, responsible—"

"Okay, okay," he said, cutting her off gently, because he felt a little embarrassed by the over-the-top compliments.

"Well, I'm just saying you don't want to waste that. There are plenty of women who'd love to sink their hooks into you and latch on for dear life."

"Sounds appealing."

He spotted a parking space, and, cutting the wheel sharply, he slid backward into the spot. Meanwhile, Sally finally got to what she'd been dancing around. "Just thinking off the top of my head here," she said, "but have you ever met my niece, Pam?"

Oh, no. He did *not* want to be set up. He'd broken up with his girlfriend, Laura, almost a year ago, and sure, he'd love to find someone he clicked with, but not someone who lived on the other side of the country. And not someone related to Sally; the idea alone seemed smothering and incestuous.

"Seth? I asked if you ever met my niece, Pam."

"Right—uh, let me think," he said, climbing out of the car and squinting his eyes against the afternoon sun. "Pam . . . Pam . . . we might've met once or twice." When they were kids, but that wasn't where Sally was going with this. Not down memory lane—down *matchmaking* lane. No, thank you.

"I really think you two should spend some time together while you're home," Sally said, taking his arm while they walked down the sidewalk. "I have a feeling you two would really hit it off. And it's perfect, because she's going to moving out west soon." He started to feel the claws tighten around his throat. How could he decline without insulting Sally?

Obviously, Sally mistook Seth's momentary silence for an invitation to discuss the topic in detail. "Pam's twenty-three," she continued, as Seth thought, *Too young for me.* "She's lovely, with long legs like a gazelle, but not lanky, I mean, graceful—like a supermodel—and she's a smart girl, like a genius almost, but not conceited about it, very humble, actually, and she's very liberated, as you young people might say, but not a hussy, of course."

Quirking his mouth, Seth wondered if Pam would appreciate this bizarre testimonial.

"And like I said, she really wants to move out west." Christ, what was this, manifest destiny? And since when was "west" synonymous with Seattle? "I just thought if Pam had a friend out there already, that would be so wonderful," Sally finished, with a note of pleading to her voice.

"Of course," Seth said, quickly latching onto the "friend" part. "If she ever needs anything, she can give me a call—"

"And like you said, you're not dating anyone right now. . . ."

"Honestly, Sally, I'm going to be so busy while I'm home. But why don't we all have lunch or something sometime? The *three* of us," he emphasized.

"Oh, wonderful! I'll make sure we do," she said, clapping her hands, as her emerald ring caught a flash of sunlight.

After agreeing to meet back at the car in a couple of hours, Sally turned and headed down the street. She moved quickly and merrily— occasionally looking back to wave. Seth shook his head and chuckled to himself. No, it didn't take long at all for him to feel at home.

Georgette ducked out from the kitchen to set a plate of apple fritters on the table Billy was using. "Help yourself, hon."

"Thanks, those smell awesome," Billy said, breathing in the

sweet apple aroma and trying not to give in to the daily temptation of working in the back, which was more of a median between the front of the store and the kitchen. A clean, cozy space, with white walls, a pink tile floor, and stainless-steel shelves neatly stockpiled with cake boxes, rolls of wax paper, and stacks of paper cups, it was where Billy decorated the cakes. It was also the place where Georgette deposited remainders for the staff to eat—baked goods that didn't look right, but still smelled and tasted delicious, and still had roughly a zillion calories.

Pausing at the kitchen door, Georgette asked, "By the way, what the hell's a soy nut?"

If Billy recalled, it was pretty self-explanatory. "It's just a roasted soybean, I think." (Well, it might sound self-explanatory; she never said it sounded *good*.)

"Oh, for chris*sake*," Georgette scoffed irritably, plowing her hand into her fluffy white rooster 'do.

"Why, what's wrong?"

"Melissa says I gotta start offerin' 'soy-nut alternatives' for vegans, or some bull crap like that." Behind her clunky pink glasses, she squinted her eyes angrily. "And we all know, whatever the princess *wants*—"

She stopped short of saying "she gets," as the alleged princess walked through the door. Georgette turned on her heel to retreat back to the kitchen, when Melissa stopped her. "Wait a sec, Georgette! I have something for you."

"What is it now?" she barked, and snatched the yellow piece of paper out of Melissa's hand.

"Two new recipe ideas from the suggestion box," Melissa replied.

"But—"

"Donna already approved them."

With that, Georgette scowled and slapped hard on the kitchen door. Once she was gone, Melissa simply shrugged off her tantrum and filled a paper cup with coffee from the old-fashioned pot in the corner. She leaned against the table and blew on her cup. "Oh, is that for the jubilee?" she asked, eyeing the sheet cake Billy was working on.

"Yeah, what do you think?" Billy asked, stepping back.

"It looks awesome so far." Georgette slammed pans around in the kitchen while Melissa rolled her eyes, and Billy couldn't help but giggle.

"By the way, do Katie and Des need my help out front?" Billy asked, just realizing she'd been working in the back for over an hour.

"No, don't worry; the lunch crowd already cleared out. Of course, Des's sleep-inducing diatribe on 'constructional imperialism' doesn't exactly entice one to linger." Billy laughed, recognizing that as Des's platform on the Big Dig, only about a decade too late. "By the way, how's Mark?"

"He's fine," she replied with a smile.

"So, are you guys still hot and heavy or what?" Melissa asked.

"I guess," Billy said, though "hot and heavy" wasn't quite it. *Mark* was hot, Billy's *fantasies* were hot, but when the two worlds met . . . her expectations fizzled.

Somehow the idea of kissing Mark was always more exciting than the reality. Billy honestly didn't know why—she was physically attracted to him, and she *wanted* to love kissing him. She wanted to melt inside, to sweat all over, to throw him down on the hood of his car and tear his shirt open with her teeth. Instead, while she enjoyed being near him, kissing him was merely pleasant. There was just something about Mark's lukewarm, very moist lips pressed on hers that didn't stir immediate and electrifying passion.

Still, she wasn't ready to conclude that the chemistry was simply wrong. What seemed far more realistic was that the passion between them would intensify as their relationship developed. Especially when they became more emotionally involved and closer to making love.

"Is he still working for that supply distribution company?" Melissa asked. "He's never here anymore."

"Oh, I know. With his promotion, he's been assigned to a different set of stores." If that sounded vague, she supposed it was, but Mark never went into a lot of detail about his job. "And he has longer hours now," Billy added, "which is why I don't get to see him as much as I'd like."

"Really?" Melissa said, arching an eyebrow.

"Yeah," she said, wondering why Melissa looked skeptical. Was she doubting that Mark had long hours? Or that it was the reason Billy didn't see him enough?

Shaking her head, Melissa remarked, "I still can't get a feel for what Mark's type is."

"What do you mean?" Billy asked, leaning against the table and accidentally smudging the side edge of the sheet cake. "Oh, shoot," she said, turning back and bending to fix it with her frosting spatula.

"Hey, Billy," Katie called, ducking her head in, "there's someone here to see you."

"Huh?"

"About the jubilee."

"Oh! I totally forgot." Damn, she really wanted to finish this cake first. Gingerly Billy worked her hands under the cardboard tray, shimmied the cake off the table to balance in her hands, and carried it to the freezer. Melissa opened the door for her.

Then Billy wiped her hands on her apron, brushed back some loose strands of hair that had fallen away from her ponytail, and headed to the front.

Suddenly she stopped short. And in less than a second, the dull but comforting predictability of life abruptly turned on its axis.

"Billy?"

"Oh, my God," she said, coming closer, barely having enough time to process the handsome, achingly familiar man standing on the other side of the counter. No . . . it *couldn't* be!

Seth Lannigan? After all this time?

"I can't believe this," he said, smiling warmly, with a touch of wonder crossing his face.

"Um, what are you doing here?" Billy asked, feeling choked by shock, as her heart fluttered frantically in her chest.

"I'm here representing Churchill and the Jubilee Planning Committee. What, you work here?" Grinning self-deprecatingly, he plowed his hand into his hair and said, "Okay, obviously you do."

"Yeah," Billy said with a laugh that was mostly nerves. "My friend got me the job a couple months ago," she added, motioning toward Melissa on the other side of the counter. That was when she noticed Melissa, Katie, and Des all watching like they'd paid for seats. Abruptly, they averted their eyes and pretended to straighten things behind the counter.

Seth must've noticed, because his eyes dropped to the floor as his mouth curved into another grin. Then he looked back up at Billy. And she really took him in—the darkly golden hair, the navy sweater that covered his broad shoulders and strong chest, the fresh-looking softness of his skin—*Wait*. Seth was clean shaven. Back in the day he'd exuded a scruffy kind of sexiness; his favorite outfit had been jeans and a hooded sweatshirt. Now he looked more clean-cut. Older, more filled out. The same, only better.

Swallowing hard, Billy tried to steady her nerves, which were still reeling. For the most part shock had worn off, and the reality of seeing Seth again had begun to sink in.

Automatically, her body and mind responded to his presence— especially the vivid déjà vu rushing through her mind, reminding her of Seth's magnetism. His sexy grin, his hypnotic gaze, the rich sound of his laugh—it all just rattled her senses.

Wiping her palms on her apron, she stopped fiddling and snapped into focus. "I lost my job at Net Circle six months ago, so I've been working here until I find something else. What about you? Are you just home visiting?"

Seth explained about his mother's move to Dublin, and selling her house. Though it wasn't logical, the notion of Seth selling his family's beach house stung Billy a little. She supposed, in the corners of her mind, she was still touched by memories of holding Seth on the beach . . . of Seth kissing her softly, deeply, under Fourth of July tiki torches and moonlight.

". . . so when Sally asked me to fill in for her today and meet with the caterer, I figured it was the least I could do."

Smiling, Billy continued to nod, feeling vaguely like a PEZ head.

Seth asked, "Should we sit, or . . . ?"

"Oh, right, good idea," Billy said, moving past him, feeling some heat emanating off Seth's body as she passed. This reunion probably called for a hug, but the counter had been between them before, and now it felt like the moment was lost. She stopped short at a free table and turned quickly, accidentally brushing her shoulder against Seth's elbow, which sent a shiver rippling up her arm. She swallowed away the tightness in the back of her throat. "Okay, let's sit right here—except I forgot my— Oh!" She almost bumped into Seth as she whipped around. Now his eyes looked deeply into hers, and a rush of heat flooded Billy's chest. "I forgot the order book," she explained, smiling almost shyly. "I'll be right back."

When she walked behind the counter, she caught Melissa, Katie, and Des all huddled by the register, staring again. Rolling her eyes, she almost laughed. "Could you guys be more obvious?"

she whispered as she passed by them and pushed on the door to the back.

Immediately Melissa and Katie followed. "Omigod, when he came in, I didn't realize he was *Seth*," Katie said approvingly.

"So *that's* Seth? The 'one that got away'?" Melissa asked, then whistled. "I swear, I don't know how you snag these guys."

"What do you mean?" Billy said, a little surprised by that comment.

"No, no, I just mean . . . he's a hottie."

Somehow that wasn't clarifying much, but right now Billy was too flustered to pursue it. Seth was out there, and there was catering business to be dealt with.

Oh, yeah, and she also had to remember how to breathe.

"What do you think—should I lose the apron?" she asked. On the one hand, Billy was tempted to keep it on to cover her recent weight gain, but on the other, her red sweater and blue jeans said "cazh," while the apron said "serving wench."

"I'd lose it," Katie said.

Melissa held out her hand for Billy to relinquish the apron.

Just then Des ducked his head in. "Hey, what's going on in here?" he asked. His shaggy locks were dipped over one eye, and his mouth was curved into a small frown.

"Des, you have to go back to the front," Melissa said. "You can't leave the register unattended." She refrained from adding, *Duh*, but it was loudly implied.

With a heavy sigh, he retreated.

"Well, go on," Melissa said to Billy. "You really don't want to leave Des out there with Seth. He'll start pontificating on the meaning of life, pretending, of course, that he has one."

A strangled laugh escaped Billy's throat—part nerves and part giddiness at the bright, unexpected turn her day had taken.

Sucking in a breath, she clutched the order book to her chest and headed to the front, her mind going blank of everything but the nervous excitement buzzing through her. She wasn't thinking clearly—or maybe at all—in fact, it was times like these she envied Des Aggerdeen's flair for conversation.

Chapter Four

God, to see Billy again! Seth thought, his surprise barely settling as he rapped his fingers anxiously on the tabletop. She looked the same as she had four years ago, except her hair was a dark red color now, and pulled back from her face, which was prettier than he'd remembered—prettier than that photograph depicted.

Rap, rap, rap.

He felt keyed up; seeing her again was the last thing he'd been expecting, and now all his senses were on alert; his pulse was pounding. In the months following his move to Seattle, Seth had been so busy with work that he'd put all speculation about her out of his mind. But now, his first day back, she appeared before him. Billy was right there—right *here.*

Damn, he still couldn't believe it.

"Okay," she said, returning to the table, balancing two cups of coffee and a thick binder. Immediately he stood to help her, but she shook her head. "I've got it," she said, leaning over to set everything down on the table, then pulling out the chair across from him. Her apron was gone, and abruptly he noticed her body. Back when they'd dated, she had been shapely and voluptuous—a hot little rocket—and now Seth could see that nothing had changed. Her curves were still round and sexy. He noticed the arousing way her jeans hugged her body, and the mouthwatering arc of her breasts against her sweater.

A jolt of lust shot to his groin, and he swallowed hard, thinking about her body without clothes. God, he bet she still had the most luscious ass, the softest, most succulent breasts—

"You still take your coffee black, right?" she asked, breaking his lusty trance.

"Yeah, thanks."

Flipping open the order book, she ran through the specifics for the jubilee. "Everything's on schedule. All the pastries will be made fresh that day. Our baker, Georgette, will be on hand to replenish items, as needed. And I'm almost finished decorating the sheet cakes for the night's finale."

"You changed your hair."

She seemed caught off guard by the nonsequitur, and ran her hand over her ponytail.

"It looks really nice," Seth added, but stopped himself from saying more—like how her dark red hair next to her pale blue eyes was like a sultry, fiery burst of color. Christ, how did she look so innocently pretty—with the light dusting of freckles across the bridge of her nose—but so sexy at the same time, fitting right into his darkest, most erotic fantasies?

She blushed, and Seth wondered how red she'd turn if she knew the graphic ideas running through his mind right now.

He passed her the last-minute notes from Sally and the planning committee, and couldn't help zeroing in on the fringe of Billy's long, dark lashes as she scanned the list. When she glanced up, she caught him staring again. Quickly Seth softened his gaze, trying to tamp down his intense resurgence of sexual attraction before Billy read it all over his face.

After jubilee business was out of the way, Billy handed Seth the final invoice. He took it and slipped it into his back pocket, but made no move to go. "So how's your family?" he asked, resting his arms on the table. "Your parents? Corryn and Kane?" After she told him about her parents' recent cruise and her sister's success in real estate, she mentioned Corryn's divorce. "Oh, I'm sorry," Seth said.

"No, don't be. It's been two years; Corryn's doing great." Smiling, Billy added, "Well, except for the fixation about how all men are bastards."

"Sounds about right," Seth said, and Billy laughed. She still had a lilting kind of giggle—the same one he used to love, and still did.

"What about you?" she asked. "How're your mom and brother?"

"Good, good," he said, and went on to give her updates.

While he was talking, Billy couldn't help but notice that Des was lingering around their table. Right now he was on about his tenth lap around with the mop, blatantly eavesdropping on their conversation. (The way his hair was combed behind his ears and his head cocked abnormally to the side each time he neared their table kind of tipped her off.) Not that she particularly cared; she and Seth were having a perfectly benign conversation on the surface, and Des was harmless anyway.

She thought about the way Seth had been looking at her a moment ago. Hungrily. No, that couldn't be right. *She* was the one who was hungry—starved—for some sexual satisfaction. (So what else was new?)

Just then everyone heard a loud bang. Des had accidentally walked into the pie case and sent his broom plummeting to the floor. "Oh . . ." he mumbled, leaning down to get it. "Whoops."

"Nice job!" Melissa called to him. Des ignored her and looked over at Billy, who smiled kindly at him before turning her attention back to Seth.

"So tell me about your life in Seattle," she said. Maybe for a moment her inner two-year-old wanted Seth to say that life was bleak. Dreary, loveless. Maybe the dark part of her wanted him to regret his decision to leave their burgeoning relationship behind.

But the feeling passed quickly. He'd always been a decent, caring person, and she honestly hoped he'd done well for himself. And it definitely sounded like he had. According to Seth, he'd started his own consulting firm two years ago, and now it was thriving.

"Wow, that's so impressive," she said, smiling, and reached out to touch his arm. "I'm so proud of you!" Shrugging off the compliment, Seth dropped his eyes to Billy's hand, and she quickly withdrew it.

"Can I take that cup for you?" It was Des, who'd somehow sidled right up to the table. Billy nodded and thanked him as he grabbed her empty coffee cup and lingered for a few seconds before leaving.

"What about your job at Net Circle?" Seth asked, leaning forward. "How come you quit?"

"Wellll . . . I wouldn't exactly use the term 'quit,' " she replied, making quotation marks with her fingers. He gave her a quizzical look. "The company went under," she explained. "It came as a total shock to me, which was crazy, because I really should've seen the signs."

"What signs?"

"Well, a few days before I got the news, moving men came in and took some desks out of the office."

"Oh . . ."

"And then the phone company disconnected the fax machine."

"Ah . . ." he said with a nod.

"And, of course, there was the fact that when I tried to access the company homepage, it said: 'Error—Web site does not exist.' " Seth had to laugh at that, and Billy giggled, too. "I guess I was kind of in my own world."

"Listen, I still have a lot of business contacts here in Boston," Seth said, turning more serious. "I'd be happy to make a few calls—"

"No," she interrupted. "No, thanks, I'll find something." She refrained from adding that she really had no clue what she was going to do next, but whatever it was, she was fairly certain she could do it on her own.

Just then Des reappeared. "Billy, can I get you another cup of coffee or . . . ?"

"No, I'm set, thanks," she said, wishing Des weren't being such a lurker today. Here she'd been talking to Seth for a while, and she still hadn't found out whether he was married. Pure idle curiosity, of course.

"Hey, I don't know what you're up to later," Des said, leaning his weight on the pole of the mop, literally making it his crutch, "but my band's having a jam session at the old abandoned warehouse. You should stop by."

Hmm . . . could that sound *more* unappealing?

"Oh, that sounds fun," Billy lied, "but I'm meeting my sister for drinks." Actually, that last part was true; after work they were having raspberry crushes at the Rack.

"Are you sure? Because I was gonna show you the new manifesto I've been working on. I'm thinking of putting it to music and just turning it into a song. You know, so I can reach more people. It'd be so cool to have your creative input."

Okay, Des was a sweet guy, but *please*—not another manifesto of logical fallacies and convoluted calls to some muddled kind of action. "Sorry—maybe another time," she said.

He nodded and retreated to help a flock of incoming customers, and once he was gone Seth looked at his watch. "You know, I should probably let you get back to work. I don't want you to get in trouble."

"Oh, I suppose you're right," Billy said as they both stood up. "What time is it anyway?"

When he told her the time, she couldn't believe it. An hour and a half had flown by! And her coworkers hadn't even called her away. Jeez, she'd taken shameless advantage of the situation . . . yet she still wasn't ready to say good-bye.

"By the way . . ." Billy said, careful to keep her tone casual, "are you going to be at the Dessert Jubilee on Saturday?"

Seth paused, then curved his mouth into a grin. "It's a possibility," was all he said. And then a silence stretched between them; Billy suddenly felt shy, and didn't know exactly how to end the conversation. Standing next to Seth she became acutely aware of his height, and of her neck arching to look up at him. Her eyes zeroed in on a small spot along Seth's jaw that he must've missed with his razor. If she let herself remember, she'd recall exactly how those sandy whiskers felt rubbing along her cheek, brushing against her lips, and burrowing between her breasts. (It was a good thing she wasn't letting herself remember.)

"Well, take care," she said finally.

"You, too," Seth replied, then leaned in for a hug.

As he closed the space between them, Billy's heart kicked up, and suddenly all the nervous energy she'd tamped down came skittering back. Her stomach clenched into a tight, almost painful ball of tension as her breathing became ragged, almost shaky. A combination of apprehension and lust that she prayed Seth couldn't detect.

What's come over me?

She was so damn nervous and terrified . . . but exhilarated, too, as Seth tightened his embrace—pulling her closer, wrapping his heat around her, and trapping her inside. Sliding her eyes closed, Billy stood on tiptoe, cupped Seth's shoulders, and concentrated on the feel of him. Broad, solid . . . *sexy.* God, he was strong—she could feel it in the restrained way he held her. He'd filled out over the past four years, probably worked out a lot. *That makes one of us.* *Ohh . . .*

Her mouth ran dry as Seth's muscle and heat enveloped her, and some thick, invisible energy rose off his body like steam off hot pavement. She felt that steam seeping into her skin, melting her inside her clothes; and to make matters worse, with his face pressed against her hair, hot puffs of his breath tickled the rim of her ear, arousing her beyond belief.

Barely stifling the urge to moan, Billy struggled to understand the chemistry crackling between them—struggled not to enjoy the burning throb that had kicked up between her legs. Not to enjoy it *too* much, anyway.

Just then Seth rubbed his cheek gently against her hair. Hazily, Billy wondered if he was acknowledging the sensuousness of the moment, if he was as turned on as she was. But who, besides her, was sex-starved enough to get turned on by a simple hug?

"Billy?" he said softly.

Swallowing hard, she savored the gravelly thickness in his voice that took her back—reminding her of the intimate way he used to speak to her. Holding her by the ocean, whispering in her ear about the future, sliding his hand gently over her breast, groaning, and whispering, "This is mine." In return, she'd run her hand between his legs, a little less gently, feeling the worn denim and the swollen bulge in the front, and say, "*This* is mine." And he would bury his face in her hair and murmur, "You're right."

"Billy?" he said again, and she snapped into the present. That was good, because reveries were silly; every relationship was passionate and full of possibilities after only a few months. Suddenly she realized that Seth was trying to pull back from the hug . . . and that she was still clinging to him . . . and with *abandon.*

She all but jumped, dropping her arms and stepping back to put some much-needed space between them. Inhaling sharply, she tried to clear the fog from her mind as her heart kept slamming against her ribs and her cheeks burned with embarrassment.

Seth was flushed, too. Dropping his gaze to the floor, he plowed his hand through his soft blond hair—a nervous habit, if she recalled—and then flashed her a brief smile. "I should really get going," he said, in a low, almost husky voice.

"Right, okay . . ." she agreed, backing up even more. "Um, it was great seeing you again and catching up . . . take care of yourself and— Oh!" She yelped as something rubbed up against her back. Turning, she saw that she'd stepped back too much—right into a plant. "Hmm, I didn't notice that there . . . anyway . . ."

"Well, I guess I'll be seeing you," Seth said with a brief nod.

He moved past her out of the bakery, and only after he was gone did Billy release the heavy sigh that filled her chest. *What a day!* There never seemed to be a way to prepare for the sporadic, non-dull moments in life that surprised her. *But it's probably better that way,* she thought happily as she pressed a hand to her heart, savored the *zing* of Seth's hug, and ignored the taunting leaves that prickled against her shoulder blades.

Chapter Five

When Billy got to the Rack, it was vibrating with loud, pulsing music and the clatter of Wednesday's happy hour. She didn't see her sister anywhere, so she pushed and shimmied her way through the throngs of people, apologizing to the air as she went, and finally made it to the bar.

Shrugging off her coat, Billy tugged lightly on her sweater to fan herself off, because the run across town was just catching up with her. Midfanning, she accidentally caught the eye of a skeevy-looking meathead in a flesh-colored, mesh muscle T. *Eww.* Predatory and desperate—she was just so flattered.

As his eyes roved over her body, Billy turned her head and mentally willed him not to approach. The last thing she wanted was to be hit on. Not that it happened often, but really, why start new traditions? Especially when she was determined to focus all her romantic energy on Mark. It was the least she could do after she'd gotten embarrassingly hot and bothered over her ex-boyfriend that afternoon.

And speaking of Mark, she hoped she got to see him before the weekend, because the Dessert Jubilee in Churchill was going to take up her whole Saturday.

The jubilee . . . That got her thinking about Seth again . . .

God, it had been so invigorating just to hold him again. Warmth washed over her body and pooled with urgency between her legs as she remembered. What was up with her? Why couldn't she get Seth out of her mind? Why couldn't she stop picturing him naked?

Why couldn't she stop fantasizing about lying under him and feeling his big, swollen erection push into her?

Because I'm sick, she reasoned. *I'm repressed, horny, and sick.*

Or maybe she was just fixating on sex because it had been a while. Maybe it was time to step up her physical repertoire with Mark. Now *there* was an idea. So far they'd kissed and touched, but, as her fantasies crept back into her mind, Billy bit her lip, sucked in a shaky breath, and knew she needed more. Her body was screaming for passion—excitement. Like a pink neon sign flashing in her brain: *Hot Sex.*

Someone tapped on her shoulder, and she turned around. "Hey," Corryn said, blowing some long, dark wisps out of her big, dark eyes and away from her face, which was pretty even when it was frowning. She was five-two like Billy, but Corryn was slim and petite like their mom. Billy, on the other hand, was "sturdy."

Corryn looked up and around the crowd. "Two seats just opened up at the bar. Wanna sit over there?"

"Sure," Billy replied. She followed her sister to the bar, and they both hopped onto their stools.

"Sorry we had to meet here," Corryn remarked as she slid off her tailored leather jacket.

"Why? I don't mind this place."

"No, it's great, except it's a pickup joint, the music's too loud, and half the guys are muscleheads." After she folded her jacket and set it neatly on her lap, she shifted to get comfortable on the stool.

Billy brushed off her sister's cynicism and tried to make eye contact with the bartender, who ignored her for a few laps around the bar before finally approaching. "Ladies, what can I get you?" Up close, Billy noticed that he was cute in a hulking, musclehead kind of way. He also had that perfunctory Boston-bartender attitude down: barely a smile, acting like he was doing them a favor.

"Raspberry liqueur, vodka, and Diet Sprite with crushed ice," Billy said.

"Make it two," Corryn interjected as she toyed absently with the clunky silver heart that hung around her neck. Incidentally, it was the only thing her ex-husband, Kane, had given her that she'd kept—the only thing that didn't somehow reek of their marriage.

"So how was your day?" Billy asked.

"Not bad," she replied with a shrug. "I showed a luxury condo to a punk band."

"Hmm."

"And apparently the Patriots lost last night, so Annette was in a shitty mood." Annette Beefe was Corryn's boss at Blue Sky Realty, whose garish Patriots parka was practically sewed to her body. "What about you? Anything new?"

Billy was about to tell her about seeing Seth when the bartender slid their sparkly pink tumblers forward. After he turned to another customer, Corryn took a sip of her raspberry crush. "Enh, this is weak," she said, making a face. "Sorry, what were you saying?"

"Well . . . I saw Seth today," Billy said.

"Uh-huh—*wait*. You mean Seth as in Seth from four years ago?" After Billy nodded, Corryn's eyes widened. "Oh, my God! Okay, back up; I need major details."

Billy explained about Seth's return to Massachusetts, his reason for coming to Bella Donna, and the pleasant chat they'd had that afternoon. After she was finished, Corryn pointed out that she'd omitted the most important part. "So how does he look?"

"Great," Billy admitted, and took a drink. As the tangy, bubbly liquid slid down her throat, she tried not to dwell on *how* great. Unsurprisingly, though, it didn't work, and a soft sigh escaped her lips.

Seth still had that warm, sexy grin, those sultry hazel eyes, and that easy, unassuming handsomeness that could stop her heart.

"Come on, there must be something wrong with him," Corryn said, reaching inside her jacket pocket for a cigarette. Then she froze—as she always did when she remembered there was no smoking in bars—and sighed irritably. It wasn't a particularly new rule, but alcohol always triggered her nicotine craving. "How's his hair?" she asked.

Hmm . . . she could say it looked gorgeous, darkly golden, and feather-soft to touch, but she knew that wasn't what her sister meant. "Not receding," Billy said with a smirk.

"His waistline?"

Billy shrugged. "He looks like he's in great shape"—mouth-wateringly great, and *felt* like it, too—"even better than when we were going out."

"Well that's annoying."

"Valid," Billy mumbled, grinning in spite of herself. "So, basically, we're talking no comb-over, no belly that could be detected, and no weak chin, either, if that was your next question."

By the dissatisfied frown on Corryn's face, it was. Shrugging, she said, "Well, so what? You look the same, too. Only better."

"Oh, does 'better' have more than one meaning?"

"I'm serious. You're so pretty, and that hair color is *sexy*. Besides, you know my motto: If he's hot, he's probably a cocky asshole, and who needs the aggravation?"

Oh, *that* motto. Definitely not one you'd needlepoint on a pillow, but Billy supposed there was a certain logic to it. Especially from Corryn's perspective after Kane Bentley, the cookie-cutter-handsome, supercunning lawyer, had broken her heart.

Still, life and love weren't always that simple or predictable. In fact, Billy was willing to take hot guys on a case-by-case basis. For instance, Seth Lannigan might be handsome, but she still believed he had a good heart. And Mark Warner was not only good-looking, but kind and affable, too.

But Billy generally looked for the good more than her sister, who was a hard case like their mom. Corryn and Adrienne viewed the world in black and white; they also viewed each *other* that way, which was probably why they didn't get along.

"By the way, how's Mark?" Corryn asked now. "Have you guys gotten busy yet, or what?"

"No, I'm still waiting for the right time," Billy said deprecatingly. "I just hope it comes in this century." Corryn grinned, and then Billy giggled, because she knew it was just her savage hormones talking. "The thing is, I want to be intimate with him, but I want us to work *up* to that. We just haven't spent enough time together to work up to it yet. I definitely don't want to jump into bed with him. I want us to be closer. I want to know him on a deeper level."

That was the way she'd always been; sex was on her mind a lot, but when it came to the actual act, it was too intimate and special for her to do without a strong emotional connection. Of course, that was why she was twenty-seven years old and had slept with only one man—her ex-boyfriend, Ryan Crennan, whom she'd dated after Seth.

She'd always wished it had been Seth.

Thinking about him now resurrected memories of this afternoon. Yet again. Billy shivered as her body stirred, reliving the sensations of Seth wrapping his arms around her and breathing against her ear. She'd always sensed a powerful kind of sexuality about him. It was in the hungry way he used to move his hands on her—the feral, almost pained expression on his face when he was aroused.

A flush of heat washed over her skin and snaked between her legs, where she was damp and wanting. Aching . . .

Meanwhile, her sister was saying something. "Wait, what?" Billy said, confused.

"I asked what time you're going to Mom and Dad's on Friday night."

"Oh. Around seven, I guess. What about you?"

"Seven's okay. Assuming I can make it."

"You can make it," Billy warned.

"You're right," Corryn scoffed. "It's a Friday night—of course I can make it."

"That's not what I mean. I mean you can't leave me there all by myself."

"Why not? Mom likes you."

"To a point," Billy said glibly.

"Look, Mom's great; I love her; she gave me life and all that. But I'm tired of her backhanded comments," Corryn said. "I'm tired of hearing that I'm thirty-four years old and that I need to get 'out there' again. It got kind of stale around the four hundredth time."

Nodding, Billy said, "You know, I think you two are in this holding pattern of passive-aggressive comments. You just need to break the cycle. Next time Mom says something that annoys you, tell her straight out."

"Fine, but I just can't understand how she's not annoying *herself*," Corryn muttered, and Billy had to laugh.

"Well, I wouldn't wait for *that* to happen."

"Anything else, ladies?" the bartender asked as he cleared away their empty glasses. He wiped a towel along the bar and barely looked up.

"Yeah, two more," Corryn said, "and put some vodka in this time."

That got his attention; he looked up and quirked a smile at her. She almost smiled back, but stopped herself just in time.

After he poured them fresh drinks, he wiped his hands on his towel, then slung it over his shoulder. "Ten-fifty," he said, apparently not charging them for the first round. That was another thing about bartenders in Boston: They picked their moments to turn on the charm.

Corryn reached for her wallet, but Billy stopped her. "It's my treat this time, and don't argue," Billy said firmly. Corryn had been trying to shield her from poverty ever since she lost her job at Net Circle, even though she kept telling her that she still had semidecent savings.

The bartender disappeared with the money, and Corryn thanked Billy and asked, "By the way, do you think you'll see Seth again?"

"Maybe. At the jubilee on Saturday. But maybe not. I don't know. I'm casual either way." Instantly she knew that sounded silly, but oh, well; it was only her sister. "Oh, and you're gonna watch Pike for me then, right?" With Lady McAvit still in a snit, Billy didn't want her baby getting into any trouble, but she'd feel too guilty to seal him up in the apartment all day and into the night.

"Sure, absolutely," Corryn said.

Smiling, Billy thanked her, then excused herself to go to the bathroom. She wove through a maze of pool tables and girls in black pants and tank tops, until she noticed something that made her stop short. Some*one*, actually. A woman who looked like Melissa on the other side of the room. The Rack was a spacious place, though, so it was hard to get a good look. Tall, skinny, dressed in black, with thick, curly hair pulled back into a ponytail.

When she turned more to the side, Billy got a better look at her profile. It *was* Melissa, and she was talking to a man whose face was in the shadows.

Suddenly she glanced over her shoulder and made direct eye

contact with Billy. Immediately Billy smiled and waved, but, even though their eyes were locked, Melissa didn't wave back. Pausing momentarily, she then turned back around.

Huh?

Is it Melissa or isn't it?

"You're blocking my shot," someone behind her barked, and Billy turned. She was right next to a pool table, and the guy holding the cue was glaring at her. He was some college punk kid with a baseball hat and a Northeastern sweatshirt, who blew his so-called shot as soon as she unblocked it. Continuing on to the ladies' room, Billy turned once to get another look at the girl who resembled Melissa.

Only now the girl was gone.

The following morning Corryn shoved her way onto the smelly, jam-packed E line. She wasn't trying to be a snob, but really, was this train ever *not* wall-to-wall crowded with people breathing and coughing on each other?

She'd trekked out to Jamaica Plain to show a one-bedroom off Huntington, and her appointment had never shown. So annoying. Realtors in Boston might have a reputation for being dismissive and short-tempered, but was it any wonder sometimes?

Now Corryn tried not to breathe—a strategy that obviously didn't last long. As it was, the little pocket of air she had smelled vaguely of sweat and stale bagels. And dirty socks. Christ, did someone have their shoes off, too? Wasn't there some kind of a law?

Frustrated and suffocated, she pushed through a mass of congestion, chanting, "Excuse me," as she went, and finally made it to a tiny clearing in the back.

After ten long minutes, the T was rattling underground. Then it jerked hard to a stop. The impact sent Corryn's head shooting up, and she suddenly found herself staring into a pair of vividly green eyes. Defogging her brain, she processed the whole image and realized that the green eyes belonged to the tall, broad-framed guy standing next to her.

When he smiled down at her, Corryn realized she was staring, so she quickly dropped her head and looked, instead, at the filthy, stinky floor. Much better. Really, who needed to make long, lingering eye contact with a guy on the T? He was probably a psycho, anyway.

"Crowded enough for you?" he said.

Her eyes flew up. He was still grinning at her. Yes, definitely a psycho.

Still, she smiled briefly at him. "I know—this is awful," she said, and noticed his green eyes sparkle. They really were so clear and beautiful . . . in fact, his face wasn't bad, either. Tiny lines of age around his mouth and eyes, with brown hair that had hints of gray running through it. Corryn guessed he was in his forties, but he was better built than any forty-something she knew.

Swallowing hard, she darted her gaze out the window at blackness streaming past as her heart rate kicked up.

She suddenly felt acutely self-conscious, like maybe this man was still watching her, and how did she look to him? She felt on display and a little nervous, because the guy was so damn attractive— an atypical observation on her part, because she hardly ever felt flustered like this, much less focused on whether or not a man was attractive. Billy would say she was too picky; Corryn would call it discerning, but in her heart, she called it *smart*.

Now she could hear the choppiness of her breathing as her body and mind zeroed in on the man beside her. She was too aware of his close proximity, too intrigued by his size, and too paranoid, because she could literally *feel* his powerful presence. Were those ice-green eyes still on her? Could he *sense* Corryn's instant attraction to him?

Just forget it, she told herself. *Focus on real-life stuff.* Like her schedule—what did she have left to do today? Oh, right, after a few more appointments and some paperwork, she'd eat dinner alone in front of the TV, then check her e-mail, find her inbox flooded with spam, and be in bed before most fifth graders. Yeah, her real life was just rolling right along.

The handsome guy next to her shifted his stance, bringing him a fraction closer. In response, Corryn's stomach muscles pulled tight and the breath hitched in her throat. Her heart was beating frantically. She was so goddamn nervous, and over nothing! God, why did she have to be so bad with men and relationships? And why did she have to let it get to her?

Sometimes she wondered if Kane had ruined her for love. Then again, maybe she'd always been screwed-up, and he'd just made things worse. Not that he was abusive—just anal, critical, and pathologically dishonest. And rather than use direct insults, he'd made passive-aggressive remarks that even a toddler could see through. *Yeah, he was really something special,* Corryn thought, *and on top of everything,* he *left* me.

Suddenly the train jerked to another jarring stop, and the doors to her left flew open. Instead of people getting off, more just piled on. Shifting her body, she attempted to get semicomfortable, but it was impossible. Not only was she sweaty, bitter, and short on breathable air, she was squished beyond belief, and could no longer reach the handrail.

"*Christ,*" she mumbled, just as the man next to her—who must've sensed her frustration—said, "Here, hold on to me," and set his hand gently on the middle of her back. Corryn jumped at the contact, but grabbed on to his arm anyway, because she was about to fall over. Now he was practically enveloping her, holding her back steadily and warmly with one hand, while she held on to his other arm.

As the T rocked and swayed, Corryn felt confused. Her body was zinging, on full sensory alert; she was clutching on to a total stranger and honestly didn't want to let go.

As the train shook, her hip brushed against his thigh and he pressed more firmly on her back. A jolt of heat speared straight to her crotch. *Insanity,* she thought, even as her panties burned on her skin.

It had been so long since she'd been touched by a man—so long since she had truly, deeply wanted to be. The guy next to her had to be releasing pheromones like crazy; it was the only logical explanation.

Sharply, she pulled away from him. A look of sudden confusion crossed his face. "I'm fine now," Corryn said by way of explanation, smiling politely and pretending she was having no trouble balancing as the T bumped and swayed. She had to collect herself and get back in control. Suddenly the train stopped short, pitching everyone forward, and as Corryn tried to steady herself, she felt something like a pinch on her breast. A pinch and a twist.

What the hell!

"Hey," she barked, tapping the man's upper arm, which was thick and rock solid.

"Huh?" he said, angling his head to face her. "What?"

"You pinched me!" she yelped. Well, she wasn't about to scream, *You tweaked my nipple,* at top volume, but clearly they both knew that was what she meant.

"What are you talking about?" he asked, looking baffled. "I was just offering you my arm—"

"Of *course* you'd turn out to be a pervert," she mumbled to herself.

"Hey, you didn't *have* to take my arm," he said defensively.

"I'm not talking about your dumb arm," she said, rolling her eyes. "I'm talking about . . . the other thing."

"What other thing? Lady, I don't know what the hell you're talk-ing about."

Right. Who else was within tweaking distance, besides the bag lady in the adjacent seat, snoring? Just then Corryn's eye caught the gleam of the shiny police badge attached to the man's belt, and her mouth fell open. "You've got to be kidding me—you're a *cop*?"

The T screeched to a stop at Copley. This was where Corryn was getting off, and she couldn't get off fast enough.

Latching onto the mass exodus for fear of getting left behind, she was still fuming when she got to the street. Well, that settled it, then. All men were pigs—not just the ones she knew personally.

Chapter Six

"You know what gets me?"

"What?" Billy said conversationally, sipping her raspberry crush as people moved and mingled around her. Earlier Katie had suggested that everyone go for drinks at the Kenmore Pub after work. Now she and Georgette were on the dance floor around the bend, and Billy and Des were standing by the bar, talking. (Or *Des* was talking; Billy was standing there nodding, with one eye on the door.)

Melissa was the only staffer missing tonight. She'd had the day off, but she wouldn't have come anyway. Ever since the one time she'd had too much to drink and drunkenly confessed the whole sordid story of her parentage, she tended to shy away from after-work activities.

Apparently Melissa had been the result of a one-night affair between her mom and a drifter who'd been passing through town. For the first twelve years of Melissa's life, her mother had supported her with odd jobs. When she'd met Des's dad, Jim Aggerdeen, everything changed. A widower with a young son, Jim had wanted a wife and a family again. And according to Melissa's drunken ramblings, he was a great stepdad, but she was still forever determined to find her real father someday.

After such an uncharacteristic display of vulnerability, it was really no wonder that Melissa now kept a somewhat professional distance from the rest of the Bella Donna crew.

"What gets me," Des continued now, "is the way nobody keeps it honest anymore." *Fresh topic.* "Can't anyone see how life has become just a co-opted travesty of social indoctrination?"

"Hmm, that's true," Billy replied absently, and slipped another glance over Des's shoulder. She was expecting Mark any minute now, and she was really looking forward to seeing him. Once she hugged him and looked into his handsome, smiling face, she'd put everything—i.e., Seth—back into perspective.

After a ten-minute monologue about social conventions and the corporate-industrial complex, Des said, "But I guess that's just what makes you and me different, Billy. We live outside the box, you know?"

She was about to respond when Mark came through the door. "Hey, there," he said, smiling as he came closer.

"Hi!" she enthused—so damn happy to see him, so damn happy that he was there to remind her that he was *real*, that he was a part of her life.

Mark folded himself into Billy's hug, but pulled out before it even got going. "Hey, what's up?" he said, extending a hand to Des. "You work at Bella Donna, too, right?"

"Yeah, hi," Des mumbled, barely returning the handshake.

"Well, later, Billy," he said, and walked away from the bar.

"Okay, I'll come find you guys," Billy said lamely to his back.

"Later, man!" Mark called after him, smiling like they were already great buddies. This, Billy noted, was so typically Mark. He was just one of those over-the-top, outgoing people who had a thousand friends. Not that she minded; she liked that he was so amiable. It made her feel special to be the girl he picked out of the hundreds he seemed to know.

Okay, okay . . . occasionally Mark's constant need to be "on" got to her. Ever so slightly worked on her nerves. But she wasn't going to think about that now. She'd been waiting anxiously for Mark to show; she wasn't about to start nitpicking. Tonight was about romance. Tonight was about reconnecting with the man in her life.

With one arm she leaned into Mark for another squeeze, and looked up into his handsome, perennially happy face. It was no wonder Mark was so popular—he was like a yellow burst of sunlight. So positive, so upbeat. *He's really special,* Billy told herself firmly.

"So, have I missed anything?" he asked, running his fingers playfully down her back.

"Nope. Before you got here, I was on the dance floor doing the cabbage patch, but that's about it."

"Sure you were," he said with a laugh, and turned to order a beer. "By the way, what are you drinking?"

"Raspberry crush," she said, though she couldn't help thinking, *Doesn't he know that by now?* Just then a rowdy bunch of college kids barreled into the bar area.

"Excuse us, guys," Mark said, flashing the crowd a winning smile as he and Billy shifted over to make room.

"So how was work?" Billy asked, wincing as a kid accidentally knocked into her side.

"Work's great," Mark replied brightly. "Just terrific, I'm loving it."

"Oh, good," Billy said for lack of anything else. "Anyway . . . I missed you this week." Smiling sweetly from under her lashes, she leaned in closer, trying to flirt.

Mark turned back to the bar to pay for their drinks. "Thanks, thanks a lot!" he gushed to the female bartender. "Thanks again!" He turned back to Billy. "Want to go sit down? I think I see your coworkers over there."

She had to stand on tiptoe to see over the crowd, but finally spotted Georgette's white pompadour. Katie and Des were sitting with her at a table across the room.

"Let's go join them," Mark suggested cheerily.

"Okay, but . . . well, it's just that I missed you this week," Billy said again—which, by the way, sounded a little lamer the second time around.

"I missed you too," he said, and dropped a light kiss on her lips. "Come on, let's go over and say hi."

"Okay," Billy said, trying not to feel too disappointed. True, she was the one who'd suggested Mark meet her out with her coworkers, but she'd hoped he'd focus more of his attention on her. At least for a couple of minutes . . .

But she should've known. That was Mark. He had an overactive friendly gene, and she supposed she was being a little bratty. As they approached the table, Billy noticed a fourth person there: a thin, wiry man in his thirties, hunched in the seat next to Georgette. "Hey, guys!" Mark said, and shook each person's hand. "How's everybody doing?"

"Hi, Mark," Katie said affably. "Hey, have you met Georgette?"

"No, I've never had the pleasure," he said brightly. "Georgette, is it? It's great to meet you."

"Hi, there," she said, capturing Mark's hand in what appeared to be a very tight squeeze. "I'm the baker," she added, and Billy noticed her words were a little slurred. "And this here's Louis," she added, gesturing loosely toward her new friend.

"Hey, there, Louis!" Mark said, greeting a total stranger with his usual zeal. "Great to meet you, buddy," he added, obviously unfazed by the fact that Louis remained as still and silent as a stone. Meanwhile mild irritation worked its way into Billy's mind, but she tried to push it aside. *Stop nitpicking,* she scolded herself. *Stop being such a brat!*

So what if Mark needed to be the life of the party? So what if he was ridiculously *on* right now? He was a jovial, savvy guy—what, was that a crime now? Would she rather he be *off*? A.k.a. a stoic dud—a.k.a. Louis?

After Billy said hi to the dud in question, she grabbed the empty seat next to Mark.

"Hey, where's Des going?" Katie said, tipping her wavy blond head to look behind Billy. Everyone turned and saw Des disappear onto the darkened dance floor. Katie shrugged. "Anyway, Georgette, show Billy the picture you just showed me."

Georgette passed Billy the wallet-sized photo she'd apparently taken out of her pocketbook. It was a little tattered, with bent corners and a crease in the middle. "Who's this?" Billy asked.

"That's Georgette!" Katie said. "Can you believe it? She looks so different."

"I look like a damn idiot," Georgette said with a snort and took a drink. "Idiot" wasn't what Billy would've said; "Betty Crocker knockoff" would've been a more apt description. The woman in the photo had a prim-looking upsweep, a doily collar, a string of pearls around her neck, and a serene expression on her fresh, youthful face. Squinting, Billy looked closer, and then the resemblance clicked.

"It's pretty, Georgette," was all she said about the picture before Georgette reached across the table to take it back.

"It was back when I was young and stupid," Georgette added bitterly, and took another swig of her drink.

"So, Georgette, how long have you been working at Bella Donna with Katie and Billy?" Mark asked congenially.

"Three years. Ever since my asshole ex walked out on me." *Here we go,* Billy thought, anxious to dodge the usual anti-Gary rant.

"Oh, I'm sorry," Mark said sympathetically.

"Don't be," Georgette stated bluntly. "Loser number two—but I'm over it."

Yeah, that was obvious. "At least *this* one I didn't marry."

"Really?" Katie said. "I didn't realize you were married before Gary."

Georgette nodded. "It was a long, long time ago. It soured me on the whole damn institution. He was older than me—broke my heart. One day just up and disappeared."

She hunched over a little in her seat as an awkward silence settled over the table.

"So . . . Louis," Mark spoke up, smiling and placing his hand gently on Billy's back—which, admittedly, was a nice touch, and definitely helping his case. "How do you fit into this whole picture? Do you work in the Copley area, too?"

"No, I just met him on the dance floor," Georgette interjected, and turned to her new companion. "You can really move, Louis. Where'ya from?"

"Worcester," he said, and offered no elaboration.

Mark perked up even more. "Worcester? Hey, no kidding, small world! I have a lot of really good friends in Worcester!" *That's different,* Billy thought sardonically, as Mark and Louis struck up a more of a conversation.

Several minutes later Katie hopped up to get some water, and Billy noticed that as soon as she approached the bar, a flock of young, preying men immediately began to circle, which wasn't surprising, because the girl was supercute. Grinning, Billy looked back at Mark, who was busy, waving to someone in the distance.

"Who are you waving to?" Billy asked conversationally, and rubbed his leg gently under the table. She was trying to get more of a physical connection humming between them; she figured it would help entice him to take her home and kiss her and touch her, and, well . . . the more quality time like that they shared, the closer they would get to taking the relationship to the next level. (Next level being sweaty nakedness.)

"Oh, just a girl I met last summer," Mark replied. "She was going out with a friend of my cousin's roommate." He said it as if it were perfectly normal that they be tight.

Then Billy asked him if he wanted to get going, but he told her he wanted to finish his drink, and what was the rush?

While Mark chatted more with Louis, Billy nursed her raspberry crush and noticed that Georgette was really hitting the sauce. "Hey, Billy!" she said loudly, slurring her words more than before. "Who was that fine piece of ass you were talking to in the bakery yesterday?"

At first Billy's defenses went on alert. She hadn't gotten a chance to tell Mark about running into Seth, and she didn't want him to be jealous or concerned. But then she relaxed, because Mark still wasn't paying any attention—lucky her.

"So who was he?" Georgette pressed. "I only caught a quick glance, but what an *ass*!"

Smiling feebly, Billy said, "Yeah, that was my . . . It was Seth Lannigan. He's . . . you know, with the Churchill people."

Letting out a loud wolf whistle, Georgette slapped her hand on the table. "Boy, I wouldn't mind gettin' a piece of *that*!" Billy's weak smile froze in place as she tried not to picture that. "I mean it," Georgette went on drunkenly. "That is *exactly* what I'm lookin' for—a young stud who will wipe all thoughts from my mind except gettin' laid!"

Billy cringed. God, this was getting embarrassing! Did Georgette have to make her aching horniness a matter of public record? Hell, Billy was horny too, but usually she just sulked about it, sucked it up, suffered in silence . . . basically, she handled it with dignity.

"Just a young buck to ride me till tomorrow and back!" she continued at top volume. "I mean a real young stallion with a real big—"

"Georgette!" Billy whispered sharply, holding her hands up. "I get it; I understand." Oblivious, Georgette slumped against the booth and drank more tequila.

While Mark turned to chat with strangers at a nearby table, Billy looked around restlessly. Suddenly she spotted a couple over by the bar: a short brunette woman and a tall blond man who somehow reminded Billy of herself and Seth, back when they were a couple.

God, she had to get a grip! Why couldn't she stop thinking about him? Why couldn't she just put him completely out of her mind?

The blond guy leaned down to kiss the brunette gently on her lips, and absently Billy sighed and ran her fingertips over her mouth, remembering Seth's soft but possessive kisses. Gentle with a sense of restrained hunger—that was Seth.

Okay, if she didn't stop fixating on him, soon she'd be reliving the day they'd met. . . .

It had been a rainy Tuesday afternoon; she remembered the silvery wetness streaked across the windows at the Prudential food court. She often took her lunch breaks there, and on that particular day Seth had been in front of her in the line for Chinese. When he'd glimpsed her standing behind him, he'd turned and smiled.

"After you," he'd said, which came as a shock, because whatever chivalry wasn't dead in this world was rarely reserved for her. Instantly she'd had a crush on him. And not because he was cute, or because of the sexy, rusty timbre of his voice. But because he'd given her his place in line. Once she was seated at a table, with an overflowing plate of orange chicken, he'd approached her. "Uh, I don't mean to bother you," he'd said, "but was it just me, or did we have some really good eye contact over by the egg rolls?" After that, lunches had turned into dinners, movies had turned into romance, and Billy had started to fall in love. . . .

Just then, Mark stood up. *Yay, are we finally leaving?* "Anyone want another drink while I'm up?" he asked.

Billy slumped back down in her seat.

Oh, well. There was no point in complaining (much). Meeting out had been her idea—her fault and nobody else's. She had just wanted to kill time after work, and she'd mistakenly thought that soon after Mark got to the bar, they would head back to her place.

But she supposed there was plenty of time for that. *What time does this place close, again?* she wondered.

Now, as she watched Mark approach the bar, Billy felt a twinge of jealousy. Girls were eyeing him left and right, and he was smiling like he was the most approachable guy in the world. But it was okay; Billy knew she was the one he wanted. At least at this point—while she watched Mark chat excitedly with the cute female bartender—she was pretty sure she was.

Chapter Seven

"That's it; I've officially given up on women."

Seth shot his friend Joe a look that said, *Yeah right,* as the waitress set down their Cokes. They'd stopped in a grubby little diner known for its juicy bacon cheeseburgers and tangy sea-salt fries. The two men had met several years ago when Seth's older brother, Ian, had played on Joe's charity baseball team.

"No, I mean it," Joe insisted, picking up his glass. "All the women I like end up being high-maintenance and insane." He took a giant gulp, as if to strengthen his resolve.

"They're not all like that," Seth said with a laugh. "You're just picky."

Joe shrugged. "Fine, then I'm picky." Earlier he'd told Seth what had happened on the subway—how he'd bumped into a knockout brunette, how she'd had dark, sexy eyes, how he'd thought they'd shared a moment, and how she'd called him a pervert. "And the thing is, *I* was the one trying to help *her*," he said, revisiting the subject for about the tenth time. Seth nodded, also for the tenth time. "I already had the handrail—I was the one trying to balance *her*."

"Uh-huh," Seth said, restlessly twisting his straw wrapper through his fingers while he glanced around the diner. With a checkered counter with shiny chrome stools and Formica tables with black vinyl booths, the cozy little place was comfortingly the same as it'd always been.

"Women," Joe said with exasperation.

"And speaking of women," Seth said, anxious for a segue—they'd only been talking about the psychotic brunette for the last half hour—"Did I tell you who I saw today?"

Joe arched a questioning eyebrow.

"Billy." Damn . . . saying her name out loud made her seem closer somehow, almost there. He expelled a shallow breath, remembering her face, those eyes—*her*. How it felt to hold her warm, cuddly little body in his arms again; she'd folded right into him like it was the most natural thing in the world. Heat stirred in his groin as he recalled how hard he had gotten when she'd clung to him. How his dick had ached, and how the smell and feel of her had nearly sucked the breath right out of his lungs.

"Billy? Hey, no kidding," Joe said, breaking into a smile and coming more alive. "How the hell is she? God, she was a great kid; I really liked that girl."

"I remember," Seth said, grinning. In fact, Joe used to act like a protective older brother with Billy, as if she needed to be protected—and from Seth.

"What's she doing these days?" Joe asked. "Still working at that company downtown?"

"No. Actually, she's working at a bakery now," Seth said, running his hand along his jaw, which was starting to feel bristly. "Decorating cakes."

"*What?*" Undoubtedly Joe was surprised because he'd always considered Billy particularly bright, artistic, and intelligent; if it were up to him, she'd be drawing aesthetically pleasing blueprints for NASA.

"She's between jobs right now," Seth explained. "I offered to try to help her, but she said no."

"Help her how?"

"Call some contacts," Seth replied. He still had quite a few in Boston.

"How is business, anyway?" Joe asked.

"Fine—shit, that reminds me! I was supposed to call Lucas and check what happened with the Dore account," Seth said, patting his pant pockets for his cell phone. Fuck, how could he have forgotten? Dore Research Institute was the firm's biggest client—Jesus, it was *important.*

No cell in his pocket. He'd forgotten that, too, and left it back at the house. Where was his brain today (besides in his cock)?

"Here you go," the waitress said, setting down their plates. The salty aroma of bacon cheeseburgers and golden-brown fries wafted through the air. Inexplicably more enticing than the takeout Seth charged to his company whenever he worked late. In the back of his mind, he sometimes wondered if his plaintive discontent was typical. Was it only natural to question the present order of things? And was the hollow ache he'd been feeling in his chest lately normal?

Maybe he was just more pensive these days because his thirty-second birthday was coming up in November. And even though he was happy for his brother, Ian, maybe hearing how much fuller and better his life was with his wife by his side made Seth feel even lonelier.

"Anyway, if you see Billy again, give her my best," Joe said, biting into his burger.

Seth nodded as his mind echoed the words, *If I see her again.* In that moment, he knew that he would. He would go to the Dessert Jubilee that weekend, which up until yesterday he'd had no intention of doing. The truth was, he felt almost tormented by the intense pull to see Billy again—to talk to her, just to get close to her. Even if it was only as friends, he wanted to know her again.

Of course, they hadn't been able to be friends back when he'd first moved to Seattle; Billy had said it was just too painful. But now, with so much time having passed, why not? True, she still aroused the hell out of him, but he could handle that . . . right?

Anyway, the past was water under the bridge; he didn't even know why he kept dwelling on it. He had to admit it was a little fucked-up that he had so much intense residual desire for Billy Cabot, and not for his ex-girlfriend, Laura, whom he'd broken up with less than a year ago. Then again, he and Laura had played things out and discovered they weren't a good match, while he and Billy had never gotten that chance.

"So is she married?" Joe asked now, breaking Seth's reverie.

Seth shrugged. "I didn't see a ring." Damn—he'd said too much. Cocking a brow, Joe grinned. "So you looked for a ring, huh?"

Seth didn't bother defending himself; he just said, "Oh, shut up, will you?"

Joe just laughed.

"Well . . . bye," Billy said softly, leaning up to kiss Mark on the mouth. He returned the gesture with a few moist lip presses before pulling back. She'd wanted to walk him out to steal a few more kisses, but now she wasn't quite sure why.

"Good night, cutie," he said with a smile. "Make sure you lock up." With a happy-go-lucky bounce in his step, he disappeared down her darkened street. Billy stood on the front steps of her brownstone, smiling after him—bemused and a little sleepy.

After they'd spent a couple (interminable) hours at the Kenmore Pub, they'd come back to Billy's apartment, watched a little TV, and made out on the couch. It had been nice. Very, very nice. He was a man; she was a woman. Nice.

Now, as Billy turned to go inside, a chill cut sharply across her chest. She hugged herself while wind whistled low through the air and sent leaves sweeping and fluttering down the street. It was a crisp, eerie kind of night, emphasized by the blackened windows of the brownstone. In fact, the only apartment lit up was hers, on the third floor.

As she slipped her key into the lock, she heard a rustling in the shrubs behind her. Abruptly she spun around, but there was nothing there. Nothing she could see, anyway, so she turned back to the door. Then she heard it again.

Instinctively, her pulse kicked up. The wind had stopped, so what was that rustle?

Probably a raccoon.

A twig snapped loudly behind her. *That's not a raccoon,* she thought, just as her key got jammed in the old, tarnished lock. Leaves crackled behind the shrubs, and even though she still couldn't see anything, her chest shuddered with fear. *Damn it!* She struggled with both hands to turn the key, but the lock rattled and resisted. Her heart pounded in her ears, and her palms began to sweat.

Finally the key turned. Shoving hard on the heavy front door, Billy hurried inside and leaned all her weight on it so it would close quickly. With a hand to her heart, she glanced back through the side window. Nothing. It must've only been an animal. Sighing with relief, she thanked God it had been only her imagination running rampant, and jogged up the stairs to her apartment.

Twenty minutes later Billy was showered and balled up on her sofa under her favorite afghan, with Pike resting lazily near her lap. With a contented sigh she thought how much she loved this apartment. There were unfinished paintings and stacks of books all around, and oversize furniture that should've made the place feel cluttered, but instead, just made it feel cozy. White and colored lights glowed warmly in her living room, and a pumpkin-scented candle flickered brightly on the coffee table.

Coffee! That was a good idea. On the way to the kitchen she stopped at the table in the front hall because she noticed the flashing red "2" on the answering machine. That was right—she'd ignored the phone when she and Mark had been cuddling on the couch. Now she hit play.

"Billy? It's Mom. Aren't you home yet? Belinda, if you're home, pick up. Okay—I guess you're not home. (Another pause.) Well, I called to see how you're doing—and also to tell you I got the number of that headhunter I told you about. Remember Gladys Belding's son, Kip? Gladys said you should call him right away to set something up. Apparently he's new, but he's already doing fantastic with it. I want you to call him." She recited Kip Belding's number, and repeated it four times. "Don't forget to call him," she added. "He'll be able to get you some interviews and find you a real job. And call me after you talk to him, and tell me what he says. Don't forget to let me know. Okay, I'll see you tomorrow night for dinner. I love you. Call me about Kip—bye."

She hit next to hear the second message, but there was nothing. A little static, then silence. But there was no dial tone, indicating that the caller was still on the line when the machine was recording. A trace of anxiety crept into Billy's chest as she listened to the charged silence that stretched across the line, and then—

Brriinng!

She jumped, startled by the loud shrilling of the phone. Pike leaped off the couch, barking. "Hello!" Billy said, after snatching up the receiver.

"Hey—are you okay?"

"Oh, God," she said on a breath, and clutched her chest. "You scared me."

"Why?" Corryn asked. "Is something wrong?"

"No, no, it's nothing," Billy said, catching her breath, and resting the cordless between her ear and her shoulder. She petted Pike and rubbed under his chin to calm him down. "There was just this hang-up call on my machine, and then the phone rang. . . ." Her voice trailed off as she realized how silly she sounded. What was wrong with her today?

As she trailed into the kitchen, Pike followed, barking again. "Shh, be quiet, sweetie," Billy said, petting him, "or Lady McAvit will call Animal Control."

"Oh, God, would she *really*?" Corryn said.

"Who knows anymore?" Billy replied, and reached for the sack of Columbian coffee beans she kept in the freezer.

"Hey, want to hear a real asshole story?" Corryn asked.

"Is this a trick question?"

"Okay, so I'm on the E line today, and the guy next to me tweaks my nipple."

"What!" Billy froze mid coffee grinding. "Are you *serious*?"

"Oh, but wait, that's not even the best part," Corryn said. "The guy's a *cop*."

"*What!*"

"I know! I couldn't believe it. Just when I thought I'd seen it all, I discover yet another dimension to the pathetic desperation of men."

"Seriously. Did you say anything?" Billy asked.

Corryn went on to give her a full account of what had happened on the train, including the part about how she hadn't actually *seen* the green-eyed, overdeveloped guy do it, but it just had to be him. "Anyway, how was your night?"

Billy filled her in on the Kenmore Pub—namely, how it was fun until Mark the boyfriend turned into Mark the politician. "I don't know," she said now. "I just wish he didn't have to be on all the time."

And she wished *she* could be more on—*turned* on.

"Yeah, Kane was on all the time too," Corryn said. "On the *prowl*."

Just then Billy remembered the cute female bartender, and every other girl whose face lit up for Mark. "That isn't making me feel better," she said.

"Oh, no, no! I'm sorry; I didn't mean anything about Mark. I was just ranting."

So what else was new? Sporadic male-bashing had become a staple in Corryn's conversations. Not that Billy minded, but she just wished that Kane hadn't made her sister so relentlessly cynical. They chatted for a few more minutes; then Billy said, "Okay, I'll see you tomorrow night at Mom and Dad's."

"Um . . ."

Uh-oh—she knew that tone of voice.

"Corryn, don't even *think* about punking out tomorrow." Her sister was guiltily silent on the other end. "If you think you're leaving me to fend off two weeks of Mom's pent-up nagging, you are very wrong."

"Fine," she relented. "I'll be there."

"Thank you," Billy said brightly. "Love you."

"Yeah, yeah. Love you, too."

After Billy settled back on the sofa with her freshly brewed coffee, Pike settled in beside her. The TV was on, but she wasn't paying much attention. Instead, images kept flashing through her mind, taking her back through her romantic history—back to her first time with her ex-boyfriend, Ryan. He'd worked in the sales department of Net Circle, and he was a cute, funny guy, even if he did have a bit of a Napoleon complex. They'd slept together on their five-month anniversary, which probably had had less to do with Billy imagining herself in love with Ryan, and more to do with Billy's body screaming that it was ready.

It wasn't that she was a prude; it was just that she'd gotten off to a late start with the opposite sex because she'd attended Catholic girls' schools until she was eighteen. When she'd entered college, guys had been everywhere, yet dating was aberrant. Hooking up for empty, drunk thrills was more the standard protocol, and that just wasn't her. Sure, she'd kissed a few guys back then, but she'd hoped for something more substantial—more meaningful.

Inevitably, because of her naïveté, she'd fallen hard for Seth. He'd been her first real boyfriend, and she'd thrown herself so deeply and blindly into their relationship—for the short time it had lasted, anyway. Ryan remained the one guy Billy had been with, and sex had just been getting good when he dumped her. Said he just wasn't "feeling it" anymore. Two for two; it hadn't done wonders for her self-esteem at the time. But then, when Ryan left Net Circle to take a different job, Billy realized how superficial their relationship had really been, because once he wasn't around, she didn't think about him much.

She sighed now, thinking how wonderful it would be to have a serious boyfriend—no waiting. Someone who was her best friend, soul mate, and sex slave, all wrapped up in one. She'd rest her cheek on his chest and listen to his heart, and he wouldn't have to get up early in the morning. Or if he did, he wouldn't care.

Despite Billy's minimal sexual experience—or maybe because of it—her dreams that night were fraught with dirty, carnal images. They flashed through her mind like bursts of fire; they licked flames up her body. One dream was particularly vivid in her mind: Seth tearing her blouse, spreading her legs, and thrusting his fingers roughly inside her. There was a fierce hunger to it that in no way represented Seth's gentle soul, but maybe it captured the raw sensuality Billy had always suspected was lurking beneath his kind heart. The idea of that kind of hungry, savage desire was what aroused her beyond belief.

She woke up sweaty, with her pajama pants sticking to her inner thighs as the dampness between her legs made her crotch feel soaked. Squeezing her legs tight, she twisted in her sheets and tried desperately to slip back into the dream. To finish what they'd started. To find out what it would be like to have sex with Seth—even if only in her mind.

Chapter Eight

The following day Seth was hammering a new wooden railing to the back deck stairs, trying to pound away the thoughts of Billy that kept rumbling through his mind. An hour earlier he'd called Lucas to check on business, and after giving him a positive status update, Lucas had thrown in his usual offer to buy Seth out. It was a running joke between them—the kind that was dead serious at the same time—and until recently, Seth had never considered taking Lucas up on the offer.

But over the past couple of months, the idea had gained appeal. What would it be like to sell the company and leave Seattle? To move back and start over?

He'd become almost romantically numb with constant work, but it was the kind of numbness that went undetected unless it was contrasted. And he couldn't think of a more distinct contrast to his increasingly solitary existence than Billy Cabot, a girl who exuded a natural kind of magnetism. He wanted to be around her—to feel some of her breezy optimism, to push the envelope of his raging desire, to be important to her again.

What am I saying? Seth thought as he flipped over his hammer to pull a nail out of the wood; he'd just banged it in crooked because he was paying no attention, and instead letting his imagination run off without his sense.

They'd shared a cup of coffee, for chrissake. (Suddenly he remembered the long, hot, arousing hug they'd shared, too. Then again, he couldn't say for absolute certainty that the lust and frustration hadn't been all on his part.) For all he knew, she had a serious boyfriend already. For all he knew, she had no interest in him anymore. For all he knew, she didn't like the idea of a long-distance relationship any more now than she had four years ago. For all he knew—

"Seth? Are you home?"

Startled, he looked up and saw Sally winding around the backyard with a basket in hand. Her face lit up when she saw him working on the deck, and she gently elbowed the tall young woman who was with her. "Hi," he said, smiling, and then abruptly realized he was bare-chested. With a hint of shyness, he reached for the T-shirt he'd pulled off about half an hour ago.

"I hope this is a good time," Sally said, coming closer.

"Sure, sure, of course," he said, hastily pulling his shirt on, then ruffling his hand carelessly through his hair.

"This is my niece, Pam," Sally said, climbing onto the deck with the picnic basket in one hand and Pam's arm in the other.

Of course, he should've guessed. Although, in fairness, he had agreed to the three of them getting together. Fine, as long as Sally didn't plan on going anywhere. "Hey, how're you doing?" he said amiably, and shook Pam's hand.

"Hi," she said, running some of her brown pageboy haircut behind her ears. As she restlessly shuffled her feet, the iridescent parachute suit she wore made swishing noises. She reminded him of an elementary school gym teacher—one who played for the WNBA in her spare time.

"We brought lunch," Sally explained. "We figured you were working hard back here, so we wanted to give you a nice break." She nudged Pam again. "Right, Pam?"

"Huh? Oh, yeah, right," she said.

"Thanks, that's so nice," Seth said, taking the heavy basket for Sally and setting it down on the picnic table. "You didn't have to do that," he added, grinning, as he peeked inside the basket. "What's in here, anyway?"

"We brought lobster salad sandwiches and sushi rolls from Jacques's Bistro."

"That sounds great," he said, though he planned to skip the sushi. "Well, here, let me clear some room." After he shifted his scattered tools down to the other side of the thick oak picnic table, Pam and Seth sat down, while Sally spread out the plates, napkins, and food. Then she pulled out three small bottles of chilled Perrier and three straws.

"So, Pam, Sally mentioned that you're planning on moving," Seth said conversationally. As he peeled the foil off his sandwich, he tried to ignore Sally's beaming expression as she darted encouraging glances around the table. "Where do you live now?"

"I'm an EMT in Newton," she said flatly. "But I want to move to the West Coast in the next few months or so."

"Oh, what's out there?"

Shrugging indifferently, she bit off a big hunk of her sandwich and replied with her mouth full: "I don't know; I just want to see other places, like California."

"And Washington state, of course," Sally chimed in. Pam mumbled in agreement.

"By the way, Sally, how's everything coming together for the jubilee tomorrow night?" Seth asked.

"Oh, everything should go smoothly. And thanks again for going to the Bella Donna Bakery for me the other day."

"No problem," he said casually, not revealing how much his visit to Bella Donna had affected him.

"Speaking of the jubilee," Sally said, "Pam's going to be there, too. Right, Pam?"

"Uh-huh."

"So, then, uh . . ." Sally began, smiling broadly, looking from Seth to Pam, Pam to Seth. "We'll all be there then. Tomorrow night. That's good; it'll give us a chance to get to know each other better. Of course, you both already know *me*, so . . ."

"Hey, Seth, where's the head?" Pam asked, rising from the table. At this angle his eyes had to travel absurdly far up to make contact with Pam's.

"Just inside," he said, motioning to the sliding glass doors. "Go through the kitchen, and turn left in the hallway."

When she was out of earshot, Sally leaned over and said, "Isn't she gorgeous?"

"Yeah, she's a cute kid," Seth replied benignly, deliberately making the point that he had no interest. But just in case he wasn't making it clear enough, he added, "Sally, you realize that I'm not looking to meet someone new, right?" Not exactly the truth, but it would suffice for the moment. "I hope you're not getting any ideas."

Sally's eyes shot wide open as she placed an elegant, manicured hand to her chest. "Me?" she said innocently. *"Ideas?"*

Oh, no . . .

"My girls!"

"Hi, Mom," Billy said brightly, and met Adrienne for a tight hug in the open doorway.

Corryn trailed two paces back. "Hey, Mom," she said, entering their parents' house and shutting the door behind her. Adrienne hugged her next.

"Oh, this is wonderful, dinner with my girls—" She stopped midsentence, sniffed Corryn's shoulder, and grimaced. "You smell like smoke."

"Gee, I wonder how that happened," Corryn said sarcastically.

Adrienne brushed off the comment. "Anyway, I hope you girls are hungry. Billy, I hope you're not too full from the bakery."

"Mom, I *work* at the bakery, not test the merchandise." Unless you counted the plate of fudge brownies Georgette had left on the counter today—but then, Billy had had only four of those.

"What's that?" Adrienne said, motioning to the small white box in Billy's hand tied up with pink string. Incidentally, this wasn't going to do much to help demonstrate Billy's point.

"Coconut cupcakes," Billy replied, then held up her hand in her own defense. "Georgette was just going to throw them out, and I know you probably don't want to eat them, Mom, but I thought Corryn and Dad might like them."

Adrienne flashed her quintessential pursed look of disapproval and said, "Because I love my family, I can assure you those are going right in the garbage."

"Love me a little less, Mom—thanks," Corryn said, taking the box from Billy and shrugging out of her coat.

Then Adrienne spun around. "Nobody's said anything yet."

"About what?" Corryn asked.

"How I look." She spun again. "I've lost four pounds; didn't you notice?" Honestly, their mom was always so petite, it was hard to tell. "God, I just feel so healthy and alive!"

"That's great, Mom," Billy said.

"Thank you, honey. *Anyone* can do it, you know. With a little discipline, some exercise, a proper diet."

Billy shot her sister a knowing look before they headed into the dining room. As Adrienne carried in a covered dish from the kitchen, Corryn made raspberry crushes at the minibar next to the china cabinet.

"Hey, where's Dad?" Billy asked after her sister handed her a drink.

"He's out looking for a new fishing pole," Adrienne said. "He'll be back soon." She lifted the cover off of the serving dish and revealed a red, watery casserole that lurked underneath. "It's vegetable lasagna," she explained. "I found the recipe in a tofu cookbook."

Already off to an inauspicious start. But Billy made the best of the meal, forking through layers of thinly sliced tofu and chunky vegetables, and at least she had her raspberry crush to wash it all down with a zing.

"Too bad Dad missed dinner," Corryn remarked, pushing a hunk of wet parsnip around on her plate.

"No, he already ate," Adrienne said with a wave of her hand. "A sausage-and-pepper sub from the deli down the street." Hmm, suddenly a trip to the mob-front hoagie shop around the corner sounded pretty good. "He's being so difficult. He keeps refusing to eat a healthy diet—even though *anyone* can do it," she finished, looking straight at Billy.

When Billy got up to clear the dishes, Corryn said, "Let's break out the dessert."

Adrienne shook her head, lips twisted in disapproval. This from the woman who used to buy Entenmann's cookies and eat half the box at the blinking light on the way home. A little too excitedly, Corryn snatched a coconut cupcake from the box on the bar and announced that she was going outside for a smoke. After she left, Adrienne lamented to Billy about what the tar and saturated fat were doing to her sister's innards at that very moment.

Forty minutes later everyone was in the family room. Their dad was home, tinkering with his guilty pleasure, the ancient slide projector, while Billy slouched comfortably in a cream-colored recliner, Corryn lay on the sofa, and Adrienne sat in a green, high-backed chair that resembled a throne. While they waited for the cruise slide show to begin, Adrienne moved in for the kill. "So what's new with Mark?"

"Nothing. I saw him last night," Billy said.

"Mark," Billy's dad echoed. "Mark . . . Do I know him?"

Adrienne rolled her eyes. "Get with it, David. Billy's been dating him for over a month now."

David just shrugged. "Doesn't sound familiar."

"Have you found out what he makes yet?"

"No, and I don't plan to," Billy said, thoroughly bored by the question.

"Nobody ever tells me anything," Adrienne said huffily. "At least tell me you called Gladys Belding's son, Kip."

"Um . . ."

"Belinda. If you don't call him, I'll be humiliated. I *promised* Gladys you'd call."

And you did that because . . . ?

"Slide show's all set up," David said. "Anytime you're ready, Addy."

The first twenty slides were pictures of David boarding the boat, walking to the cabin, opening the cabin door, and unzipping his suitcase. Obviously Adrienne had been holding the camera. Next she showed slides of all the people she'd met on the cruise, even if only for a minute, and narrated their myriad ailments and dysfunctions.

"See the one with the chubby knees and loud vacation prints?" she said. "That's Louise Moonie. A sweet woman, but no tolerance for dairy. We played pinochle together on day three." She clicked to the next slide. "Oh, now *that's* Maeve Byrnes. She has a son who sounds *very* interesting—Corryn, are you paying attention?"

When her sister didn't answer, Billy glanced over and noticed that Corryn's eyes were closed, and her mouth was curved softly and sleepily against the throw pillow.

"Corryn?" Adrienne said again, and Billy discreetly shook her sister's foot.

"Oh, um, what?" Corryn said, her eyes fluttering open.

"I think I found an interesting man for you."

"Oh . . ." she said, stretching, and slowly sitting up. "Sorry, Mom, but I'm giving up interesting men for Lent."

"Don't be smart. I'm serious; Maeve Byrnes has a son around your age who is single and looking."

"Desperate, in other words."

"He's *not* desperate. In fact, he's tall, dark, and handsome."

"What, according to his *mother*?" Corryn said with an incredulous laugh, sending a look around the room that said, *Is it just me, or does our mom need an intervention?*

"Look, Corryn, I know you're not crazy about setups—"

"No, I love them, really. They're right up there with getting my period in white pants."

"Can we please change the topic?" Billy said, glaring at her mother. "If Corryn doesn't want to be set up, then that's it—end of discussion."

Adrienne heaved a frustrated sigh. "Fine, I'm done trying to care. I'm gonna stay completely out of your life from now on."

"Thank you," Corryn said.

"If you want to end up alone like Aunt Penelope—"

"Addy, please . . ." David implored, rubbing his temple.

"Mom, can't we all just enjoy the slide show?" Billy asked, realizing that "enjoy" was pushing it, but at least they could avoid controversial topics like Corryn's love life, and the fact that Adrienne's older sister had never married.

In fact, Billy was particularly short on patience when it came to criticism one of her favorite aunt. So she had never married, so she was almost sixty and still lived in the house she'd grown up in. Why did Adrienne have to obsess about it? Why did she always have to panic that Corryn and Billy would end up miserable, lonely spinsters just like Aunt Pen—who didn't seem the least bit lonely or miserable?

Aunt Pen had started her own interior design business over

twenty years ago, and since then it had flourished into an undeniable success. She could afford to live almost anywhere, yet she chose to stay in the house she'd inherited from her parents, which Billy considered a gesture of pure heart, and just another indication of Pen's warmth and sincerity.

"Fine, I guess I'm *always* wrong," Adrienne mumbled now, still sulking because no one was supporting her attempts to set up Corryn. "I just want the best for my girls because I love them, and I'm wrong *again*."

Calmly, Billy said, "Mom, you're not always wrong. You just have a compulsive need to criticize. No matter what Corryn or I do, you'll always find something else we should be working on. Face it: You're never satisfied."

Defensively, Adrienne yelped, "That's not true! How can you say that to me? And what about all the good I do? Do you ever remember that?"

"Okay, okay," David said quickly, in his most pacifist tone. "I think everyone's getting a little too worked up here. Addy, I know you want to help, but Billy and Corryn are both adults now. They have to make their own choices."

Adrienne's face scrunched in bafflement.

"Anyone for espresso?" he asked affably, and went into the kitchen. Corryn slipped outside for another cigarette. After she returned there was a silence in the air—one that seemed to echo things that had just been said and magnify how absurd they really were.

"So . . . are we all still good friends?" Billy asked, smiling coaxingly at her mom and her sister. Corryn smirked at her mom, who responded by sticking her tongue out. Billy let out an exasperated laugh; they were both so damn alike.

Adrienne switched the lights back on and shut off the slide projector. "I had something else I wanted to talk to you girls about. But now I see how you *really* feel about me . . ."

"Oh, Mom, come on," Billy said lightly. "What is it?"

"Well, I had an idea for something fun that the three of us could do together."

"Uh-oh . . ." Corryn said.

"I have two words for you," Adrienne continued, sitting back down in her chair. "Adult. Ed."

"What about it?" Billy asked.

"How about we all take a class together? One of those fun night courses. Ever since I lost weight and changed my lifestyle, I've wanted to take a cooking class, and I was thinking it would be a good excuse for some mother–daughter bonding. It'll be my treat; I'll take care of everything," she finished with her hands perched together, prayer style. "What do you say?"

She just looked so excited about the idea that Billy couldn't bear to say no. "Okay, I'll do it," she said, and looked over at Corryn, who she was pretty sure would go along, too . . . though she might make Adrienne sweat it out a little.

After a pause, Corryn shrugged. "Fine, as long as it's only one or two nights a week."

"Oh, great!" Adrienne enthused. "I'll just go get the course book."

After she left the room to fetch that, David returned bearing espresso and Sausalito cookies. "Don't let your mother see these," he whispered, grinning, and offered them to Billy and Corryn. Corryn took one, but Billy passed, despite the sensory receptors in her brain that always buzzed for chocolate.

"Dad, I brought cupcakes," she said.

He shook his head and said quietly, "No—too messy. I'll sneak one later." After he bit into his cookie, he said, "By the way, I like this adult-school idea. It'll be good for you to spend time with your mother. She misses you when you're not here."

Corryn scoffed, obviously not buying it.

"It's true," David insisted, absently spilling pieces of cookie on his shirt and the hassock. (Not exactly a master of subterfuge.)

Corryn sighed. "If she misses us, why does she antagonize us the minute we walk through the door?"

"Her heart's in the right place," he said tritely but sincerely. "She just wants you to be happy—and she doesn't want you to smoke. None of us do."

"It's true," Billy agreed softly.

Just then Adrienne bounded back into the room with the adult-school course book, but quickly got sidetracked by all the cookie crumbs. She bickered with David about using a plate—or how about giving up junk food altogether?—while Billy rolled her eyes, and Corryn fell back on the sofa, mumbling, "I need a cigarette."

Chapter Nine

The next day Billy got to the Copley Mall early—stopping at Doubleday's to buy that new Renoir book—before heading to Bella Donna to check on her cakes for the jubilee. She'd finished them yesterday, and wanted to make sure they were safe and sound, their decoration pristinely intact. She also wanted to place candy leaves around all the edges, which she couldn't do until now, because if she had put the candy pieces on too early, moisture from the icing would have broken them up.

When she got to Bella Donna, she said hi to Des, who was cleaning the rotating pie case. "Is Donna here?" she asked.

"Yeah, up in her office, making the schedule for next week."

Nodding, Billy went to the back and crossed the pink tile to the walk-in freezer. She lifted the cover off the first cake, but the freezer was too dark to make anything out clearly, so she propped the door wider to let some light in. And then her jaw dropped.

Oh, no . . .

What happened?

Smeared icing—waves and sunset swirled together into a tye-dyed blob of pastels. Her stomach knotted as she scanned the cake in disbelief. This one was her favorite of the three, too. Sudden panic seized her chest, and she raced to the freezer to check on the others.

Damn it all! The other two cakes were also a mess; the trim was mashed and the images distorted. What the hell had happened? And what if she hadn't decided to come in and check on the cakes before the jubilee tonight?

Holding back frustrated tears, Billy sucked in a breath and tried to figure out what to do. First of all, it was suddenly clear what had happened: Someone must have been ambling around in the dark freezer, accidentally knocked over the stack of cakes, and not had the guts to own up to it. She was really disappointed at the thought, because she considered her coworkers friends. To give them the slight benefit of the doubt, whoever had done it surely hadn't realized the extent of the damage. A lot of good that did her—Jesus, what now?

Time to get it together and solve this mess. Of course, she could simply show Donna, who would undoubtedly suggest that Billy wipe off the frosting, recoat the cakes with white icing, and forget it. The defeatist in her might be tempted, but ultimately that wasn't how Billy wanted to handle this. She'd been excited about the sheet cakes; she'd spent the past few days slaving over them, and she wanted to present something special tonight. She didn't want to cop out with something generic.

At the same time, there was something about having to redo something you'd labored over that was more daunting and awful than simply starting a whole new project. *Hmm . . .*

Looking around the room, she caught sight of her little plastic Doubleday's bag, inside which was her new book on Renoir.

And suddenly she had an idea.

By the time Billy got to Churchill that night, she was wiped out and exhausted—not exactly an ideal feeling when you were about to cater a party. She definitely needed a cup of coffee before the Dessert Jubilee got under way. After spending hours slaving and redecorating, she'd managed a simplified but pretty re-creation of *Les Grands Boulevards*, which spread panoramic style across all three cakes. Obviously she was no threat to the art-forging world, but she still thought it was pretty damn fabulous for cake.

As she walked down Main Street with a café mocha, she took in her surroundings, noting that Churchill was one of the cutest, coziest places she'd ever been. It had storybook charm, with cobblestone streets, wrought-iron street lamps, and sidewalks lined with maple trees. People milled around the quaint boutiques, old-fashioned bookshops, and elegant little bistros.

The plush expanse of green lawn that served as the town square was surrounded with thick foliage and benches, and right in the center was a statue of Mort Churchill—town father and famed dessert connoisseur. From what Billy understood, the annual Dessert Jubilee was a kind of founder's-day event, existing as both a fundraising affair and a tribute to Mort Churchill's memory. Right now the town square was festive, filled with tables and chairs, and crepe-paper party lights strung along utility poles.

This was Billy's first catering gig since she'd begun work at Bella Donna a couple months ago, but Katie had told her it was a snap. Basically they were supposed to keep the coffee brewing, consolidate half-empty trays, replenish napkins, plates, and utensils, and make rounds with champagne cocktails. The sheet cakes weren't being wheeled out until later in the evening, as a finale. It all sounded manageable, but it would have been even better if Billy weren't about to drop from exhaustion.

Donna had come earlier, but when she saw that Melissa had everything under control, she'd left. Now Georgette was in Marie's Café—the restaurant that annually volunteered its kitchen—and Des and Katie were on the lawn, setting up the last of the chairs.

Billy and Melissa were spreading out tablecloths when Billy suddenly remembered something. "Oh, Melissa, I saw you at the Rack the other night. But I don't think you realized it was me."

Melissa regarded her with a blank expression.

"You know, on Wednesday night?" Billy said by way of clarification. "I waved to you, but I guess you didn't recognize me."

Furrowing her eyebrows, Melissa shrugged. "Wasn't me."

It wasn't? Billy had thought for sure . . .

Then again, the bar had been dark, the woman had been far away, and Billy had been drinking raspberry crushes. She must've been mistaken.

Just then Mrs. Tailor passed by with two trays wobbling in her hands. "Oh, here, let me help you," Billy said, coming quickly to her side.

"Oh, thanks so much," she said, smiling, as Billy set the trays down on the buffet table.

"Sure, no problem. Listen, if Melissa asks, would you tell her I went to the bathroom?" She knew she could use the bathroom inside Marie's Café, but she preferred to go across the street to the pavilion on the fringes of the beach. It would give her an excuse to amble around a little more before getting back to work.

Once she'd left the brightness of the town square, Billy realized how dark it really was outside. It was only seven o'clock, but there was an eerie blue-black sky hovering over the coast. She spotted a wide stone building that looked like a little house, with two doors. The one on the right had an engraved sign that read, "Ladies."

As she reached for the handle, a cold wind blew across her face. Trees rocked from side to side, and leaves fluttered wildly through the sky. Then she heard voices.

She looked around, and through a stream of fog she saw two men arguing down by the water. One was big and burly, with a dark gray beard. He wore a long black coat and a cap. The other had dark, slicked-back hair and a flaming-red neckerchief flapping crazily in the wind. Both men jabbed angry fingers at each other and motioned toward the water.

Suddenly the one with the neckerchief turned his head and caught Billy watching. Abruptly she looked away and ducked into the ladies' room. When she came out five minutes later, both men were gone.

An hour later the jubilee was in full swing, and the town square was jumping; people were milling around chatting, hugging, and, of course, eating. Eating with abandon. Not that Billy could blame them. In fact, if her stomach weren't clenched and nervous, she might contemplate a pastry or two herself.

Instead she kept checking to see if Seth had arrived yet. Could she be more desperate to see him? She didn't think so—not that she'd ever admit it out loud. Really, she'd promised that she'd put him out of her mind, yet every other second she was scanning the crowd, hoping to catch a glimpse of his dark blond hair.

Finally, in the midst of making the rounds with champagne cocktails, she saw him. Her breath caught in her throat as she watched him move through the crowd. She swallowed deeply, pushing down a lump of emotion clogging her throat. Just as she was about to turn and finish passing out cocktails, Seth glanced over, and their eyes locked.

He grinned and started walking toward her. Billy's mouth ran dry, and her tongue felt like thick cotton with each step he took. She didn't even register the weight of the tray in her hand, or the ache in her arm from holding it up for so long. Her pulse pounded in her ears, and she couldn't remember the last time she'd felt so nervous . . . so excited . . . so inexorably filled with anticipation.

Out of sheer survival instinct, then, she turned away—and smacked right into someone else. "Oh, I'm sorry!" she yelped, startled, and relieved she hadn't tipped over the drinks on her tray.

"Quite all right, madam." She instantly recognized the man she'd collided with. His slicked hair and flaming neckerchief kind of gave him away. It was one of the men who'd been arguing on the beach. Up close, she took note of his pronounced widow's peak, olive-green blazer, and tan linen pants. If he recognized her, he didn't show it. Nodding briefly, he offered a fleeting smile. "Please do excuse me," he said in a quasi-English accent, then called into the crowd, "Leslie, you look stunning! And Harlan, my good man!" Certainly a far cry from his irate behavior on the beach earlier.

"Excuse me."

Billy turned. There was a tall man with a gray beard and a long black coat standing beside her. Wait a minute . . . talk about eerie! It was the *other* man who'd been arguing on the beach. It was like a bizarre little reunion, but luckily neither of the men seemed to recognize her. Instinctively, Billy whipped her head around to look for the one in the neckerchief, but he had disappeared into the crowd. "Excuse me," the bearded man repeated, louder this time and with a surlier edge.

"Oh, I'm sorry," Billy managed. "Do you need something?"

"Do those have nuts in them?" he asked, motioning to the platter of chocolate-chip cookie bars on the table behind her.

"No, I don't think so. . . ."

"Because I'm allergic to nuts," he said loudly. "Can't have nuts." Just then Billy noticed that his champagne flute was empty. With his empty hand he reached for a fresh champagne cocktail from her tray. He appeared a bit haggard, half his face shadowed with an unkempt beard, and the other half dominated by dark, drawn eyes. Before Billy could say anything else, the man brushed past her, set his empty flute down on the table, and snagged a cookie bar. Billy observed him walking off, swaying a little, and she wondered how many drinks he'd had that night.

Just then someone tapped her shoulder. It was a fleeting but gentle touch. Instinctively she knew who it was, and with her heart in her throat, she turned around.

"Hi," Seth said, smiling down at her.

"Hello," she said, as a crazy image popped into her head: jumping up, wrapping her legs around Seth's waist, and covering his face with kisses. And, besides the fact that he'd probably slip a disk, the idea was extremely tempting.

Finally Billy started to feel a dull ache in her arms from holding her tray up too long.

"Do you need some help?" Seth asked, as if sensing her discomfort, and took the tray from her. He set it down on a nearby table.

"Oh, thanks . . ." she said stupidly. Yeah, she supposed *she* could've thought of that . . . if her mind weren't too booked up with other ideas—with silly, futile thoughts. "So . . . I'm glad you could make it," she said, smiling.

"Me, too."

Chewing her lip, Billy willed her heart to slow down, but it continued thudding hard in her chest. *It's only Seth,* she told herself, but it didn't do much good. "How's it coming with your mom's house?" she asked.

"Let's see . . . I've fixed the railing on the deck and the latch on the fence. Next I'm repainting the gazebo in the backyard. My mom called yesterday and said she can't decide if she wants it to be cream-colored or beige. Personally, I thought they were the same thing."

Grinning, Billy said, "And here I thought fix-ups happened *after* the house was sold."

"Hey, I've gotta keep busy," he said glibly, then glanced down at her body. "I like your uniform."

"Yeah, right." Billy laughed, rolling her eyes.

"No, I mean it. You look cute."

Blushing, she joked, "Please, I look like a waiter." Then she held up her hand. "Don't say it; I know—I *am* a waiter."

He laughed, and it was a warm, familiar sound that inexplicably relaxed her.

"Oh, Seth, *there* you are!"

Billy turned to see a well-dressed older woman hurrying toward them, dragging along with her a tall, skinny woman in a purple warm-up suit. The older woman looked vaguely familiar, but Billy couldn't place her. The younger one appeared to be in her early twenties; she had angular features, and moved with a lanky kind of clumsiness that probably came with being over six-four.

"Hi, Sally," Seth said—Sally, that was it! Billy had met her once at Seth's house—then smiled pleasantly at the tall girl. "Hey, Pam. Are you two enjoying the party?"

Sally replied, "It's wonderful! Of course, I can't eat all these sweets like I used to. I'm just not lucky enough to have *Pam's* knock-out figure and dynamite metabolism."

"Uh-huh," Seth managed. "By the way, Sally, this is Billy. I'm not sure if you two met a few years ago."

"Yes, we did, briefly," Billy said with a short wave. "Hi, it's nice to see you again."

"Oh, hello . . ." Sally replied, a little flustered; either she didn't remember, or she wasn't prepared to be diverted from her obvious matchmaking designs.

Meanwhile, Billy couldn't help but feel a twinge of jealousy at the thought of Seth going out with another woman—redwoodesque or otherwise. Sighing softly, she started chewing on her bottom lip again.

"How do you know Seth?" Sally asked her.

When Billy hesitated, Seth piped in, "We're friends." Somehow the words cut through Billy's heart, which wasn't logical because she and Seth *were* friends now, and a week ago they hadn't even been that.

"Sally!"

They all turned and saw the man with the neckerchief coming toward them, with a man and a woman alongside him. Jeez, could this be a more annoyingly small world?

"Oh, hello, Greg," Sally said, smiling, and made the introductions. The man with the neckerchief was Greg Dappaport, owner of the Churchill Art Gallery, and the couple with him were mutual friends, Marion and Frederick Thames.

"You look familiar," Greg said, squinting a little while he studied Billy's face. "Have we met before?"

Hmm . . . she wasn't sure if he was referring to the time he had spotted her eavesdropping on the beach, or the time she'd bumped into him like a total klutz—which was only about fifteen minutes ago, so she supposed she hadn't made much of an impression on him. Either way, neither exploit was particularly flattering. "No, I don't think so," she said, smiling politely.

While everyone exchanged small talk about the jubilee and about other residents of the town, Billy felt uncomfortably like a seventh wheel. But she didn't want to walk away from Seth—not after she'd waited all night to see him, to talk to him. "Oh, Seth!" Sally said suddenly. "Look over there! That's the man I was telling you about."

Billy, Greg, and the Thameses turned to see the bearded man swaying his way through a cluster of people. "What man?" Seth said.

"You know, that new fisherman in town, Ted Schneider. The rude one I told you about."

"Oh, right," Seth said, nodding but not exactly sounding bowled over with interest.

"Don't even get me started on Ted Schneider," Greg Dappaport said, grimacing. The Thameses shook their heads, presumably in agreement.

"He came up to me before," Billy remarked, trying to add to the conversation. "Apparently he's allergic to nuts, because he was asking me about some of the food."

Greg Dappaport chortled and nudged Frederick Thames lightly in the ribs. "Now *that* might be an effective way to eliminate our interloper. Slip him some pecan pie, and assuming he doesn't get most of it in his beard . . ."

"Oh, Greg, you're terrible," Marion chided.

He chortled again and then shook his head in self-reproach. "You're right, terribly macabre of me. But tell me, is it all right if I transfer my murderous thoughts to his hideous excuse for a boat?"

After a few more minutes of chitchat about the apparent town outcast, Greg Dappaport and the Thameses left, and it was just Sally, Seth, Billy, and Pam again. Sally turned to Pam. "So what kind of day did you have, dear? Did you have to save a lot of lives?"

Pam shrugged. "A couple, I guess."

"Wow, what do you do?" Billy asked, impressed and even more jealous, damn it.

"EMT," Pam replied, at the same time Sally said, "Doctor." Rather than debating the point, though, Pam brusquely excused herself to go to "the head."

"I know she hasn't been overly talkative," Sally said after Pam left, "but once you get her going, oh, my, she will blow your mind with intellectual discussions."

"Sounds fun," Seth said dryly, and turned to Billy, who was now being summoned by Des.

"Shoot," she said, nodding at Des, "I've got to get back to work."

"Oh, okay," Seth said, sounding disappointed. "Well, I hope I'll see you later."

Billy hoped so, too. That was the problem.

* * *

"Hey, what's up?"

"Sorry to pull you away," Des said, flipping his head to get some shaggy locks out of his eyes, "but I can't find Katie. Have you seen her?"

"No, but I haven't been paying much attention." *Too busy obsessing over Seth.* "She must be around here somewhere."

"I found her charm bracelet on the ground; she must've dropped it," Des said, and held it up. Billy recognized the small but clunky silver chain, and took it from him.

"Oh, I see Mrs. Tailor over there," Billy said, spotting Katie's grandmother in the distance. "I'll give it to her to give to Katie."

Billy approached Mrs. Tailor at the same time the infamous Ted Schneider did. Just as Billy was about to mention the charm bracelet, Ted drunkenly grabbed another champagne cocktail off Mrs. Tailor's tray and asked her about nuts. "Do the brownies have nuts in them?" he asked, slurring his words.

"Uh . . ." Mrs. Tailor looked to Billy a little haplessly, then turned back to Ted. "I don't think so, sir, but—"

" 'Cause I can't have no nuts," he barked. "I'm allergic. You should have a goddamn sign or something, telling what the hell has nuts." With that, he took a quick swallow of his cocktail, so quick it showered both sides of his beard with champagne. He didn't seem to notice. "How the hell am I supposed to know what I can eat and what's going to goddamn *kill* me?"

Poor Mrs. Tailor; she was a little old lady, and a big drunk sailor was lashing out at her. Nobody needed it. "You know what?" Billy piped in. "Why don't you come to the kitchen and talk to our baker? She can tell you everything that has nuts in it."

"Oh, that's a good idea!" Mrs. Tailor agreed. "Come with me;

I'll introduce you to our baker and she can answer all your questions." Billy decided to go, too, feeling protective of Katie's grandmother, and afraid that if this big slobbering guy tipped over too far, he would absolutely crush her. Anyway, it was nearly time for Billy to take her sheet cakes out of the refrigerator so they could warm to almost room temperature.

They all headed across the street to Marie's Café, where Georgette was working busily in the kitchen. "Georgette," Mrs. Tailor said delicately, obviously not wanting to interrupt.

"Yeah, what?" Georgette said, sounding gruff and impatient.

"Uh, this gentleman has some concerns about a nut allergy. . . ." Georgette angled her head back to look at him, then quickly turned back to her ovens as Ted asked her what items on the buffet tables had nuts. While Billy gingerly pulled her sheet cakes from the fridge, she overheard Ted saying that he couldn't have even a trace of nuts or it would trigger a dangerous allergic reaction. Well, he said this using his own slurred and brash style of conversation, which was fine, because social niceties were usually wasted on Georgette.

After Georgette told Ted what items, specifically, contained nuts or nut oil, she continued her work, implicitly dismissing him. Most of the exchange was a dismissal, really, since Georgette had barely spared him a glance. Again, Ted didn't seem to notice. He muttered a cursory thanks and headed back to the town square.

Billy had hoped to see Seth again that night, and she got her wish about an hour later. But first she had to wheel out the sheet cakes, and she could've used some help, but Melissa had left early with a bad headache, and Des was busy with other tasks.

"Mrs. Tailor, have you seen Georgette? She wasn't in the kitchen."

"Oh, no, I'm sorry, I haven't," she replied as she consolidated some scattered pastries onto one tray.

Damn—two people could push the carts out together and present the cakes in the panoramic style Billy had intended. She couldn't do it herself, but she didn't want Mrs. Tailor to strain herself, and Georgette was currently MIA. Luckily, Katie was coming by at that moment, carrying an empty tray with her. Billy had forgotten all about her charm bracelet! After she gave it back to her, Katie helped her wheel out the cakes.

The reaction was more than Billy could've hoped for. The crowd went on about them, some reactions even touched with awe, filling Billy up with an indescribable sense of pride and accomplishment.

"I'd recognize that artwork anywhere," a voice said. When she turned around, she found Seth standing behind her. "Billy, those cakes are unbelievable. It really looks like a painting; I can't even believe it." As he shook his head, wonder crossed his face. "You're amazing."

"Thanks," Billy said, blushing hotly—overwhelmed by the compliments, the rush of creating something, and by Seth's just being there.

Suddenly someone bumped into her from behind and pitched her forward, right into Seth. "Sorry," a tipsy female voice called in the distance, as Billy stumbled. She would've fallen over completely if it hadn't been for Seth lurching out to catch her, cupping her arms with strong but gentle hands.

"Are you okay?" he asked in a low, soft voice.

Blurrily she nodded, while his sensuously heated touch undid her senses and muddled her mind with sexy, forbidden thoughts.

Fluidly, his hands slid over to her shoulder blades and tenderly caressed her through her white cotton shirt. Maybe it was purely a comforting gesture, but Billy perceived it only as seductive. The heat from Seth's hands branded her back, seeping into her skin, and rushed through her veins—straight to her crotch.

God, why did Seth turn her on so much? (And was it wrong to ask God about this?)

Now she noticed that his gaze was burning, just like his hands. With smoldering intensity, he bored through her with his eyes, and Billy's breath stalled in her lungs. Their faces mere inches apart, she zeroed in on Seth's mouth. Sensuous and tempting . . . she remembered what it was like to kiss that mouth. The way Seth always folded his mouth gently over hers and then slid his tongue in like a snake. A random but achingly sexy image popped into Billy's mind: Seth tearing open her shirt, sending buttons flying, and burying his face in her naked cleavage. It might be worth getting arrested for public indecency just for the hot, racy thrill of losing control with him, of feeling his open mouth on her breast—

"Billy . . ." he said huskily, lowering his face to hers. *Oh, God, it's really happening,* she thought hazily, raising herself on tiptoe, bringing her lips magnetically toward his. Blood thundered through her veins as the hot, suffocating chemistry between them reduced her breathing to shallow panting. She wanted to devour him, to lie down right here, right now, to peel off her panties and—

"Aaahhh!"

A woman's scream rang through the air, startling everyone, including Billy and Seth, who jumped apart.

"Aah! Ahh!" the screamer continued. "He's dead! He's dead!"

Dead?

Dead!

Feverishly, people rushed over toward the center of the square. Billy hurried, too, but being five-two was a hindrance, because she couldn't see anything over the heads of everyone else. Somehow she wormed into a tiny space and saw a man lying lifelessly on the ground. With a gasp she covered her mouth and turned into Seth, who wrapped his arms around her. "Oh, God," Billy choked, not as prepared as she'd thought she'd been to see a dead body.

"Don't look," Seth whispered, hugging her and letting Billy bury her face in his warm, solid chest.

"Oh, my God, it's Ted Schneider!" she heard Sally say.

"What happened?" someone called out.

"One minute he seemed fine, and the next he just collapsed," someone else replied.

"Pam, you're a doctor," Sally said. "Maybe you should examine the body."

"I'm not a doctor," Pam stated flatly, then shrugged. "Maybe he had a heart attack. But someone should call the paramedics." (Thank God for Pam's vital expert advice.)

Pockets and purses rustled in a mad rush for cell phones, and Billy pushed out of Seth's hug. Hurriedly, she moved through the crowd and dropped to her knees in front of Ted's body. He wasn't dead, only passed out. That was what she told herself as she fearfully pressed her fingers to his throat, desperately hoping to feel a pulse. But there was nothing, only stillness, lifelessness, and up this close she could see that his eyes weren't even closed, but at half-mast. *Oh, dear God . . .*

"The paramedics are on their way!" Greg Dappaport announced. "I called Deputy Trellis, too."

The manic chattering that followed seemed to drown Billy, descending into a miasma of empty clamor as she swallowed away a lump of anxiety and fought back the irrational tears that stung her eyes. She didn't deal with death well; ever since her best friend had died in a plane crash when she was twelve, Billy's heightened awareness of her own mortality had been a black mark on the back of her mind.

Death up close shook her, rattled her almost frantically, and thank God Seth was beside her again, coaxing her to her feet and into his arms. Shutting her eyes, she buried her face in his chest and tightened her arms around him as he gently rubbed her back. The dead man was a stranger to her, but for some reason what she did know about him seemed unsettling. He was new in town, obviously not too popular; he liked champagne cocktails, was allergic to nuts, and he'd been the burly, bearded man arguing on the beach— so angry and so alive just a few hours earlier.

Chapter Ten

Corryn was freezing in her green cotton scrubs, which was kind of ironic, because she was trolling for ice cream. A craving had hit her between episodes of *Trading Spaces*, and she figured Pike Bishop could use the walk, so she'd thrown her fleece pullover on top of her pajamas, wrapped a scarf around her neck, and headed around the corner, onto Newbury Street.

"Come on," she said, tugging lightly on Pike's leash when he stopped to sniff something on the sidewalk. After she took one last drag, she tossed out her cigarette. "Come on, sweetie." Relenting, Pike walked with her down three steps to the left, into a tiny espresso and ice-cream shop almost lost between two trendy, glittering restaurants.

While she was waiting in line, Corryn caught a glimpse of her reflection in the chrome of the ice-cream case. Holy hell, she looked like complete crap. And wait a second . . . what was *that*?

Squinting, she hunched down for a better look at the dark, thick smudge along her jaw, and realized it was a remnant streak of the mud mask she'd donned during *Seinfeld*. Using her sleeve she rubbed, but it was all crusted over, so only half of it flaked off. Oh, who cared how she looked anyhow? She was just here to stuff her face with ice cream and walk it off at the same time. With any luck she'd be in bed (alone) by eleven, with Pike guarding her front door.

Sounded perfect—and with the exception of Billy's dog, a typical Saturday night.

"Next!" called the kid behind the counter.

"Hi," Corryn said, stepping forward, "can I have a waffle cone with a scoop of Chocolate Chunk and a scoop of Mocha Madness—"

"Yeah," the kid said, turning to get it.

"And a scoop of Mint Chocolate Chip," she finished.

"Oh—okay, yeah," the kid said, sounding surprised by her appetite.

After she paid, Corryn hurried out of the shop, because Pike was getting restless. Once he was out in the night air, he became more himself—alert, protective, and stopping every few feet to sniff the sidewalk. Gently, she nudged the leash. "Come on, come on, sweetie," she urged. Balancing her giant cone with only one hand was trickier than she'd thought.

Just then, a dog barked loudly across the street. Pike jumped into action, barking like crazy, as Corryn let out a startled yelp and tried to rein him in. He was practically circling in place, trying to get to the hyper dog across the street. "C'mon, settle down," Corryn coaxed, tightly gripping the leash and no longer paying attention to her ice-cream cone, which had started to tip. Finally the other dog disappeared with its owner, and Pike settled down—just as one of Corryn's ice-cream scoops rolled out of the waffle cone and onto her sneaker with a splat.

"Oh, *damn* it," she cursed, "damn it, damn it!" Passersby doled out pitying looks, while Corryn lost her anger and bent to wipe some of the semifrozen slop off her Nike with the one-ply napkin she'd gotten inside the ice-cream shop. It wasn't exactly working wonders.

"Need some help?"

Corryn looked up and saw a tall man standing above her, bearing napkins. The streetlight wasn't falling his way, so she couldn't make out his face, but she was too preoccupied with her cold, wet shoe to notice. "Thanks," she said, eagerly taking the stack from him, "thank you so much. God, I don't know how I do these things."

"Hold on," he said, and ducked into the shop. Seconds later he returned with more napkins. As Corryn finished drying off her sneaker, the kind stranger bent to pet the dog. "Well, take care," he said.

And as he moved past her, Corryn's eyes caught the shiny glare of something on his belt. A police badge . . . and then she placed the voice. No, it *couldn't* be. Whipping around, she squinted into the darkness, trying to see if the man walking away from her now was the pervert from the T. Inevitably, there was only one way to find out.

"Hey!" she shouted to him. "Wait!" He stopped and turned, and now the streetlight was hitting his face, which looked confused—not to mention extremely familiar. "It *is* you!" she said.

"Huh? Oh . . . *Christ.*" Obviously it clicked for him, too. Running his hand over his face, as though tired already, he walked back toward her.

On her guard, Corryn held her back straight, while her heart pounded hard in her ears and blood thundered through her veins. She couldn't believe it; she'd never expected to see him again! "Hi, there," he said when they were only a few feet apart. "I'm Joe. Joe Montgomery." He held out his hand, and she recoiled like he had fleas, so he set it back down at his side. "Look, about what happened on the subway the other day . . . I'm not sure what I did to offend you, but I'm sorry I made you upset."

"Are you saying it wasn't you?" she asked suspiciously.

"Wasn't me what?"

"Who tweaked my nipple," she replied with exasperation, and Joe snorted a laugh. "It's not funny!"

"No, no, you're right—I'm sorry, it's just . . . I don't know; it sounds funny." Just then, as if automatic, his gaze dropped to her breasts. Corryn swallowed hard, grateful for the heavy fleece concealing her nipples, which were probably prickling under her scrubs right now. Loser or not, this guy was *hot*. "Anyway, I can promise you it was not me," Joe went on. "That train was so packed, it could've been anyone."

Hmm . . . she supposed he had a point.

Now he smiled gently at her, and she noticed little lines around his eyes that matched the ones around his mouth. There was something rugged about him—something craggy and sexy—and without thinking, Corryn dropped her gaze to his left hand. No ring. *Jesus, what am I thinking?*

"So, do you forgive me?" he asked lightly. "Even though I'm innocent?"

"Well . . ." After a pause, Corryn grinned. "I suppose."

Joe bent down to pet Pike's head again. "I never got your name," he said, looking up at her.

"It's Corryn."

"Joe," he said, extending his hand again, and this time she took it. His smile was easy, sexy, and . . . suspicious. No, she did not trust that smile, even if she did like looking at it.

Grinning, he said, "So what do you do when you're not getting groped on the E line?"

Vaguely she heard the question, but was mostly sidetracked by Joe's chest. He wore a sweater and a lightweight coat, and he was just so massive-looking, especially compared to her, that she couldn't help wondering what it would be like to sleep with a big, overpowering guy like him . . . and where else might he be big and overpowering?

Not that she intended to find out.

Oh, please. Not like *he* intended to show her—what, with her tantrum on the subway, and now tonight's five-star appearance.

"Okay, I'll start," he said when she didn't answer. "I'm a homicide detective."

"Oh, right—I'm a Realtor."

"That sounds interesting."

"It *does*?"

Joe chuckled, then said, "Listen, I don't know what you're doing now, but would you maybe want to go for a cup of coffee? There's a little place down the street. My treat."

"But I don't even know you," Corryn said, scrunching her face warily.

"Hence the cup of coffee," he replied, grinning.

She realized how socially inept she looked, but he'd caught her off guard. Anyway, why should she go for coffee? She was just going on an ice-cream run, and Pike was restless; besides, if she wasn't mistaken, there was a *30-minute Meals* marathon on in half an hour. Obviously she had a full night, and anyway, she was suddenly feeling tired.

Shaking her head, she tugged lightly on Pike's leash. "No, no, I don't want to," she said, then amended, "I mean, I can't." In the back of her mind, she wondered why she was acting like a rude asshole, but she couldn't seem to stop herself.

"Okay, no problem," he said with a brief nod. "Take care." When he disappeared down the street, Corryn realized her legs were trembling a little. It had been a long time since she'd gone out with a man, and . . . well, of all the men to go out with, a cocky, muscular cop just seemed like the stupidest choice. One driven solely by hormones, which made up the most destructively oblivious part of herself.

A gust of wind blew, and as she bundled her scarf up tighter, she felt something hard along the side of her chin. What the— Oh, *damn*. She'd forgotten all about her crusty mask residue, which had been on her face the whole time. Talk about embarrassing! With a hapless sigh, she buried her face in her hands. *Oh, hell*. So much for her typical Saturday night—a muddy beard, a hunky stranger, her heart still racing, and no fucking chocolate.

Ted Schneider's dropping dead put a damper on the jubilee. Things had wrapped up quickly after the paramedics came and took the body away. Deputy Trellis had arrived on the scene, looking like he was barely out of high school. Apparently Sheriff Mueller was on vacation in Marblehead for the next two weeks. With him Trellis brought the medical examiner, who stated that Ted Schneider had died from an allergic reaction to nuts.

Jesus.

After the medical examiner noticed pronounced swelling in Ted's neck, he realized that Ted's throat had closed up and that he'd died, in fact, from suffocation. Once Billy and Mrs. Tailor said that Ted had mentioned a nut allergy, the case was closed as far as the ME was concerned.

Of course, Deputy Trellis questioned the catering staff, but considering that Georgette had told Ted specifically what foods to avoid—with Billy and Mrs. Tailor as her witnesses—there wasn't any reason to assume that Ted, in his apparent drunkenness, hadn't simply gotten confused and eaten one of the items Georgette had warned him about. The ME highly doubted the possibility of "cross-contamination"—or that Ted had ingested something that touched something *else* with traces of nuts—because he said that whatever Ted had eaten most likely had a very high concentration of nuts to kill him so quickly.

It was a terrible allergic reaction, and one that was chalked up to carelessness on Ted's part, especially considering that he'd had no EpiPen on him. The death was an accident, pure and simple.

Yet ... the tasteless joke Greg Dappaport had made earlier about killing Ted by slipping him pecan pie ... it kept echoing in Billy's mind.

Georgette had resurfaced in the middle of all this, apologizing to Billy for cutting out on work to go "necking" with a man she'd met that night. Suffice it to say, Billy was too unnerved by everything else to care. Too disturbed by the image of Ted Schneider's big, sturdy body lying limp and crumpled on the grass.

Most of the guests had filed out and headed home when Seth offered Billy a ride home. She declined, though, because she had promised to share a cab with Des to Brookline, since Melissa had taken the Aggerdeen wheels when she'd left the jubilee early. So Billy headed home, wishing that Des exuded the same kind of comfort that Seth did, but knowing that he didn't. Listlessly she stared out the taxi window, watching the start of pelting raindrops, watching the city lights float by, and watching the moon. Wasn't it funny the way it appeared to be moving? As if it had a destination. And wasn't that somehow the trick of it all?

When Billy got to the Bella Donna on Monday morning, she found her coworkers talking about the man who'd died at the jubilee that weekend. Billy shared Katie and Des's confusion, but Georgette remained wholly unapologetic. "I told him what he shouldn't eat; that's all ya can do," she'd stated more than once.

By the early afternoon, everyone had become preoccupied with work. Billy was decorating the bottom tier of a lemon-vanilla wedding cake when Katie ducked her head into the back. "Hey," she whispered, "your man's here."

Billy turned around, pastry bag in hand. "Mark's here?" she said, surprised.

"No, no, your *other* man. You know—*Blondie*."

"Oh . . ." Billy said, feeling the familiar tightening of nerves in her abdomen. "Okay," she said, setting down the pastry bag and wiping some loose strands of hair away from her face with the back of her hand.

When she walked into the front, she saw Seth waiting for her, looking handsome and golden and a little scruffy. He particularly stood out in the crowd of young professionals that had just entered the bakery, all looking like carbon copies of each other: the guys in khakis and blue button-downs, the girls in black pants and pale-colored blouses.

"Hi," Billy said, smiling, as she led him down to the far side of the counter, away from the register. "What's up?"

"Hey . . . is this an okay time?"

For what? That was the question. "Yeah, sure. Is everything okay?"

"Oh, everything's fine, but I was wondering . . . well, I'd love to take you to lunch today. I mean, if you don't have other plans already."

Other plans . . . interesting concept. Did that include sitting alone in the food court while she stuffed her face with orange chicken? If so, then she had other plans quite often.

"No, I don't have plans," Billy said, smiling. "I'd love to have lunch." And why not? It was perfectly innocent; it wasn't like she was cheating on Mark. In fact, she'd be sure to tell him all about it the next time she saw him—which wouldn't be for five freaking days, anyway.

"Katie, do you mind if I take lunch now?"

"No problem," Katie said brightly. "I've got it covered."

"Thanks," Billy said, and turned back to Seth. "Let me just grab my bag." On the way to the back, she took a few deep breaths and reassured herself that this was fine—it was a nice, friendly gesture on his part, because Seth was a nice, friendly guy. So that was settled. They'd have lunch, make pleasant small talk, and relax.

She just had to make sure there was no hugging involved.

While Seth was waiting for Billy, a white-haired woman stormed out from the back, flapping a piece of paper in her hand. "Where the hell is Melissa?" she shouted.

"Still not here," replied the blond girl behind the register.

Heaving a sigh, the older woman said, "Well, maybe you can tell me something. Who the hell eats *pears* on a sandwich?" The blonde looked confused, so the woman showed her the sheet of paper. "Look at this list! When the princess said 'sandwiches,' I thought she meant bologna and cheese. Not 'bean sprouts, pears, and Fontina,'" she read, then slapped the paper. "'Bok choy pesto and mizuna'—who the hell's even *heard* of half this stuff?"

Whirling around angrily, she stopped short when she made eye contact with Seth. Shit, he hadn't meant to stare.

"Hey, you're the guy from the jubilee," the white-haired lady said, sounding intrigued.

"Yes, hi," he said, "I'm Seth, a friend of Billy's."

"Georgette Walters," she said, reaching out to shake his hand—or to clutch it, as the case may be. "So if you're a friend of Billy's, will we be seein' more of you around here?"

"Uh, I really don't know . . ." he began, just as Billy came back out with her coat and bag, and suddenly everything was brighter.

"Ready?" she said, walking toward him.

"Your friend Seth and I were just gettin' acquainted," Georgette explained with a wink, squeezing Seth's hand once more before releasing it. As they walked out of the bakery, Seth heard Georgette call to him. "Make sure ya come again," she drawled suggestively.

He smiled briefly and kept on going, but he almost had to laugh. This lady wasn't really coming on to him in the middle of the store, was she? Christ, maybe it had been a while for him, but when he finally broke his dry spell, it sure as hell wouldn't be with Billy's coworker.

And he had to keep reminding the insane voice in the back of his head that it wouldn't be with *Billy*, either.

Chapter Eleven

"So what's good here?" Seth said, as they looked over the Cheesecake Factory menu.

"Everything, I think," she replied, resisting the urge to say, "Cheesecake."

As she scanned her menu, Billy swallowed a lump of nervousness and ran her hand over her fluttering stomach. From across the table she could smell a hint of Seth's clean, masculine scent.

"So . . . thanks for inviting me to lunch," Billy said, sipping her Diet Coke. "That was really nice of you." God, had she ever been more banal?

"Sure, I wanted to do it," Seth said, then leaned forward, resting his forearms on the table. "So how are you doing after what happened on Saturday night?"

Oh . . . she'd temporarily forgotten about that. The way Ted Schneider had looked lying dead on the ground.

"What can I get you?" their waitress asked as she approached their table. Billy ordered chicken Romano, and Seth ordered a burger. After they ordered and the waitress left, a silent pause stretched between them. Under the table Billy accidentally brushed Seth's calf with her foot. "Oh, sorry," she said, sitting up more and pulling her legs in. Her chest tightened with longing. Ridiculous—so she'd dreamed of having sex with Seth too many times to count. Did that mean every single interaction had to be shrouded in frustration?

As she watched his fingers rapping lightly on the table, she noticed how sexy they were . . . how strong . . . how they might feel sliding inside her panties, climbing up between her— *Wait, what was the question again?*

"Billy?"

"Huh?"

"I asked what you were thinking."

Well, hell, she wasn't about to tell him *that.* "Oh, nothing," she said, "just wondering about your company. You never really told me the details. What's it called? What do you do? Do you like it? What's a day in the life?"

"Okay, okay," Seth said with a laugh. "Let's see here. It's called Lannigan Consulting. Very inventive, I know. As of August we're finally in the black, which is great. And basically what we do is help start up small companies."

"Wow, that's amazing!"

Seth shrugged as if it were no big deal, but there was a hint of pride behind his modesty. "What about you? Are you looking to get back into Web design? Or do something different?"

"Something different, but I have no idea what," she said with a sigh, feeling like a post-Gen-X cliché. "Part of me thinks I should— I mean, of course I *should*—but . . . I don't know. I guess what I like about working at Bella Donna is the freedom . . . the independence. The cake decorating is fun, and sometimes I can really use my imagination—sometimes I'll work in the back on a cake for a couple hours, and I won't even realize so much time has passed." She shrugged. "It's fun. And also, I have more time to myself, when I can just sketch or paint at home. . . ." Suddenly she realized she'd been droning on, so she decided to cut straight to her larger point. "Basically, I'm clueless."

"Ah," he said, grinning. "I see."

The waitress came over and set down their meals; Billy ordered

another Diet Coke, and Seth told the waitress to bring some extra lemon when Billy forgot to ask. He actually remembered that?
Interesting . . .

"Well, whatever you do after Bella Donna, I think it should be
something artistic," he said, picking up his burger. "You're such an
incredible artist. Hey, do you still carry your sketch pad everywhere?"

"Yeah, I guess," she said, grinning at him.

"Do you remember that time we went to Starbucks, and there
was a drawing class there?"

"Oh, my God!" she exclaimed, the memory hitting her like a
bolt of lightning. How could she have forgotten? A group of students who'd come into Starbucks to sketch customers and attempt
to capture the local culture. Each seemed to zero in on one person
as their subject, and the girl who'd sketched Billy had ogled her relentlessly, making it extremely obvious that she was drawing her,
and then didn't even have the decency to draw something flattering.

"She made me look like a big Weeble," Billy said now.

Seth laughed, shaking his head. "It was only because you were
wearing that big wool sweater, and you had your hair all pulled up."
He remembered that, too.

"You're just trying to make me feel better," she said with an almost flirty tilt of her head.

The way Seth smiled at her touched her heart; it was casual, like
he knew her well, like they were really friends again. Suddenly her
palms felt itchy and clammy, and, unwittingly, she rubbed them on
her thighs, burning up the denim but barely noticing. He was too
damn tempting. But she just had to remember two little words: *Mark
Warner.* Synonymous with two more little words: *future potential.*

"Listen, Billy," Seth said, setting down his burger. "I . . . well, I
asked you to lunch for more than just catching up." He looked like
he was struggling for the right words. "Well the truth is . . . it's just

so great to see you again, and . . . I wanted you to know that I'm really sorry about the way things ended."

"It's okay," she said quickly, anxious to segue to a new topic.

"No, really, I just want you to know that . . ."

God, what? That he regretted the past? She did, too, but the past was what it was, so why bring it up now? Their breakup was old news, and even though they'd dated only a few months, it was *painfully* old. "Seth, it's ancient history." *Hint, hint.* "Don't even worry about it. How's your burger?"

"Well, I just wanted you to know that it was really hard to leave, but I felt it was the opportunity of a lifetime—"

"Of course," Billy piped in. "It's totally understandable. Let's just be friends and move on." Okay, that sounded lame and trite, but she was a desperate woman. Getting dumped gracefully was one thing; having to talk about it was another. Besides, there actually was some truth to what she was saying. She *did* want to be friends with him now, whereas four years ago she couldn't deal with that prospect. In fact, after one or two e-mails, she'd stopped keeping in touch altogether because it was the only way she felt she could get over him.

"Okay," he said, smiling, and touched her wrist affectionately. Breath hitched in her throat at the contact. He didn't let go. Her heart raced as Seth's fingers lingered on her skin. Slowly, almost imperceptibly, his thumb applied gentle, seductive pressure, and it sent heat shooting right to her G-spot.

Wait a minute, what the hell was going on here? Did he want to be friends or not? If she wasn't mistaken, Seth was charming her now—working her, arousing her—in a way that seemed anything but platonic.

"Billy . . ." he said, circling his thumb on her wrist with a maddeningly slow rhythm. Braving a glance up at him from under her lashes, Billy found his gaze locked on her, hungry and potent, and she blurted the first thing that came to mind.

"I have a boyfriend."

Inevitably, this was the guilt talking. For Pete's sake, she was having a clandestine lunch with her ex, and getting turned on at the table. Talk about Guilt Central. And the really frustrating part was that this wasn't like her at all. She was fiercely loyal by nature, and she *liked* Mark; she didn't want to jeopardize anything there, even if he did occasionally annoy her with his social-butterfly routine.

"Oh," Seth said, sounding caught off guard. Withdrawing his hand, he sat straighter in the booth. "I mean, that's great that you have a boyfriend. I'm not surprised—you're a catch, Billy," he added lightly—casually—and went back to his burger. "I'm glad things are going so well for you," he threw in.

Uh-huh. Well, this lunch had just taken a bizarre turn . . . but then, who was she kidding? Practically every moment since Seth came back had been off-puttingly surreal.

Ten minutes later, while Billy was asking the waitress for a third Diet Coke, Seth was sitting there feeling like an asshole. Who the hell did he think he was? Of *course* Billy had a boyfriend. The girl was sweet, smart, fun, pretty, and lusciously sexy. Her eyes were pale blue and guileless. Her personality was warm and inexplicably magnetic. Christ, what on earth had he been thinking?

But that was just it: He *hadn't* been thinking. Just acting on instinct. Just going with the moment. It seemed like every time he was with Billy, his body raged out of control. His cock throbbed, his balls ached, and he lost all common sense. Hell, it was stupid anyway; he had a life and a business in Seattle. He was only going to be in Massachusetts a couple more weeks—why was he so fixated on being with her?

Okay, that was it. Things were going to be different now. He had to focus on what really mattered: selling his mom's house, keeping up with his business, and getting back to Seattle in a reasonable amount of time. If he kept focusing on his lust for Billy, he'd never get anything done. *Get your head straight,* he thought. *Both of them.*

Chapter Twelve

"So what did you say?" Corryn asked.

"What could I say?" Billy said, stirring her drink. "I told him I was seeing someone. I'm sure I misread it anyway. He was probably just being nice. Nothing even happened, but I still feel so guilty."

"Then I guess Mom's done her job."

They'd met after work at George, a dim, moody bar on Boylston. This was the first chance Billy had had to fill her sister in on what happened at the jubilee on Saturday night and her lunch with Seth today. She supposed part of what made this afternoon so unsettling was the recollection of that long, sizzling moment at the jubilee—right before the scream—when she could've sworn Seth was about to kiss her.

"What did Seth say when you told him about Mark?" Corryn asked now.

"Nothing, really," Billy replied with a shrug. "Except that he's happy for me. Jeez, does he always have to be so *nice?*"

Corryn let out a laugh. "Yeah, what is up with you and these nice boys? First Seth, now Mark—and both are decent-looking. What's your secret?" Billy just rolled her eyes as she slurped her raspberry crush. "Is anything else bothering you?" Corryn asked gently.

"No . . ." Except that she couldn't stop thinking about kissing Seth, and that was frustrating—plus, she knew that thinking about it was wrong, so *that* was frustrating. If only she could replace her spicy, erotic fantasies about Seth with ones of Mark, but it was hard.

"Well, speaking of men," Corryn said, "guess who I ran into on Saturday night while I was hanging out with Pike?"

"Who?"

"That guy from the T." Billy looked at her sister questioningly, and Corryn clarified: "The charmer who tweaked my nipple—but it turns out he didn't."

Billy's eyes shot up. "Ew, him? Wait—he didn't do it? You mean you actually *asked* him about it?" she said, giggling.

"Of course. I couldn't just let it go. But I believe him. Now that I talked to him, it doesn't seem like his style."

"How long did you guys talk?"

"Not long. And then I basically made a fool of myself."

"How?" Billy asked skeptically, because Corryn's portrayals of herself often lacked authenticity.

"He asked me to go for coffee, and I acted like a complete dumbass. I acted like I never even *heard* of coffee."

Billy laughed. "Why do I have the feeling you're exaggerating?"

"No, it's true—oh, but I did find out his name. It's Joe Montgomery. He's a homicide detective."

"Wait a minute," Billy said. "Joe Montgomery? I know him!"

"*What?*"

"I know Joe," Billy said again, her face lighting up with a smile. I mean I *used* to know him. He's friends with Seth."

"Oh . . . wow," Corryn said, feeling a pang of disappointment. Somehow this Joe thing had been *her* little intrigue. Knowing that he was connected to Billy and Seth made her feel more exposed—more vulnerable. "Small world . . ."

"God, this is great!" Billy continued excitedly. "Joe is *such* a nice guy; you should totally go for it!"

"Whoa, go for what?" Corryn said, putting up her hands to

slow her sister down. "He's cute, but we talked for two minutes. I'm not planning to see him again."

"Why not? You like him; I'm sure he likes you—*you're* single; *he's* single—"

"Billy, please, I've told you, I don't want to date," Corryn said, then, "He's single?"

"Divorced," Billy replied eagerly. "Oh, that's perfect, too—*he's* divorced; *you're* divorced—you guys can sit around bashing your exes together."

"What a treat."

"C'mon, if you're not going to have a hot romance for yourself, then do it for *me*," Billy pleaded. "Let me live vicariously through you."

Corryn scoffed. "What are you talking about? You have Mark."

Hmm . . . Interesting theory. But did anyone really *have* Mark? Billy was beginning to wonder. Sure, everything seemed great on the surface, but it was hard to get close to someone who had a million friends and little free time. Then again, an everlasting relationship and a soul-deep connection were probably a lot like hot sex—they would simply come with time.

Or so she hoped.

She had the next day off from work, so she figured it was finally time to meet Kip, the wonder headhunter, and watch him work his magic. Adrienne was home right now, literally waiting on bated breath, salivating for details about Gladys's son, the powerhouse.

Yet when Billy arrived at the shabbily run-down building off of Tremont Street and climbed three flights of creaky steps to the Belding Personnel "suite," she began to doubt Kip's power. Maybe it was wrong to jump to conclusions, but it was kind of hard not to when her first impression of Belding Personnel was peeling paint and dry rot.

She knocked lightly on the door and heard papers rustling frantically on the other side. Then feet shuffling . . . then the thump of someone tripping . . . then someone whispering, "Shit!" Finally the door swung open. A skinny guy in his twenties with a frosted goatee, who was slightly out of breath, smiled down at her. "Hi, Kip?"

"Hello, doll," he enthused, and offered her a cool, clammy handshake. "Come in. God, I feel like I already know you, the way my mother always goes on about you!" That seemed hard to believe, because Gladys had met her only once, and had persistently called her Bailey. Kip led her over to his desk, which was about a twelve-inch journey. The office had a musty kind of quality that hopefully came from not opening the windows enough, and not from asbestos. "Please have a seat," Kip said. He dropped into his chair and wheeled it forward with a squeak.

"I appreciate your meeting with me on such short notice," Billy said, tenderly sitting down in the wobbly, torn chair that faced Kip's desk.

"No problem. I was thrilled to finally match the name with the face," he said.

Which name? she thought sardonically, then pushed her flippancy aside. Really, she should be serious about this—this was her career at stake. Working at the bakery was a fun, diverting sideline, but she was twenty-seven years old already. She needed to be hitting the proverbial pavement, breaking back into the corporate scene, and, with any luck, Kip would help her do that.

While Kip got organized, Billy shifted a little in her seat to get comfortable. As it was, she didn't feel quite like herself today in a black pant suit and high heels. It was her standard interview outfit, which was considerably tighter today than when she'd bought it six months ago. She'd obviously gotten spoiled working at Bella Donna in soft, warm sweaters and faded blue jeans, and right now she missed the worn comfort of her battered green velvet coat.

"Okaaaay . . . let's seeee here . . . Got your résumé," Kip said, rooting around on his desk for the sheet that Corryn had faxed over for Billy that morning. "Let me just find it . . . *un momentitooo* . . ." After a few more minutes of shuffling, he said, "Well, while I'm looking for it, why don't you tell me more about yourself?"

Billy gave him her professional history, in brief—which wasn't difficult, because it *was* brief—and Kip nodded profusely while he rooted around his office. "Ah! Here it is," he said, finally locating her résumé and scanning it briefly. "Looking good . . . Web design experience, advanced computer skills, degree from BC—nice. The old-boys' network *loves* that."

Billy supposed that was a good thing—to an extent.

"Let's see here . . . Net Circle . . . three and a half years. So what happened there?" Kip asked, looking up.

"Oh, the company declared bankruptcy. It just couldn't bear the declining market."

"Ouch," he yelped sympathetically, and set her résumé down on his cluttered desk. "Okay, let's be honest. You're looking for a thriving, fast-paced environment where you can apply your natural creativity, and where you can grow, right?"

"Yeah, definitely," Billy said, perking up. Gee, when he put it like that, it sounded pretty good. She recalled the surge of elation she'd felt when she'd presented the Renoir cakes at the jubilee. She wanted to feel that rush again, and if she could get paid for it, even better.

"Fabulous, because it just so happens that I have a *supremo* fit for you."

"Really?" she said, leaning forward with anticipation.

"There's a position that's just opened up for a smart, detail-oriented, and fabulously creative individual—how does that sound?"

"Wow, that sounds great! Where's the job?"

"Tuck Hospital in Dorchester," he replied . . . much to Billy's disappointment. Okay, not to be a diva, but working in a hospital hadn't been remotely what she'd had in mind. She supposed it had to do with her heightened fear of her own mortality—similar to why she'd never watched *ER*, also why she compulsively avoided televised surgeries and movies about killer viruses. It was a little quirk of hers.

But, on the other hand, the mature thing to do would be to keep an open mind. "Okay . . ." she said now, trying to conceal her uneasiness. "And what would I be doing there?"

"Well, in the terrific position that's currently available, you'd be working in the Infectious Disease Unit—you know, greeting incoming patients, and attending to some basic administrative needs."

Hmm . . . "Basic administrative needs" was suddenly not sounding so creative, and the prospect of greeting patients *before* they got treated for their infectious diseases wasn't all that enticing. "Kip, I'm sorry," she said, chucking maturity out the window. "But I really don't want to work in a hospital. It's just a personal preference—a *strong* personal preference."

Kip looked flummoxed by that one. "Well, it's a great job, Billy," he said, with an edge to his voice that hadn't been there a moment ago.

"I'm sorry," she said again. "It's just not for me."

Now he looked a little peeved. "O-kaaaaay," he said, and shuffled some more papers on his desk. "If you're suuuure . . ."

"I am, but thanks for thinking of me," she said brightly. "Um, are there any other positions open that I could interview for? I'm pretty open, you know, besides hospitals." Oh, wait, maybe she should specify that she also wasn't crazy about cemeteries, prisons, and nuclear-waste dumps, before they had another misunderstanding.

But as it turned out, there was no need. Kip cut the meeting short, saying, "You know, let me look through my client portfolio and give you a call, okay, doll?" Even though he'd called her "doll," Billy sensed that Kip's flamboyant positivity had dwindled.

"Okay, great, just give me a call," she said, smiling amiably, and left his office.

As soon as her high heels hit the pavement, her cell phone rang. Jeez, did her mother have some kind of sixth sense?

"Yes?" she answered, without bothering to check the number.

"Hello, may I speak with Billy Cabot, please?" It wasn't her mom—it was a man. With some sort of an accent, too.

"This is Billy," she said, pressing her free hand to her other ear to block out the sound of traffic as she walked toward Government Center.

"Why, hello!" he said. "This is Greg Dappaport of the Churchill Dappaports." Now she recognized that accent! (Did she say accent or affectation?) It was the quasi-English man with the slicked hair and silk neckerchief whom she'd met at the jubilee. The one who'd been arguing with Ted Schneider on the beach.

"Am I catching you at an inconvenient time?" he asked.

"Um, no."

"Oh, wonderful, because I would love to discuss your work." *Huh? What work?* "I got your mobile phone number from Sally Sugarton; I hope that's all right."

"Sure, sure," Billy said, still zeroing in on the word "work." What had he meant?

"The reason I'm calling is that I am interested in commissioning you for a mural at my gallery."

What!

"A street mural," he explained. "Of course, I'm sure you're busy with many of your own projects, but would you have time this week to meet with me at the gallery? I could tell you more about what I have in mind."

For a moment Billy remained speechless. This didn't make any sense—how did he know about her love of painting? Had Seth told him to call her? "I'm sorry, Mr. Dappaport, I'm confused. Could you back up here?"

"Oh, of course, I apologize," he said with a chuckle. "It's just that when I get excited about a new artist, I tend to forget myself. You see, I became a fan of your work at the jubilee this past weekend. The cakes you decorated were nothing short of breathtaking. The detail was nearly flawless—it blew me away. Everyone was talking about it, you know."

Clutching her stomach, Billy swallowed a hard lump of surprise. "Thank you, thank you so much. But . . . well, you realize that those images weren't original? I mean, that wasn't really my work—it was a very loose recreation of Renoir's *Les Grands Boulevards*."

"Oh, I know, of course, but you really made it your own!" Dappaport enthused. "It was quite delightful—and I really fancy your flair for contrast."

Shock and excitement struck her, as well as the pressing need to ask, *Is this a joke?* How could sheet cakes have made such an impression?

Then again, she sensed that Greg Dappaport wasn't exactly married to the mainstream. In fact, from his clothes to his affected accent, he seemed a bit eccentric. They talked briefly, and set up a meeting for the following day. When Billy hung up her cell, she smiled into the air—grateful for this unlikely chance, and for unconventional people like Greg Dappaport.

That night, in the spirit of tempting fate, she told her parents about the street mural. She didn't have any of the details, and maybe it would be a lemon of a job, but she was excited and she wanted to share her news with the people she loved most. It was too bad Corryn had begged off on dinner tonight, because it would've been fun with her there, too.

"I still don't understand," Adrienne said, rinsing a plate and handing it to Billy, who set it in the dishwasher. "This Mr. Dappaport is going to pay you to paint on the *street*?"

"It's a kind of mural," Billy said, explaining the concept to her mother yet again.

"I don't know. Painting on the *street*? Sounds pretty strange, doesn't it, David?"

Billy's dad shrugged. "I don't know, the street seems as good a place as any."

Rolling her eyes, Adrienne murmured to Billy, "Ignore him." David remained clueless at the coffee grinder, while Pike Bishop ambled around the kitchen. "Also, I don't know if I like the idea of your being outside all that time. It's freezing this time of year."

"It's not freezing. Besides, I'll be wearing long sleeves and a smock, plus I have my coat in case."

"What, that beat-up old green one that looks like its been through the trenches?"

"I give up," Billy mumbled, burying her face in her hands, as David interjected to ask who wanted lemon peel in their espresso.

"I'll have lemon peel," Adrienne replied, "but no espresso. Just put the peel in a cup of tepid water." Billy's head shot up at that bizarre order, and she glanced over at her father, who looked equally bewildered. "Caffeine retains water and depletes calcium," Adrienne explained in the supercilious, health-conscious tone that had become her regular voice.

Sighing, she turned to Billy and said, "I'm sorry"—gee, she didn't *sound* too sorry—"but I don't like this whole idea. Working for some strange man, painting on the street—what's wrong with getting a *real* job? Where you work in an office like a normal person?"

Please, what was normal? Everyone had their own way of doing things, including her parents. Adrienne had tinkered in all different kinds of jobs over the years, while David had remained steadfastly loyal to three basic things for the past forty years: Adrienne, fishing, and his software company—in that order.

"Look, Mom, this *is* a real job. This is a chance for me to paint my own mural and get paid for it. Don't you get how exciting that is?"

"Okay, relax, relax. I'm only trying to take an interest." *An interest in making me crazy?* "Well, do you at least know how much he's paying you?"

Struggling to control her frustration, Billy replied tightly, "I told you, we're discussing it *tomorrow*."

As Adrienne rinsed the steel pot she'd used to boil root vegetables in fat-free, sodium-free chicken stock for dinner, she sighed. "Fine, Belinda. Do what you want. Don't get me wrong; I want you to be happy. I know you like to draw, and that's nice, but . . . I just don't want this to interfere with your finding a real job."

Ech. The term "real job" was really starting to grate on her nerves. "Look, I went to see Kip Belding today; he said he'll call me if something comes up. In the meantime, this might be a huge opportunity." There was no way Billy was telling her mom about the job opening in the infectious-disease ward of Tuck Hospital. Adrienne would just tell her to wear a gas mask and suck it up (figuratively speaking)—and find an eligible doctor for Corryn.

"Well, I, for one, am very proud of you, honey."

Startled, Billy looked over and saw her father smiling at her. "Whatever mural you paint, I know it will be beautiful. You really have the eye." With that, David carried his espresso into the family room.

Billy nodded after him, looking fondly at the kitchen door he'd just exited, then glared back at her mother. "Take a lesson," she said, and left Adrienne alone with the dishes.

*   *   *

Twenty minutes later David was reading in his chair, while Adrienne and Billy were sitting cross-legged on the floor, filing cruise pictures into old photo albums. There was something implicitly sad about photo albums, but her mom was addicted to them. She would always say they would be something for Billy to show her grandchildren someday—and there was something implicitly sad about *that* statement, too, but nobody seemed to see it but her.

Now, as Billy flipped open one of the soft-covered binders, a gentle puff of dust floated up into the air, and images of dauntingly dated moments in Cabot family history stared back at her.

"How's Mark?" Adrienne asked casually, though her gaze was pointed.

"Fine," Billy said simply, though, in truth, she hadn't talked to him recently enough to confirm that. She'd tried his cell a few times that day, but each time she'd heard a recorded message saying the number was currently "out of the service area." She figured he would call her whenever he was finished with work.

"By the way, don't forget about our cooking class," Adrienne said. "It starts this week."

Hitting her hand to her forehead, Billy said, "That's right! I'll remind Corryn, too."

"Oh, don't worry, I already left several messages on her machine."

As Billy flipped to the midsection of the album, she came across pictures of her aunt Penelope with her parents—pictures she'd never seen. She'd seen Penelope smile before, but gentle, kind smiles, not the radiantly happy expression that she wore in these photos. "Mom, what are these from?" she asked, as she turned the page and found more of the same.

"Hmm . . ." Adrienne said, pausing for just a moment. "Oh,

those were from a summer vacation your father and I took about twelve years ago. We rented some cottages on the coast of Maine."

"Really? Where was I?" Billy said, not recalling the trip.

"You were at sleepaway camp, remember? The Sisters of Sacred Heart Camp for Virtuous Teens?"

"Oh . . . right." How could she have blocked out *that* rollicking good time? "So Aunt Penelope went with you and Dad?"

"Actually, she invited us," Adrienne said, as she shuffled through the stack of cruise photos in her hands. "Oh, wait. Now I remember. She brought a man with her."

Just as her mom said that, Billy flipped the page and found two photos of Aunt Penelope holding hands with a tall, broad-shouldered man. In one picture he was squinting and holding his hand up to shield the sun. In another he held a fishing pole and smirked at the camera. Billy studied the second photograph, seeing something familiar in the man's face.

And then it clicked. . . .

Holy shit!

No cap—a salt-and-pepper beard, instead of a gray one—but it was *him*. Her aunt Penelope had been holding hands with the late Ted Schneider!

Chapter Thirteen

"Mom, who is this man?" Billy asked, because she knew only his name, but had no clue how he'd fit into Aunt Penelope's life.

"Yes, that's him," Adrienne said, leaning over to look at the photo Billy was holding up. "That was the man Penelope brought with us on vacation. It was her boyfriend at the time. Or whatever one would call it. Personally, I'd call him a no-good lothario. Remember him, David?"

"Hmm?" David mumbled, ensconced in his book.

"What was the name of that man Penelope dated about twelve years ago?"

"Which one?" he asked, turning the page.

Rolling her eyes, Adrienne echoed, "Which one? Practically the only one." Then she glanced at Billy. "Aunt Penelope barely dates," she added gratuitously. "Probably why she has never married."

"I know, I know," Billy said impatiently, tired of her mother's obsession with Aunt Penelope's love life. She knew Adrienne loved her sister, but for some reason she acted more judgmental than proud of her. Aunt Pen was a self-made woman—independent, successful, and kind. Sometimes Billy really had to wonder what her mother's problem was. "So she dated this guy, and what happened?"

"Ted!" her mother exclaimed, just remembering. "That was it; his name was Ted. Pen was *crazy* about him."

"How did they meet?"

Adrienne paused to consider that. "You know, I can't remember. Oh, wait, they might have met at the hardware store, believe it or not." She shrugged. "Anyway, I suppose they hit it off right away." Billy resented the way her mother said "suppose"—as if she had trouble picturing her reserved older sister dazzling someone. Maybe Billy was reading into it, though, because she'd always adored her aunt. There was just something inherently warm and comforting about her. (Once again, Adrienne could take a lesson.)

"Well, were they serious?" Billy asked, still confused and a little anxious.

"Yes, at least Penelope thought so," Adrienne said. "But after only a couple months, he left."

"What do you mean? Where did he go?"

"I don't know what happened. To be honest, Penelope never seemed to want to confide in me about it." *Shocking.* "But after Ted left, she seemed to give up on men altogether—and as you know, she never married."

"Yes, Mother, I think we *all* know that," Billy said.

"Anyway, even though Penelope didn't talk much about it, I could tell she was just devastated. Remember, David?"

David was somewhat zoned out, with his book resting on his lap. "She was better off without him," he said simply, as though further analysis was silly.

Adrienne softened then, and spoke with more genuine sympathy. "It's true. He obviously didn't appreciate her."

God, Billy couldn't believe this; it was just too crazy. Aunt Penelope and Ted Schneider? Not only had they been involved, but the relationship had apparently been a turning point in her favorite aunt's life, and she'd never even known.

"Oh, David, do you remember that night all four of us went to that new restaurant and Ted got into a quarrel with our waiter?" Before David answered, Adrienne turned to Billy. "It was a little uncomfortable. I remember now—we were having dessert, and Ted got angry because he found some chopped nuts in his cake after he'd specifically asked the waiter if the cake had nuts—of course, I don't know why he was surprised. If I recall, it was some really rich, heavy layer cake with everything but the kitchen sink thrown in." Jeez, how the hell did she remember that? Her mother had issues. "I remember Pen was worried, too, because he didn't have anything on him in case of an emergency."

Billy swallowed hard as Adrienne closed the photo album in her lap and set it aside. "Does Aunt Pen ever talk about him anymore?"

Shrugging, Adrienne said, "No, but I wouldn't expect her to. She probably thought he was her last chance." Billy rolled her eyes at that; no, that was obviously what *Adrienne* thought. *Tsk*ing, she added, "I told her not to sleep with him until she had a ring on her finger, but maybe she didn't listen."

"Hey, do you mind?" David said, obviously irritated. "This is my *sister*-in-law you're talking about."

"Sorry," Adrienne said, making a guilty face of regret. "I shouldn't have said that." No kidding, but what else was new?

Anxiousness fluttered in Billy's chest, and she felt agitated, wanting information that she knew was out of her immediate grasp.

"What's wrong?" Adrienne asked.

To tell or not to tell, that was the question. Or it was *a* question; Lord knew there were many others. What had really happened between Ted and Penelope? Why had he left her? Where did he go? And why would someone who was obviously conscientious about his allergy, even back when he was dating Pen, suddenly be so careless as to eat something at the jubilee that contained nuts— something that Georgette had *specifically* warned him about? It just didn't make sense.

But something kept her from divulging anything to her mom. At least for now. She didn't want to tell her about seeing Ted at the jubilee, or the fact that he'd died there, until she knew more. Besides, it was really none of her mother's business. If it was anyone's business, it was Aunt Penelope's.

"Are you sure I'm not interrupting anything?" Billy said, sitting on the rose-colored silk of her aunt's settee. Pen's library was a testament to her elegant taste, an ornate yet beautifully cozy blend of colonial dark-wood furnishings and assorted antique pieces. Small brass lanterns were fixed to the walls, which were high and lined with colorful hardbacks.

Pen's eye for colors and interior design had always represented the kind of creativity and artistry that Billy admired. She might think she got her artistic side from her aunt, but actually her mom was creative, too. Among her sideline careers over the years, Adrienne had designed jewelry and greeting cards, dabbled in flower arranging, and even tried creating custom-made welcome mats for a while, but none of those pursuits lasted too long. Adrienne had always been much more interested in her family than her work.

"Don't be silly," Aunt Pen said now, sitting across from Billy on a pale green armchair with rose embroidery that matched the settee. "I'm always happy to see you. You know you can stay here whenever you want, honey."

Billy smiled. "Thanks," she said, feeling tempted, as usual. Aunt Pen's house was a perfect sanctuary, like one of those big, shadowy old houses seen in movies, where there was always a study and a fire in the fireplace.

She'd come with Pike to Pen's house after leaving her parents' because she couldn't stop thinking about what Adrienne had said: that Ted Schneider had not only dated Aunt Pen over a decade ago, but very possibly broken her heart. Now she sat across from her aunt, who was a soft, full-figured woman with short hair colored light brown. Billy spent the next hour chatting about innocuous things— i.e., her life—and the whole time she was trying to figure out how to bring up the subject of Ted Schneider. Then debating whether she should even bring it up at all. Finally she bit the proverbial bullet and told Pen about the pictures she'd seen in Adrienne's photo album.

"Oh . . . yes. Ted," Pen said calmly, and just a bit plaintively. "We weren't involved long, just a couple months, but I really cared about him."

Billy nodded, suddenly feeling furious with Ted for leaving, even though she had no idea *why* he'd left. "What happened?" she asked gently.

Pen shrugged. "Even now, I'm still not really sure what happened. We were happy. I mean, I thought we were." She reached for her china mug and sipped the tea she'd set down for them. "I never really wanted to talk about it—at least not at the time, because I was so upset, and . . ." Her voice trailed off momentarily, but Billy could guess why Pen hadn't wanted to talk about it: Venting was not her style. Very reserved by nature, Pen had always been more of a listener than a talker.

Except that now it seemed that she *wanted* to talk. And Billy couldn't help feeling flattered that she would be viewed as a confidante. "It was really strange. I cared about Ted so much, and in some ways I felt like I really knew him. But . . ." She sighed, sitting back against the armchair. "After he left I thought about it, and I realized there was so much I didn't know."

"What do you mean?" Billy asked.

"Well, he told me once that he'd grown up around here, but he didn't like to talk about it. I never pressed, because I figured he'd open up more in time. Then, after he was gone, I wished I had pressed, because it might've explained things more."

"Explained how?" Billy said, confused. She didn't want to tell her aunt about Ted's death yet—okay, in truth, she didn't want to tell her at all—because she didn't want Pen to get upset. Billy was hoping she would be able to gauge better what she should tell Pen once she learned a little more about how the relationship with Ted had ended.

"You see, Ted used to get these ominous phone calls at his apartment. I don't know if they were hang-ups or what, but at first he'd just make light of it, joke it off and try to distract me so I'd forget. Finally I told him I was getting concerned and I needed him to be honest with me. That's when he told me that he owed some people some money, but that he didn't want to get me involved."

"Who did he owe money to? What, like a bookie or something?" (In the back of Billy's mind, she couldn't believe she'd actually just used the word "bookie" in a sentence.)

Pen shrugged. "Again, he said he didn't want to talk about it, and stupidly I didn't press. I figured he'd tell me the details when he was ready. But I did offer to loan him the money." She blushed then, shaking her head and putting a soft-looking hand to her cheek. "I know that must sound crazy, but I cared about him so much, and . . ."

Billy swallowed, feeling a lump of indescribable emotion form in her throat. "Well . . . um . . . did you ever loan him the money?" she asked.

Pen shook her head. "No. He was very proud and old-fashioned; he felt strange taking the money from me, but he finally said he would think about it. The next thing I knew, he was gone." Billy waited for her to say more. "He left me a Dear John letter, telling me that he was sorry, but that he had to leave Massachusetts. He said someone from his past was after him and he couldn't bear to get me involved."

"Someone from his past?" Billy echoed, as unsettling anxiousness frittered manically in her chest, making her breath come up short. "Is that who he'd owed money to?"

"I don't know; I guess," Pen said with a sigh of resignation. "That's why I wish I had asked him more about his background. Where exactly he'd grown up, what his life was like before he met me. Maybe then I would've been able to make more sense of things." She looked down at her hands folded on her lap for a moment, and when she looked back up her eyes were a little glassy. "Oh, look at me, will you?" she said, smiling wanly. "I'm just an old fool, still letting myself believe there was any truth in that Dear John letter. It was all a lie, I'm sure. Ted left me and gave me a ridiculous story, and to this day I still like to tell myself that maybe, just maybe, the story was the truth."

Billy's heart sank. Her gut tightened into a tense knot and churned with frustration. On the one hand she felt terrible for the hurt and rejection her aunt had suffered. *Been there, done that.* She and Seth had dated only a few months, too, but when he'd left Billy had been crushed. Almost unbearably sad. Not to mention in denial and a little desperate to rationalize.

Still . . . Billy wasn't so sure Pen *was* rationalizing. She wasn't so sure that Ted's Dear John letter had been the absolute truth.

Oh, God, it was so crazy, but . . .

What if Ted's death had not been an accident after all?

Her mind raced frantically with the disturbing but undeniable facts. Ted had grown up in Massachusetts. Nobody in Churchill seemed to like him, yet nobody seemed to *know* him, either. Or so they claimed. Sally Sugarton and her friends had joked loudly about Ted's nut allergy—an allergy that he'd obviously been careful about, yet he somehow managed to ingest a high enough dose of nuts to kill him in a matter of moments.

He'd told Penelope that he owed someone money. He'd said

someone from his past had been after him. God, was it possible that that someone had finally caught up with him? Had someone from his past finally gotten him after all?

"Billy, what is it? You look like you've seen a ghost."

She wasn't even going to touch that. "No . . . it's nothing." Okay, she could not tell Pen about Ted's death. Not yet. Not when so much was left unexplained. Billy did not believe for one second that Ted had died by accident or because of pure carelessness. Not anymore, not after what Pen had told her.

Pen . . .

She still thought that Ted had dumped her cold. That he'd provided a bullshit excuse, abandoned her, made a fool of her. Billy didn't believe that, but she couldn't be absolutely positive unless she found out what had really happened to the elusive Ted Schneider—both then and now.

Stroking Pike Bishop's fur, Billy gazed into the fireplace, watching flames flicker and listening to wood crackle as Penelope sipped her tea. If Ted had been murdered, Billy was determined to find out why. Now, of course, her interest was personal.

When she got home that night, her machine was blinking. There was a message from Mark explaining that his cell was dead. He gave her another number to call, and when Billy dialed it, there were two rings before a woman answered.

"Oh, hi . . . is Mark there?" Billy asked.

"Hold on," the woman said. "Who's this, please?"

"This is Billy," she said, wanting to ask the same question, but the words didn't come quickly enough.

A few moments later Mark came on the line. "Billy?"

"Yeah, hi. Who was that woman? And what number is this?"

"Oh, that was my friend's girlfriend. They've been over here hanging out, and she let me borrow her cell phone to call you. She said I could give you the number to call me back."

"Oh, I see," Billy said, knowing the explanation was reasonable, but she couldn't help feeling irked. If Mark had time to hang out with his friends on a weeknight, why didn't he have time to hang out with *her*?

"So how was your night, cutie?" His superupbeat, thrilled-to-hear-from-her demeanor softened her annoyance. They talked for about fifteen minutes. She told him what happened at the jubilee, but didn't mention Aunt Penelope's connection to the man who'd died. She didn't feel like getting into it at the moment, but she'd do it in person—which reminded her . . . "So when can I see you?" she asked. "How about a sleepover one night this week?"

"Let me think. . . ."

"C'mon it'll be fun," she said coaxingly, then joked, "I won't try anything, I swear."

Mark chuckled. "I'd definitely love to do that, Billy, but . . . well, let me check my work schedule and get back to you. I'm going to some pretty out-of-the-way stores this week, so I'll need to get an early start. Plus, I'll probably get a better night's sleep in my own bed."

"Well, I don't mind having a sleepover at your place . . . ?" she offered, hoping he'd take the bait. Leaning against the wall, she inhaled a frustrated breath, realizing that inviting herself over was not exactly her idea of being swept off her feet, but it would have to do.

"You know, this week I honestly think it'll be tough," Mark said jovially. Meanwhile, Billy felt like disappointment had punched her in the stomach. She and Mark obviously liked each other, but if they didn't spend more time together, how were things ever going to advance to the next level? How were they ever going to grow closer—into a loving couple?

And putting love aside—what did this boy care more about:

sleep or cheap thrills? She was honestly beginning to wonder . . . was it *her*?

"Okay, I understand," she said, finally relenting on the sleep-over idea. For now.

"Great, thanks, Billy, you're the best!" Mark said merrily. "Listen, thanks a lot for being you." She had to roll her eyes at that one. After exchanging a few more pleasantries, he told her he couldn't wait to see her that coming weekend, and then they hung up. Billy threw off her coat, stripped out of her clothes on the way to bathroom, and then jumped into a hedonistically long, hot shower.

Afterward she rubbed some raspberry-scented body lotion on her legs and arms, slid into a cotton pajama pants and a faded sweatshirt, and curled up on the sofa. Once she was settled under an afghan, she realized that she was craving chocolate, so she flipped on the TV for Pike, who was on the sofa, too, and padded into the kitchen, pulling her wet hair up into a ponytail on the way. Instantly she went for the king-size Special Dark bar in the freezer, but, feeling guilty, she broke it in half. Grabbing an ice-cold Diet Coke from the fridge, she nudged the door closed with her hip and went back to the living room.

Once Billy was settled back on the sofa, she thought again about Ted Schneider's death. She couldn't get it out of her head that there had been foul play involved, and now that she was home and relaxed, she could really mull over her strategy. She was determined to do some investigating, but where would she even begin?

The sudden blasting whir of sirens shattered her calm. She put a hand to her heart, a little unnerved as the strident shrill of the siren, which was getting unbearably and unendingly closer. Then she felt a fleeting stab of panic: Maybe her building was the one on fire!

Quickly she threw back the afghan, climbed off the couch, and headed over to her bay window. With a crisp snap, the shade flew up.

"Aah!" she yelped, jumping away from the window, startled out of her wits. Her heart slammed hard and frantically against her ribs, and her chest tightened in acute, choking fear. "Oh, my God," she said softly, shaking her head. "Oh, my God."

Pike started barking like crazy. He must've sensed something was wrong, and, as always, he was right. Something red was smeared all over the outside of her window, and she could only shudder to guess what it was. Blood? Guts?

Whatever it was, it was chunky-style.

God, I'm gonna be sick, Billy thought, clutching her roiling stomach and trying not to panic. Only after a few deep, ragged breaths was she able to take a closer look at the window. *Wait a minute . . . no . . . yes.*

Fucking . . . crazy!

The red on her window wasn't blood, and it wasn't guts. The goddamn mess was tomatoes.

Chapter Fourteen

"Tomatoes?"

"Uh-huh. Last night I was pretty sure, but today, with the sunlight, I could tell."

"What the *hell*?" Melissa said, gripping her black coffee and looking pissed on Billy's behalf as she leaned against the table. She'd come to the back to give Georgette a list of new menu ideas from the suggestion box—told her to "make them happen," because they'd already been cleared with Donna. Now there was a lot of cursing and pans slamming around in the kitchen, but Melissa just ignored it while Billy filled her in on last night's events.

"And you really think your neighbor did it?" Melissa asked.

With a sigh, Billy exchanged the tip of her pastry bag for a narrower one. "I never would've thought Lady McAvit was capable of something like that, but . . . I mean, who else? She's obviously still mad about Pike eating her tomatoes."

"Ah, so the tomatoes on the window is what—her psychotic, emblematic statement?"

"I guess," Billy mumbled, shaking her head and crouching down to draw a perfect orange jack-o'-lantern on the fudge frosting. She was in the process of decorating four dozen Halloween cupcakes for the front of the store. "I just can't deal anymore," she continued. "I knocked on her door this morning to try to reason with her, but there was no answer. Should I go to the police?"

"Hmm ... that's a tough one," Melissa said, mulling it over. Billy hoped that, as a law student, Melissa might have some keen insight about these kinds of disputes. The only other person Billy had told so far was Corryn, who'd been beyond livid. In fact, it had taken Billy an hour to convince her sister not to storm the brownstone, and to just let her handle it.

Now Melissa set her coffee down and crossed her arms over her chest. As always, her sleek all-black designer clothes contrasted loudly with Billy's attire—a lilac-colored sweater and bootleg khakis that were tight on her boot. She told Billy about a case she'd learned about in a law seminar: Two petty neighbors brought every squabble they had to court, until they both ended up too broke to keep their apartments. "I mean, I just want you to keep in mind this is your *neighbor* we're talking about," Melissa said. "You've got to live with this person, so unless you have proof it was her, getting the police involved might only make things tenser and more unbearable. And you don't want to get into a situation where she sues you, claiming you made conditions in the brownstone 'unlivable.' "

"What! That's crazy. I—"

"I know, I know, it sucks," Melissa said sympathetically. "But it's just one of those sticky situations."

True ... and Billy was torn. Last night, after she'd calmed down, she'd paced around her apartment—or maybe she'd paced first *to* calm down?—and then decided to sleep on it. Lady McAvit was the obvious culprit; who else would expect Billy to understand the significance of tomatoes smeared on her window? It made sense to confront her, but by the same token, if Lady McAvit *had* done it, could she be anything other than certifiably demented? And in that case, Billy didn't relish the prospect of exacerbating her dementia.

Besides, she couldn't prove anything. This morning she'd polled some of her neighbors across the street, but none of them had seen anything. That wasn't surprising, though, because of the large oak tree outside the brownstone, with thick, leafy branches that hung right in front of Billy's fire escape.

Still, the fact remained: She couldn't let Lady McAvit continue to fester in this bizarre pool of animosity. "Okay, I won't get the police involved yet, but what are my other options?"

Melissa shrugged. "Be nice to her. Kiss her ass." The advice sounded funny coming from a girl who rarely kissed ass and, if anything, inspired others to do so. Still, there was a certain logic to it.

"All right," Billy said after a moment of reflection. "I will try one more time to smooth things over." Although she'd already apologized twice, and sent a basket of fruit last week, but fine. A little more groveling and maybe the grudge-holding, psychotic battle-ax downstairs would see the light. Then they could settle this and finally move on.

"It seems like your best bet for now," Melissa agreed. "Be extra friendly when you see her; maybe hold the door for her, bring in her mail."

Okay, let's not go that far. She wasn't her butler, for chrissake. But she understood the basic concept, and decided to put Lady McAvit out of her mind for the moment.

And instead she focused on Ted Schneider. What had happened to him? Who *was* that mysterious stranger? Curiosity stirred wildly inside her; she just couldn't let it drop. And maybe it sounded crazy, but Billy thought if she could find out who killed Ted, then maybe she'd have something to tell her aunt Penelope. If Billy could prove that Ted had been telling the truth—that someone really *had* been after him—then Aunt Penelope would know, once and for all, that he hadn't been lying to her. That he'd left because he'd *had* to.

Well, she was going to Churchill tomorrow to meet with Greg Dappaport anyway; maybe when she was there, she could do some snooping around.

Just then Des sauntered into the back. "Hey, what are you guys talking about in here?"

"Tomatoes," Melissa replied, then smiled sweetly. "You know, those little round things people throw at you and your band?"

"Ha-ha," he mumbled, rolling his eyes.

Billy grinned and turned her attention back to the Halloween cupcakes, starting to draw a witch on one, when Katie popped her head through the door to tell them there was a line of customers out front.

Billy set down her pastry bag to go, when Melissa stopped her. "No, Billy, you finish what you were doing. Des and I can handle it. C'mon," she said, giving her stepbrother a light shove toward the front. He grumbled something about the gluttony of "white-collar sellouts"—i.e., Bella Donna's clientele—and then they were gone.

Leaving Billy alone with her thoughts, and way too many cupcakes.

That afternoon was windy with the biting chill of autumn. After her shift at the bakery, Billy headed to Churchill to meet with Greg Dappaport. Now, as she turned the corner, she tossed out her café mocha to hug her arms across her chest and rub some heat into her bones.

The Churchill Art Gallery was a pristine stucco building about two hundred feet from the ocean, with a manicured side lawn and a giant weeping willow. There was a wide stone threshold in front. Was that where her mural would be?

Sucking in a nervous breath, Billy climbed the white steps that led to the entrance. Clutched to her chest she had her portfolio, which included some of her graphic designs as well as her own drawings. She'd even worn the tried-and-true interview suit, yet was much more nervous for this meeting than she'd been for the one with Kip Belding. Who, by the way, still hadn't called, apparently unable to tap into any open positions besides glorified orderly at Tuck Hospital in Dorchester.

The interior of the Churchill Art Gallery looked the way one would expect: pristine white carpet, pristine white walls, and splashy paintings all around. Freestanding sculptures filled each corner, and classical music played quietly overhead.

"Billy?"

Spinning around, she saw Dappaport shuffling toward her wearing a double-breasted burgundy suit with a blinding yellow neckerchief flapping in his wake. He extended his arms as he approached, and though she felt utterly ridiculous about it, Billy hugged him. "Greg Dappaport," he said by way of reintroduction. "It's lovely to see you again!"

"Hi," Billy said brightly. "I was so flattered by your call."

"I know Sally introduced us briefly at the jubilee, but did I meet you before that?"

Of course, she hadn't planned on mentioning the incident on the beach, but now that Dappaport had brought it up, she realized it might be a good way to get some information about Ted Schneider, so she pushed her pride aside. "Actually, I did see you on the beach before the jubilee began," she said tentatively, studying his reaction.

Quizzical for a moment, Dappaport said, "Oh, yes, that's right! How dreadful—I'm afraid you didn't see me at my best. I was having an unfortunate argument with that horrid fisherman who insisted on keeping his obscene eyesore of a boat docked in a prominently visible slip. I'm sorry—I know it's tacky to speak ill of the dead—but the man seemed intent on ruining the décor of the jubilee, not to mention the *town*." She nodded with feeling, because he was a potential employer, but inside, she was suppressing a grin. If Dappaport had such a disdain for the tacky, then what was up with that blinding neckerchief? Although, in fairness, it looked somewhat more natural on him than on Fred from *Scooby-Doo*.

"In fact, the boat's *still* docked in the Churchill marina, and I suppose it will be until the man's affairs are settled. The SS *Drifter*, if you can believe that name. It's just sitting there, silently mocking us all. Anyway, I've decided to give up the crusade." He ran a hand over his widow's peak and smiled genteelly at her. "Now back to our business."

He went on to explain what he had in mind for the smooth expanse of stone in the front of the gallery: namely, an evocative mural to capture Churchill's "essence." Billy showed him her portfolio, and he seemed impressed. "I notice you have a real affinity for landscape painting," he remarked, flipping through the drawings.

Smiling, she said, "I suppose it's my favorite." She was about to add that she was open to other approaches when Dappaport told her he liked that—or "fancied" that. (The accent kind of came and went.)

"Images of nature are timelessly gorgeous," he said with a touch of awe in his voice. "And what's so brilliant is that a picture of the ocean is so expected in a coastal town like ours, it's *un*expected. You know?"

"Yes, I see what you mean," she said, nodding and thinking, *This is really going to happen. I'm going to be commissioned for a mural.*

Dappaport said, "Ever since I acquired the gallery this past spring, I've been looking for something that will just make it pop. But I was waiting to be hit with a bolt of inspiration, and then when I saw those cakes of yours—so ornate, so intricate, so *fresh*—I knew I'd found my artist."

Billy's face flushed with heat, and her chest swelled with pride. How could cakes have made such an impression? Even if Dappaport was a little quirky, there had to be something truly special about them . . . didn't there?

After they discussed details—like materials, hours, and, of course, money—Billy thanked him again for the opportunity, promised she wouldn't let him down, and prayed she could keep her promise. She agreed to start as soon as possible, and only as she was heading to the door did she remember the rest of her mission in Churchill today.

"Oh, Mr. Dappaport?"

"Yes?"

"Can you tell me where the sheriff's office is?"

"The sheriff's?" he echoed, looking surprised.

"I just want to say hi," she improvised. "Old friend of my family's." A lie of course; she wanted to stop by and see what she could find out about Ted Schneider's death. The sheriff probably wouldn't tell her anything, but hey, it wouldn't hurt to try.

"I see. Well, regrettably, Sheriff Mueller is still on vacation in Marblehead. His office is across town, near the library. I believe Deputy Trellis is filling in."

"Oh, okay. Well, thanks again," she said, and left the gallery. She practically floated up the street, elated by this new job, this new development in her life, and it was in this hazy state of fulfillment that she literally ran into Seth.

"Oh!" she said, jumping back. "I'm sorry, I— Seth!"

"Hey," he said, sounding very pleasantly surprised. "What's up? What are you doing here?" After she explained about the streetscape project, he congratulated her.

"That's great; you must be psyched. You're going to take the job, right?"

"Definitely."

"Good, then I guess I'll see you around town more often, huh?"

Nodding, Billy felt a golf ball take shape in her throat. "So . . . how are the home repairs going?" she asked.

"Not bad. I'm on my way to the hardware store now for some

paint. Listen, if you get a chance, you should stop by and see how the place is coming along."

No, she should *not* stop by. After they'd almost kissed at the Dessert Jubilee, and after the simmering, erotic tension at lunch the other day, Billy knew that being around Seth was not a particularly sane idea.

Then again . . .

If she went over to Seth's, she might learn more about Ted Schneider. Living in such a small town, even temporarily, had to yield its fair share of information. Not to mention that Seth's friend Sally seemed acutely plugged in; surely she would know some local gossip that might be useful.

Once that comfortable rationalization was in place, Billy said, "Okay, I will."

"Great," Seth said. "Let me give you directions in case you forgot."

A few minutes later, after they said good-bye, Billy turned to watch Seth walking away. Biting her lip, she admired his sexy butt moving like the rest of him: with unassuming charm. She sighed, almost wistfully, thinking about how freaking *hot* Seth was, and then forced herself to focus.

The case. Her mission was to find out who killed Ted, and she didn't want to get distracted. No matter how potent Seth's presence was, no matter how good he smelled, and no matter what dirty thoughts ran through her less-than-Catholic mind.

Chapter Fifteen

After an hour at Marie's Café, where Billy had jotted down ideas for the streetscape (and had a piece of lemon pie), she walked across town to the sheriff's office, where she found a *Gone Fishing* sign posted on the door. Deputy Trellis was obviously working hard.

Next she headed to Seth's, referring to the directions he'd given her. It was getting close to five—soon it would be dark out. As of now, the sky had a grayish-blue tint, almost like twilight.

As she approached the Lannigans' beach house, memories came skittering back, reminding her of the brief time she'd shared here with Seth. One weekend in particular stood out. They'd house-sat for Seth's mom, and spent three sultry, unforgettable nights together down by the water.

How they'd never consummated their relationship during one of their late-night swims Billy would never know. She could still remember Seth's steel-hard erection, the way it pulsed when she touched him underwater. She remembered the hungry, intense expression on his face, the restraint it had taken not to shove the crotch of her bathing suit to the side and invite him in—not to take his bulging cock up between her legs. . . .

Now she dashed up the front steps and knocked on Seth's front door. She waited and knocked again. Still no answer. Suddenly she heard banging coming from the back, so she wound around the side of the house, hearing leaves crackle beneath her feet. And then she saw him. He was down on one knee, hammering the floor of the gazebo that sat above a stone wall in the enclosed backyard.

God . . . he was beautiful without his shirt on. Biting her lip, Billy watched him work—watched the muscles in his sleek, smooth back flex. Heat seeped into her bones and thrummed between her legs, and she let out a breathy sigh of frustration.

He must've felt her burning gaze, because he turned around and caught her staring. In that moment she wished more than anything that she could simply go to him—climb onto him, press her mouth to his hot, smooth skin. Wished that she could feel his hands under her sweater, beneath her bra, closed firmly over her bare breasts.

Now, instead of waving hello, Seth let his eyes bore into her, then quickly scanned her body. Even though she wasn't wearing anything alluring, the intensity of his scrutiny made her feel exposed, nearly naked, and only vaguely aware of the chill in the air. Which reminded her . . . if Seth had his shirt off in this weather, he must've really been working up a sweat. *Oh, wow* . . . The thought of Seth sweaty *really* turned her on.

Finally he came to his feet and walked closer to her. She met him halfway. "Hey," he said, in a low, almost husky voice. "I didn't expect you till later . . ." he added—explained, really, as if he were apologizing for being only half-dressed. What was he, crazy? Up close his body was the stuff of fantasies. His chest was strong and powerful, with light brown hair that trailed sexily down to the waist of his jeans. His arms had subtle but mouthwatering curves of muscle, and there was no doubt: The yum factor was in full, screaming effect.

"I'm sorry," Billy mumbled absently. "Is now a bad time?"

"No, no," he said quickly, coming right in front of her, towering over her, close enough to reach out and touch, and Billy swallowed hard, averting her eyes to clear her head. Not her brightest move, considering that her eyes fell to his stomach, which was thrillingly close to a six-pack. Smooth, soft flesh covering solid strength—she wet her lips as her mouth ran dry and heavy arousal pooled between her legs.

"I'm glad you're here," he added as he led her onto the deck and through the sliding glass doors to the kitchen. Suddenly Billy was hit by a memory: cooking dinner for Seth on their house-sitting weekend. She'd accidentally undercooked the fish, and joked that her special was "baked sushi."

"What are you smiling at?" Seth asked her now.

"Oh, nothing," Billy replied, taking a seat at the kitchen table.

"Can I get you a drink?" he asked as he reached inside the fridge and pulled out a can of Coke for himself. Billy resisted the urge to ask if he had Framboise, vodka, and Diet Sprite on hand, and settled instead for water. It was almost evening, but she didn't want to look like a lush—and it would mostly be for her nerves, but she didn't particularly want to look nervous, either. Besides, she might as well keep her wits about her if she was going to try to get information about Ted Schneider's murder. That *was* her purpose for being there—the half-naked-hottie factor was just a plus.

"Have you heard anything about that guy who died at the jubilee?" she asked, trying to sound casual.

Seth shrugged as he pulled out the chair across from her and took a seat. "No, not really, why?"

"Just curious." She paused, running her thumb carelessly up and down over the condensation on her glass. "So Sally and her friends really didn't like him too much, huh?"

Seth shrugged. "I guess he didn't fit in enough," he said dryly. "But Sally mentioned that she ran into Deputy Trellis yesterday, and he said that Bob closed the case on it right away—which is always great with Trellis, who rarely handles anything more taxing than kitten rescue."

"Who's Bob?" Billy asked.

"Medical examiner."

"Oh."

"Not that there was anything to close, really. It was obviously just a terrible accident."

"I doubt that," Billy mumbled.

"What?" Seth said, tilting his head, confused.

"Nothing," Billy said quickly.

Slanting his eyebrows, Seth said, "You don't think it was an accident?"

"No, no, I mean . . . I'm just saying, it's easier for Deputy Trellis to assume it was an accident than to try to figure out if something else might have happened."

"Like what?" Seth said skeptically.

Billy shrugged and toyed with the wet rim of her glass. "I just think it's strange that Ted would eat something with nuts in it when he'd just finished asking half the bakery staff what foods he should avoid."

"Yeah, but you said he'd been drinking, right? So he was drunk, confused."

"Hmm . . ."

"What other explanation could there be?"

Billy deflected the conversation a little by asking, "Do you know if Ted had problems with anyone in town? Anybody specific?"

"I don't really know," Seth replied, leaning back in his chair. "According to Sally, nobody in Churchill really even knew him that well."

"How does Sally know so much?" Billy asked, genuinely curious.

With a laugh, Seth said, "Excellent question. I've stopped trying to understand that. But somehow she's got her finger on the pulse of everything that happens in this town—not to mention everything that *could* happen, and everything that didn't happen but almost did."

"Oh, I see. So nobody really knew Ted, yet Sally and her friends disliked him enough to make that comment about killing him," Billy said, remembering the joke about slipping Ted something with nuts.

Seth let out a short, incredulous laugh. "Oh, come on, they were only kidding! Granted, it wasn't remotely funny." Looking sincerely at her, he softened his voice. "Billy. Seriously, what's going on? Where is all this coming from?"

"I'm just curious, that's all."

"Oh, really?" Seth said, curving his mouth into a grin, as if amused by her attempt at secrecy—as if he *knew* when she was lying. Shaking his head, he absently ruffed his hair with his fingers. (Billy recognized the adorably scruffy habit, but tried not to dwell on it.) "C'mon, really. Do you really think the guy was murdered?"

Although she'd had the best intention to keep a low profile—really, she did—when Seth's hazel eyes stared her down, the effect was like truth serum, and before she knew it she was spilling everything she knew about Aunt Penelope's relationship with Ted, and what he'd told her about someone being after him.

"And that's why I think there could've been foul play," she continued. "And I'm thinking that maybe the someone from his past—the someone who was after him—finally got him."

Seth hesitated, as though searching for the most diplomatic way to phrase his next question—though there was really no need, because Billy could guess what it was. "Is it possible he was just portraying something to your aunt . . . you know, giving himself an out?"

"Well, anything's possible," Billy remarked with admitted triteness. "Maybe it wasn't someone from his past. Maybe it was someone in town with a whole different agenda, but it wasn't an accident, and I'm gonna prove it."

"Uh-huh—whoa, wait a minute here. What do you mean, 'prove it'?" Seth asked warily. "What do you plan on doing?"

"Nothing," Billy replied quickly. "Just . . . trying to piece things together for myself, that's all." It was true to a point; that *was* her overall plan. But it was subject to adjustment if an actual lead fell her way.

"I'm sure if there was anything suspicious, there would've been an investigation."

"But you said yourself, Deputy Trellis is totally inexperienced."

"Did I say inexperienced?" Seth remarked. "I meant to say *dumb*. But anyway, Bob examined the body; it was obviously all routine."

"I agree that it *looks* that way," Billy conceded. "Do they at least know what, exactly, Ted ate that triggered the fatal reaction?"

"Well, Sally said he was cremated."

"Already?"

Seth held up his hand. "I know how it sounds, but apparently Trellis found Ted's will on his boat; it specified that Ted wanted to be cremated right away in the case of his death. I guess he had a thing about having his body lying dead, something about not wanting to decompose. I'm not sure; I was only half listening when Sally was telling me all this. Anyway, since he had no family to speak of, and there wasn't going to be an investigation, the sheriff's office and the coroner didn't see any reason to wait."

"Convenient," Billy mumbled, more to herself. Seth just squinted, a little intrigued, a little bemused, as though not sure what to make of her and her theory at the moment. "I know it might sound weird, but I still want to see what I can find out. Something seems off here. Oh, but don't mention this to anyone, okay?" She knew he wouldn't if she asked him not to—not even busybody Sally would get it out of him.

"I won't," Seth said, still looking skeptical. Billy knew he didn't honestly believe it had been murder, but he let it drop for now.

"Thanks." As Billy lifted her glass of water, another pain shot up her arm. "Ow," she whispered, and rubbed her triceps.

"What's wrong?" Seth asked, and leaned forward with concern.

"Oh, it's nothing. I think I just pulled a muscle or something carrying that tray around at the jubilee." Then, with a self-deprecating grin, she added, "I'm at the top of my game these days; can't you tell?"

When she winced again, Seth came to his feet and walked behind her chair. "Here . . ." he said, and set his hands on her shoulders.

"What are you doing?" she asked, hearing her voice almost crack at the contact. Seth's hands were on her—powerful and warm—and melting her into a weak, spineless puddle.

"Hold on . . ." he said, as he gently massaged her shoulders. His hands thoroughly worked her muscles, rubbing her shoulders down to her upper arms. *Oh . . . God.* Billy's heart shot up to Olympic speed, and perspiration seeped into her palms, which were clutching the fabric of her pants. She needed to calm down, but she couldn't. The way Seth's fingers dug soothingly into her flesh was intoxicating . . . drugging . . . especially now that he was working his way back up and sliding his warm palm underneath her hair.

"Um . . . thanks, that feels better," she said weakly, nearly moaning as Seth used two fingers to knead the back of her neck. It wasn't just the sensuality of his movements—it was Seth himself. He'd always emanated a potent physical energy, and now the scant space between their bodies felt charged with it. The air was thick with suffocating heat, reducing Billy's breath to short, shallow puffs, and her body to liquid flames.

As he deepened his massage, she bit her lip, fighting the urge to drop her head back. God, she was ridiculous; he was trying to work a kink out from her very out-of-shape body, and she was turning it into foreplay. His hands were so strong, his fingers so warm, and it felt so good, she didn't want him to stop. That was normal.

But was it normal not to want him to stop *ever*?

Suddenly she heard him breathing, and knew he'd leaned down and gotten closer. His breath fell deeply and heavily, so she knew he was turned on, too. Instinctively she squeezed her legs together, because her vaginal muscles were throbbing and her thighs were trembling, and suddenly she felt his lips on her ear. "W-what are you doing?" she asked brokenly.

"I don't know," Seth replied softly—roughly—and licked inside her ear.

Fire raged between her legs, and before she could even think straight, Seth was rubbing her shoulders again and sucking hard on her earlobe. The sensation of his hot, wet mouth tugging on her ear and his roughened cheek against her neck was all too much, and Billy's head lolled back just as strong hands slid under her arms, urging her out of her chair and turning her around. Instantly, Seth's mouth descended on hers, capturing her in a gentle but possessive kiss. It didn't take long, though, for the kiss to deepen—turning wet, urgent, and so goddamn *sexy*.

"Oh, God," she whispered when their lips parted. Seth groaned huskily, tilted his head, and sank deeper into their next kiss, which became almost endless.

With her breasts crushed against his ribs, and her body arching and straining to relieve its sexual hunger, Billy was slightly losing her mind. Seth's sexy gruffness was all coming back to her as he tightened his embrace and whispered huskily about how good she felt.

Billy slid her hands up his bare chest, getting more turned on by the feel of his naked flesh, and then coiled her arms around his neck as she kissed him back with fierce hunger. She'd temporarily lost reason and good sense, but she just didn't care, because Seth's licking into her mouth was the most thrilling thing that had happened to her in so long.

She could feel the dampness between her legs, the stickiness of her panties against her flesh—the near pain of wanting sex so much. Not flowers or sweetness, not right now. Just sex with Seth. Just Seth's cock, rock-hard and pumping inside her.

And speaking of hard cocks . . . *Ohhh!*

Suddenly she felt his erection. It was straining the fly of his jeans—how could she have missed that? It was one of the most beautiful things she'd ever felt. As Billy assailed Seth's mouth, she undulated against his pelvis, trying to align his crotch with hers, to fit their lower bodies together like puzzle pieces.

Groaning, Seth kissed her harder and slid his hands down her back to cup her bottom. In one sharp motion he squeezed her and pulled her up against him.

"Ohh . . ." she moaned, rubbing against his erection, and breaking the kiss to get her breath back.

"Oh, Jesus." Seth groaned, moving them back until Billy's butt hit the kitchen table. And then she was flat on her back, and Seth was spreading her legs wide before he climbed on top of her. In a matter of seconds he was lying on her, rubbing her breasts and burying his face in between while he ground his erection into her aching crotch. Each thrust of his hips was punctuated with a sharp, lusty moan from her—one that implicitly begged for more.

How had she gotten here? she wondered hazily, lifting her pelvis off the table in sharp motions, totally succumbing to lust, grinding hard with Seth, and practically having sex through their clothes. How would it feel *without* clothes? If he yanked her jeans down now, would she even try to stop him?

They were both nearly panting; it seemed inconceivable that a kiss had gotten so out of control so fast. Make that a shoulder massage. Make that stopping by to investigate the death of . . . What was his name again? Oh, who cared?

Seth tore his mouth off hers and lifted himself up on his hands. As he rocked his body against hers, he whispered raggedly about how good she felt, how much he wanted her, how she drove him crazy . . . but Billy could barely hear over the blood thundering in her veins and her heart pounding like a bass drum in her ears. She couldn't remember the last time she'd felt so excited—not with her ex-boyfriend Ryan, and so far, not with Mark.

Mark!

Oh, Christ—she'd forgotten all about him! She was totally betraying him, even if they weren't officially exclusive yet.

Abruptly, then, she pushed on Seth's shoulders to move him off of her. But he was so turned on, he didn't seem to realize what was happening. An anguished-looking expression crossed over his face as he continued to pant and pump his hips.

Then he leaned down to kiss her, but Billy turned her head . . . leaving Seth to trail kisses across her cheek and down her neck.

"Ohhhh . . ." she moaned traitorously again as Seth licked her pulse point.

But somehow she shook herself back to reality. "Seth, wait," she said, and gave his arms another shove.

"Wha . . . ?" he said, pulling back, confused.

"Wait," she said again, and started to sit up.

Seth rolled off her and onto his feet, his blond hair rumpled, his face flushed, and his expression dazed. "What's wrong?" he asked huskily, plowing his hand through his hair.

For the first time Billy could feel the flaming heat on her face and the pull of her inner thigh muscles, which were definitely not used to that kind of stretching. "I'm sorry; I can't do this," she said, and climbed down from the table. Her tailbone was a little sore, too, but that was probably a good thing. Knowing that this encounter hadn't been *all* ecstasy-filled rapture might help ease her guilty conscience later. A girl could hope, anyway.

"What's wrong?" Seth asked again, his voice gravelly. "What is it—that other guy?"

"Yeah," she replied. Of *course* it was. Mark wasn't her official boyfriend yet, but that was obviously where they were headed, so how the hell could she have simply forgotten his existence, even for a few moments? She was a grown woman; there was no excuse for this kind of impulsiveness. And when she thought about the way Mark's huge and ecstatic default grin would falter if he knew she'd made out with her ex-boyfriend, her heart just sank. "I'm sorry; I never should've let this happen," she said, straightening her sweater, which had gotten twisted, and brushing some hair out of her eyes. "I've got to go."

"Wait," Seth said, following her out of the kitchen and through the hall. Gently he caught her arm as she reached the foyer. "Billy, I'm sorry. I didn't mean to come on so strong—"

"Don't be sorry; let's just forget it," she said, turning around and catching a glimpse of Seth's erection, which was still straining hugely against his jeans. Definitely time to go. "Listen, I'll see you around . . . you know, Churchill or whatever . . . um . . . take care."

Her exit scene was marred when she yanked hard on the front door, only to spring forward because the door was locked. "Here," Seth said, coming up behind her and unlocking it. He must've sensed she was frazzled—nearly shaking—as she stepped out into the cold. Earlier she'd wished she had the guts to attack Seth, but now she could see that she hadn't been nearly ready for that. Too much sensory overload. Too much longing. Too much emotional baggage that came with knowing Seth again.

She inhaled the fresh, cold air, hoping it would help, but instead her chest constricted. It was as though a giant fist were squeezing her lungs, making it hard to breathe. Irrational tears stung the backs of her eyes as the fist closed on her throat, making it hard to swallow.

It was all flooding back to her now. The way it had been back when he was hers—the way it had hurt when he left. The way it would hurt when he left *again* and went back to his real life in Seattle. Emotions rumbled inside her, fast and turbulent, as she thought about Seth, and how the air around him always felt like a thick force field.

If she stepped through it again, she'd be lost.

Chapter Sixteen

By the time Billy got home, she was frantic with guilt. The last thing she needed was an interlude with a very pissed-off Lady McAvit.

"Well, thanks for jinxing my tomatoes."

"What?"

"Forget it," the woman muttered, scrunching her pruny face with disdain, and brushed regally past Billy in the front hall of their brownstone.

"No, really," Billy said, trying to keep her voice extremely even, calm, solicitous—in other words, taking Melissa's advice and kissing ass.

Pausing at her open apartment door, Lady McAvit said, "Ever since your mongrel got into my greenhouse, my tomatoes have been wilting and shriveling up on the vine." Billy couldn't help noting the similarity between McAvit and her vegetables. "I want you to know I'm filing a complaint with the management company. Pets may be allowed in this building, but there have to be *some* limits," she snapped and slammed the door shut in Billy's face.

Some limits? Did that include *vandalism?* The woman was certifiably insane! Furiously, Billy raised her sore arm and knocked hard on Lady McAvit's door. No answer. "I want to talk to you," she called, and knocked again. "Did you smear tomatoes on my window? That was you, wasn't it?" Still no answer. Billy released an infurjated sigh. "You'd better leave me alone, or *I'll* file a complaint, too—with the police."

Darting up the stairs, she slammed the door to her apartment angrily and went straight for the phone. She paused before she dialed Mark's number, though, because she wanted to calm her nerves before she talked to him. God, she hoped his cell was working again, because she really needed to talk to him, and it was the only phone he had. Apparently his old roommate had convinced him it was cheaper than having a phone line in his apartment. Three rings and Mark answered. "Hello?"

"Hi, it's me," Billy said, sinking into the rocking chair by the door. She brought her feet up so she could curl her cheek comfortingly against her knees. "I need to talk to you."

"Hey!" Mark greeted her, superjovially as always, which only made her feel worse. "What's up, cutie?"

"Um, can I come over to your place? I need to talk to you tonight—in person." She wanted to confess what had happened with Seth, and apologize. And she wanted to find out where he stood with her *after* her confession, which she could see only in person.

"My place?" Mark echoed, his inflection wavering. "Um . . . well, why don't you just tell me over the phone? It's late and everything. . . ."

"I know it's late," Billy said on a sigh. "But it's kind of important, Mark."

"So let's talk now," he offered cheerfully. "What's on your mind, cutie? I'm here; talk away."

"But why can't I just come over to talk to you?" she asked, confused.

"Listen, Billy . . . it's just not a good time."

Since when? What happened to "I'm here, talk away"? "What do you mean?" she asked with frustration. "I'm telling you that I want—"

"Look, this is all too much for me tonight," he interrupted.

"Huh?" How could this phone call be "too much" when she hadn't even gotten into the part about kissing her ex-boyfriend yet?

"It's just been a tough day, and I'm really tired," Mark added, sounding nearly frantic to get off the phone. "I'm sorry; I've really got to run."

"What's that noise?" she asked, picking up voices in the background. "Do you have people over?"

"No, it's my TV," Mark said quickly. "Anyway, I think I just need a little breathing room, okay? It's not you; it's me. Um, you're a great girl; you really are—don't change, okay?"

"Mark, what the hell are you talking about!" she nearly yelled. "You're not making any sense."

"Look, I think it's best if we just lie low, taper off, and regroup for a while," he went on hurriedly, "but we'll do lunch real soon—*my* treat! Bye, Billy."

Then he hung up.

For endless minutes Billy sat in her rocking chair with her forehead pressed to her knees, not fully grasping what had just happened. What planet was she living on? Here she'd wanted to talk to Mark about what'd happened with Seth—she'd wanted to apologize, because she'd had all these doubts about where they stood. And now, it seemed, she stood alone.

Suddenly her phone rang, and Billy's heart jumped. "Mark?" she said on a startled breath, assuming it was him calling right back. (Assuming he wanted to explain his behavior, like maybe that he'd forgotten to take his anti–psychotic asshole medication.)

But the line was quiet. Dead, almost . . . except there was no dial tone. There was only the barest trace of breathing on the other end.

"Hello?" she said, waiting for a response as uneasiness crept into her chest. Unnerved by the quiet, she swallowed a hard lump of anxiety. "Mark?"

No answer. But just as Billy was about to hang up, someone finally spoke. "Go away," the low voice hissed. "Just go *away*."

With her heart slamming against her ribs, Billy dropped the phone.

"So you're telling me there's nothing you can do?" Billy said incredulously as she hugged Pike, who must've sensed her fear, because he was wagging his tail, on full alert.

"Look, I'm sorry," the police officer said for the tenth time, sounding more bored each time he said it. "If you get more calls, we can put a trace on the phone. But don't be surprised if the call was made from a pay phone anyway—we get that all the time."

"Great," she mumbled. She'd also told him about the tomatoes on her window, but he hadn't exactly been rabid for details.

"Like I said, we'll talk to your neighbor, but unless the call's traced to her home or office, we've got no proof it was her. What does she do for a living?"

"Besides terrorize me?" Billy said, frustrated. "How do I know? She's psycho tomato woman."

"So there's no one else you can think of who'd be playing pranks on you?" he asked in more of that flat, bored tone. Billy didn't appreciate his attempts to minimize vandalism and a threatening phone call by referring to them as "pranks."

"I can't think of anyone except my neighbor," she said honestly.

"An ex-boyfriend maybe?"

"No." Please, Seth would never, ever do anything to hurt her, or even scare her; he had too good a heart. And Mark was a decent guy, too, even if he *had* just dumped her. Her only other ex-boyfriend was Ryan Crennan, and Billy couldn't believe he'd spent even one minute thinking about her in the last two years.

"How about an ex-girlfriend?" the cop asked with a less than covert snicker.

"No," Billy said, rolling her eyes. *Pervert.*

"Fine, well, you can come down to the station tomorrow to file an official complaint. In the meantime, keep your doors locked."

"Yeah, thanks, genius."

"What?"

"Nothing."

"And if anything turns up, we'll let you know. But don't be surprised if—"

"If you don't find out anything, I know," Billy said, and hung up the phone. She sighed. Honestly, she hadn't meant to take out her fear on an innocent civil servant, but her nerves were shot tonight. First Lady McAvit picked a fight with her downstairs, then Mark told her he needed space, and now a threatening phone call and some ineffectual bureaucracy, to boot.

Sighing again, she hugged Pike closer, and decided to do the only thing that might make her feel better. She reached for the phone and called her sister.

The following day Billy filled Melissa in on the latest savagery with Lady McAvit, and the mysterious "prank" call.

"So what are the police going to do?" Melissa asked as she reached for a stack of new napkins from the supply shelf.

"Absolutely nothing," Billy replied with lingering resentment.

"Well, I guess there's not much they can do," Melissa offered sympathetically. "So you're sure it's your neighbor then? This all seems so over-the-top for some little old lady who gets her kicks growing indoor tomatoes."

Billy smirked at that, although truthfully, Melissa's sentiments matched her own. In fact, all night she hadn't been able to get it out of her mind: It *was* too over-the-top for Lady McAvit. They'd lived in the same brownstone for over two years; she'd never shown a trace of zealous vigilantism. So why now?

It might sound crazy, but the truth was . . .

Last night it had occurred to Billy that the vandalism and the threatening call coincided exactly with her decision to look into Ted Schneider's murder. It didn't make much sense, since she hadn't even gotten to talk to the deputy—the only person she'd told her suspicions to was Seth . . . right? But still, she couldn't shake the possibility that there was a connection. Was it possible that someone was trying to scare her away from snooping? Was that what the raspy, whispering voice had meant by, "Go away"?

But who could know what she was up to?

It was very possible that whoever it was had used tomatoes out of convenience; if Lady McAvit had forgotten to lock her greenhouse again; anyone could've swiped some of them and thrown them at Billy's window.

She considered telling Melissa her theory, but decided against it, because it wasn't her place to blab Aunt Penelope's business, a concept that Adrienne had never quite grasped.

"What are you working on now?" Melissa asked, motioning to the cake on the table.

"Oh . . ." Billy said, turning back to it. "*Window* by Matisse." Melissa shook her head, smiling, and Billy grinned back. "Isn't it funny?" Ever since the jubilee, word of mouth about the Renoir cakes had spread, and now Bella Donna constantly got requests for famous-painting cakes. Of course, Donna always cleared those orders with Billy first.

Between that and the streetscape, Billy should be having an awesome time, but last night's phone call kept playing in her head. And whenever her mind took a break from that, it switched over to the erotic encounter on Seth's kitchen table—rerunning graphic images of them entwined and frantic and barely in control.

Just then Georgette slammed the kitchen door open and carried a bin of frosting to the walk-in freezer. Huffily, she threw the freezer door open, dropped the bin down, kicked the door closed, and stomped back to her lair.

Melissa shot Billy a questioning look, then shook her head. "She has had such an attitude lately. Ever since my promotion. Have you noticed?"

Of course. Who the hell hadn't? "No, not really," Billy said, trying to stay diplomatic.

"Ech, she is *so* annoying," Melissa went on, rolling her eyes with disgust. "It's like, don't blame me because you're old and fat and your husband left you."

"Melissa!"

"What?"

"Come on, that's mean."

"Well, what's her problem?"

Shrugging, Billy said, "I just think maybe she's not crazy about all the new recipes."

"Well, I'm sorry, but this isn't a cafeteria. We can't serve mac-'n'-cheese and Tater Tots all day long." Reserving comment, Billy reached for the pastry bag. "What?" Melissa said.

"Nothing," Billy replied. *Just . . . sometimes the things you say.*

"Whatever," Melissa said with a shrug, and carried her stack of napkins to the front. As soon as she was gone, Georgette angrily kicked open the door from the kitchen. There was flour on her pink Superfly glasses, and her white pompadour was in savage disarray.

"I heard every word that bitch just said," she declared with steely, biting hatred. Guilt pitted in Billy's gut as embarrassment stained her cheeks. God, she hoped Georgette wasn't too hurt by what Melissa had said—and she hoped she didn't think that *Billy* felt the same way. "I was a cafeteria lady for twenty-two years and I'm damn proud of it."

"Oh, really, don't pay any attention to Melissa," Billy said feebly.

"I swear, one of these days," Georgette added seethingly, "I'm going to *kill* that girl!"

"Hold the elevator!" Billy called as she frantically rushed into the adult-school building, hoping she wasn't too late on her first day of class. She was supposed to meet her mom and her sister over fifteen minutes ago, but she'd taken the B line from work, and, predictably, the subway had crawled the entire way. "Wait, please . . . please hold that. . . ."

The scrawny man in the elevator ignored Billy's pleas, staring ahead as though he didn't see or hear her, and then very obviously reached up to press "door close." The elevator sealed two inches from her face. "Thanks a lot," she grumbled after it was too late to matter, then took the next one to the seventh floor and skirted around the hallway to find her classroom.

As soon as she entered the room, she was hit with the déjà vu of high school home ec. Tiny desk-chair contraptions made up half of the room; kitchen appliances and countertops made up the other. From what she could tell, the students in the class ranged from mid-twenties to mid-fifties. In front, a woman with a short blond coif and an apron was speaking to the class.

Carefully Billy crept along the wall, discreetly trying to find an empty seat. "Thank you for joining us," the teacher said loudly. Billy froze as all the students turned their heads to notice her. To-night was the first of six sessions of "Intro to Refined Cooking," and so far she wasn't off to a great start.

"Oh, thanks," Billy said, smiling feebly. "Sorry I'm late." Then she made brief eye contact with her mom and sister, who were seated in the front row. Corryn grinned at her, while Adrienne shot her a chiding look before turning back to her notebook. Just then Billy noticed the little weasel who'd shut the elevator on her, sitting on the other side of Corryn.

"Ow!"

Billy whipped her head around. "Oh, sorry!" she whispered, realizing that she'd accidentally kicked someone's foot, which had been sticking out in the aisle. A few people angled their heads back to look, and the teacher paused dramatically. Once Billy dropped down in an empty seat in the last row, the teacher resumed her lesson. "As I was saying, my name is Judy Smith, and for the next six sessions I'll be teaching you some wonderfully inventive and lusciously delicious techniques for enhancing your recipe oeuvre."

Suddenly a hand in front went up. Billy stifled an eye roll as she rooted around in her bag for a pen. Come on, a question already? The teacher had barely said anything. "Hello," the student said in an instantly familiar voice. "My name is Adrienne Cabot, and I just wanted to tell you that I'm really, really looking forward to this class."

Okay—so her mom was a brownnoser.

"Well, thank you, Adrienne. I assure you, we're going to have a terrifically abundant and gloriously luxuriant time in this class." Addressing the rest of the class, Judy continued, "Now, I assume we're all here for the same reason—to enrich our lives, as well as our palates."

Adrienne's hand shot up again.

"Yes?"

"The truth is, I'm here because I'm looking to incorporate more healthy foods into my cooking. You see, I've recently lost some weight, and it's changed my whole way of thinking and living." Yeah, four pounds could really do that to a person.

"That's absolutely glorious, Adrienne," Judy said, smiling at her new pet. "And I can assure you that in this class you'll never be wanting for new ways to prepare truly inspiring, delectably ravishing meals that are resplendent with nutrients."

Adrienne scribbled frantically in her notebook, obviously trying to capture every adverb, while Billy continued feeling around in her bag for a pen. No luck. Not even her sketch pencil, which must've dropped on the way here tonight.

While everyone took notes on olive oil, Billy looked around, hoping to catch someone's eye. Finally she tapped on the shoulder of the woman in front of her, who claimed she didn't have an extra pen, and sat farther forward.

"Is someone talking?" Judy said suddenly, darting her eyes suspiciously. Billy slumped down in her chair, hoping she didn't look too guilty. "Yes, Adrienne?" Judy said, calling on Billy's mom, who had her hand raised yet again.

"Regarding the oil issue"—now it constituted an *issue*?—"back when I was heavy, canola oil was a constant theme in my cooking. Would olive oil be a better substitute?"

As Judy replied with a flowery spiel about burning temperatures, Billy gave up her quest for a pen. When she looked over at Corryn, who was half slouched in her chair, she laughed to herself, imagining the expression of apathy on her older sister's face.

Corryn wondered how much more she could stand, sitting next to a dorky guy who couldn't stop sneezing. She'd glared at him briefly, and from the quick look she'd gotten, he was a petite little man with ruddy cheeks and a poorly executed comb-over.

"Aa-ah-ah-*choo!*" he burst out again, and a few wisps of Corryn's hair flew forward. *Yuck!* She screwed up her face and leaned away with blatant disgust. Who cared if it was rude; had he ever heard of tissues?

"Now everyone pick a partner and go to a kitchen station," Judy said.

Corryn was about to turn to Adrienne when she felt someone poke her arm. "Excuse me. Would you like to be my partner?"

It was the sneezer, looking hopeful. Now she felt guilty. "Oh . . . thanks," she said, smiling politely, "but I'm pairing up with my mother—"

As she said the words, Adrienne called to Billy, "Honey, come be my partner!"

"Right . . . the three of us are partnering actually," Corryn explained, tugging on her mom's sleeve.

When Adrienne glanced back, she must've noticed the man lurking around Corryn, because she said quietly, "Well, maybe all four of us could work together."

"What?" Corryn whispered back, definitely less than thrilled. "Mom, I thought we were here to bond."

"We are, but that young man has been staring at you for the past hour." Wait—was that supposed to be appealing or creepy? "And besides, just because we came together, there's no harm in meeting someone new. In fact, it would probably do you a lot of good."

Before Corryn could tell her mom what, exactly, would do *her* a lot of good, Adrienne was extending her hand and introducing herself. "Hi, I'm Adrienne, and that's my daughter Billy," she said, motioning to Billy, who was making her way up the center aisle.

Holding back a sigh, Corryn joined in. "And I'm Corryn."

"Nice to meet you," he said, looking mostly at Corryn. "I'm Roynald. Roynald Membrano."

"Well, we'll just go grab a kitchen station," Adrienne said way too quickly, taking Billy's hand and pulling them both forward. "You two can meet us over there."

Corryn held back an eye roll, but it took a mammoth effort.

Puh-lease. Did her mother actually believe this partnership was going to lead to romance? Besides trading outfits, Corryn wasn't seeing a big future with Roynald Membrano. Not that a guy had to be built for her to like him, but . . .

Hmm . . .

Joe Montgomery was built, and she definitely liked him. Lusted after him, really. A rugged cop with killer green eyes . . . she'd bet he looked so achingly sexy without his shirt on. Even though she hadn't seen him since they'd run into each other on Newbury Street, Joe still crept into her fantasies . . . especially when she was alone and horny in her bed at night, fantasizing about sex. Picturing Joe naked and on top of her, his overpowering body almost crushing her as he drove into her like an animal and satisfied her basest needs.

"Corryn?"

"Oh . . . right," she said, snapping back into focus. "We should go over to our station." Which she would do on autopilot, because she was anxious to get back to her fantasy—especially since fantasy was all it could ever be. Joe might be sexy and very much her physical type, but as she'd learned from Kane, that made him dangerous. Ultimately, it was safer and wiser just to be alone.

"Excuse me," Judy called across the room. "Please find your own station." Corryn looked over and realized she was talking to *her.*

"Oh, no, the four of us were going to work together—"

"Absolutely not," Judy said strictly, shaking her head with rapid but mechanical jerking motions. "Two to a station," she added firmly.

Adrienne offered Corryn a halfhearted look of apology, and Billy barely stifled a grin. "Oh, good, it's just the two of us," Roynald said. "Is this your first adult-ed class?"

"Um, yeah. What about you?"

"No, I take classes all the time. It's a great way to meet some really interesting people." Corryn managed a nod, though she was suddenly feeling a little smothered.

"Judy? Am I doing this right?" Adrienne called out. Judy glided right over to her.

Corryn exchanged knowing looks with Billy; then she laughed. Hey, it could always be worse. Sure, she'd just been thrown at a total stranger by her hopelessly Machiavellian mother, but at least she wasn't stuck working with the teacher's pet.

Chapter Seventeen

A couple of days later Billy was in Churchill, working on the street mural. Dappaport had gotten her a slew of supplies, and he basically left her to do her own thing for as long as she wanted. He told her he just needed to know when she arrived and when she left; the rest was up to her. She loved the autonomy, because it made her feel like a legitimate artist.

Now, as Billy breathed in the clean, temperate October air, she realized that she loved being in Churchill, too. It was a gorgeous little town in the fall. Trees glowed amber and gold as leaves scattered colorfully across the ground.

Suddenly her cell phone rang. "Hello?"

"Billy? Kip Belding here."

"Hi, how are you?" she said brightly.

"Fabulous, doll." Oh, good, it sounded like she was off his shit list. "I'm calling because I've found you the premier position of the new millennium."

"Really?" she said, stretching over to dab paint in the far right corner of the mural. "What position?"

"How do you feel about an energetic, challenging work environment?"

"Sounds great. Where?"

"Well, it's in Dorchester," he said, "right off the orange line."

"Mmm-hmm," Billy said, not thrilled about riding the most dangerous subway line in Boston, but trying to keep an open mind. "What's the company?"

"Well, it's a really large, multifaceted institution, with a constantly evolving client base. . . ."

"Right . . ."

"And I'm sensing a lot of growth potential here, doll."

"Kip, the company?" Billy pressed a little impatiently . . . and suspiciously.

"Tuck Enterprises," he mumbled quickly as he cleared his throat.

"Wait," she said, pausing with her paintbrush in midair, "this isn't Tuck *Hospital*, is it?"

"Um . . ."

She rolled her eyes and sighed softly. "Kip, I really don't want to work in a hospital," she reiterated. "It's just a strong personal preference."

Now Kip sighed—and loudly. "Billy, the job market's a real bitch these days. I mean, if you want me to work with you, you're going to have to be more accommodating." Billy held her tongue, but only for her mother's sake, and Kip gave more details about the open position with a lot of growth potential (ER file clerk).

When he finished, Billy said, "I appreciate your thinking of me, but I'm going to have to pass. If anything opens up in Web design, though, definitely give me a call." She was being as polite as possible, because Adrienne was friends with Kip's mother, Gladys, and Billy didn't want to burn bridges. As she snapped her phone closed, she heard someone coming up behind her.

"Hey, there," Seth said as Billy whipped around.

"Hi," she said with a breath of relief. "You startled me." Instantly heat suffused her cheeks as memories of their hot and heavy makeout session suddenly popped into her mind. If only she hadn't moaned and writhed and carried on like a sex maniac, she might not be so embarrassed right now.

"I'm sorry," he said. "So how's it going? Wow, that looks awesome so far." He moved past her to survey her mural-in-progress. Pride flooded Billy's chest, in spite of the nervous fluttering, and she thanked him.

"What are you doing out here?" Billy asked.

"I was over at Marie's Café, fixing a loose wheel on a rolling cart," he said, motioning with his thumb toward the center of town. "I guess Sally mentioned to half the town that I'm decent with a screwdriver. Anyway, I just wanted to stop by and say hi."

"Oh."

"Yeah."

Glancing down at the ground, Seth cleared his throat almost awkwardly; good, so it wasn't just Billy who felt foolish and flustered about the dry-humping-on-the-kitchen-table bit from the other day.

"I also wanted to tell you what I found out about Ted Schneider," he said.

That took her by surprise. "What?" she asked, wiping blue fingertips on her smock.

"According to the rumors Sally heard, Ted was a regular at the Rusty Canoe." Billy squinted questioningly. "It's a little hole in the wall tavern outside of town—right on the wharf."

"Hmm . . ."

"So I was thinking . . . maybe when you get done here, we could go check it out."

"We?" Billy said, surprised . . . and more than a little intrigued.

"Well, there's no way I'm letting you go alone," he said.

"I'll be fine alone," Billy said, assuming it was true, and assuming she brought her pepper spray. "I mean, I wouldn't want you to be bored. I know you probably think it's silly that I'm looking into what happened, anyway."

"I don't think it's silly," was all he said. Obviously Seth wanted to come; and of course Billy wanted him to come, so further pretense seemed silly. And tonight was a great night to do some investigating, because her parents were watching Pike, which they often did because they liked hanging out with him. Still, she couldn't help wondering why Seth was doing this. A few days ago he hadn't seemed too convinced that Ted's death was murder. Was it possible that he just wanted to spend time with her?

Images of their hot, frantic kiss rushed through Billy's mind, as arousing sensations rippled through her lower body. Softly, she sighed. He still turned her on.

"So should I pick you up here, or do you want to meet at my house?" Seth asked.

"Pick me up," she told him, because she remembered the last time they'd been alone at his house.

The Rusty Canoe lived up to its name in terms of oxidation. It was a dusty little bar, big on fishnetting, dim lighting, and the potent smell of dubiously "fresh" catch.

As Seth and Billy made their way in, Seth took Billy's hand. She didn't know if it was a romantic kind of gesture, or just a familiar one—or maybe he sensed her apprehension—nevertheless, she held it tight. "Let's grab a table," he said, and led the way to a booth in the far left corner.

Before Billy slid in, she realized she had to pee, so she excused herself in search of the ladies' room. Off toward the back were two adjacent doors labeled *Mensch* and *Wench*. So, in addition to its other repellents, the Rusty Canoe was overtly chauvinistic.

After using the facilities, Billy noticed the dim, cracked mirrors and the graffiti on the walls. Right in front of her someone had scribbled, *I'm a nasty freak*—which was followed by the rebuttal: *So's your mother.* A sudden protective urge came over her, as she thought of her aunt dating Ted Schneider and having to spend time in a dank, seedy place like this because she loved him.

Aunt Penelope, Billy thought firmly to herself, *you can do so much better.*

Back at the table, Seth was making some headway with the waitress, who seemed to have taken a liking to him. She looked to be around forty, with deep lines of age marked into her tanned, leathery skin, and wore a name tag that read, *Leah.* "Haven't seen you around," she said, smiling broadly. "And believe me, I'd remember."

"I'm new to the area," Seth remarked casually. "Just wanted to check out the local scene."

"And you came *here*?"

"Yeah, well, this place has a lot of . . . personality," he said, looking around. Leah snorted a laugh, and Seth continued, "I wonder if you could tell me about a man who used to come here—"

"Oh, you're gay," she said, obviously disappointed. "I should've known."

"No, no," he said with a soft chuckle, "I'm not gay." Please, it was all he could do to tame his fierce attraction to Billy—not to mention his dick, which had gone from semihard to aching in the last twenty minutes. But how the hell could he look at her—hear her voice—and not recall what had happened the other day on his kitchen table? How could he block out echoes of Billy's sexy, throaty moans, and the feel of her hard nipples against his palms? She'd told him to forget about it, but she was asking the impossible.

"You're not gay?" Leah said, perceptibly cheered. "Then why are you looking for a guy?"

"He's an old friend of the family's, but he lost touch a few years ago," Seth lied. "I wanted to find out what happened to him. From what I understand, he used to come here."

"What does he look like?" she asked. After Seth described Ted, Leah nodded with recognition.

"Hey," Billy said, sliding into the booth.

"Hi," Seth said, smiling at her, then turned back to Leah . . . whose face dropped, suddenly losing its flirty expression.

"So what are ya having?" she asked brusquely, and flipped her pad open. Seth could only assume her demeanor had changed because she mistook Billy for his wife or girlfriend.

"I'll have a Sam Adams," he said, then looked to Billy.

"Nothing for me," she said. It was hard to trust the cleanliness of the glassware in a place like this.

After the waitress left, Seth turned to Billy and dropped his voice. "Listen, how do you feel about sitting at the bar for a few minutes?"

She didn't have to look over at the bar to know how she felt—like a piece of chum swirling among a few inebriated sharks. In other words, clobbered, smothered, not exactly thrilled. "Why?" she asked, confused. "I thought we were gonna ask the waitress about Ted Schneider first, and then work our way through the crowd." At least, that had been the plan they'd discussed on the ride over here. Although Billy still didn't know why Seth was so intent on helping her with her investigation. She hadn't told him her theory about the vandalism and threatening phone call, because she hadn't wanted him to worry. Besides, she couldn't prove there was a link between that and the Ted Schneider case.

"I know, but I get the feeling that Leah will be more talkative if it's just me."

Billy scrunched up her face, not getting it, and then—abruptly—she got it. "Ohhh, I see. It's 'Leah' now, huh? She *likes* you."

Grinning, Seth shrugged. "It's been known to happen from time to time."

"Okay, fine," Billy said with a smirk, and slid out of the booth. "But promise me you'll give me the signal as soon as I can come back."

"Of course I will."

"And drink your beer out of the bottle," she added.

"I promise."

With that, Billy headed to the bar, which was a horseshoe-shaped strip densely populated with dirty old men. At least that was how they looked; maybe they were all pillars of the community. (The dirty-old-men community, that is.)

She ducked her way through the crowd, hopped up onto an available stool right in front of the tap, and tried not to touch the bar, which had something sticky on its surface.

"What can I get ya?" the bartender asked, pointing at her. He was a thick, stout man with a bushy mustache and a short manner; Billy knew she had to order something to stay in his good graces.

"Hi, I'll have a Diet Coke," she said, forcing a bright smile in the hopes it would help her blend in. Hey, while Seth was working the waitress for information, Billy might as well work the barkeep. "So . . . been working here long?" she asked casually.

"Yup."

"Oh, that's interesting."

No response.

"I guess a place like this attracts a lot of regulars," she fished.

"A place like what?" he asked, setting her Diet Coke onto the bar, and spilling some as he pushed it toward her. (Well, at least the carbonation might help dissolve the mystery ooze at her place.)

"Um, you know . . . just a real down-home kind of rustic establishment." He looked at her as if she were nuts. "A nice, quaint little . . . joint?"

He turned to another customer. "Hey, Coop, another beer?"

Hmm . . . she hadn't even gotten close to a conversation, much less asking him about Ted Schneider; maybe she was pussyfooting around too much. Maybe she needed a much more direct investigative approach. "Excuse me," she called, lifting her butt off the stool so the bartender would notice her over the tap. "Excuse me!" she called again, motioning to him with her finger.

"Yeah, lady, what?" he said impatiently, while he dunked some used glasses in a tub of grayish water, shook them out, and then put them on a drying rack. *Ewww.*

"I was just wondering . . ." she began, trying to position herself casually along the bar without actually touching anything. "Did you happen to know a man named Ted Schneider? He used to come in here sometimes. A big guy, tall, gray beard."

He nodded. "What about him?"

"Was he a regular?"

"Regular enough."

"Did he usually come in alone, or—"

"Hey, lady, what do I look like, friggin' Chuck Woolery? I'm not running a dating service here." He said that last part a little loudly for her taste, then headed to the other side of the bar, calling out, "Turk, another brewsky?"

Meanwhile, Billy swallowed tremulously as she noticed several of the Rusty Canoe's barflies staring at her.

"So you're looking for a date, huh?"

Startled, she turned and found a tall bald man right next to her. He wore trousers with long underwear and suspenders, and his smushed, sour face screamed, *Elongated troll.* Somehow he'd slithered up so close he was practically breathing on the top of her head. "No, no," Billy said, edging toward her left. (That side wasn't much better: a bucktoothed man with rabid freckles and a disconcerting resemblance to the kid from *Problem Child*.) "Just trying to find someone," she said. Wait, that didn't come out right.

"Well, look no further," the tall one said, smiling and revealing a few less teeth than was ADA-recommended. "Your ship's come in."

A burst of laughter erupted at the bar, and someone let out a wolf whistle.

Almost grimacing, Billy said, "No, I meant I'm looking for some information. Did you by chance know a man named Ted Schneider?"

"Hold on there—I don't give any information till I get a slow dance."

What! Okay, that was *so* not happening. "I don't dance," Billy lied. "But thanks. So about Ted Schneider—"

"C'mon, *one* dance. One dance won't kill ya. I'm Willy, by the way," he said, and held out his hand to shake hers. Billy and Willy? It would almost be too precious if he didn't look like the crypt keeper on growth hormone.

"No, really," Billy insisted, "I . . . I sprained my ankle the other day, and it's still recuperating. But thanks. Now about this man—"

"Like I said, I don't bite the line unless you bait the hook."

More chortles and whistles. Okay, that was it. She'd tried. For-*get* it. She had no reason to think the troll even knew anything. "I said no," she reiterated for the last time, and turned around on her stool. She stretched up and looked over at Seth's table for the go signal. But Seth wasn't looking her way; he was talking to the waitress. Billy hoped at least *he* was getting somewhere . . . and she hoped he'd get there fast.

"Where's your date?" Leah asked, after setting down Seth's beer.

"My date? Oh, you mean my sister. She's over at the bar."

"So you were asking about some guy before?" Seth gave a description of Ted, and Leah recognized it right away.

"Did you know him well?"

Leah shook her head. "No, but he seemed like a nice enough guy. Never really hassled me. Well, except when he drank too much. Anyway, I never knew his name till I saw his picture in the paper—wait, you know he's dead, right?"

Seth tried to act surprised to see what more he could learn. "No, actually I didn't. How did he die?"

"Some kind of allergic reaction," she said with a shrug. "I read about it in the *Gazette* after it happened. It wasn't too detailed, just a little bit piece about him."

"Ah, I see. What was that you said about Ted drinking too much?" Seth asked, because he suddenly remembered that Ted had been intoxicated at the jubilee. Or at least he'd seemed that way.

Leah nodded. "Yeah, that was the only thing. He was pretty decent, but sometimes when he drank, he didn't seem to know when to stop. And he didn't always hold his liquor too well."

"What do you mean?" Seth asked curiously.

"When Ted got drunk, he got—"

"Mean?"

"Stupid," she finished. "No, stupid's not the right word. Forgetful. Like he'd order the same thing twice, wouldn't remember he already ordered, or he'd ask me about the specials a million times."

"I see . . ." Seth said, nodding pensively. What Leah was telling him only seemed to confirm the possibility that Ted, in his drunkenness, had simply gotten confused at the Dessert Jubilee, and accidentally eaten something he shouldn't. Still, Billy was convinced Ted's death was no accident, and Billy had always been bright and intuitive. Seth was skeptical, of course, but he had to admit there was a possibility that she was right. "Did he ever mention how he liked Churchill? Why he moved here? Or where he was from?" Seth said.

"No, he pretty much kept to himself," Leah replied. "But he hated rich people; I know that. I overheard him going off about it a couple of times. About how the rich thought they could buy everyone. That's why I could never understand why he liked that woman he always came in with."

"What woman?" Seth asked, his gaze sharpening.

"His girlfriend, I guess," Leah said.

Interesting. In all of Sally's gossipy rants about Ted Schneider, she'd never mentioned his having a girlfriend. Maybe the woman was from out of town. And more important, maybe she knew something about Ted's death. At least it was a place to start. "I don't suppose you know his girlfriend's name?" Seth asked. "Or where I could find her?"

Leah scratched her head with the eraser of her pencil. "Jeez, I don't have a clue. She was old, kind of the prissy type, looked like she came from money." Tilting her head, Leah smirked. "Boy, you sure are interested in some guy you don't even know," she said. "Let's talk about something else, like *me*."

This definitely seemed like a good time to give Billy the signal. When he glanced over at the bar, he saw her perched on her stool, looking around aimlessly. Her big eyes seemed to take in everything, but never linger too long in any one place. And damn . . . she was pretty.

As soon as Billy made eye contact with Seth, she couldn't hop off her stool fast enough. She scurried back to the table and slid into the booth just as the bartender called out, "Hey, Leah, we're not running a welcome wagon here!"

Rolling her eyes, Leah turned to go, but Seth stopped her. "Wait, can we have some fried calamari and steamed oysters over here?" After Leah left, Seth grinned boyishly at Billy and said, "I realized I was kind of hungry."

"Oysters?" she said, grinning back. "Just don't get any ideas."

His face darkened then. Now he was a man, not a boy, undoubtedly remembering that incredibly sexy encounter on his kitchen table, and Billy's cheeks flamed as she recalled it, too. Then she sucked in a sharp breath and reined her sanity back in.

"So how did it go? Did you learn anything about Ted?" she asked. Seth told her what Leah had said about Ted Schneider having a girlfriend, and Billy mulled it over. Then she tapped the tabletop as though she had a revelation. "Ow!"

"What happened?" Seth said, instantly concerned.

"Oh, nothing, I think I just got a splinter," she said, studying her finger, then shook off the thought. "Anyway—you know what we need to do?"

"What?" Seth asked, hoping that if she wasn't going to say, *Fool around,* she'd at least say, *Eat.* But he had the distinct feeling she was about to cook up another errand for them to run, and before his meal came.

In the meantime he used her splinter as an excuse to touch her. Taking her hand in his, he examined her finger, then rubbed it gently and said, "No splinter."

"Thanks," she said, smiling. She tried to pull her hand back, and Seth reluctantly let go.

"You said, 'You know what we need to do,' " he reminded her.

"Oh, right," Billy said, remembering now. "Break into Ted Schneider's boat."

"*What?*" He almost choked on his beer, and as he set it back down he let out a laugh. "I know you're joking. . . ." Yet the intense look in her pale blue eyes said that she was quite serious. "No, Billy. No, that's not a good idea."

"Why not?" she pleaded, sounding a little like a kid pleading with a babysitter to let her get away with something. "Come on, it's key, don't you see? If we want to find out who his girlfriend was, we need to find out more about who *he* was. Starting with looking around his boat. I don't know why I didn't see it sooner. That's where I've been going wrong here."

"Oh, is *that* where?"

"Seriously, Seth . . . please?" she said, smiling extra sweetly. She knew she could do it alone, but she didn't want to. Seth was her partner now, and anyway, it was creepy down by the water at night.

He shook his head again. "No way, that's a terrible idea. We don't even know what we're looking for—we don't even know *how* to break into his boat. Oh, and on a side note, it's against the law."

"We won't get caught," Billy protested, hoping that was true.

"Anyway, what are we gonna find that'll point to Ted's killer? I mean, I know Deputy Trellis is kind of a dumb shit, but he must've at least checked out the boat."

"Yeah, but it was just mindless procedure to close the case—he didn't even know what to look for."

"And we do?"

"At least we have a lead. We know Ted was dating someone. Please, Seth? I'm not talking about damaging property or anything. But maybe . . . I don't know, if the boat is really this dilapidated old wreck, I'm thinking maybe it won't be that hard to get onto. It might not even be locked." She touched his shoulder, and despite the tingling electricity that traveled up her arm, she didn't let go, but squeezed him gently. "Please?"

Seth looked intently back at her, and finally released a sigh. Billy was looking at him with those beautiful blue eyes, searching his face, and there was a crackle there—an excitement—he could tell she liked this investigating . . . even though, when it came to the two of them, it was like the blind leading the blind.

But it wasn't like he had anything better to do.

Okay, that wasn't it. Really, he liked spending time with Billy . . . and he hoped she liked spending time with him, too. "Come on," she coaxed, tugging on his sleeve; his eyes dropped to where her hand clutched his shirt, and her palm slid off.

His eyes shot back up, meeting her expectant gaze. He wished she'd touch him again, and with more than her hand. "Okay," he finally said. "But no damaging property."

"Agreed."

"And if anyone comes, you run. I don't want you getting in trouble."

With wonder touching her smile, Billy said, "But what about you? If someone comes, I'm not gonna run off and forget about you."

"Don't worry about me. I have a way with the people in this town." She giggled, and Seth shook his head with exasperation. "Come on, let's go," he said, leaving a twenty on the table and sliding out of the booth. "Could you cancel that order?" he called to Leah on their way out the door.

As they left the Rusty Canoe behind, Seth felt an odd sense of ease, despite the crime they were about to commit, and despite how much he still ached to make love to Billy. God, there was just something about her. She was a calming, comforting presence, but an electric jolt of excitement, all at the same time. That was Billy . . . a sweet little spark of fire.

Chapter Eighteen

"I can't believe you talked me into this," Seth whispered as thunder banged and cracked loudly overhead. By the time they'd left the Rusty Canoe, it had gone from drizzling to pouring-down rain, and violent bursts of light blazed through the black sky. "If you get struck by lightning, I'll never forgive myself."

"Don't worry; you're taller," Billy said glibly. "You'll be struck first."

"Yeah, thanks."

Billy grinned at him and scanned the marina to make sure no one was watching them as they broke onto Ted Schneider's boat—the SS *Drifter*. "Don't worry; this'll be fun," she whispered, and snapped on the flashlight they'd taken from Seth's glove compartment. Raindrops pummeled her face and plastered her hair to her head as she looked up at him. Gently Seth reached over to move a clump of wet hair out of her eyes. He kept his hand poised there for a moment before dropping it.

"Fine, since we're here," he said, grinning, "but your idea of fun needs work."

Seth went first, climbing up onto the deck of the boat and then holding out his hand to help Billy up. Just as she put her foot on the floorboards, a sonic boom of thunder hit. With a yelp she squeezed his hand and jumped forward. "Don't be scared," Seth said comfortingly, over wind and rain.

"Okay," Billy said. "I mean—I'm not."

"You know, we can still forget this whole thing and go home. It's pretty damn crazy, anyway. I mean, of all places during a thunderstorm, the ocean? Not smart."

"I know, but if we hurry, we'll be all right," Billy said. "We'll just take a quick look, and get the hell out of here, okay? I promise." Normally, fear of electrocution would be enough to keep her away, but she was too curious to turn back now. Not to mention that she had a vested personal interest in seeing this through.

Using the flashlight, they found the door that led to the main cabin, but it was sealed with a heavy padlock. "Locked," Seth said, turning back to Billy. Accidentally she shone the flashlight in his face, and he held his hand up to block the light. "Hey, put that down."

"Oh, sorry! Hmm. Well, let's break one of those windows," she suggested, motioning to the three glass portholes along the side of the cabin.

Tilting his head, he said, "We agreed—no damaging property."

"Oh, right . . . well, what about the lock? Can you break that?" Before Seth could be a goody-goody about that one, too, she said, "Come on, a rusty old lock doesn't constitute 'property.' "

"Okay, let me just find something," he said, taking the flashlight from her and shining it around until he found a thick iron shard lying on the deck. He bent to pick it up, then returned the flashlight to Billy, who was just taking it all in as rain beat her back and thunder shook her nerves. "Get back," he called.

Then he banged hard on the lock. Once, twice, three times, and it gave. Old and rusty, just like Ted's favorite bar—perfect. "You did it!" Billy said excitedly as Seth pulled the remnants of the shattered lock off of the latch and led the way into the cabin.

The interior of Ted's boat was the calm *during* the storm. Rattling thunder seemed far less ominous, and flashes of lightning were less daunting through small porthole windows.

"So where should we start?" Seth asked, plowing his fingers through his wet hair.

"I-I'm not sure," Billy replied through chattering teeth. Suddenly she became acutely aware of her sopping-wet blue jeans, which clung to her body, and her drenched, battered jacket that looked dark green instead of light. "I guess we should just look around and see if we can find something that will point us in the direction of Ted's girlfriend. Let's just hope there's something here that gives us a clue who she is." Along the wall was a long, deep shelf that held various supplies. Rope, first-aid kit, pocket knife, and—

"Fabulous!" Billy snatched a flashlight off the shelf. She flipped it on and flooded the space between she and Seth with even more light. "Here," she said, handing Ted's flashlight to Seth. "We can split up."

"Okay," he said, "but be careful."

As Seth looked around the main room, Billy ducked down another step to the blackened bedroom quarters. It was a bit claustrophobic, with a double bed that barely fit, and not much space to walk around. The mattress was thin, the sheets were rumpled, and the room smelled like a cross between halibut and mildew—or maybe halibut *with* mildew—but she was hardly an expert on fishy stenches.

Ted's girlfriend—whoever she was—had been a good sport to go along with these accommodations.

Rain thumped rhythmically on the metallic roof of the boat, and thunder rumbled through the sky. "Have you found anything?" Billy called out as she reached over to the shelf beside Ted's bed and picked up a small leather-covered box. Then she sat down on the bed, hearing the springs squeak and snap.

"Just some fishing gear," Seth called back, "some hooch . . . a hunting magazine . . ."

"Oh, God!" Billy yelped, and tossed the box onto the bed the moment she realized its contents. A shudder ran through her, and Seth called out to her.

"Are you all right? What did you find?" he asked, coming to her.

"Hold me!" Billy said in a tinny little voice, coiling her arms around his waist and pressing her cheek into the wetness of his chest.

"What happened, sweetheart?" he asked gently.

"Toenails," she mumbled.

"Huh?"

Inhaling a sharp breath, Billy said, "Apparently Ted kept his clipped toenails in a box by his bed. And I *touched* them!"

Seth laughed. "Oh, man, you really had me worried for a second." He tightened his arms around her, and Billy couldn't resist snuggling into him for a few moments. "Hey, what's that?" he said suddenly, pulling out of her embrace and walking past her, toward the bed.

Billy turned and saw that the flashlight she'd carelessly tossed on the bed was casting light directly on a book. Seth reached over to pick it up and read the title aloud: *"Puss in Boots."*

His eyebrows quirked in silent question, and Billy shrugged. She leaned down to grab the flashlight, then held it over the book as Seth flipped it open. There was a yellow Post-it note stuck to the first page, with feminine handwriting scrawled across it. *Meet me at TRC at nine-thirty,* Billy read, thinking that TRC obviously stood for the Rusty Canoe. Then it clicked. "His girlfriend—oh, of course!"

Suddenly a loud crack of thunder, like an oak tree splitting down the middle, shattered the air and shook the boat. Billy jumped, and Seth plowed his hands through his air. "Jesus."

"Oh, my God, we've gotta go," she said hurriedly, retracing their steps to the deck. "We've gotta get out of here before lightning strikes the boat!"

Grinning in spite of the storm, Seth followed her and murmured, *"Now* she says that."

* * *

Once they got inside Seth's house, fat drops of rain were sluicing down off their bodies and from their hair. Billy couldn't bear to ruin the beautiful hardwood floors, so she stayed frozen in place—literally—shivering her butt off. A blast of thunder sounded then, only a reminder that the storm was still in full effect, and that she had a hellish commute back to Brookline waiting for her. The next train didn't leave for another forty-five minutes, though, so there was really no hurry.

"Okay, first things first," Seth said, absently ruffling some of his wet hair. His jaw was a little bit scruffy, and his cheeks were ruddy from the rain, which brought out the green in his hazel eyes. "We need to warm you up."

Billy tried to say, "And to warm you up too," but her teeth were chattering.

"I'll get you a towel and some dry clothes," Seth said. "You can change in the bathroom right there." He pointed down the entry hall, and Billy managed a jerky nod. Tilting his head, he studied her, as though he wished he could do more. "Sweetheart, your lips are kind of purple. Oh, Jesus," he said, leaning over to hug her, and then he must've remembered that they weren't boyfriend and girlfriend anymore, because he quickly pulled back. "Uh, let me get that stuff for you."

As Billy trotted across the foyer she felt guilty about the puddles left in her wake. Once inside the bathroom she stripped naked, and felt much warmer without her clothes on. Her nakedness made her feel a little vulnerable as she waited for Seth. Finally she heard a knock on the door.

"Okay," she said, and cracked the door enough to reach through and grab the clothes he was offering. "Thanks!"

"Sure," he replied through the door. "Listen, I'm gonna have a drink to warm me up. Do you want something?"

"Yeah, that sounds great. Whatever you're having is fine."

She heard Seth disappear down the hall, and then looked back at her reflection in the mirror. God, she was really standing there in Seth's house, buck-naked, and it had been a crazy night, but now that it was settling down, an amorous, exciting sensation seeped into her body and filled her bones. Hot wetness pooled between her legs, and a heavy kind of fullness stimulated her breasts.

Speaking of her breasts . . . Almost unthinkingly Billy ran her palms over the naked tips, and felt them ripen against her hands to aching hardness. She slid her eyes closed for barely a second, just fantasizing about Seth touching her there . . . and everywhere . . . of Seth bursting into the bathroom, pushing her up against the sink, and having sex with her right there.

Abruptly, then, she snapped herself out of this train of thought. *Enough fantasizing—it's not getting you anywhere.*

And she had to stop thinking about the fact that he'd called her "sweetheart" a few moments ago, and the gentle rasp of his voice when he'd said it.

She finished drying off, and slipped into the clothes Seth had given her. They were soft sweatpants, fresh wool socks, an old T-shirt, and a heavy sweatshirt. And they all smelled like him. Not even attempting to fix her hair, which was a straggle-plastered, dark-cherry mess, Billy left the bathroom and found Seth in the family room.

He'd changed into blue jeans and a sweatshirt, and had started a fire in the fireplace. "Your wine's on the table," he said as Billy came in. He was bent down, moving logs around with the poker, and Billy found her gaze zeroing in on his butt. (Well, she did have *eyes*, after all.)

She bit her lip, staring at his perfectly hard, rounded ass and the muscular line of his legs beneath his pants. Now, this was a time when a wolf whistle was actually called for.

"Thanks," Billy said, taking her wine and sinking down onto the cushy, warm sofa. When the fire got going, Seth moved the screen back in place, picked up his wineglass, and moved closer to her.

"It's so perfect here," Billy blurted, relaxing into the upholstery, feeling instantly soothed by the Shiraz.

"Yeah, it is," Seth replied almost absently, sliding his gaze to hers for a brief but intense moment. God, this setting was totally romantic and seductive. . . . What a waste, considering that Billy had promised herself she wouldn't get involved with Seth again.

"So how's your family?" she asked, anxious to cut some of the tension.

"Scattered," he replied. "My brother lives in Alaska, my mom lives in Dublin, I live in Seattle, and our house is in Massachusetts. Something's wrong with this picture."

Smiling gently, Billy thought how lucky she was to have her family so close, even though her mother's idea of conversation involved driving her daughters to the brink of madness in regular fifteen-minute intervals. Sighing, she thought about her family and felt a flush of happiness and gratitude fill her chest, which was warm from the wine already.

"I guess you miss them a lot," Billy said. She'd never met Seth's older brother, Ian, or his father, who'd died years ago, but his mother had always been sweet. "How often do you talk to your mom?" she asked, sipping more of her wine and feeling the effects of the smooth, heavy Shiraz now as it slid thickly down her throat, swimming through her like a wave of heat and going to her head . . . among other places.

Seth explained that he'd spoken to his mother just the day before, when she'd called to see how the house was coming.

"It looks beautiful," Billy remarked. "When are you putting it on the market?"

"I don't know," he said briefly, but there was a slight edge to his voice. It made Billy wonder if he was having second thoughts about selling the house. Maybe he'd keep it for himself, leave Seattle, and come back to live in Massachusetts forever.

Jesus, she had to slow down on the wine.

"Hey, do you still like to go Rollerblading in Boston Common?" Seth asked, diverting the subject away from his plans, and back to Billy. He sat down next to her on the sofa.

She grinned at the memory of Rollerblading with Seth. Those had been some of their most romantic dates, even though Seth's Rollerblading skills were excellent, and Billy's were, well, spontaneously adopted. In fact, on their third date, when Seth had asked her if she liked outdoor activities, the word "yes" had flown out of her mouth before she'd had a chance to think. Sort of a lie, but she figured it was a harmless one. It'd always reminded her of that Lemonheads song: "I lied about being the outdoor type. I never owned a sleeping bag, let alone a mountain bike."

Anyway, it hadn't taken long for Seth to see through her pretense. He'd been careful with her, encouraging her to hold on to him—to wrap her arms around his waist from behind and grip him as he careened down Boston Common—and she used to squeeze her eyes shut, but would keep opening them because it was all so fast and wonderful, watching life spin around her. Of course, Rollerblading had never been that exciting without Seth there, too.

"I haven't done it in a while," Billy said now. "The last time I was holding on to Pike's leash, thinking we could both get our exercise at the same time. . . ."

Seth winced, as though he knew what was coming, and Billy

pushed up her pant leg to reveal an ugly, blockish scar just below her knee.

"Oh . . ." he said, brushing the skin gently with his thumb. "That must've killed."

"Yeah," she said, her breath catching at the sensation of Seth's touch. His fingers were warm and tender when he touched her scar, and he just let his hand linger there, until his eyes darted up and locked with hers.

Billy tried to swallow away the rise of tension as Seth's gaze burned through her and the heat from his hand seeped into her skin and slinked up her leg.

A log dropped loudly in the fireplace, startling them both out of the moment. Seth withdrew his hand, exhaled a breath, and went over to tend to the fire, while Billy sat back against the couch cushions, trying to regain her self-control.

But it was hard. . . .

Her blood was boiling—a combination of animal lust and strong wine—and she didn't know how long she could resist throwing herself at Seth tonight. She pulled her legs up until her feet were planted on the sofa cushion, and pressed her cheek against her knees. Acute arousal stirred in her lower body, making her clamp her thighs together to ease the tension, but it wasn't working. Even though Mark had pretty much called a halt to their relationship, Billy still didn't want to fall into bed with Seth. Well, she *wanted* to—madly, desperately, hungrily—but she couldn't let herself. There were just too many emotions tied into sex—*especially* sex with Seth. The smartest thing to do would be to leave and head to the train station right now.

But she stayed on the sofa, inexorably frozen in this warm, insulating moment, as Seth set the poker back against the bricks and the screen back in place. He returned to the sofa, but allowed a bit more space between them this time. With one arm draped along the edge of the couch, he said, "By the way, are you gonna tell me what you were thinking on the boat?"

Huh? What boat? And who could think straight with Seth sitting so close, emanating a potent sexual energy and looking so goddamn yummy?

"Oh, right," Billy said, and pushed some still-wet clumps of hair behind her ears. "Did you notice that Ted's copy of *Puss In Boots* was from the Churchill Public Library?"

"No, was it?"

"Yeah, there was a stamp imprint in the back of the book that said, 'Property of CPL.' "

"Oh."

"So that's it."

"What's it?"

"Ted's girlfriend works at the Churchill Public Library."

Seth paused, cinching his eyebrows quizzically. "How do you figure that?"

"It just makes sense," Billy said. "Obviously Ted's relationship with this woman was a secret, because no one in town has a clue about it. The Post-it note asking him to meet was probably just stuck in some random book and passed off to him at the library. Also, the waitress at the Rusty Canoe said that Ted's girlfriend seemed prissy. That fits the librarian theory to a tee."

"Nice," he said, grinning, then sat farther forward. "Okay, I might be buying this. Especially since the library closes at nine, and the note said to meet at nine-thirty—"

"And it takes half an hour to get from the Churchill Public Library to the Rusty Canoe?"

"Yeah, about that."

Smiling, Billy said, "Oh, my God, we're actually getting somewhere!" Laughing softly, Seth agreed it was a possibility, and Billy asked, "So what now?"

"Hmm . . . I could find out from Sally who's working at the library these days—see if anyone fits the description: prissy and wealthy."

Billy giggled then, a little giddy with the wine, and said, "Seriously, though, if this woman was intimately involved with Ted, she might be able to tell us something about his past. She might even have an idea who killed him, but doesn't want to come forward, because she'd have to publicly admit the affair."

"True. You know what? I wanna call Joe—see what he thinks about all this."

"Okay—oh! I forgot to tell you about Joe." She filled him in on Corryn's run-ins with Joe on the subway and Newbury Street (leaving out the specifics of their misunderstanding, since Corryn probably wouldn't appreciate her nipple being small talk).

Seth laughed. "God, that was *Corryn*?" Then he leaned over to grab the phone off the end table and dialed. "Hey, what's up?" he said into the receiver. "Listen, I need you to check something out for me. . . ."

After he told Joe about what happened at the jubilee—minus Billy's personal reason for looking into it—he asked him to find out whatever he could about Schneider's past. "Maybe he has a record or something—just anything. Call it morbid curiosity. . . . Yes, I know you have a life, you schmuck. Just do it, and call me if you know something, okay? . . . Yeah, okay."

"Oh, and tell him to be nice to my sister," Billy said, smiling, leaning over Seth's shoulder to speak into the phone.

"By the way, Joe, you know that psycho brunette that you couldn't shut up about?" Seth said, grinning. "That's Billy's sister."

After Seth hung up the phone he picked up his wine, and Billy realized she was still perched up on her knees, leaning over him, their faces only inches apart. When he turned to look at her, her eyes zeroed in on his mouth. Parted and wet . . . sexy and delicious.

Tempting the hell out of her. Like a tongue snaking up her inner thigh and hovering between her legs.

Words died in her throat as his gaze dropped down to her lips, and without warning he slid his hand up under her hair, cupped her nape, and pulled her down to kiss him.

Once their lips touched, Billy felt an immediate spark of pleasure. Moaning softly, she curled her fingers into the fabric of Seth's sweatshirt, tugging and pulling as he opened his soft, hot mouth and flicked the tip of his tongue against hers.

Then, abruptly, she pulled away, because she was losing herself—again. "I-I think we'd better stop," she whispered. "I mean, I think I'd better go."

"I'm sorry," Seth said. He sat back and ran his hand down his face in frustration. "Christ, it's so hard to be near you again and not touch you."

For some reason that admission really turned her on. Weakened her defenses, which were laughable, at best. As she climbed off the couch, Seth rose to stop her. "Wait, why don't you just stay here tonight?"

No—that would be trouble and beyond. Seth was looking around the beach house casually enough, but there was an intensity burning in his eyes, and his voice was thick and almost raspy, as if crackling from the tension that still stretched between them.

"No," she said, shaking her head emphatically because she was also trying to convince herself.

"Why not? Do you have to be at the bakery early tomorrow morning?"

"Eleven," she said.

"So stay."

"But . . . where am I supposed to sleep?"

"My bedroom," he said, motioning to the stairs with his head. She gulped hard, fear and excitement coursing through her body at the idea of sharing Seth's room—his bed, his *body*. Her crotch began to sweat.

"I'll sleep in my brother's old room."

Oh.

Well, it didn't make sense for Seth to give up his room, since Billy was the guest, though there was something acutely tempting about sleeping in Seth's bed, tangling in his sheets, inhaling his scent on the pillows, even if he wasn't there. "No," Billy said again. "I mean, thanks for the offer, but this is silly. I'll just go home."

Seth paused, then nodded. "Okay, if you're sure. I'll drive you home."

"All the way to Brookline? You don't have to do that."

"I want to."

"No."

"Why?" he asked with a hint of exasperation.

"Because"—*I don't want to go. I really, really don't want to*—"you've been drinking."

He barked a laugh. "One glass of wine? Believe me, I'm fine. I'm Irish, remember?"

Rolling her eyes, she laughed nervously. "You're a savage."

Seth grinned. "Seriously, I'm fine to drive, but if you don't feel comfortable . . ." His voice trailed off for a second, and he set his wineglass down on the coffee table. "Come on, Billy, just stay here. It's pouring out, and you'll have to change trains at Back Bay, anyway."

True—then walk three blocks from the T stop. It was stupid. She knew he was fine to drive; she just didn't want to leave. And right or wrong, she just couldn't get her feet to move. "Okay, so which way to my room?"

* * *

Two hours later, complete restlessness and sexual frustration had kicked in, turning Billy into a sweaty, sleepless ball of raw animal lust. Her mother would be so proud.

The thunder and lightning had finally stopped. Now wind rattled the shutters, and rain rapped rhythmically on the windows. Billy lay staring up at the ceiling, aching for Seth to burst into the room, rip the comforter off her, and climb on top of her—aching to feel him touch her and slide inside her. Well, just plain *aching*. She was past the point of debating whether these thoughts were right or wrong—they were what they were: constant.

Sitting up, she looked across the room and out the bay window that was across from Seth's bed. All she could see were glittering streaks of rain that flickered in darkness. It didn't make any sense that four years had gone by, that Seth had been a memory—not quite a distant one, but still a memory—and now it felt like no time had passed. It felt like they were building up to something, like it had been then, except the sexual attraction now seemed even more palpable and harder to ignore.

Finally Billy flopped onto her back with a sigh. This wasn't working. She sat up, pushed Seth's thick comforter off her body, and headed downstairs. Giving up on sleep, she decided to sit in the family room for a while, maybe finish the wine she'd left there.

Billy huddled by the fireplace, fighting off a sudden chill. She'd gotten warm in Seth's sweatshirt, so she'd taken it off and left it upstairs. Now she was wearing just his T-shirt and sweatpants. As she looked at the glowing embers, she tried to push thoughts of sex out of her mind. She supposed she was battling more than lust—also fear. The experience she'd had with Ryan had been so paltry, she wondered if she would be able to keep up with Seth between the sheets. Not that she had firsthand experience when it came to Seth's style of making love, but seeing how thoroughly aroused he got from kissing and from touching her breasts, Billy figured he had to be an animal in bed. She shivered at the thought, and suddenly heard, "You okay?"

Her head shot up, and she saw Seth standing there in boxer briefs. He was shirtless, his hair was rumpled, he looked a little scruffy, like he'd just woken up, and in that moment he'd never been more breathtakingly sexy.

Now, scratching his bare muscled chest, he said, "Are you cold? Do you need a blanket or anything?"

"No, I just couldn't sleep," Billy said.

"Me, either."

"What time is it anyway?" she asked, looking back at the fire-place, pretending she was captivated by the remnants of the fire, rather than Seth's half-naked body.

As he walked into the room, she felt a pang of self-consciousness about the T-shirt she'd borrowed. By the tight way it clung to her breasts and belly, she could only assume it dated back to around the seventh grade. She felt a little embarrassed to have her soft stomach and heavy breasts on display.

Then Billy noticed Seth's eyes drop. When she glanced down, she saw that her nipples were erect and protruding . . . and when she glanced up, she found Seth still watching her—staring glazed-eyed at her breasts. His nostrils flared almost imperceptibly, while his chest rose and fell. Billy trembled and bit her lip, looking away to break the spell, and that was when she noticed the bulge in Seth's boxers.

Her breath caught in her throat, her mouth ran dry, and sud-denly, in two steps, Seth was in front of her—dropping down, just as Billy was climbing up—and hazily she thought, *This is going to be amazing,* as Seth pulled her to him.

Chapter Nineteen

Billy tugged on Seth's neck, pulling herself up higher as she crushed her mouth on his. He felt so unbelievably good pressed against her—so warm, so strong, so powerful. God, she never wanted to let go of him.

With their mouths fused, the kiss turned savage and devouring. Groaning, he licked into her mouth and sent shivers rolling through her body—right to the apex of her thighs, where she was already damp and trembling.

"Ohh," Billy moaned from deep in her throat. "Ohh . . ."

She angled her head to take more of him, and felt herself losing her balance. Seth gripped her to him, and with one of his arms around her waist and the other just below her butt, they both sank onto the floor. Then he tore his mouth from hers and ran his tongue down her neck.

Rocking her hips, Billy felt her crotch flame as Seth trailed his tongue back up her neck and took her earlobe between his teeth . . . then sucked it . . . then slid his tongue deep inside her ear. She squirmed and moaned while flames licked up her legs and blood rang in her ears, and she couldn't even think straight when Seth shoved up her tight little T-shirt. "Oh, *God* . . ." she cried out as Seth trailed his tongue up her stomach and over her swollen nipples.

"God, I want you so much," he murmured frantically, and sucked a nipple into his mouth. The sensation jolted her. She plowed her fingers through his soft, blond hair, and gripped his head to hold him in place. When he finally released her nipple, he buried his face between her breasts, pushing them together with his hands. Billy twisted and groaned as her legs fell open. "You wanna go upstairs?"

"No," she said, pulling on his hair to drag him up for another kiss. "No . . ."

He slid his tongue inside her mouth, and they rolled over together so she was on top, nestling his hard cock into her soft crotch . . . then, feverishly, they rolled again, and Billy ended up flat on her back—with her legs spread wide, and Seth's hand digging into her sweatpants.

As his fingers brushed her bare flesh, he grunted. "Jesus Christ, you're not wearing panties."

"They were wet from the rain," she explained brokenly, as Seth growled and rubbed two fingers against her. Back and forth, he sensually glided his fingertips over her opening until they were both panting. "Please . . ." Billy begged breathlessly. "Do it . . . *do* it."

He must've understood, because abruptly he slid both fingers inside her.

She cried out sharply as her back arched off the floor. The intrusion was painful, but in a sexy, thrilling way that made her ache for more.

Seth withdrew his fingers and thrust again . . . and again . . . until finally he shoved Billy's sweats all the way down, and when her bare butt hit the carpet, he thrust again. She met his movements with sharp cries of pleasure, unknowingly coaxing him to go deeper—harder—until she almost couldn't take it. Her body felt weak, trembling, nearly battered, and they hadn't even had sex yet.

With a shove Billy pushed on Seth's shoulders, and he rolled with her until he was on his back. She captured his mouth in a deep, sucking kiss while her hand reached for his penis, squeezing and stroking until the tip was wet. "Ohh . . ." Seth groaned, as Billy ran a finger over his testicles, pressing gently in between. "Oh . . . *Jesus.*"

Boldness overtook her, and she crawled down his body until her lips brushed his cock—and then she started to suck. Sliding his fingers into her hair, Seth made harsh, guttural sounds, and it was all happening so fast, in such a blur of passion, that Billy barely registered the exact taste of him, or the tangible reality of what she was doing.

Finally Seth slipped his hands under Billy's arms, pulled her up, and rolled her again. "I'm gonna burst," he whispered as a tiny flicker of light from the fireplace cut across his face. He was so savage and beautiful when he was aroused. Suddenly he pulled away and came to his feet.

"Where are you going?" Billy asked hazily—but fretfully. *Please don't stop now.*

"Condoms."

Thank goodness. He was back in no time, completely naked except for a condom, and he fell right back into place, tossing a couple extra condoms down on the floor beside them. After he climbed onto Billy's wilted, wanton body, he lifted himself on his hands and stroked her G-spot with the tip of his erection. She arched her back off the floor, and they both moaned. Seth pushed his penis harder against her opening, and Billy squeezed her eyes shut and heard her own choppy breathing. Locking her legs around him, she tried to piston her lower body off the carpet so she feel him.

"Oh, man," he whispered, his voice sounding strained, then gently rocked his pelvis until he was partway inside her, and already she felt a heavy pressure between her legs. "Jesus," he muttered tightly. "You have done this since we broke up, haven't you?"

"Barely . . . *ohh* . . ." She groaned as he moved a little deeper. "Yes . . . *please* . . ."

With a long, low groan, Seth thrust all the way inside her, and

Billy's body shot up, shocked by the fierce penetration . . . but excited, electric . . . inflamed. "Oh, God, oh, God," she said, "Keep going. . . ."

Seth's thrusts picked up rhythm as Billy moaned and twisted on the carpet, and the longer it went, the closer she felt to orgasm. With each hard plunge, his cock drove deep inside her and her back arched. She let out a strangled yelp every time she felt him slide into her, and a tortured moan every time he slid back out—almost all the way, but he was never far, never gone. God, he was there, really doing this to her, this dirty, sexy, raunchy thing, and—*Oh!*

Finally the friction became unbearable, and Billy began to shake. Panting and sweating as her climax racked her body, she cried out in ecstasy.

And Seth pumped faster, his mouth dropping open, his eyes rolling closed, and seconds later he started to come. Billy moaned at the pleasure of her subsiding orgasm, the sound of Seth's low groan, at the feel of his body convulsing and his back muscles contracting.

Afterward it took several moments for her body to stop shaking. Seth gathered her up in his arms, still breathing hard, and rolled them so they were lying side by side on the carpet. Sleepily, his lids dropped closed, and Billy smiled a faint, weak smile. She couldn't help thinking that no matter what the consequences, what had just happened between her and Seth had been better than anything else she'd ever experienced in her life.

For this one perfect moment, there was only her and Seth.

About an hour later, Billy stirred beside him on the carpet, suddenly cold and aware of her own nakedness. "Mmm . . ." Seth murmured, nuzzling his face against her hair as he pulled her closer. She felt limp lying there, but anxious at the same time. Instantly she became aware of sensory details—like the musky, lingering scent of sex, the residual smell of burning wood, the sound of Seth's breathing, the trickle of drizzle across the windowpanes.

"Hi," he whispered, and leaned over to brush a kiss across her cheek. It seemed innocent enough . . . until she felt Seth's open mouth running down the back of her neck. Almost soundlessly she sighed as Seth's hot mouth rekindled her libido.

Smiling, she reached her hand up to cradle the back of Seth's head. Her fingers laced through his feather-soft blond hair, and she savored the reality of Seth's body lying right beside hers. He murmured, turning her head enough to kiss her. It was slow, deep, and wet—he tasted a little tangy from sleeping, but mostly he tasted . . . familiar. Holding his head with her hand, Billy kissed him back, drowning in the sensual movement of his tongue.

"I can't believe that happened," he said thickly when the kiss broke. "I've fantasized about that for so long."

Her eyes widened. "You have?"

"Hell, yeah. You are the sexiest girl I've ever met."

"Please," Billy said, stifling a laugh.

"You are," Seth insisted, and kissed her again.

"I've fantasized too," Billy said. "When we were going out, I used to think about making love with you all the time."

"You did?"

"Constantly."

"But I thought you weren't ready," he said, studying her face.

"Well, I wasn't *yet*, but I was definitely getting there. Then you moved."

She shouldn't have thrown in that last part; she didn't want to reopen that topic. But Seth just let out a strained laugh, shook his head, and buried his face in the crook of her neck. "Jesus, don't tell me that. You're torturing me."

She giggled. "What do you mean?"

"You're telling me that if I hadn't moved we would have been having sex like this for the past four years? Christ, I think that is the most tragic thing I've ever heard."

Of course he was only kidding, but still . . . did he really think the sex was as hot as she did?

Maybe he read her mind then, because he rolled back on top of her and kissed her deeply. Billy wrapped her legs around him until her heels touched his thighs. His erection was hard and probing, but he didn't inch forward. With her eyes half-closed in arousal, she smiled at him.

"Listen, Billy . . . I want to tell you something."

God, she was afraid she knew what was coming—afraid Seth was going to spoil this moment by dousing her with a bucket of ice water called reality. *No, please . . . I just want to have this moment.* "No, don't say anything," Billy said softly, her eyes searching his. "Just kiss me."

"But I just want to explain the situation—"

"I already know the situation: You live in Seattle now, and you're going back in a couple of weeks." He didn't deny it, so she threw in, "And my life is here." Not that it was all that rip-roaring of a life, but it wasn't bad, either. Her family was here, Pike was here, and it wasn't like Seth was going to ask her to move, anyway. If he hadn't done it four years ago, he certainly wasn't going to do it now that they'd been barely hanging out for two weeks. She needed to let him know that he shouldn't worry about apologizing for making love to her when there was no real future there; and more important, she needed to save some face.

"Oh," Seth said after a pause. "Yeah, I mean, you're right. I just . . . well, I'm glad it happened anyway."

"Oh, me too!" Billy said, smiling at him and kissing his mouth, his cheek, his jaw. "It was so unbelievable, so . . . *good,*" she added for lack of a better word, because her mind was still a little dizzy, and then she coiled her arms around his neck and hugged him tighter.

When they were nestled this close, his penis found the target on its own, and Billy let out a soft, strangled moan in . . . frustration? anticipation? "Please . . ." she whispered, as Seth slid inside her, and they both cried out at the pain and the pleasure of such a tight fit. He began to move, thrusting slowly and deeply, again and again—he had to be getting rug burn on his knees—and Billy rolled her head on the carpet, antsy with the need for direct stimulation at the exact speed and pace and that would make her come.

As Seth pumped his hips faster, with his face buried in her neck, Billy used two fingers to rub herself hard until she climaxed; Seth followed her mere seconds later.

An hour later Seth was wide-awake and Billy was fast asleep, curled in a little ball on the carpet like a cute, round angel. Smiling down at her, he draped a blanket over their lower bodies and strummed his fingers lightly down her arm. For the first time in a while, Seth felt a fullness in his chest—it was like something was finally filling up the void inside, the hollowness he'd started getting used to. In Seattle he constantly filled his mind and his world with work, with numbers, with building client networks, and now that he'd left it behind—it was a huge fucking cliché—but a weight had been lifted. He supposed it was counterintuitive to be hollow and weighed down at the same time, but life was full of contradictions—in fact, one of his favorites was lying right beside him.

It made no sense that he hadn't seen Billy in four long years, but that she still seemed to hold the power to make him happy.

But then again . . . she'd been right: His life was in Seattle, and hers was here. Would it really be fair to ask her to pick up and move across the country so they could . . . what? Date? *Please.* He almost laughed at how stupid that sounded. They could always try a long-distance relationship, he supposed, but . . .

Wait, he was getting way ahead of himself here. Jesus, he still didn't know what was going on with that other guy in her life! In fact, that other guy might be the real reason Billy didn't want to talk about the future—maybe she wanted a future with someone else.

It was better if he simply enjoyed this fling with Billy and didn't analyze it. In another week or so his mom's house would be fixed up and on the market, and Seth could return to Seattle. Back to his empty apartment, back to his real life.

Just then Billy stirred in her sleep, and Seth leaned down and kissed her cheek. He smiled as he remembered how flustered she'd been at the Rusty Canoe, looking like she'd rather be shunned than hit on. Or the way she still jumped at thunder and lightning—but not enough to keep her from breaking into Ted Schneider's boat. Now *that* had been fucking crazy. How had she talked him into that one?

Sighing softly, he whispered, "I think I'm falling in love with you again." But he could barely hear himself over the strong gust of wind blowing outside, the tree branches swatting against the house, and the deep, even breathing of this girl he loved.

Chapter Twenty

Billy's eyes snapped open, and it took her a minute to realize where she was and what she'd done. Seth had carried her upstairs to his bedroom in the middle of the night, and now he was lying next to her on his stomach, with one arm buried under his pillow, the other lying loosely across her abdomen.

She crept out of bed while Seth continued to sleep with his face half-buried, his blond hair messy and sticking up in all directions. Once Billy had used the bathroom and the mouthwash, she studied her reflection in the mirror above the sink. Her hair was a messy firestorm of tangles, and her cheeks were glowing pink.

With Ryan sex had been good but not great. It wasn't really his fault; it had just been so new to her then that she hadn't had an overflowing amount of confidence in that area. But with Seth it was so different. She still wasn't very experienced, but when he'd looked at her last night—when that compelling, unstoppable moment had descended upon them—she'd known what to do.

Eyeing the marble tub in the reflection in the mirror, Billy decided to take a quick shower before Seth got up. Then she'd get dressed, run to the train station, and hopefully make it to Bella Donna by eleven.

Her shower lasted longer than she intended, but the beating hot spray felt like a massage, and as she ran her hands over her body, she noticed that everything seemed to possess a new kind of sex appeal.

Her hips, her breasts, even her belly—the beast. Instead of feeling like a bulging little butterball this morning, Billy felt . . . well . . . *sultry.*

Turning off the water, she reached for a towel and stepped out of the tub. "Hello," Seth drawled, leaning against the doorjamb, sexy and rumpled with a hell of a morning erection pushing against his boxer briefs. *Yum.*

"Oh, hi," Billy said, clutching the towel to her body, suddenly feeling shy. Seth didn't seem to notice, though. He crossed the bathroom, pulled her into his arms, and smiled down at her before kissing her deeply . . . passionately.

Mmm . . . He'd visited the mouthwash, too, that morning. Billy moaned softly, lifting up on tiptoe to savor the kiss.

Then a rush of cold air washed over her naked body, and she heard the towel hit the floor. "Hey!" she yelped, feeling apprehensive about being naked in the light of day.

"You don't need it," Seth murmured, kissing her again and walking them back to the wall. Okay, she was over her apprehension now. She reached in between their bodies to grab the elastic waistband of Seth's briefs. He groaned as she started to pull his underwear down, and brought one hand up to help her shove them down to his ankles. Running her tongue down his neck, Billy massaged the head of Seth's erection—squeezing his shaft and rubbing her thumb over the tip—and Seth responded by inserting his hand between her legs, stroking her and sliding inside her. Choppy moans sputtered out of them both as Seth fingered Billy almost roughly, bringing her to the brink of ecstasy.

Then he dropped to his knees, and before she knew it, she was lying on the soft bathroom rug, and Seth was kissing and licking the most intimate part of her. She arched and twisted and moaned, until she finally burst and her muscles rippled with contractions. He held her tightly while she climaxed.

Cuddled on the bathroom floor on the rug, with Seth flat on his back and Billy smiling into his chest, she said teasingly, "Why do I always end up on the floor?"

Seth just laughed. But Billy knew the answer: It was the most fitting place to be when you were getting down and dirty.

"Okay, I gotta go," she said, drinking the glass of orange juice that Seth had poured for her. She'd thrown on her sweater and jeans from the day before, which Seth had washed and dried for her, and now they were warm and cozy on her skin. After she pulled her hair into a ponytail, she shrugged on her battered green coat, which had been through the dryer, too, and somehow made it through alive.

"Wait," Seth said, pausing at the cabinet. "I can make you breakfast if you're hungry."

"No, really, I'm gonna be late. But thank you."

"When will you get out of work tonight?" he asked.

"Seven-thirty or eight," she replied, and scurried over to him, leaning up to kiss his cheek, but he made this even harder by turning his face and giving her a slow, passionate kiss. She kissed him back, trying not to feel sad that this was just a short-term fling.

No, a fling would be too painful; she could *never* handle a fling. More like a one-time-only thing. *That* she thought she might be able to deal with. Something she could tell her grandchildren. Well, not quite, but still . . . making love with Seth was something she'd always wanted to do—always wondered about—and now she'd had the experience. But to continue sleeping with him was just begging for heartache. Which brought her to her next point.

"Seth," she said, pulling back. "About last night . . . well, it was wonderful. Of course, you know that. But I think it's best if it doesn't happen again." His face darkened a little, but he didn't say anything. "It's just that I don't want to make things too complicated."

"What's complicated about it?" Seth asked, an edge to his voice. "The other guy again? What's the deal with you guys anyway?"

"Oh, no—I mean, he and I are kind of on the outs right now. That's not it."

"Then what?"

Hello . . . She didn't want to get hurt again; couldn't he see that? "I just think it's better that way," she said.

The thought saddened him, made him feel frustrated almost to the point of anger. But he tried to play down the wealth of turbulence that went with the depressing prospect of sleeping with Billy only once. Jesus, if he'd known the last time would be the *last* time, he would've prolonged the sex even more. Definitely would've brought a condom into the bathroom with him that morning. As it was, he'd honestly planned only to brush his teeth and give her a kiss good morning. Finally he shrugged, his expression blank. "Okay, if that's what you want."

"Yeah. Um, I think that would be best," Billy repeated firmly, trying to convince herself—her new pastime, apparently. "But you're still gonna come with me to investigate our librarian lead, right?"

"Oh . . . yeah, definitely," Seth replied, because even though he was disappointed and his ego was bruised, he didn't want Billy sleuthing around by herself. Somehow he had the feeling she'd only get into trouble. And the truth was, he liked helping her; the Ted Schneider mystery was a refreshing distraction from the daily grind. "I'll ask Sally today about who works at the Churchill Public Library," he added.

"Okay, great," Billy called over her shoulder on her way to the front door.

"I can drive you," Seth offered.

"No, it will take longer with all the morning commuter traffic," she said, turning to say good-bye, because Seth had followed her to the foyer. Jeez, she wished he'd put some clothes on. He was parading around in just his boxers, and he looked so sexy it was hard to think.

"Oh, don't forget this," he said, picking her cell phone off the table by the stairs. He must've taken it out of her pocket before he'd tossed her coat into the dryer.

The green message light was flashing. Flipping the phone open, Billy pressed the button to hear her voice mail, expecting her mother's prying, or her sister's sarcasm, or even Kip's sugar talk, but instead she heard a voice that was harsh, whispering, and terrifyingly familiar: "I hate you, you bitch! Why won't you just go away?"

"Oh, God," Billy muttered, feeling the color drain from her face. Her chest constricted with fear. Fear of being watched—of being targeted.

"What is it?" Seth asked, coming closer. "Billy, what's wrong?" She hadn't told him about the other weird phone message she'd gotten, or the tomatoes smeared on her window . . . or, come to think of it, that eerie hang-up call she'd gotten last week, or the mysterious rustling she heard in the bushes outside her brownstone the night she'd met Mark at the Kenmore Pub. But wait—surely the last two incidents weren't related to the threats, because they predated Ted Schneider's murder. They had to be coincidental . . . right?

God, she was just so damn confused.

Swallowing hard, Billy passed Seth the phone, and he listened.

"I don't get it," he said, looking pissed as hell. "Who would say something like that to you?"

"Oh, why is this happening again?" Billy moaned, clutching her stomach, which was skittering nervously.

"Wait a minute, what do you mean? Has this happened *before*?"

She filled him in as best she could, but she still had so many unanswered questions. For example: If these threats were somehow connected to Ted's murder, how did anyone even know Billy was looking into the case? She hadn't said anything to her parents or

Aunt Penelope yet. The only people she'd told were Corryn and Seth. Sure, she'd asked Greg Dappaport about his argument with Ted on the beach before the jubilee began, but she'd never shared her suspicions with him that Ted was, in fact, murdered. Besides, Dappaport hadn't seemed too fazed when she'd brought up the argument; he'd explained it away as a simple squabble over where Ted had docked his boat.

"At first I thought it was my neighbor," Billy said now—rambled, really—"but now I don't. I just can't believe she'd keep stalking me over some stupid tomatoes. Then I thought maybe it was someone who knew something about Ted Schneider's murder—like maybe they wanted to scare me off so I'd stop snooping. But I've barely even gotten anywhere with the investigation yet. I don't know; I just don't know—"

"All right, calm down, sweetheart," Seth said soothingly, trying to calm her. "Have you gone to the police yet?"

"Yeah, but they just think of these things as pranks, and at this point they say they can't do anything. I'm scared," she said.

"Don't be," he said, and slid his arm around her shoulders. Protectively he hugged her to him. "I'm not gonna let anything happen to you. I promise."

In that moment Billy believed him. Partly because she wanted to, partly because she needed to, and partly because it was Seth and he had integrity. If he said he'd look out for her, she knew he would, and she was unspeakably grateful. Now the question was: What and who were they even looking out *for*?

No matter how much she analyzed each piece of her recent situation, she couldn't seem to fit it all into one cohesive puzzle.

Seth said, "Okay, now I'm driving you to the city, and please don't argue. But first I'm calling Joe to see what he thinks about all this."

* * *

Luckily, Joe was a little less worried, telling them how common pranks like that truly were, and how 99 percent of the time they were harmless. But he promised to drive by Billy's apartment regularly to make sure there was no one lurking, and said that if anything else happened, to give him a call. Plus, he said he was still trying to find out whatever he could about Ted Schneider's past, and when he did, he'd be in touch.

Billy had also asked Seth to see what he could find out about Dappaport. She didn't want to believe there could be anything sinister about him—not when he was her quasi-benefactor, commissioning her for her first mural and telling her how much he liked her work. She didn't want to believe he could have any other agenda, and she wanted it so much that she was afraid she was deliberately avoiding the possibility. Obviously, with the threats continuing, she couldn't afford to do that anymore.

Around noon Seth dropped Billy off in front of the Copley Mall, and she thanked him profusely for the ride. Even though traffic had made her late to work, she was grateful not to have ridden the T today. She'd been shaken up, and in no mood to be on a crowded subway, alone in a city of strangers.

"Billy?" Seth said, as she stepped out of his car.

He wanted to tell her he was falling in love with her again, that last night was fucking amazing, that he wished she'd skip work and spend the day with him, that he'd protect her. But words that were futile stayed clogged in his throat.

Finally he said, "Just be careful." She smiled softly at him, and then she was gone.

* * *

Just when life couldn't get any more surprising, Mark showed up at Bella Donna with a bouquet of flowers and his own jovial version of remorse plastered across his face. But before that happened, Katie, Georgette, and Billy were congregated in the front, talking. It was funny, but once Billy got back to the bakery, back to her routine, she didn't feel quite as vulnerable.

"So what ever happened with that guy Louis you met at the Kenmore Pub?" Katie asked Georgette as she hopped up to sit on the counter. Right now there were no customers, and Donna was in her back office writing up next week's schedule.

Georgette scoffed. "Nothin'. I asked if he wanted to go back to my place, and he said no, 'cuz it was gettin' late." It sounded like she was definitely harboring some bitterness about it. Snidely, she added, "Wasn't my type anyway. Too old."

"Wasn't he only, like, thirty-something?" Katie said with a laugh.

"Yeah, but what I need is a young stud who can get it up and get it *done*, if ya know what I'm sayin'."

Georgette seemed to think that if she kept saying it, it would come true. But still . . . for once Billy did know what she was saying. All too well. There was definitely something to be said for great sex. Hot, relentless sex you could still feel the next day. Flushing, she recalled last night—the way she and Seth had fallen so passionately into bed—but first, onto the floor. Each time they'd made love, it had been with an intensity that left her limp and weak. And then this morning, in the bathroom . . . heat washed over her as she remembered every detail.

Not that it would ever happen again, but was there really any harm in reenacting the encounter a million times in her head?

Katie said, "By the way, what are you guys doing for Thanksgiving? Because my grandma said anyone's welcome to come to our place for dinner."

"Oh, that's so nice," Billy replied, "but I'm going to my parents' house with my sister." Thanksgiving was still a few weeks away, but that was what they did every year—though she almost shuddered to think what concessions Adrienne would make to accommodate her new health kick.

"What about you, Georgette?"

"Just having dinner with my son," she said flatly. "Then he goes to visit my asshole ex, his asshole wife, and their asshole kids." Sounded like a plan, though somehow Billy had to draw the line at calling the kids assholes.

Up until two weeks ago, she'd toyed with the idea of inviting Mark for the holidays, but obviously now, after he'd told her he needed "space," that wouldn't be happening. She supposed in the recesses of her mind, she was still trying to decipher their last bizarre exchange.

And like fate listening in, Mark came in bearing flowers. Billy barely registered her surprise as he walked into the bakery, smiling hugely and presenting her with a big bouquet of carnations (which, by the way, she truly hated—and not because they were cheap, but because they always reminded her of funerals).

"Hi, there," he said, donning a hopelessly broad grin. Then he tilted his head. "Can we talk?"

Patting Billy's shoulder, Georgette headed to the kitchen, while Katie went to help a customer who'd come in behind Mark.

"Mark," Billy said, walking down the counter so they were away from the register. "Um . . . I'm really surprised to see you here after what happened—I mean after what you said. . . ."

"I know, I'm sorry," he injected quickly, pushing the flowers forward again. Relenting, she took them. "Please, Billy, I want to explain. I'm sorry for that whole phone conversation. I was just taken off guard by your call, and . . . well, I guess I was just at that turning point in a relationship where you question where it's going, if you want to get serious, that kind of thing."

Quietly she took that in and swallowed a lump of awkward discomfort. What could she say? That wasn't as legitimate an excuse as full-on dementia, but it wasn't all that unreasonable, either. They'd barely been dating for seven weeks; it only made sense that there would be a pivotal moment when they decided whether or not to get serious. She herself had had moments at which she'd questioned their future.

Of course, that still didn't excuse his behavior.

And could she simply resume things with Mark when they now had this big secret standing between them? The one about sex with her ex just twelve short hours ago?

"Mark, the truth is . . . well, I really needed to talk to you last week."

"I know, I know, you needed me, and I dropped the ball," he said apologetically. "Billy, I can't tell you how sorry I am for freaking out about us, but all I can do now is step it up, get it in gear, and raise the bar."

Huh? It would be nice if Mark could do sincerity without talking like a motivational speaker. Then again, she supposed he wasn't too accustomed to groveling. After all, he was tall, handsome, charismatic, and insanely popular. He was also successful, interested, and a resident of Massachusetts. The neon sign in her head started flashing again: *Future Potential.*

Future. The word kept echoing through her mind. And she did truly *like* Mark. Did she just want to blow that off?

"Listen, let's talk about this; let's work through it," he urged, taking the bouquet from her and laying it down on the counter so he could clasp her hands to his chest. "Have dinner with me tonight."

"Um . . ."

"Please don't say no. I have a surprise planned for us. I want to show you how important you are to me—how important *we* are to me. What time's your break?"

"Six," she replied, feeling a little like a traitor with Mark's hands on her, when Seth's had been there just a few hours before. Of course, that begged the question of whom, exactly, she was betraying.

"Meet me in Copley Square at six-fifteen," he said. "Please? I promise you'll love it."

"Well . . ." Billy agreed, feeling she owed Mark that much. Or maybe she was doing it for herself, mostly. Out of guilt . . . obligation . . . curiosity?

"Great," Mark said, a big smile sliding across his face, and leaned down to press a moist kiss to her lips, similar to a sponge dabbing a stain. "I'll see you at six-fifteen."

As he left Bella Donna, Billy watched him go, still feeling vaguely taken off guard, and Katie finished with her customer. "Thanks, have a nice day," she said, then turned to Billy. "So are you and Mark still off? Back on? What's the deal?"

Billy sighed. "I wish I knew."

Just then Donna ducked her head through the door to the back. "Billy, I've got a cake order on the phone—can we give them something in a Degas?"

"Um, sure, I can try." She'd told Donna she'd try almost anything—except Dalí. "What's the occasion?"

"Ten-year-old's birthday party."

She had to laugh at that. Still, she felt a spark of excitement for the project, which reminded her that tomorrow she was going to spend all day in Churchill working on her other project—the gallery streetscape. Greg Dappaport's smiling face popped into her mind then, and she remembered that Seth was going to find out more about him. Billy just hoped that nothing suspicious turned up, that nothing in Dappaport's background would point to a connection between him and Ted Schneider. She wanted to believe he was being sincere when he told her he believed in her talent. She wanted to believe he was exactly what he seemed. *Please, please don't let Dappaport be the killer.*

Donna thanked her for taking the latest cake order, and added, "Billy, you're a godsend. What would I do without you around here?"

A sense of pride filled Billy's chest, just as Melissa came into the bakery, setting her bag down with a plunk. "Hey," she said, sounding a little edgy, and filled a large cup with coffee.

Billy and Katie said hi at the same time; Donna had already gone to the back.

"Hey, was that Mark I saw on the escalator just now?" Melissa asked, reaching for an apron on the wall.

"Oh, yeah, he stopped by," Billy said.

"So you guys worked things out?" Melissa asked.

"He brought her a big bouquet of flowers," Katie piped in, motioning toward the carnations lying on the counter.

"But what about Seth?" Melissa asked, sipping her coffee. "You two looked pretty into each other at the jubilee."

Billy's face blushed hotly, which apparently gave her away, because Katie said, "Oh, my God, did you guys hook up?"

"Well . . ."

Melissa's mouth curved into a cynical-looking smile. "Wow, Billy, hooking up with two guys at once—way to go."

Jesus, did she have to make it sound so tawdry? It really wasn't like that. Mark had ended things, and what happened with Seth wasn't just about sex; she was practically falling in love with him— *No, no! It's not love; it's a post-amazing-sex delirium.* (She was pretty sure she'd read about those). *Please don't fall in love with Seth when he's leaving in a couple of weeks. . . .*

"Next week's schedule is posted," Donna called. Everyone flocked to the back to check it. Melissa tapped Billy lightly on the arm and said quietly, "I meant to ask you, how's it going with your neighbor? Have you been kissing ass like I told you?"

"Um . . . I tried to kiss ass, but she wasn't too interested. But don't worry; I really think everything's gonna be okay."

Chapter Twenty-one

"Surprise!"

Mark was standing in the middle of Copley Square, where he'd set down a blanket and a bag from Burger King. Was it just Billy who noticed the ice-cold wind cutting across their faces, or the fact that the ground beneath the blanket was nearly frozen?

"Dinner under the stars," Mark announced, beaming at her, and Billy instantly felt a pang of guilt. It was a sweet gesture, and besides, she wasn't having dinner with Mark for the luxury of it; she was there because they desperately needed to clear the air.

"Thanks," she said, and sat down, crossing her legs and getting her butt used to the cold, unforgiving ground. But it was to no avail, as the chill of the concrete seeped through Billy's jeans, sending shivers up her back.

"And I got you your favorite," he said, reaching inside the bag. "A BK Broiler with some fries for us to split."

She thanked him again, even though cheeseburgers were her favorite, and jeez, couldn't she have her *own* fries?

Ahem . . . Food was hardly the point at the moment. "Listen, Mark, I appreciate your doing all this, but I'm not sure we can just pick things up where we left off—"

"Billy, please just listen," he interrupted, holding up his hands in a gesture of entreaty. "When you called me the other night, you

needed me. You were trying to reach out to me and I blew it." *Valid.*
"I'm sorry I did that. I am so sorry; that's all I can say. I guess I wasn't
sure how I felt about us advancing to that next level, but now I am
sure."

"Mark, there's something you should know—"

"Please let me finish," he went on.

But wait! She had to tell him about Seth; it might change his
mind about getting back together.

Taking her hands in his, he said, "Can we go back to the way we
were? Can we just forget the stupid way I acted, and start seeing
each other again?"

Can we? After she'd been so passionately in the arms of another
man? Could she simply blot out the image of Seth naked and tender and rumpled and gentle? After a long pause, she told Mark that
she needed to think about it.

"Okay, totally understandable," he said, nodding. "Take whatever time you need." Jeez, why was he so open with his feelings
now? So freaking approachable and devoted to their relationship?
What was up with men and their bad timing, anyway? "Let's eat!"
he said, as he enthusiastically lifted his fat, juicy double Whopper to
his mouth.

When Billy picked up her broiled, slightly limp chicken sandwich, a big leaf of mayonnaise-y lettuce slid out from the bun and
landed on her jeans with a greasy splat. Dabbing it with a napkin,
she reached for a drink, only to notice that there wasn't one.

"Oh, duh, I forgot the drinks!" Mark exclaimed, and hopped to
his feet. "Here, I'll run across the street and get us something."

As she watched him jog across Boylston, Billy recounted all his
wonderful attributes. Mark was kind, affable, and considerate. Okay,
his idea of a "special surprise" could use an upgrade, but still . . .
fundamentally, he was a nice guy.

When he returned, however, he had only one cup in hand. "We can share this," he said, handing the small cup to Billy first. "It's more romantic that way!"

After one sip, she was pursing her lips. It was regular Coke, which, to a Diet Coke hound, tasted beyond putrid. When she handed the cup off to him, he took a long, thorough gulp, followed by a protracted, "Aaahhh."

Just then a ketchup packet blew off in a sweep of wind, and Mark jumped to his feet and tried to save it. "Mark . . . Mark, don't worry about it," Billy called as he lurched for it. The wind kicked up and blew their napkins all around.

"It's good ketchup," he called back. "It's free—we shouldn't waste it!" He lunged down to the ground, releasing a sigh of relief as he swiped the ketchup packet up and dropped it into his pocket. When he turned back to Billy, his mouth spread wide with unabashed glee.

Feebly, Billy smiled back. Try as she might to understand Mark, sometimes he still managed to elude her.

Later that night Billy punched out and left the bakery, expecting to find Corryn waiting for her. She'd insisted on making sure Billy got home safely in light of all the creepy things that had been happening lately. But it wasn't Corryn waiting outside Bella Donna. It was Seth.

As their eyes met, Billy felt an immediate surge of excitement. "Hi, there. What are you doing here?"

"I came to make sure you got home okay," Seth said, coming closer.

"You didn't have to do that," she said.

He ignored the comment. "Listen, I talked to Sally today. First of all, she told me that Greg Dappaport is from a prominent Connecticut family she's known for years and years. Apparently she became friendly with Greg's sister, Bethany, all the way back when they were in private school together, so she's known Greg practically all his life—though they didn't become particularly friendly until he moved to Churchill three years ago. Anyway, it sounds like everything with him is on the up-and-up."

"Oh, good," Billy said with a sigh of relief, and Seth went on to repeat what Sally had told him about Greg's educational and professional history. Afterward Billy said, "So what's second of all?"

"Based on Sally's description, I think the head librarian at the Churchill Public Library, Claudia Dibbs, might be the woman we're looking for. Uptight, prissy, rich. Plus, she's not married. A widow."

"Interesting," Billy said, chewing her lip. "But you never met her?"

"No. Apparently she moved to town not too long ago."

"Oh, my gosh, we have a real lead; this is great! When should we talk to her? How about tomorrow? I have to be in Churchill working on the streetscape, anyway."

"Okay. But maybe you should leave the talking to me."

"Why?"

"Because . . . you know, I live in town. I know Sally—"

"And you think you're smoother than me, is that it?" she said, grinning.

His mouth curved teasingly. "Well . . ."

"Just because you schmoozed our waitress at the Rusty Canoe?" Seth just smiled. "We can work out the details tomorrow, how about that?"

"Billy!"

She looked over and saw her sister rushing through the mall, with her dark hair flying loosely around her face. "Hi, I'm so sorry I'm late— Seth," she said suddenly, just registering him. "Hi."

"Hey, Corryn. It's good to see you again. How've you been?"

"I'm fine, and you?"

After they exchanged pleasantries, Seth said, "Well, I can see you're in good hands here, Billy. But let me give you two a lift so you don't have to take the subway."

"Seth!"

They all turned around and saw Joe heading over. Okay—this was getting weird now. "Oh, my God, Joe!" Billy said, smiling. "How are you? What are you doing here?"

"Hey, kid, what's up?" he said, tapping her shoulder affectionately. Then, abruptly, his attention was diverted by Corryn. "Oh, hello," he said, and cleared his throat. "Small world, huh?"

"Yeah," she replied, "claustrophobically, freakishly small." Billy could tell she was only kidding, but Joe cinched his brows, as though he didn't know how to take that. Jeez, did her sister always have to be so sarcastic?

Again Billy asked, "Joe, what are you doing here?" Then it hit her. "Did you find out something about Ted Schneider's murder?"

"Murder?" he said, looking thoroughly confused, and glanced at Seth.

"Yeah, I didn't tell you the whole story," Seth said after a pause.

"Oh." Another brief pause. "Well, Seth mentioned you were getting out around eight. I finished my paperwork early, so I thought I'd swing by and check on you," Joe said to Billy.

Billy let out a laugh. She couldn't believe all these people had cared enough to come just to check on *her*. "That's so sweet," Billy said, very subtly nudging her sister's side. Corryn shot her a warning glance, and Billy added, "Really—thanks, you guys."

"Hey, why don't we all go somewhere?" Seth suggested. "Maybe get something to eat."

Even though Billy had eaten a BK Broiler a couple of hours ago, she was already hungry again. "Sure," she said, and turned to Corryn. "Want to?"

Corryn hesitated, glancing at Joe, who looked intently at her.

Billy sensed a kind of electricity between them, something palpable, and when Corryn finally agreed, Joe did, too.

They were all seated at Uno's on Boylston, much more relaxed now that Billy and Corryn had raspberry crushes in front of them, and Joe and Seth had ordered beers. The only problem was that the burn from the vodka was making Billy too acutely sensitive to every move Seth made. Every brush of his leg against hers in the tight-fitting booth, every shuffle of his feet under the table. Memories flashed through her head like a dirty slide show: his naked, muscled legs, his thick, hard penis, the mushroom-headed tip when it was wet and scorching. . . .

Billy sat across from Corryn, who sat next to Joe, who kept shooting glances her way. They were so damn adorable together, if only her sister would give Joe a chance.

Seth had told Joe their suspicions, but, predictably, Joe wasn't buying any of it. As a cop, he was a stickler for evidence and "facts." *Jeez.*

Now, while they waited for their pizza, Joe told them what he'd learned about the late Ted Schneider. "Born and raised in New Bedford," he said.

"Not far from Churchill," Seth remarked, sliding his gaze to Billy, who nodded.

"Graduated from high school in 1959. Joined the army but went AWOL. According to the marriage records, he was married once to a woman named Gertrude Swain. They divorced. I called the Swain family of Michigan and asked a few questions."

"And they just answered you?" Corryn said, surprised.

Joe shrugged. "They assumed that since I was a cop, I was after Ted for something, and they were all too happy to talk then. Apparently they think the guy was a real bastard, and they had no clue that he died. Or at least that was how they acted."

"Why was he a bastard?" Billy said, leaning forward with interest. Finally she might get some real information about the kind of man Ted was—information that might actually shed some light on why he'd left Aunt Pen.

"According to Babs Swain, the matriarch of the family, Ted married their daughter Gertrude thirty years ago, but the marriage lasted less than a year. Apparently the Swains were a high-society family who viewed Schneider as a fortune-hunting lothario. That's a quote, by the way. Anyway, they offered him a payoff to leave Gertrude, nothing messy, just sign the divorce papers and disappear." With a shrug, Joe finished, "He took it."

"Oh, my God, what a dick!" Corryn blurted—obviously forgetting herself. (And did she have to say *dick* when Billy had just gotten the image of Seth's out of her mind?)

Seth said, "It sounds like the family did their daughter a favor, then. Obviously Ted didn't really love her if he took a payoff."

"Yeah, but the thing is, it backfired," Joe went on. "When Gertrude found out what had happened, instead of thanking the family for helping her see the light—Babs honestly seemed to expect that, by the way—she took off. Up and disappeared. They never heard from her again. Ted, either."

"Jeez," Billy said, sitting back against the booth upholstery. "First Gertrude disappears into thin air; then Ted disappears into thin air. A lot of disappearing going on; meanwhile I can't even hide from the company who gave me a college loan nine years ago, much less my family."

"Hey," Corryn said, scrunching her face.

"Oh, not you," Billy said, smiling at her. "Or Dad."

"Yeah, but who's to say Gertrude and Ted didn't disappear *together*?" Joe said.

True . . . Billy hadn't even thought of that. Maybe Ted and

Gertrude had gotten the payoff *and* each other. But even so, where did Aunt Penelope fit into Ted's life?

"Wait, Joe," Corryn said. "You must know something about what this guy's been up to for the past thirty years. I mean, where has he been living? What does he do for work?"

"According to the IRS, he's filed as doing odd jobs, mostly working as a contract fisherman, drifting from town to town."

"So obviously whatever payoff the Swains gave him, he blew a long time ago," Seth remarked, which made Billy wonder if Ted might have been after Penelope only for her money. Aunt Pen wasn't especially wealthy, but she did have a successful business, and that beautiful old colonial she'd inherited from her parents. And what about what Ted's Dear John letter saying that someone from his past was after him? Was it something as simple as a spurned lover—someone he'd screwed over while he was drifting from town to town? Or could it have been the Swains in search of their daughter? And were they just conveniently feigning ignorance of Ted Schneider's death?

Just then the waitress came bearing pizza and refills of beer. "Another drink, ladies?" she said.

"No, thanks," Billy replied. Another drink would only fuel her hormones, which were already raging, especially with Seth's solid thigh pressed against her. Corryn passed, too, and Billy wondered if she had similar reasons, sitting next to Joe.

"Now, Billy, I want to know more about these threats," Joe said with concern. "Seth told me you've gotten some weird calls and that someone smeared tomatoes on your window."

"Yeah, I think it has to do with the case," she said.

Joe leveled an impatient look at her. "The case? Billy, there *is* no case. Ted Schneider died from an allergic reaction to nuts at an event where there was a shitload of food. Oh, sorry." He must've felt like a gutter-mouth in front of Corryn. "Anyway, he ate something he shouldn't have and suffered a fatal reaction. It happens *all* the time."

"But what you said about Ted's background—"

He held up his hand before she could finish. "Look, Seth asked me to find out about the guy, so I did. He never said anything about you two conducting a murder investigation." Now Seth got a look from Joe, one that very clearly said, *What the fuck?*

"We really haven't done too much," Seth said in their defense.

"What, exactly, have you done?" Joe asked warily.

Seth gave him the very abridged version, and Billy said, "See? We've hardly rocked the boat."

"No, but you broke into one," Joe said, sounding frustrated. "That's a crime."

Billy was debating whether or not to feign ignorance on that one when Corryn jumped in. "Forget about this guy's death—who cares? What the hell are we gonna do about the threats?"

"Exactly," Joe said with a nod. "It's been a few calls and some vandalism, is that right?"

"Well, I also had a hang-up call that was kind of creepy the week before the jubilee," Billy said. "And I got the feeling someone was outside my building one night. But then again, my mind might have been playing tricks on me."

Joe nodded and said, "The fact that those incidents precede the jubilee only proves my point that none of this related to this guy Ted's death."

"Murder," Billy insisted.

"You have no evidence," Joe said, unrelenting and once again throwing around the E-word. "Now let's get back to reality. Do you have *any* idea who might want to threaten you or even just scare you? Anyone at all who might be angry with you? Or who even might think you'd actually find this funny?"

"No," Billy said. "To be honest, I really don't even know that many people."

"What about someone you work with?"

"No, I can't imagine—"

"Do any of your coworkers have issues with you? Think, Billy. Most of the time, in cases like this, it's someone you know. Could someone at the bakery have a problem with you?"

"Not that I know of," Billy said.

"And the messages haven't given any clue as to what the caller might want from you?" Joe asked, staring her down with intensity.

"No—whoever's behind this hasn't mentioned that at all. Just cryptic things like, 'Go away.' "

"That's not too cryptic," Corryn said sarcastically.

"Seth, is there any chance this could be connected to you?" Joe said.

"What do you mean?"

"Maybe someone might be jealous, or have a grudge against your"—he stopped just short of saying "girlfriend"—"against Billy for spending time with you." Suddenly Sally Sugarton's niece, Pam, popped into Billy's mind. No, she was harmless—even if she did seem to have designs on Seth. Anyway, how would Pam possibly know Billy's cell number and address?

"I can't think of anyone," Seth said now. "No one who'd have a grudge, and no one who'd even know we're spending time together."

"Maybe Sally mentioned something around town, or—"

Seth shook his head adamantly. "No way. I haven't mentioned Billy much to Sally." Inexplicably, the words stung, and Seth must've realized, because he looked over at Billy and grinned. "I mean I love Sally to death, but she might as well hang a sign around her neck that says, 'Town Crier.' Anyway, Billy asked me to keep this quiet."

That was true.

God, he was cute.

She wanted to kiss him so much right now.

"Okay, this is how it's gonna be." Joe was in dictatorial mode; suddenly Billy was remembering more about his authoritative demeanor. "I want you two to drop this whole investigation. That's it; you're done. I don't want to find out you've been snooping around Churchill and asking questions."

Billy paused, waiting for the rest, but so far she wasn't too impressed with Joe's vision for how things were gonna be.

"Now, I do not believe there is a connection between Ted Schneider's death and the threats Billy's been getting—and I don't believe Ted's death was murder, either—but if there *is* a connection, *I'll* find it. Do you understand?"

Seth released a small sigh, but didn't agree or disagree. Billy tried to follow his lead, but her face must've given her away, because when Corryn spoke she sounded worried. "Billy. Come on, just forget it. Who cares if Penelope dated this guy a decade ago? It's history. Jesus, I don't want you getting killed over it!"

"But if you don't think the murder and the threats are related, what's the difference if I snoop around a little?" Billy asked.

Corryn sighed with exasperation. "I just don't want you making yourself any more vulnerable to whoever is leaving you these messages." She turned to Joe and said, "Isn't there something you can do? Like put her under house arrest or something?"

"Hey!"

With a short, dry laugh, Joe slanted his gaze at Corryn, about to respond when, for a moment, their eyes seemed to lock. His mouth parted a little, and for a few crackling seconds the air felt charged with tension.

Seth spoke up. "All right, we'll drop the whole thing."

"But—" Billy began to protest when Seth lightly squeezed her thigh under the table. Her breath caught, and almost instinctively she stilled.

"Joe, please just find whoever's behind the calls," he said, sounding gravely serious. Almost commanding. Billy swallowed hard at the thick, masculine power in Seth's voice. Could he be more fucking sexy?

Chapter Twenty-two

Seth drove Billy home, because he wanted to make sure she got there safely, and Joe drove Corryn home for that same reason—not that Corryn was being threatened, but Billy wasn't about to argue.

"I'll be fine now," she said, turning the lock of her brownstone. "You can go."

"I think I'll wait until you get inside."

They headed up the stairs to Billy's apartment, and came to a jarring halt at the top of the stairs. "Oh, my God—what's *that*?"

"What the hell . . . ?" Seth stepped forward and snatched the sheet of paper that was taped to Billy's door. In big, blocky letters it read, *I hate your fat face—go away, you bitch!* "Christ," he muttered angrily, and reached back to grab her hand. "C'mon, sweetheart." The endearment soothed her, even though it sank in only blurrily as her mind raced frantically with fear. Gently Seth guided her into her apartment, with his hand on her back, and as soon as he locked the door behind them Pike Bishop bounded over.

He attacked Seth first, jumping up on him, sniffing him, snarling at him, and barking, of course, but Seth dropped down to pet him. "Hey, boy," he said, rubbing his neck until the dog warmed up to him. Next Pike went to Billy, who petted him and let him lick her hand. "Hi, baby," Billy said, fighting the choking fear climbing up her throat.

It was suddenly hard to breathe—to think. Somebody had been

in her building. Of course, Lady McAvit had a key, but Billy didn't believe in her heart that her neighbor was the culprit. So who else could've gotten in? She supposed that whoever it was could've slipped into the brownstone when a resident came in or out of the front door. But the thought of someone lurking there, waiting for an opportunity to slip inside, sent shivers all through her. As she shuddered, Seth slipped his arms around her.

"C'mere," he said in a low, soothing voice, pulling her to him so her back rested against his chest and his arms coiled around her waist. Softly he spoke into her ear: "Don't be scared. We're gonna figure this out, I swear. Joe will check the note for fingerprints and interview your neighbors to find out if they saw anyone strange in the building tonight."

Billy nodded and leaned back, letting Seth's chest take her weight. "You're right," she mumbled. "I just hate this. Do you think Joe was right? That none of this is related to what happened to Ted?"

"I honestly don't know what to think at this point."

"It has to be related, Seth—I *know* it is."

"Maybe, but I think Joe's right. We have to lay off the investigation and just let the police take things from here."

Sucking in a breath, Billy straightened up and turned around. "What are you talking about? I thought you were only agreeing with Joe at the restaurant to humor him and Corryn. You mean you don't want to talk to Claudia Dibbs anymore?"

Seth sighed and ran his hands along her upper arms. "Billy, it's not that I don't want to, but I don't want you getting into danger—"

"I'm already in it. What harm can it do now?" Before he could argue, she said, "Look, this started out being about my aunt Pen—trying to bring some closure to her relationship with Ted and why he left her—but now it's about more than that. If somebody out there is threatening me, I have to figure out what's going on. It's self-preservation."

Seth paused.

"If you don't want to help me, I guess I'll do this myself," Billy said, praying that wouldn't happen. She didn't want to do this alone; Seth was her partner, her support, and he made her feel safer.

"Okay," he said finally. "We'll talk to Claudia Dibbs, find out if she knew Ted, see what she has to say, and that's it, right?"

"Right," Billy said. "But . . . well, a lot depends on what she has to say."

Silently, Seth relented.

As Billy led him farther into her apartment, he said, "This place is great. A lot bigger than your old place downtown."

"Thanks, I really love it here," she called over her shoulder on her way to the kitchen.

He stopped to peruse some of her paintings that were leaning against the wall. One in particular caught his eye. It was of a man resembling himself, except he had a black mustache, horns, and a serpent around his neck.

Seth let out a laugh.

"What?" Billy said, coming back into the room with a bowl of food for Pike.

"What's *this*?" he asked, holding the painting up to her.

"Oh . . . uh . . ."

"Why do I have *horns*?"

"Well . . . I've never been good at drawing ears," she said, and took the painting from his hand. It was a silly picture from four years ago—but, okay, she supposed she didn't have to have it framed.

Seth stepped closer to her, and suddenly Billy felt his heat—the potent energy that lifted off his body in strong, intoxicating waves. He didn't even have to do anything; just his being there aroused her senses, making her want nothing more than to hold his naked body in her arms . . . and to feel his hot, wet mouth tugging on her nipple.

But would she hate herself in the morning?

Probably.

Though she really did not want to, it was best if they said good night. "Well, thanks for seeing me home," she said, breaking the charged silence and motioning toward the door. "I'm pretty tired, so I'll just walk you out. Thanks again," she added brightly, then stupidly held out her hand for a shake.

Understandably, Seth didn't take it.

"What?" Billy asked, trying to act casual, even though her apartment suddenly felt as hot and sticky as last night's sexcapades.

"I'm staying here tonight," he said simply.

"But why?" she asked, feeling her pulse kick up and her stomach tighten with anxiety . . . or was it anticipation? "I-I thought you just wanted to make sure I got home safely."

"That was before we found a note on your door. Now I'm staying. Please don't argue."

Please, how could she argue? She was scared out of her wits, and only Seth seemed able to calm her nerves these days.

"Actually, I'd love it if you stayed with me." Seth's face brightened. "Stayed here on the couch," Billy finished, and headed to the bathroom.

"But—"

"Please don't argue," she called out, and shut the bathroom door with a thud.

Inside the bathroom she pulled her hair up into a ponytail and slipped out of her clothes and into her pink-and-purple kimono. After she washed her face and brushed her teeth, she came out and stopped in the entry hall to check her messages. "Hey, doll, Kip Belding here. Something sweet's just come up. Call me." She pressed save, figuring it wouldn't hurt to give him a call tomorrow. The next one was from Mark. "Hi, cutie, it's me. Gimme a call back—oh, wait, what time is it? Almost ten, that's too late. Okay, if you get this message, call me back before ten. But not after ten, okay? I have to get up early tomorrow. Anyway, I'm so glad we talked and had dinner together under the stars! Can't wait to see you soon for some more great times! Bye-bye!"

She braved a glance over at Seth, who was sitting on the couch, looking off to the side as though he were oblivious, but his jaw was clenched. ·

The couch was not exactly what he'd been hoping for. But he wasn't too surprised; she'd told him this morning that sex had been a mistake. *Jesus.* He ran a hand over his face with frustration, and tried to swallow his fierce jealousy of the guy who'd left a message on Billy's machine. Mark. This other *fucking* guy. The thought of Billy passionate and naked with any other man made Seth's blood boil. But how serious could Mark and Billy really be if Billy had slept with *him* last night?

As Billy walked into the living room, she smiled gently at him. "Thanks for looking out for me. And thanks for . . . everything."

"No problem," Seth replied curtly, kicking off his shoes.

"I mean it, I really appreciate all you're doing to help me with the Ted Schneider case. I just don't know *why* you're doing so much."

"I just want to see it through," was all he said.

"Okay. I'll get you a blanket and a pillow," she said, and went into the bedroom. Pike Bishop didn't follow her into the bedroom; instead he kept hovering around Seth—sniffing his shoulder and his neck then letting out a sudden bark.

"I knew her first, you know," Seth muttered wryly, and Pike barked again. "Okay, okay, boy," Seth said, patting the dog's head until he warmed back up to him and quieted down.

Billy returned with a pillow and a blanket. Her kimono covered her whole body, so why did she look so fucking sexy right now? Maybe it was just the vivid memories that kept pounding through his brain—of Billy's full breasts jiggling and bouncing in passion, of her hard nipples in his mouth, of his fingers up her—

"Here you go," she said as she spread out his blanket. Tossing the pillow behind his head, Seth leaned into the sofa cushions, fighting the burgeoning erection he feared was futile tonight. Not to mention painful. "Okay, well . . . see you in the morning," Billy said, now on the threshold of her bedroom.

"Okay—oh, wait. Billy?"

"Yeah?" she said, peeking her head out her bedroom doorway.

"Before I go to bed, can you do me a favor? A really small one, I swear."

"What?"

"Kiss me," he said. "Just a kiss good night."

The suggestion hung in the air, and Billy swallowed, feeling her mouth run dry. Of course, she *wanted* to kiss Seth again, but this was forbidden territory.

Then again . . . she'd vowed not to have shameless, uninhibited sex with Seth, but she'd never said anything about *kissing*.

"Please," he said huskily, his voice thick and full of desire. It was the voice of her mind—the desire of her body. "C'mon, *one* kiss."

"What are you, Willy from the Rusty Canoe?" she said, trying to lift some of the tension that hung heavily between them. The air in her apartment felt thick and almost oppressively humid—stifling. Tightness pulled between her legs, tearing her body with keen arousal. She desperately wanted to feel him inside her, like the night before.

Well, in all honesty, she still *could* feel him inside her from the night before.

"Billy . . ." he said, his eyes dark and hungry. As if magnetically pulled, Billy walked over to him. Sitting gingerly on the tip of the couch, she leaned down and pressed a light, sweet kiss to his mouth.

Light and sweet was okay with him, too, it seemed, as Seth tipped his head and feathered his lips across hers. Cupping her arms gently with his palms, he rubbed his thumbs in circles that burned right through the flimsy fabric of her kimono.

Then, slowly, he folded his mouth into hers, drawing her into a deep, sensuous kiss. It was slow and wet and drugging, and when he pulled back Billy staggered a little, feeling the dazed expression on her face.

Heat crackled in the scant space between them, and neither pulled away. Seth was still rubbing her arms, holding her close. Damn him—just the touch of his soft, seductive lips on hers, and Billy was aching for more.

So in the spirit of being a sex-hungry martyr, she threw her arms around him. Seth cupped the nape of her neck and kissed her. Soon she was totally lost in the sensations of his hot, probing tongue and his choppy breath intermingling with hers as they kissed hungrily.

"Oh, God," she whispered brokenly, and Seth bounded off the couch, lifting them both to their feet and walking them backward toward her bedroom.

Seth had her robe off before they reached the bed. She had only a tank top and panties on underneath, and just as the backs of Billy's knees hit the edge of the bed, Seth dropped to his knees, yanked her panties down, and buried his face between her legs.

Billy cried out in surprise—in ecstasy—and fell flat back as soon as he slid his tongue inside her. With her neck arching and her head lolling on the comforter, Seth gripped her hips and made love to her with his mouth. Then he drove two fingers inside her, and she nearly screamed.

"How does that feel?" he whispered on a breath, withdrawing his fingers.

She moaned in response as her knees shook and her hips writhed on the bed.

"Do you like *this*?" he asked, and plunged three fingers in at once. Now she *did* scream. It was just too much—she was going to come—when Seth rolled over, taking her on top of him, and she rolled again, out of her mind, shuddering violently, and they both fell onto the floor. Hurriedly, Seth reached into his back pocket and took a condom from his wallet. Billy helped him off with his pants. Panting, Seth coaxed her to sit astride his lap, and in a giddy delirium Billy murmured, "Not the floor again . . ." as Seth's erection slid inside her.

Her eyes drifted shut as heat exploded in her veins, and everything else blurred out.

"So this is it," Joe said as he turned the lock on his front door. Corryn walked inside his apartment along the hardwood floor into the living room. Her shoes were high-heeled boots that clunked loudly as she moved, and she could feel Joe's overwhelming presence right behind her.

"It's nice. You live here alone?" she asked, turning to face him.

"Yeah, I live alone," Joe said, grinning. "My wife doesn't want to cramp my style, so she lives in the suburbs."

Corryn smirked. "Funny."

"Hey, can I take your coat?"

"Oh, yeah," she said, sliding the leather jacket off her shoulders and handing it to him. She was feeling nervous—too nervous for what the situation called for. Why had she agreed to come here? Joe had said maybe they could watch a movie and talk. Was that really all he wanted? But she didn't believe he'd lured her here so he could get laid, because he'd originally suggested her place. She'd said no, of course, because her place was a mess.

"Can I get you something to drink—something fruity?" he asked. So he'd been paying attention.

"Okay, a glass of water." *Truly inspired.* "If it's no trouble." *Shut up, shut up now.*

She'd come here tonight for the simple reason that she was so damn physically attracted to this guy, like nobody ever before. And while she couldn't deny that the thought of ending up alone held no appeal to her, the thought of ending up with someone like Roynald Membrano from cooking class held even less appeal than being alone. Not that Roynald was a bad person, but he'd spent the whole last class asking her all kinds of nosy, prying questions, in between juicy sneezing fits, and her mother kept ogling them from across the room, desperate to believe it was the love connection of the century.

Positioning herself gingerly on the arm of the couch, Corryn said, "So how long have you lived alone?" She'd meant to ask how long he'd lived *here*, but *alone* had just slipped out.

"Uh, almost ten years now, but I'm kind of getting sick of this place, actually," he called from the kitchen. "I'm divorced. You are too, right?" Joe said, coming back with a glass of water for each of them.

"Yeah, how did you know that?"

"I did some checking," he replied with a grin.

"Oh, I see." So he'd asked Seth about her. Suddenly her heart kicked up, and she just barely suppressed her smile.

"What happened with you guys?" Joe asked casually, referring to Corryn and her ex-husband, Kane, whom she rarely felt like discussing unless she could curse up a storm.

"He was a cheater," she replied simply, and hoped Joe would leave it at that.

"Oh, I'm sorry," he said. "I can sympathize."

"What, with being a cheater?" she said, her defenses on full alert.

"No, no," he said quickly, sitting down on the love seat across from her. "I mean my ex-wife cheated on me, too."

"Really?"

She hadn't meant to sound that shocked, therefore revealing how unbelievably sexy she found him, but Joe just nodded. "It sounds clichéd, but I really think she didn't like being married to a cop. My hours were a lot crazier before I made detective, believe it or not. Unless she liked being married to a cop *because* of my crazy hours, because I was never around, so she could do whatever she wanted. I really don't know."

"Oh . . . that sucks. I'm sorry. How long have you been a cop?"

"Sixteen years. Eight in homicide. What about you? Tell me about real estate."

"Why, are you looking?" she asked. "Just kidding—I'm off duty tonight." God, he made her nervous.

"Seriously," Joe said, grinning. "You work at Blue Sky Realty, right? How do you like that?"

Grimacing, she said, "It's okay, if you like dealing with the public all day."

"Tell me about it," Joe said. "I pretty much hate the public now. The first thing you learn as a cop is that *everyone* is lying."

"Really? Everyone?"

Joe nodded. "Yeah, it's Academy 101. You can't believe anyone. The suspects, the perps, the victims on the scene, no one. That's the only way not to be surprised or taken in. Assuming people are lying is the only way to keep a cool head—kind of like that old riddle about the two guards."

"Oh, wait. One always lies, one always tells the truth?"

"Right. Even in that, the only way to figure the answer is by focusing on the guard who's a liar. Only using logic with the assumption that being lied to is the only way to deduce the truth." So far

Joe was refreshingly easy to talk to, and it threw Corryn's wisecracking defenses out of whack.

Relaxing more, she said, "Well my boss's 101 is ABC."

"Always be closing?"

"No. Apartments before condos." Joe tilted his head. "It's true for the most part," Corryn said, "at least in this town." Annette Beefe's theory was based on Boston's constant inundation of college kids, who were always looking for short-term leases. Corryn's boss, Annette, was always looking for a quick score.

"By the way, are you still up for a movie?" Joe asked. "We could see what's on TV. Or I'm sure I have some videos around here. . . ."

"Okay," Corryn said, sinking into the couch cushion, feeling more at ease. Joe flicked on the TV and sat next to her. Glancing over, she noticed the curve of his biceps, which were powerful beneath his shirt.

As they sat in silence, Corryn could feel the heat rising between them, the cloying feeling between her legs, and suddenly Joe leaned over. She turned her face, and just like that, he kissed her. It was very gentle, just a brushing of his lips across hers, and afterward she ducked her head, then refocused on the screen.

She just wasn't ready, and Joe seemed to understand, because he draped his arm along the back of the couch and seemed perfectly content to watch TV by her side.

The next morning Billy heard the crinkling of the shower curtain, and Seth climbed in behind her. Just as she turned to face him, he pulled her into his arms. "Wait," she said.

"For what?" he mumbled into her neck.

"Just wait." She'd woken up that morning limp and sore and very much in need of a reality check. She and Seth were turning into a fling, and she hated that. It was a cheapened version of an actual relationship, and that left her feeling . . . sad. "It's just that everything's happened too fast with us, and . . . well, it's not like you have any plans to move back to the East Coast, right?"

He hesitated, pulling back a few inches. "No," he said finally. Of course, he fantasized about it sometimes—about selling the company to Lucas, about living in Churchill, about starting over with a new company that wouldn't take as much of his time—but ultimately he wasn't ready to do it. It was too big a change—too risky, too unstructured. He hadn't even laid the groundwork for a new company. No, it just wasn't realistic.

Even though Billy was expecting Seth to say no, her heart plummeted. A tiny part of her had imagined him saying yes, or at the very least, saying maybe.

"So then where is this going?" she asked, feeling inexplicably defensive, yet trying to sound casual, as if she weren't on the verge of tears.

"I don't know . . . I mean . . . I just like being with you. Obviously I'm extremely attracted to you. And it's not like you're gonna leave Boston anytime soon, right?"

"No," Billy said, even though she might if he asked. Or she might be willing to try a long-distance relationship for a while—but she already felt too vulnerable and exposed to propose all this when she didn't even know where Seth stood on their future. She was waiting for *him* to say something.

Meanwhile, Seth paused as though he was about to speak, but then stopped himself.

"So this is, what . . . a harmless fling?" Billy said finally, trying not to show her anger, her embarrassment, her irrational frustration with Seth and his whole sick need to live in Seattle.

Irritably, he replied, "I'm not sure what you want me to say. Aren't you dating someone else, anyway?"

Suddenly Billy felt like a complete fool. So a fling was *exactly*

what Seth thought this was. He thought that she was dating someone else, and he was perfectly fine with that! He didn't want a
relationship with her again—even a long-distance one—but was
perfectly content to fool around while he was here, and then blow
out of town.

No, she couldn't do it. Not again. As it was, she was already de-
veloping strong feelings for him, and knew how deeply she would
miss him when he left. Pain cut through her heart, slashing that
soft, vulnerable place inside that she'd begun to open up to him,
whether he realized it or not.

Abruptly she turned and gave him her back.

"Billy—tell me. What is it you want me to say?"

"Nothing. But I'm just trying to tell you that I don't think it's
a good idea for us to keep . . . getting involved. I care about you,
and I like spending time with you," she continued, fighting back
tears that stung her eyes. "But I just want us to be friends from this
point on."

There. She'd said it. Too bad it was all a load of crap.

She'd hoped he'd protest, but it didn't happen. "Fine," he said
curtly, and climbed out of the shower.

Seth drove down Beacon Street wondering what the hell had just
happened. After one of the best nights in his entire life, he'd sleepily
climbed into the shower to relive some of it. And out of nowhere,
Billy decided she wanted to be friends.

Friends!

Damn it all—if that wasn't the classic kiss-off. He'd asked her
what was going on with the other guy because he'd thought—
wrongly, he supposed—that she'd been fishing around about a future. But obviously if they were going to think about starting a

relationship again, he'd need to know what the deal was with this mysterious other man in Billy's life.

But as soon as he'd put *her* on the spot, she'd clammed up, wanting to drop the subject and just be friends. Fuck, he didn't want to be friends. True, after he'd dropped Billy off at work the day before, he'd done some thinking about what had happened between them. But what he'd realized was that he couldn't ask Billy to up and move across the country just for him, and he wasn't going to move back. It wasn't that the idea wasn't tempting—of course it was. He loved the East Coast; he loved that big old beautiful house he was going to sell.

But his life and work were in Seattle. Still, he'd decided to remain open to the possibility of a long-distance relationship. He'd thought Billy might feel different about that option this time around. But it was pretty obvious she was still involved with that guy, Mark; otherwise she'd be able to answer a goddamn straightforward question about him.

Oh, hell, why was he letting her get to him like this? He wouldn't deny he was having fun with her, but he was also getting way too sappy and sentimental. Thinking he was already in love with her . . . it had to be loneliness. Not that Billy wasn't lovable, but he was getting in too deep. And even when he tried to keep things light, she didn't seem to like *that*, either.

It felt like he couldn't win with her. But he did still care about her. And he knew he couldn't bear it if anything happened to her. So that settled it then. They'd be friends.

It was really the best thing for both of them.

Chapter Twenty-three

After spending most of the day in Churchill, working on the streetscape, Billy remembered to return Kip Belding's call. His phone rang half a time before he picked it up. "Hi, Kip, this is Billy Cabot."

"Oh, I'm so excited you called! I have the peach of all positions for you."

"Really?" she said, interested but skeptical.

"How would you like to grow in a versatile, consumer-driven facility, with an ample benefits package to boot?"

"Sounds interesting. Where is it?"

"It's in Dorchester."

A red flag went up. "What company?"

"Well, it's a health-oriented conglomeration—"

"Please tell me it's not Tuck Hospital again," she said, holding back a sigh.

"Um . . ."

"Look, Kip, I've told you that I don't want to work in a hospital. I'm looking for a more corporate environment." She couldn't believe she was actually saying that, especially after her blissful time away from the eight-to-five madness, but it was true. Corporate America was less scary than a hospital; she feared diseases, doctors, bugs, and private jets—end of story. What did Kip not understand about this?

"Well, it's really not *in* the hospital," he snapped defensively. "You'd be adjacent to the main building, in a large, basementlike enclosure."

Huh?

Then it hit her. No, that couldn't be it.

"Kip, you don't mean . . . the *morgue*, do you?"

He heaved a deep, martyred sigh, but didn't deny the charge. *Jesus!* Zombies might not be one of Billy's fears, but that didn't make the morgue prospect any less creepy. "Kip, I'm sorry; I'm going to pass on that one. In fact, I'm going to pass on every single position that opens up at Tuck Hospital. You have my résumé; you know my skills. If something opens up that actually involves those skills, please give me a call."

Seth's Acura pulled up outside the gallery just as Billy hung up her cell phone. "Hey," he said as she climbed into the car.

"Hi," she said brightly, trying to start this new platonic thing off on the right foot. "How's your day going?"

"Fine."

"Anything new around the house?"

"No."

"Sounds good."

They drove quietly to the Churchill Public Library. It was obvious that Seth was still peeved at her, and Billy could only assume it was because she'd put an end to the no-strings sex. But she knew he would get over it; the fact was, if Seth didn't want to be her friend, he wouldn't be here right now.

Earlier Billy had made plans with Mark for the upcoming weekend. He'd thanked her profusely, showering her with praise, and told her she wouldn't regret giving him a second chance. She'd told him that she wanted to just take it slowly, and deep in the recesses of her mind, she prayed that she wouldn't regret it, either.

When they entered the Churchill Public Library, Seth was hit with a sensation of déjà vu from when he was young. His father would take him there to listen to his mom, who used to run a story hour for the kids. Smiling nostalgically at that, Seth felt yet another pull back toward his old home.

"Now do you have it all down?" Billy asked softly as they crossed the peach-colored carpet toward the circulation desk.

"Yeah, of course," Seth said, referring to the plan they'd come up with last night, in bed, after some slow, steamy sex.

"So I'm a writer, and you're my assistant—"

"Wait, I thought I was the writer," he said, confused, as they approached the desk.

"No, I'm supposed to be . . . right?"

"Well, let's just both be writers."

"Can I help you?"

"Oh, yes, hi," Billy replied to the bored-looking teenager sitting behind the desk. "We're looking for Claudia Dibbs, the head librarian?"

He nodded and called loudly over his shoulder, "Miss Dibbs! People here for you!" God forbid the kid actually got up to get her. Seconds later, a full-figured woman in her sixties emerged, with smooth caramel-colored hair pulled into a loose bun. She wore a conservative navy dress with a timid floral print, and a string of pearls around her neck.

"Can I help you?" she asked, looking first at Seth, then at Billy.

Folding her hands on top of the desk, Billy reminded herself that bluffing was all attitude. "Yes, hello, my name is Billy Cabot. I'm a writer, and this is my assistant, Seth Lannigan."

Seth shot her a look out of the corner of his eye.

"We're here researching a book on the local fishing industry," she continued in her best writer voice, whatever that meant. "I wondered if we could talk to you. I promise I won't take much of your time."

"But what could I possibly tell you about the local fishing trade?" Miss Dibbs asked, confused.

"Um . . . well, I figured as head librarian, you'd be able to give me some important information, maybe some idea where I could begin looking, um . . . well, I figured with the prestigious role you have in this community, you know, your having an ear to the ground, so to speak, and just being more knowledgeable about this town than I'm sure most people are . . . I thought you'd be an invaluable person to talk to—that is, if you don't mind."

"Oh, well . . . of course, I'd be happy to help," Miss Dibbs said, pressing a hand to her chest proudly and stepping out from behind the circulation desk. (Sometimes flattery really *did* get you everywhere.) She sat down at a nearby table.

As soon as Billy joined her, Miss Dibbs said, "My throat's a little parched. Maybe your assistant could fetch us some water. There are Dixie cups by the water fountains."

"Oh, good idea," Billy said, looking to Seth, who was glaring back. "Would you mind?"

"Sure—no problem," he replied tightly, and turned to go find the nearest water fountain.

"The fountain on the fifth floor is the coldest!" Miss Dibbs called to him. Seth paused, then nodded. "By the way, the elevator's broken," she added, then turned back to Billy. "Handsome assistant." It could've been an objective comment, or a veiled insinuation that "assistant" was code for "gigolo." Or was that just how Billy's mind was working at the moment? Did it simply reflect the constant sexualization of nearly everything now wherever Seth Lannigan was concerned?

While he was fetching water, Billy eased into her questions about Ted Schneider by first asking Miss Dibbs a little about the history of the town, the tourist trade, and the popularity of seafood restaurants. Then she moved in for the 411. "Now, I know there was a fisherman who moved here recently and suffered an untimely end. Ted Schneider, I believe his name was. Did you know him?"

Miss Dibbs drew her lips together tightly. "Why would I know him?" she asked evasively. She'd started to clam up now, Billy could tell, so she had no choice but to pull out the big guns. She reached into her bag and retrieved the library book they'd found on Ted's boat, and she slid it across the table.

"It's from this library. I just thought if Ted Schneider was a patron here, you might've known him."

Miss Dibbs took the book in her hands and clutched it to her chest. Breathing heavily through her nose, she shut her eyes with emotion and nodded. After a long, heavy silence, she spoke. "Yes. I knew him. I knew him well."

Yes! Finally somebody knew the guy well. "Can you tell me about him?" Billy asked.

With a sigh, she took a tissue out from inside her sleeve and dabbed the corners of her eyes. "He was a kind man. He had a gruff exterior, but when we were alone, he was sensitive—gentle." She paused, looking meaningfully at Billy, and said, "In case you haven't guessed, we knew each other in the biblical sense. We were having a clandestine affair, and I just don't want to hide it anymore."

Billy nodded, coaxing her to continue, thinking, *Jackpot!*

"Teddy was very giving and generous in his lovemaking. In fact, he was the most tender lover I've ever known, and I've known quite a few." Okay, that was so not going in a book about the local fishing trade.

Trying to keep the flow going, without appearing too desperate for the info, Billy said, "That's lovely. How did you two meet?"

Sniffling softly, Miss Dibbs explained, "Ted moved into town a few months ago. I think he planned to stay here for only a little while. Teddy was like that, always on the move. He had a nomadic spirit." She made it sound so freaking beautiful that "Teddy" made a habit of leaving. *Tell that to Aunt Penelope.* "We met early one morning when I was out walking on the beach. We hit it off; there was just this spark between us. In time, he opened up to me—told me how he couldn't stand all the snobby, rich people in Churchill. Well, don't quote me on that part. Teddy knew I had my money, but he didn't hold that against me. He was on the outside of this town; I was on the inside. It was so romantic—so tragic. Like *Romeo and Juliet.*" *Yeah, just like that,* Billy thought, holding back an eye roll.

"So you knew him well?" Billy fished.

"I don't know how well you can know a man like Ted. He was somewhat of an enigma, but I still loved him so much. It's hard to explain."

"Well, what did you know about him? I mean, did he ever talk about his background?"

Miss Dibbs shrugged haplessly. "He traveled a lot, most of his adult life; he moved around. He was married once. Apparently it didn't last long. He didn't talk about her much, but I got the impression she was one of those really cloying domestic types with no life or ideas of her own. One of those women who baked all the time for him and basically just smothered him to death. A man like Ted can't be smothered or his spirit will be stifled."

Billy resisted the sudden urge to gag as Miss Dibbs continued, sounding bitter, "We had plans. We were in love; we even talked about selling the stocks my husband left me and moving somewhere far away. But all those dreams died with Teddy."

A red flag went up. The idea of Miss Dibbs selling her stocks for Ted wasn't sitting well with Billy. She asked, "Why did Ted want to move? Just to get away from all the rich people here or . . . ?"

"No—well, maybe I shouldn't say anything," Miss Dibbs said, but then shook her head. "Oh, what difference could it possibly make now?"

"What is it, Miss Dibbs?" Billy pressed.

"Claudia, please," she said. After a wistful sigh, she continued, "Someone was after him." Billy's heart rate shot up, and her palms prickled. *Now* they were getting to it. "I don't know who. All Ted said was that it was someone from his past. He needed to get away, and of course I would've done anything to be with him and to help him. I pleaded with him to tell me what was going on, but he said he couldn't bear to involve me, and I figured he would tell me everything when he was ready."

Déjà vu settled on Billy like a thick, gauzy cloud; confusion and doubt sat heavily on her chest. Why did this sound so much like what Aunt Pen had told her? Ted had needed money, Ted had needed to get away from a mysterious person from his past, but Ted hadn't wanted to talk about it. It was the same thing, except Ted had left Pen before he'd agreed to take any money from her, whereas Claudia Dibbs was all set to sell her stocks.

Billy *wanted* to believe that Ted's Dear John letter to Aunt Pen had been legitimate, but suspicion niggled in her mind. Considering what Joe had told her—that Ted had left his first wife after taking a payoff from her family—and considering that Ted had hit up both Pen and Claudia for money, Billy had to wonder if he had been just a con man. A grifter, pure and simple. Was Ted in the practice of romancing lonely women and scamming them out of their money? And if so, did that mean that no one from his past had ever really been after him? Was that all just part of the con so that Ted could later extricate himself from the relationship?

No, but that didn't make complete sense, either, because even if he *was* a bullshit artist, Billy still believed his death was murder. There wasn't a doubt in her mind. God, her head was spinning!

"Puss in Boots," Claudia said now with a humorless laugh, looking down at the book in her hands. "It was a little joke between us."

When she failed to elaborate, Billy said, "Guess you had to be there—but anyway, getting back to Ted's death—"

"Dear God, what a tragic accident!" Claudia said, pressing a soggy tissue to her breast. "I couldn't believe it when I heard. Teddy always made a point to ask about nuts whenever we went out to eat. Granted, he never bothered to carry around his EpiPen, so I always brought Benadryl with us in case, but still, it wasn't like Teddy at all to be so careless with his allergy. He knew it could be fatal."

Inhaling a ragged breath of emotion, she added, "Why would he do that when he had *me*? We had smoldering passion. He was my Teddy Bear and I was his Pussy Cat."

O-kay.

"Claudia, this might sound crazy, but have you considered the possibility that Ted's death was something more than an accident?" Billy asked tentatively.

"What do you mean?" she said, scrunching the folds of her face in confusion.

"You mentioned that someone from Ted's past was after him—at least according to him, right?"

"Yes."

"Well, is it possible that the person finally caught up with him? That whomever it was killed him at the jubilee by slipping him something to eat that would trigger a fatal allergic reaction?"

Claudia looked stunned. "But who would know Ted well enough to know how severe his allergy really was?"

Excellent question.

Just then Seth returned with the water. "There were no cups," he explained, very faintly out of breath from all the stairs. "I had to wait for the custodian to bring some up from the supply room."

"Oh, great, thanks," Billy said to her assistant. "Um, good work." Seth smirked at her, and Billy turned back to Claudia. "Just one more question. On the night Ted died, did you see anyone hanging around him at the jubilee? Did he mention exchanging words with anyone?"

"I wish I could tell you," she replied, "but I wasn't at the jubilee. I had to work that night. Even though this place was practically deserted. There was just some old man asleep in a chair, and a girl using the computers." Sniffing, Miss Dibbs added bitterly, "If I hadn't had to work that night, I could've been with Teddy when he got poisoned. He could've died in my arms. Just like *Romeo and Juliet.*"

"Now, what do you take away from that?" Billy asked Seth after recapping her interview with Claudia Dibbs.

"More than I ever wanted to know about Ted's competency in the sack?" he said dryly.

"True," Billy replied with a giggle. (She could tell Seth was getting out of his funk and she was relieved.) They'd left the library ten minutes ago, and now were walking toward the town square.

"By the way, I thought we were *both* supposed to be writers," he said. "When did I become your research assistant–slash–water boy?"

"Oh, sorry, I just got lost in the role, I guess," Billy apologized, looking sweetly sorry as a glint of amusement danced in her pale blue eyes.

"Why, what did you take away from it?"

"I don't know; it just doesn't make any sense," Billy said, pulling her crocheted mittens out of her coat pocket and slipping them on. Already she felt her nose and cheeks burning a little from the cold. "If Ted was really concerned that someone from his past was after him, like he told Claudia, why would he just show up at the town square, getting stupidly drunk, like he didn't have a care in the world? Why wasn't he more careful? More guarded?"

"Maybe he didn't expect whoever was after him to be at the jubilee," Seth said. "Or maybe the line he fed both Claudia and your aunt was complete shit; no offense."

"But if he was murdered, then *someone* had to be after him,"

Billy countered. "The same person who's after me now . . ." She shuddered as she said the words, and dark worries swam in the back of her mind, but this was nothing new, because mortality was her albatross. Seth put his hands on her shoulders affectionately, and when Billy looked up into his face, her eyes searched his. "And that's another thing. I keep thinking about what Joe said. That the person threatening me is probably someone I know, like a friend or a coworker. . . ."

Her voice trailed off as a sudden, jarring thought occurred to her. One that was just too crazy. "Oh, my God," Billy mumbled. "Oh, my God!"

"What?" Seth said anxiously, his eyes sharpening as they bored into hers. "Billy, what are you thinking?"

"Oh, Seth," she mumbled, dropping down onto a park bench to get her head straight. Her mind was frantic with thoughts that didn't make sense, yet made perfect sense. "I think I figured it out." He sat next to her, leaning forward, waiting for her to explain. "First of all, I think you were right. I think that the person from Ted's past—the person who killed him—was someone he never expected to be at the jubilee. Someone who lied to him about the foods he could eat. Someone who conveniently disappeared right before Ted dropped dead, and resurfaced only after the commotion settled. Someone who works at Bella Donna, and could easily find out my address and phone number from the employee files in Donna's office."

"Wait a minute. . . ."

"Georgette," Billy said, clutching her mittened hands together, desperate to grasp all the implications of what she was thinking. Memories came flooding back to her, fast and sharp. Georgette was married many years ago to a man who'd left her. At the Kenmore Pub she'd shown Billy a photo of herself back then, and it matched Claudia's description of Ted's first wife to a tee. When Georgette had spoken to Ted at the jubilee about the menu, she hadn't looked him in the eyes—in fact, she'd barely even turned around—and now it made sense why. She hadn't wanted Ted to recognize her after all these years.

Seth expelled a breath and said, "So Georgette Walters is really Gertrude Swain."

"There must be some way we can find out for sure," Seth said later, as they rode in his car toward the city. "Can't you just check her driver's license at work when she's not looking?"

"She doesn't drive," Billy said, remembering that Georgette had mentioned on more than one occasion that she'd let her driver's license expire many years ago. "But she has to be Gertrude Swain. Think about it: After Ted took a payoff from her family, she disappeared—like Joe said—and started over with a fake name. *That's* probably why she never officially married Gary; it would involve legal documentation. And she must be the one threatening me."

"But how would she even know you're looking into Ted's murder? Did you tell her?"

"No."

"Unless . . ."

"What?"

Seth glanced over at her, and Billy noticed the color in his face from the cold outside, and the way it illuminated the glittering hazel of his eyes. "Maybe Georgette knows about Ted's relationship with Penelope, and your connection to her. Have you ever mentioned Penelope at work?"

"Sure, sometimes."

"Maybe Georgette's been following Ted for years, watching him, waiting to get her revenge. And maybe she put it together that your aunt Penelope was the same Penelope Ted had been involved with.

Who knows, maybe she knew you'd talked to Penelope about Ted." That had been the same night that Billy had found tomatoes on her window. But did that mean Georgette had been following her? If so, was she following her *now*?

"So, what, you think that everything that's happened has all been part of some elaborate scheme?" Billy asked nervously, checking out her foggy window to see if any white pompadours were in the distance.

"I don't know," he said, sighing with frustration as he slid to a stop at the red traffic light ahead. He turned to her. "What should we do next? Tell Joe?"

"Oh, he'll just yell at us and blow us off. I mean, I know Joe's a great guy, but we're going to have to have a little more to go on before he'll take this seriously. He's never gonna believe that Georgette is Gertrude unless I come up with something more tangible than my own personal opinion." Which reminded her, the justice system really needed an overhaul. "I'm not sure how, but I have to try to find a link between Georgette and Ted. Someone is out there, someone who hates me—or wants me to go away—and I have to see this through."

"No, *we* have to," Seth corrected, smiling softly her, leaning down as though to kiss her, but then he kissed her cheek, just brushing it quickly, and pulled back to put an appropriately platonic amount of space between them.

As the light turned green, Seth turned back to the road while emotion reached inside Billy's chest, and fervently gripped her heart.

Chapter Twenty-four

"Psst."

Billy leaned farther forward, trying again to get her mom's attention. *"Psst."*

What, was her mother ignoring her? Billy had scored a seat directly behind the teacher's pet so she could grill her for information. Specifically, she wanted to see if Adrienne remembered anything Penelope might have told her about Ted's first wife. Anything that might help confirm Billy's theory about Georgette, so she'd have something to take to Joe.

Billy desperately wanted to shield her aunt from the pain of dredging up her relationship with Ted again. Ideally, she would also like to avoid telling Pen about Ted's death until she could offer her a better understanding of Ted's past, and how his leaving was in no way a reflection on her. And who better to turn to for details than the self-proclaimed expert on Aunt Pen's life, Billy's mother—a.k.a. the Great Truth Teller.

Unfortunately, Adrienne was too transfixed by Judy—too torn between gazing with adoration and taking notes like a maniac—to notice. Next to her was Corryn, lazily sitting in her chair, resting her cheek in her hand, almost looking like she needed it to prop her up. (On a side note, Roynald Membrano was sitting on the other side of Corryn, looking lovesick.)

"Today we're going to delight in the wondrousness of fresh

herbs," Judy said, standing in front of the room, talking like a Stepford chef, and making a point to pronounce the H in "herbs." "Now, can we have one or two volunteers come up front and try to guess which *herbs* are which? I've laid several *herbs* out on the table. Who will come up?" Predictably, Adrienne flapped her hand with rabid enthusiasm. "Roynald, how about you?" Possibly Judy noticed Roynald looking at Corryn instead of her, and felt like putting him on the spot as punishment.

"Yes, all right," he said, flashing a tremulous smile at Corryn, who smiled mildly in return.

"And Roynald needs a partner . . ." Judy said.

Billy expected Adrienne to jump out of her seat, and actually to vault over Judy's head like a leapfrog to get in front of the class, but instead she turned to Corryn and whispered loudly, "You go, too. Go up with Roynald. C'mon, go!" Corryn looked irritated as hell, probably because Adrienne's idea of whispering needed work, especially when it was laced with desperation. "Corryn, go up there!"

"No," Corryn hissed under her breath.

"Come on, he likes you!" Adrienne went on, making superobvious motions with her head. "Go up there!"

"Mom, stop it!" Billy whispered from behind, and Adrienne heaved a martyred sigh, followed by an *I try so hard* shake of her head. Corryn stayed planted in her seat.

After Roynald and another student guessed three out of the six herbs correctly, they were appropriately patronized by the grande dame, and sent back to their seats. Then Judy went behind the counter to finish making soufflés, using the basil, thyme, and rosemary.

As soon as Roynald left to use the bathroom, Adrienne turned back to Corryn. "He's a nice boy; why don't you talk to him? What's wrong with you?"

"What's wrong with *me*?" she asked incredulously.

Leaning forward, Billy jumped in. "Get off her back, Mom. She doesn't like him that way. It's none of your business who she likes anyway!"

"I'm her *mother*!"

"Yeah, don't remind me . . ." Corryn mumbled under her breath.

Adrienne's eyes shot over. "Well, I think that was a very *mean* thing to say. Corryn, you're mean, you're rude, and you're nasty."

"So I'm your clone, then?"

"Oh, stop, both of you!" Billy whispered. They looked back at her, both fuming. In some ways they were so alike. Neither could let anything go, and when they got frustrated they both looked like these tiny brunette fireplugs about to explode. "Corryn, just ignore her."

"But she's—"

Billy cut off her sister's protests. "And Mom, stop being a martyr. Stop butting in and pushing her on Roynald, who you claim is a nice guy, but who shut the elevator doors on me the first day of class, so as far as I'm concerned is subhuman. Now both of you just shut up!"

"*Herbs* really add delectable texture to any dish, as well as voluminous layers of rapturous flavor," Judy went on, as she greased ramekin cups for the soufflé, and Billy tried to get her mom's attention again. But now Adrienne was giving her the silent treatment. Billy could only assume it was because she'd taken Corryn's side. "Psst, Mom," Billy said, tapping her lightly on the shoulder. "*Mom*."

"Oh, what is it?" she asked, sounding irritated as she angled her head back.

"Remember how you showed me that picture of Aunt Penelope with that ex-boyfriend of hers, Ted?"

"Yes."

"Well, do you know if, when they were dating, he ever mentioned marriage?"

Adrienne scoffed. "If they did, it obviously didn't amount to a hill of beans. He left her, and, as you know, Penelope never married."

"Right," Billy said, stifling a scream, "but what I meant was, did he ever mention *being* married? In the past?"

"Well, how should I know what they talked about? Penelope's not the most open person in the world." *She's not?* "In fact, if you want to know the truth, I always felt like she looked down on me."

Oh, please—she did *not* have time for this. "Uh-huh, that's a shame, but back to Ted's background—"

"It was like she always thought she was just a little bit *better*."

"Mom, can you please focus here?"

"Miss Cabot!"

Billy jerked to attention as Judy scrutinized her under scolding eyebrows. "Apparently you're an expert on chiffonades?"

"Um . . . no. No, I'm not."

"Well, you must not need instruction," Judy continued smugly, "since you feel perfectly content to talk in my class. Perhaps there's something you'd like to share with the rest of us?"

"No, I'm sorry," Billy stammered, feeling her cheeks burn with embarrassment because all eyes were on her. On primal instinct, she turned to her mom for some sort of support or feeling of protection. What she got instead was disapproval, but at least Corryn had the decency to look back and bite her lip in sympathy.

"Now, everyone pair up," Judy said to the class, just in time for Roynald to return from the bathroom (with a tiny scrap of toilet paper stuck to his heel). "Everyone pick a partner," Judy reiterated, and Roynald's eyes darted straight to Corryn at the word "partner."

Oh, no. Billy had to protect her sister this time. "Come on, Corryn; be my partner," she said quickly, and grabbed her hand.

"Thank you," Corryn whispered on a giggle as they headed to the kitchen area.

"But wait . . ." Adrienne floundered.

"See ya later, Mom," Corryn said over her shoulder.

"Where are you two going?" Adrienne called after them as Roynald came closer. "Maybe the four of us can all work together."

Never gonna happen.

When Billy glanced back, she saw her mom and Roynald heading to a station together. She smiled at Adrienne and waved.

"Do you have anything without aspartame?"

The girl behind the counter at the tiny frozen yogurt shop, with a perpetually drooped-open mouth and a glazed, vacant look in her eyes, just shrugged.

"Mom," Billy said, leaning restlessly on the counter, "if you want it sugar-free, then probably not."

"Yeah," Corryn said, gently licking her cone. "Come on, Mom— live a little."

Adrienne paused, haplessly scrutinizing the chalkboard menu yet again before throwing her hands in the air and expelling a breath. "Oh, why not?" she said with a laugh. "I'll have what they're having." That was pretty major for her, considering that Billy and Corryn were both having large cones of Dutch chocolate with rainbow sprinkles. As it was, if it weren't for the concept of "bonding," Billy doubted her mother would even have agreed to stop at the dingy little frozen yogurt shop on Comm. Ave. after class.

The girl behind the counter, whose dim expression still hadn't changed, turned to make the cone, and Billy tapped her mom affectionately on the arm. "I'm proud of you, Mom. It won't hurt much, I swear."

Once they were all seated in a hard, plastic booth in the corner, Corryn grinned and said, "So, Mom, how was working with Roynald tonight? Is he still your new best friend?"

Billy laughed.

"Well . . ." Adrienne began, licking her cone as a form of a pregnant pause. "He's a very nice young man. . . ." Another pause. "But, uh . . ."

"Yeah?" Corryn pressed with a glint of laughter in her eyes. Their mom was stalling, and it was painfully clear.

"Well . . . I changed my mind. I think maybe he's not right for you, Corryn." She looked from one daughter to the next, then said, "To be honest . . . you were right. I suppose he *is* kind of a dud."

"Kind of?" Corryn said, shooting an incredulous look at Billy.

Then Adrienne giggled—*giggled*—and said, "And he's a little strange, too!"

"A *little*?" Corryn said.

Billy laughed, then said, "Mom, why do you think he's strange? What did he do?"

"Oh, my God, he couldn't stop asking me questions. 'Do you like cooking? Do you like our teacher? Do you like soufflés? What's your favorite number?' " She waved her hand through the air. "Oh, please, he was driving me *crazy*! Then I asked him what he does for a living, and guess what?" Billy and Corryn sat forward with interest. "He works for the Census Bureau."

"Well, I told you he was weird," Corryn said, "but you wouldn't listen."

"I thought you were just being closed-minded," Adrienne said in her own defense.

"No way. I mean, I'm sure there's someone out there for him, but he was just too odd for me."

Billy nodded and threw in, "And what about how he closed the elevator door on me the first class?"

"Oh, get *over* it already," Corryn said, giggling, and Billy started laughing again.

"This is fun," Adrienne said, and licked some rainbow sprinkles from her oversize cone. "I wish . . . I wish Penelope and I could be as close as you two are."

After a momentary pause, Billy said, "I didn't think you felt that way about Pen."

"What do you mean? She's my sister," Adrienne stated simply. It wasn't that simple. But maybe it could be.

"I know, Mom, but you just never seem . . . proud of her."

"Belinda. How can you say that? Of course I'm proud of her. She knows that. I'm sure she knows that." Except that Adrienne's voice faltered a bit; she wasn't all that sure.

"Then why do you always make rude comments about how she lives her life?" Corryn asked bluntly.

"I just don't want her to forget what's important. It's because I love her—you know, like the way I tell you two things. Out of love."

"Yeah, about that—" Corryn began.

Billy interrupted: "But how can you expect to be close to Aunt Pen when you act like a nagging, judgmental know-it-all? You know—like a mom?" Temporarily speechless, Adrienne pressed her lips together as Billy continued, "And when you're always saying that you don't want us to end up alone like her?"

"Well, wait a second. No, I *don't* want you to be alone," Adrienne said. "I want you to find someone, like I found your father, so you can have a family. I'm sorry if that makes me a bad mother."

"It doesn't, Mom, but why do you have to criticize Pen?"

Adrienne sighed with a hint of resignation. "I guess I see how much you both look up to her, and I'm afraid that you'll want to be like her. I mean, I know *she's* happy, but that doesn't mean that if I could pick the ideal lives for my daughters I'd choose the one she has."

It made sense, and Billy believed her mother, but there was

something else going on. Maybe it was something that could be defined only by the muddled dichotomy of siblings—love and jealousy, closeness and anger, fierce devotion and acute competition. Happily, Billy and Corryn's relationship was unmarred by that kind of dynamic—probably because of their seven-year age difference and what seemed to be an innate friendship.

If Adrienne wanted to be as close with Aunt Pen, she had to be a better friend. She had to stop comparing their lives. And she had to stop projecting. In fact, for the first time it occurred to Billy that her mom might actually feel a stab of envy for her older sister, who'd built a career out of her creativity, who'd accomplished something Adrienne never had, and who'd earned the respect and admiration of Adrienne's daughters. Not that Adrienne would ever trade what *she'd* accomplished, her family.

But still. Was it possible that Adrienne judged Pen because somewhere in the back of her mind, she was afraid that Pen was doing the same thing to her?

"Mom, I've been thinking. Remember how you used to sell those welcome mats and stuff?"

"Yes. What about it?" Adrienne asked, looking confused by the abrupt switch in topic.

"Well, you seemed to love that. Wouldn't you have fun if you tried something like that again?"

"Oh . . . I don't know."

"That's true," Corryn agreed. "I remember you were really into that for a while."

Adrienne shrugged. "Your father and I don't really need the money at this point."

"Not for the money," Billy said, balling up her gooey napkin and setting it to the side, along with Adrienne's and Corryn's. "Just for your own fun. Oh, I know! What about tablecloths? Remember when you made a bunch of different tablecloths that one year?"

"I just gave them as gifts," Adrienne said dismissively, but her eyebrows were cinched together. She was thinking about it; the wheels were starting to turn.

"People loved those, Mom. Don't you remember?"

"Oh, I remember I designed patterned napkins to go with the tablecloths, too," Adrienne added, her voice touched with pride.

"I know, they were gorgeous!" Billy enthused. "You should do something like that again, Mom! Not just tablecloths and napkins, but curtains, slipcovers, anything with fabrics."

"It's true," Corryn said, nodding. "You are kind of a fabric hound, Mom."

"True," Adrienne said, as her mouth curved into a smile.

"And maybe you could talk to Pen about it," Billy added, hoping she hadn't pushed it too far.

"What do you mean?" Adrienne said, tilting her head, uncertain but not unwilling to listen. Already this was progress.

"Well, maybe the two of you could work together sometimes. Maybe she'd be able to use the stuff you make in the rooms she designs. If nothing else, she could help you get started finding a market for yourself."

At this point Billy didn't know what to expect from her mother. Either she'd show a little growth by at least humoring her and saying she'd consider it, or she'd retreat behind her safe, self-righteous wall. "I don't think so," she said finally. Billy frowned. So that was that.

Then, as the three of them slid out of the booth, Adrienne said, "But I guess it wouldn't hurt to pick up some fabrics tomorrow." Billy smiled now. "Tomorrow" was really a fabulous word when it was used for good and not for evil.

Chapter Twenty-five

When Billy got to her brownstone later that night, Seth was waiting on the front steps, drinking a coffee from the Starbucks down the street.

"Hey," she said, smiling as she came upon him.

"Hey, you," he replied, coming to his feet. His dark blond hair was a little rumpled, maybe needed a haircut, and he could use a shave. In other words, he looked achingly sexy.

"What are you doing here?" she asked, a little afraid of the answer. Even though they were friends now, they'd slept together just the night before, and Billy's emotions were still all jumbled. Still, she knew one thing for sure: The more she fell in bed with Seth, the more she'd fall in love.

"I'm here to sleep over," Seth said, holding the front door of the building open for her after she unlocked it.

"You didn't have to come all the way here for that," Billy said, but she really did like the idea of him protecting her.

"Just to be on the safe side," he said. "I called you on your cell phone before to make sure you were all right, but there was no answer."

"Oh, I had my phone turned off in class." Please, she didn't dare draw any more attention to herself during Judy Smith's culinary boot camp.

As she made her way up the stairs, Billy's stomach knotted with worry that something would be on her door. Seth had given Joe the note from the night before, and Joe said he'd dust it for prints, see what he could find. So far nothing.

Now they got to the landing—thank God, nothing threatening there. Sighing, they exchanged looks; they'd both been thinking the same thing. When they entered her apartment, Pike Bishop didn't come to the door.

"Pike?" Billy called circling around her apartment and into the kitchen, "Pike?" Fear gripped her chest, and her stomach clenched into a tense knot. Oh, God, where was he? Did something happen to her dog?

Oh, please, no! I just couldn't take that!

Just then there was a galloping racket on the back stairs, getting louder and louder—and in seconds Pike came barreling through the doggie door. Billy's heart lurched.

Thank you, God.

"Oh, baby," Billy crooned, dropping down on her knees, hugging him, kissing his face, and petting his fur, which was cool to the touch. She was so relieved to see him, and she realized that everything that'd happened had shaken her up more than she had let herself admit.

"Hey, boy," Seth said, coming up to him and rubbing his chin. Pike, who was usually guarded, was immediately warmly receptive to Seth. (But then, what creature of nature *wasn't*?)

When he straightened up, Billy hugged him. She didn't even think about it; it felt like the most natural thing to do because she was so relieved and Seth meant so much to her.

"Don't worry," Seth said softly, his voice dropping to a husky timbre that raked over her skin like trailing fingers. "Don't worry about anything." When she pulled back from the hug her cheek grazed his, and she looked into his eyes. Tension crackled between them, and Billy had to bite her lip to keep from biting Seth's.

"Well . . ." Billy said, stepping back to take a breath. Shucking off her battered green coat, she tossed it somewhere on her way to the living room. "You know you have to sleep on the couch, right?"

"The couch?" Seth said, following her. "Are you sure there's enough room for both of us? Well, I guess if we're naked, we can squish in. . . ."

"Nice try."

"Thank you," he said, grinning.

"Seriously," she said, tilting her head up. "Are you still gonna stay with me?"

"Of course," Seth said, as if it were a crazy question. "I'm not leaving you alone; we've established that."

Taking a deep breath, Billy said, "Okay, well, then, I'll fix up the sofa for you." She turned to go, but he grabbed her arm and pulled her back to him.

"No. You won't."

"Seth, please don't make this any harder than it has to be. We've talked about this. I don't think it's a good idea for us to be involved that way anymore."

"Congratulations. What I meant is that you're not fixing up the sofa for me, because the bedding's all still there from last night."

"Oh."

"How about we order a pizza?" Seth asked. "I'm starving."

"Yeah, that sounds great," Billy said.

While she rooted around for a menu, Seth played with Pike, tossing a pair of Billy's socks around for him to catch, sending him crazily around the apartment. "How about peppers and onions?" Billy said, returning to the living room. She wasn't the least bit worried about onion breath, because she wasn't—repeat, was not—going to kiss Seth tonight.

"Great," Seth replied as he pulled on the socks, which were hanging out of Pike's mouth, and Pike kept shaking his head, gripping them with his teeth. "How was cooking class, by the way?" he asked her when she set the phone down after ordering the food.

"Okay. My soufflé fell and the teacher hates me, but fine otherwise."

"Did you find out anything more about Ted's first marriage?"

"Unfortunately no."

Rubbing under Pike Bishop's chin, Seth smiled down at him, then tossed the socks into Billy's bedroom. Excitedly Pike bounded after them, and within seconds there was a loud crash, like maybe all her books had been knocked off her low bookshelf. "That didn't sound good," Billy remarked, shooting Seth a look.

"Sorry."

Twenty minutes later the buzzer sounded; the pizza was there.

After they ate, Billy said good night to Seth, who climbed onto the narrow sofa and tried, futilely, to get comfortable. Damn, he didn't want to be out here; he wanted to be in the bedroom—he wanted to be in *her*. But she'd made it clear that wasn't happening, and thinking about it was only going to drive him up a fucking wall tonight.

He needed to force himself to sleep, and to try to forget that his dick had stiffened half an hour ago and now was hard as a spike. He just had to get thoughts of Billy alone in that big, soft bed out of his mind, and make himself forget how she looked when she was lying open and wet and wanting—when she was breathing hard and groaning, with her mouth dropped open as she climaxed.

Sliding a hand over his painfully hard, swollen cock, he noted that *that* train of thought wasn't helping, either.

"Well, good night," Billy said after she emerged from the bathroom, having brushed her teeth and put on her pink-and-purple robe.

"Night," Seth said, covertly rubbing his erection under the covers. His voice sounded raspy with lust, but he hoped she wouldn't notice. If she did, she didn't let on.

Poised at her bedroom door, she said, "Seth, thanks again for doing all this with me. And just remember . . . if you come in my room, Pike will attack you."

"Good to know."

After Billy shut her door, she leaned all her weight against it and exhaled a deep, shaky breath. Was she making the right decision by resisting temptation? She had to be; she was falling for him again and needed to rein in her emotions before she got crushed again.

In the meantime, Mark was more eager than ever to show her he cared, and that was flattering and sweet.

Flattering and sweet? Jeez, what about exciting? Elating? Too hot to handle?

Sighing, Billy climbed into her bed and slid under her thick red comforter. As she drifted off to sleep, she reminded herself she was being smart, being practical, that Mark Warner was every girl's dream. She told herself she could handle being friends with Seth, that nothing could scare her and nothing could break her.

And the thing was, she almost believed it.

That night Billy had a strange dream: Seth was making pancakes in Marie's Café, wearing only his jeans and a bandanna wrapped around his head. Billy wore her catering uniform. No matter how hard she pulled, her pink bow tie kept cinching tighter around her neck, and when she sat down at the table her black pants split. Georgette was there, too; she kept grabbing at Seth's crotch while Sally Sugarton and Pam the Tree looked on.

Then Billy's eyes flapped open.

She lay in bed for a few dazed seconds, processing the images still fluttering in her mind, just starting to grasp that they weren't real—and like a pile of bricks, it hit her.

* * *

"Seth, wake up! Seth!" She was sitting on the very edge of the couch, nudging Seth's shoulder, but apparently too gently, because he kept his back turned and his head buried deep in his pillow. "*Seth.*" Finally she climbed on top of him, straddled his body, and hoped she didn't break anything important.

When he rolled over, his eyes opened drowsily, and his voice was a gravelly whisper. "Billy? What's wrong?"

"Seth, I've been stupid," she said.

"Oh, sweetheart . . ." He groaned and slid his arms around her waist. She could feel his hard, pulsing erection pushing up from under the comforter.

Obviously he'd mistaken her meaning. "No, no, not about that," she said, resisting the urge to pretend it was *precisely* that. "I mean about Georgette." The dream about Georgette all over Seth had given Billy an idea.

"Oh," he mumbled, disappointed. Sighing sleepily, he rose up onto his elbow, and then into the sitting position. His hair was sticking up in fifty ways, and even by the stream of moonlight he was breathtaking. "What is it?" he asked. "Did you think of something?"

"I've figured out a way to find out more about Georgette's past." Seth waited, and Billy bit her lip before adding, "But I don't think you're gonna like it."

The next day Billy and Seth were about to have a quick breakfast when the buzzer sounded. "Who could that be?" she muttered, and pressed the talk button. "Yes?"

"Hi, it's Mark!"

Oh . . . damn. Could there be a worse time for Mark's unbridled enthusiasm?

"H-hi, come on up," Billy said, not daring to glance over at

Seth. Would he be jealous? Or merely apathetic? She didn't know if she could deal with either right now. Besides, it really wasn't like Mark to show up at her door unannounced; usually his work schedule precluded any spontaneity on his part.

Finally she looked at Seth, whose face was now inscrutably blank. "I guess Mark's in the neighborhood," she offered lamely. She knew she didn't exactly owe Seth an explanation, but at the same time there was no denying that this was awkward.

Momentarily there was a rhythmically perky knock on the door. Billy ducked out of the kitchen and opened the door, still in her tank top and pajama pants. "Hi, there . . . I'm kind of surprised to see you," she said, smiling pleasantly, and trying to actually sound surprised rather than disappointed.

"I brought doughnuts!" Mark said, holding up the bag as he entered her apartment. Bending down, he placed a damp but firm kiss on her mouth. "Have you eaten?"

"No." But when had that ever stopped her, anyway? Seth came out of the kitchen, and Mark's expression faltered. "This my friend Seth. He's in town, so he crashed on my couch," Billy said quickly, and motioned toward the living room.

Mark shot a glance over at the couch, still covered with a comforter and pillow, and his expression eased. "Hi, how are you, buddy?" he said, approaching Seth with his hand out. "It's really great to meet you. Where are you from?" The two men were at eye level, but while Mark's eyes were open and inviting like a puppy's, Seth's were dark and guarded, like a wolf's.

They shook hands, and Seth managed a brief smile, but it was nowhere near as beaming as Mark's. (Of course, neither was Ronald McDonald's, but that was a whole other issue.)

"Nice to meet you," Seth said, then turned to Billy. "Listen, I've gotta run."

"Oh, that's a shame," Mark said sincerely, "but it was nice meeting you. Billy and I should take you out to see the sights sometime this week. That would be really great!"

"Right. Later," Seth said, and left. When the door slammed closed behind him, Billy's heart sank like a stone. God, he'd seemed so . . . hurt.

While Mark ate doughnuts at the kitchen table, Billy brewed some coffee and tried not to think about the sullen expression she'd seen on Seth's face. Or the edge she'd heard in his voice right before he'd left. Sighing, she tried to figure out why it was so damn hard to be friends with him. Okay, she had to stop. Here she had a great guy like Mark, and she was more concerned about making Seth feel better than making Mark feel at home. He'd been there for nearly twenty minutes, and she'd barely paid any attention to him!

Before she got a chance to rectify that, however, her phone rang. She crossed the kitchen to answer it. "Hello?"

"Doll?"

"Oh, hi," she said, feeling apprehension creep into her chest. "Please tell me this phone call isn't going to involve Tuck Hospital," she remarked, surprised by her own bluntness.

"No, no, I've found something else," Kip said, and went on to describe an open position in the marketing department of a small finance company. *Hmm . . . not bad.* In fact, it sounded promising. And it wasn't like she could make ends meet forever working at the bakery. Getting a corporate job was the responsible thing to do (God, she sounded like her mother). The only hitch, Kip told her, was that she had to go for an interview that morning.

Billy agreed, suppressing a wave of ambivalence, and after Mark left she went to scrounge up her interview suit.

* * *

"So Kip tells me you have a lot of office experience?"

"Yes," Billy replied to her interviewer, who was disturbingly named Mrs. Cross.

"That you can type?"

"Yes, I can type."

"How fast?"

"Eighty words per minute," Billy said, adding an extra five words to the truth.

"Mmm, that's pretty good," Mrs. Cross replied with a brief nod. "And what about your communication skills? How do you feel about calling important people, greeting high-profile, powerful clients, presenting a professional and inviting image that represents the company?"

What was the right answer to that? That she felt fucking *thrilled* about it? As it was, she'd thought she was interviewing for a position in marketing, and only after she'd gotten there had she discovered that Bevlin Financial worked as an adjunct to Tuck Hospital— securing patronage and soliciting donations. At this point it was embarrassingly clear that without Tuck Hospital, Kip Belding would starve.

"The image you present reflects on me, of course," Mrs. Cross went on, glancing dubiously at Billy's hair.

Meanwhile Billy's head was swimming. The cacophony of printers whirring, fax machines beeping, and ten phones trilling at once was chaotic—maddening. She missed the serene work environment of the Churchill Art Gallery; she missed being in her own world, creating something, oblivious to everything else except the colors and images swirling in her mind.

"Now, as with all front-desk personnel, we'd provide you with a uniform of sorts so as to present a cohesive image for the company," Mrs. Cross went on. "It's a lovely melon-colored blazer with matching slacks." In other words, an orange suit. "In fact, I'd need you to try it on now, so I can see if I'll need to order a new one—assuming I decide to hire you, of course."

Okay, that was it. She wasn't going to take this job, and she wasn't about to try on a used orange suit to spare Mrs. Cross's feelings. "You know what?" Billy said, struggling to be heard over fifty ringing phones clamoring and ricocheting off each other. "I don't think this job's for me." She stood up and reached out to shake Mrs. Cross's hand, who just sat back, eyes wide, stunned, as if she'd been slapped across the face.

Actually that image brought a smile to Billy's lips. She set her hand down and said, "Thank you for your time," and turned and walked out.

Once outside on the sidewalk, she felt an incredibly liberating sense of relief. Kip had done something very important for her today. He'd helped confirm all the little ideas and doubts swimming in the back of her brain; he'd helped her see that life was too short to be trapped in a job because she was afraid to take a chance.

He'd helped her realize that what she really wanted to do—no, what she *intended* to do—was to make a living as an artist. She had no clue how she would make that happen, but she was determined to figure it out.

"Thanks for the ride," Billy said as she and her dad walked toward the art gallery. David had given her a lift, deciding to do some fishing while he was in Churchill.

"Well, let's see what you've been working on," he said jovially.

"Okay, keep in mind it's only two-thirds done," Billy said.

"All right, I know; now let's see it."

Billy went to the far left corner, picked up the rock that secured the heavy green tarp over the mural, and gingerly pulled it back.

Across the stone was a luminous water scene with a pinky-crimson sunset and translucent, phantom images that looked almost superimposed, giving the mural a touch of the surreal.

"Billy, this is beautiful," he said, smiling warmly. Giving her a one-armed hug, he added, "I am so proud of you."

Her chest swelled with pride and satisfaction at the simple words, which meant so much, especially in light of her new resolve to work full-time at her painting.

"It's beautiful," her dad said again.

"And who's this?" Greg Dappaport called from the open entrance of the gallery. Today he had on a blue-and-white, diamond-patterned neckerchief, a houndstooth jacket, and red linen pants. His shiny loafers clicked as he descended the front steps.

"Oh, hi," Billy said brightly. "Mr. Dappaport, this is my dad, David Cabot."

"Pleasure to make your acquaintance," he said, shaking David's hand. "Billy, I suppose this is a perfect occasion then to tell you some exciting news."

"What?" she asked curiously.

"Well, as you know, I've been so pleased and enthralled by your work so far that I've dropped your name to some of the gentlemen in my yacht club. In fact, I've told my polo club, wine club, and skeet club, too." He looked from her to David, letting a ripple of laughter erupt. "You'll never believe how many of them want to commission you for portraits!"

"Really?" Billy said, breaking into a laugh herself, because it was just too fabulous.

"Now, I know landscape painting is your milieu of choice, but if you can create a mural like this"—he motioned to the street where her mural was—"I'm sure you can paint a few supercilious old codgers with one hand behind your back."

Billy laughed again, excitement swirling inside her, filling her up, making her almost giddy, and she turned to her dad. "Isn't this wonderful?" she said, smiling.

David smiled back. "I'm just so proud of you."

On her way to Seth's house that afternoon, Billy's cell phone rang. It was Corryn. "Hey," Billy said.

"Hi, I was calling to make sure you're still alive."

"How sweet."

"Seriously, have you given up this whole murder investigation thing yet?" Corryn said.

"Nope."

"Great."

"How did you know I was still investigating?" Billy asked.

"Because you were asking Mom those questions in cooking class. Anyway, at least Joe's been doing drive-bys on your street. So far nothing suspicious—that's good."

Tilting her head, Billy grinned into the phone. "And you know what Joe's doing how?"

"Oh, well . . ." Corryn faltered for a second. "We've been talking."

"And?"

"Okay, and we kissed."

"What! Corryn, that's awesome! When did this happen? And more important, how was it?"

"The other night, after we left Uno's. And . . . nice." She paused, then said, "But to tell you the truth, it was over before it got going, which was my fault."

"Well, have you guys talked since?"

"No."

"Oh."

"What about you? What's the deal with Seth—you guys are friends now?"

"Um, yeah." Technically they were friends—*now*. Of course, a couple days ago they were rutting animals, humping each other like sex-starved maniacs. God, it was almost inconceivable that Billy had been so wrapped up in the investigation she hadn't had a chance to catch Corryn up to speed.

As she turned the corner onto Seth's street, Billy gave her sister the abridged version, then said, "Listen, I've gotta go, but let's have a raspberry crush night soon. It's been so long."

After Corryn agreed, they said good-bye, and Billy walked up the cobblestone sidewalk to Seth's front door. She chucked her cell into her bag and knocked. No answer. She knocked again, and then she remembered the last time she'd come knocking, and went to the back. Sure enough, there were voices coming from the deck. She saw Seth sitting across from Sally, who sat adjacent to her niece, Pam.

She wanted to do an about-face, because she had no reason to be there in the first place; she'd just wanted to see him.

When Seth saw her his face broke into a smile. "Billy. Hey, come over."

Sally and Pam turned their heads, and Sally said, "Oh, hello, I remember we all met at the Dessert Jubilee."

"Yeah, hi," Billy said brightly, even though jealousy crept inside her heart. She couldn't help it; she had the distinct impression that she'd interrupted some serious matchmaking. That the tall, skinny girl with the pageboy haircut was available and interested, which didn't mean Seth was interested back, but still . . . just the thought of him kissing or touching anyone else made Billy's heart ache.

"I didn't mean to interrupt," Billy said as she climbed onto the deck.

"You're not," Sally said. "Pam and I just brought over a gourmet lunch for Seth. Pam is responsible, actually, not me. I'm helpless in the kitchen, but Pam is a genius. Of course, there's only enough for three. Had I thought ahead, I would've brought more, but we just stopped over to talk about Pam's trip out west."

Billy swallowed uncomfortably, holding back irrational tears. So *Pam* was welcomed with open arms out west, but it never crossed Seth's mind to invite Billy. He pulled out the chair next to him for her, but Billy waved him off with her hand. "Oh, no, I can't stay. I was just working at the gallery, and I . . . Well, Seth, could I talk to you privately for just a second? I wanted to tell you something."

"Oh, sure," he said, and led her through the sliding glass door into the kitchen. "What's up?" he asked as soon as they were alone.

"Sorry to interrupt," she said again, now with annoyance clipping her tone.

"You're not. Sally just showed up."

"Anyway, I just wanted to tell you that everything's all set. Georgette's gonna come to Atlas after work tonight. You're still coming, aren't you?"

"Of course I'm coming. By the way, how did you convince Georgette to come?"

"Well, it wasn't that tough, because she loves to go dancing, but I had to ask Des, too, so it wouldn't look suspicious. So while you're probing Georgette for information, I'll keep Des busy."

"Okay," Seth said with a nod. "Now, you're sure you feel safe being with Georgette? I mean, in light of the fact that she is probably the one stalking you?"

"Yeah, because she has no idea I'm on to her. Anyway, there's a good chance that she doesn't really want to hurt me, just to scare me off the case."

Last night Billy had come up with their plan of attack and Seth had grudgingly agreed: It was no secret that Georgette found Seth attractive, so she was more likely to spill something incriminating to him, especially if she had a few drinks in her. Not that they expected her to confess to Ted's murder, but maybe she'd reveal a detail or two about her past that would at least give them something to take to the police.

"Seth!" Sally called from the deck. They could hear her through the glass and see her waving him back to the table. "Your lunch is getting cold!"

With a nod he held up his hand, then turned back to Billy. "What time do you want me to meet you at Atlas?"

She could barely make eye contact with him, because she was so filled with moodiness right now. Her chest tightened with jealousy and longing, and she hated that this girl was moving in on her man (who wasn't her man). Obviously Billy's possessiveness wasn't justified, but tell that to her churning gut and her thudding heart.

No, she had to get a grip here. Pam had every right to pursue Seth. Billy needed to grow up, to be the bigger person, and she didn't just mean her dress size. "Meet me at seven," she said as she turned on her heel. "I'll just leave you three to . . . you know . . . whatever," she added, and slid open the glass door.

Seth caught her arm before she could go. "Hey—is anything wrong?"

"No," Billy replied, her blood boiling, albeit unreasonably. "Nothing at all."

Chapter Twenty-six

"So, Seth, you married?"

Georgette leaned in closer and let her big breasts fall flat on the tabletop. She and Des were seated across from Billy and Seth in a dark booth at Atlas.

"No, I'm not married," he replied. Unfortunately he didn't elaborate (something along the lines of, "After Billy, I became celibate," would've been nice). "My company keeps me pretty busy."

"Ooh, you own your own company?" Georgette asked. "Pretty fancy."

"Not really. It's a consulting firm in Seattle. Basically we help start up small businesses." Shrugging, he added humbly, "It's a living."

"Ya know, I've always wanted to see Seattle," Georgette said. "Hey, if I ever come to town, could I stay at your place?"

Billy almost choked on her Diet Coke, while Seth floundered for an answer. "Uh . . . well, to tell you the truth, I travel a lot . . . so—"

Luckily, the waitress interrupted at that moment to bring Des a beer and Georgette a refill of tequila. Georgette threw her head back as she took the shot, while Billy struggled to understand her unreadable coworker. They'd been at Atlas for half an hour already, and so far Billy hadn't picked up any signs that Georgette had any other agenda besides getting into Seth's pants. She'd thought now that she was looking for signs, they'd be easier to find.

On the other hand, the night was still young, and Georgette

was very preoccupied with Seth at the moment. Of course, Billy was counting on that, hoping Georgette would be distracted enough by her hormones to slip up and reveal something.

"So," Seth began, "how do you guys like your job at Bella Donna?"

Des shrugged and avoided eye contact. "It's great if you like bureaucratic bullshit," he replied flatly.

"It's fine," Georgette drawled. "Same shit, different day."

"I hear you," Seth said, smiling at her, and Billy could tell he was about to start fishing. "So, Georgette . . . what does your husband do?"

"Besides bone his new wife?" she said drunkenly. "How should I know?"

"Oh," Seth said, acting surprised, "you're divorced, then?"

"No—never married the guy. Just lived with him. Basically was his *slave*."

"Oh, I'm sorry," Seth said diplomatically.

"I sure know how to pick 'em," Georgette said with a hint of a sneer, then tilted her head and winked through her big pink glasses. "Present company excepted."

Seth smiled again, and Billy twisted her napkin in her lap. She knew she should make small talk with Des so that Georgette would feel more comfortable spilling something to Seth—so Billy would look oblivious to their conversation—but she couldn't seem to tear herself away, and anyway, Des was being unusually withdrawn tonight.

"Well, at least you didn't have to go through an upsetting divorce," Seth said casually.

"Yeah, tried that once already, didn't care for it," Georgette remarked, then crept her hand further into the center of the table. With each moment that ticked by, Billy noticed pudgy, acrylic-tipped fingers walking slowly but greedily toward Seth.

"Really? So then you *were* married once?" Seth asked—probed, really, but he was so damn charming while he was doing it.

"Yeah, but that was a long, long time ago. The bastard left me—no note, nothing. Just dropped off the face of the earth; strangest thing." She took a swig from her beer chaser, then set the glass down hard on the table. "Come on; let's dance."

A mix of surprise and apprehension crossed Seth's face, and Billy could tell he was hoping Georgette hadn't been talking to him. Of course, when she tugged on his arm, all pretense was lost. "Uh—I'm really not a very good dancer," he protested as Georgette urged him out of the booth.

"Don't worry; I'll lead," she said, pulling him with her toward the dance floor. On the way Seth looked back at Billy searchingly—desperately—and Billy couldn't help grinning.

"I don't know where our waitress went," she said to Des now, who was hunched in the booth looking sulky. "I'm just gonna go to the bar and get another Diet Coke."

After ordering another soda, Billy leaned her elbows on the bar and glanced over at the dance floor. Even though tonight's business was serious, she just had to laugh. Georgette jiggled her hips and raised the roof, while Seth moved tentatively, obviously trying to keep out of the fray. She must've lost her glasses somewhere, because they weren't on her face . . . or maybe that would be her convenient excuse to grope Seth on the dance floor.

As Billy turned back to the bar, she felt a hand on her waist and almost jumped at the contact. "Oh, Des!" she said, finding him at her side. "You startled me." Just then she realized his hand was still lingering on her waist; subtly she shifted over until it fell back to his side. "What's up?" she asked brightly. "You don't seem like you're having fun tonight."

"Yeah, well vapid dens of cultural bankruptcy aren't exactly my scene," he said with acid sarcasm. Gee, he didn't *have* to come.

Yesterday, when Billy had invited him, he'd seemed thrilled with the idea, but tonight he had inexplicable attitude.

"Is something wrong?" she asked.

"No. By the way, what's up with you and that guy Seth?" he asked, flicking his chin in the direction of the dance floor.

"Oh . . . he's, you know, a good friend of mine."

Squinting, Des asked, "What about that guy Mark Warner? Our old distribution rep—you still dating him?"

"Um, yeah. Well, we had some problems, but we're working things out."

"What problems?" he pressed, which put Billy's back up a little, because this felt more like an interrogation than a casual conversation.

"It's sort of complicated," she replied, ready to change the subject to much more mundane issues, like Des's band and their possible name change from the Sophists to the Nouveau Beatniks.

"You know, it's funny," Des said with a humorless laugh. "I never thought you'd be that type of person."

"What type of person?" she said, confused.

"A total sellout."

"What?" *Excuse me?*

"Forget it."

"No, really, what are you talking about?"

"I just can't believe the guys you date," he said, sounding annoyed. "They're totally part of the corporate-industrial complex. Don't you even care?"

"Wait, I don't think that's fair," Billy said, keeping her voice calm and even. After all, Des was normally a decent guy, but maybe he'd had too much to drink tonight.

"Whatever," he sneered, and self-righteously flipped his hair.

"Seth and Mark are both really nice guys," Billy insisted, not sure why she was bothering to convince Des of this.

"Yeah, you just keep telling yourself that."

"*What?*"

"Nice guys? Please, they're corporate sellouts! They blindly con-done a system of economic opulence and capitalistic soullessness!" Whoa, this was getting insane now. "I thought you were different," Des went on angrily. "I thought you had, like, an artistic essence or whatever. But you're just like everyone else—just a perpetrator of psychosocial inequity."

"Des, *stop,*" Billy said, cutting him off. "You're really out of line. What are you, drunk?"

"No, I'm *hurt,* okay?" he said, doing a fist pump to the chest on "hurt." "Yesterday I left my latest manifesto for you to read, and to-day I find it crumpled up and thrown in the men's-room toilet!"

"What on earth are you talking about?" Billy said, shaking her head, totally confused. "Des, I didn't know you left anything for me—I never even saw it."

"Right! I put it next to your paycheck in your employee mail slot. Then at the end of my shift today, I find it in the toilet!"

"Oh, my God, Des, I'm so sorry. I swear it wasn't me. I never even saw it," she said again. He pouted, scowled, and shuffled his feet; then Billy tapped his arm. "Really, I swear it wasn't me. C'mon, you know I'd never do something like that."

Finally Des lifted his head, blew his hair back, and said, "Okay, all right. I mean, if you say it wasn't you, it's cool. I believe you."

She sighed, glad that she'd calmed him down. Jeez, she'd never seen Des so angry! Of course, the question remained: Who *had* trashed Des's manifesto? The men's room was an odd choice, too, because Des was the only guy who worked at Bella Donna. It was as if someone deliberately intended for him to find it.

"Look, I'm sorry I went off on you," Des said.

"No, it's okay," Billy said, even though it wasn't, and she felt a little overwhelmed and creeped out by Des right now. "So . . . how's

Melissa?" she asked, desperate to change the subject. Besides, there was nothing like venturing into the bizarre Aggerdeen family saga to deflect a conversation.

Des shrugged. "Same as always, totally blind to commercialized brainwashing and the emptiness of her own existence."

"Hmm . . ." Billy said, only half listening as she glanced back to check on Seth. He looked wholly uncomfortable, while Georgette housed him from behind with her white hair in wild disarray à la Albert Einstein. Suddenly she jumped in front of him. With arms spread wide, she shimmied and threw her head back with abandon.

Billy's mouth dropped open just as Georgette tried to hump Seth's pelvis.

"And now Melissa just spends all her time on the Internet," Des was saying. "Whenever I come around, she covers the screen real quick, so I can't see what she's doing. I figured it was all part of her obsession with finding her real father, but the other day she told me that she'd already found him a couple of weeks ago."

"Oh, really?" Billy said, tuning in to the conversation.

"Whatever. It's not like I can believe anything she says anyway," Des remarked with a shrug. "Like at the Dessert Jubilee—she left two hours early, said she was going home because she had a migraine. But when I got home, I found the car in the garage—still wet."

"I don't get it," Billy said, confused.

"It wasn't raining when she left," Des explained. "It only started raining on my way home. I remember, because I was sitting in the cab worrying that I might've left my guitar out on the deck." Now that he mentioned it, Billy remembered staring out a taxi window that night when rain suddenly began to pummel the glass. Des shrugged again. "Melissa's full of shit. She was out cruising with the car while we were all stuck working."

Billy reserved comment, because she didn't want to say anything against Melissa, even though she was thinking that if what Des said was true, it was a really bitchy move on her part.

"So, Billy . . . what do you say?" Des said, ducking his head down almost shyly and looking up at her with hooded eyes.

"About what?" she asked.

"You and me," he replied.

Gulp—where did that come from?

"I dig you, Billy," he said (punching his heart on the word "dig"), "and I don't wanna dance around it anymore, you know?"

Oh, Lord, what the hell was Des saying? And why did he have to pick the least convenient time to say it? Georgette and Seth were heading back this way.

"So what about it?" Des said, and ran his finger along the back of Billy's hand. She involuntarily jerked at the contact, and then felt guilty when a hurt look crossed Des's face.

"Um, well . . . Des, I like you a lot; you know that. But as I mentioned, Mark and I still have something going, and . . ." She looked off to the side for the words. "You know, we're friends."

She regretted the words, though they were necessary, because the "friends" routine never made anyone feel better. Ryan had called her his friend right before he'd dumped her.

Now Des slammed his beer down on the bar. "Whatever," he said.

"Wait, Des . . . I'm sorry, I—"

"Just forget it," he snapped, turning from her. "I thought you were different, but you're just like all the rest." He walked away, disappearing out of Atlas, leaving Billy in a vague state of shock. As she headed back to the booth, she met up with Georgette and Seth by the table.

"I'm goin' to the can!" Georgette shouted over the music.

Seth dropped into the booth next to Billy. Letting out a sigh, he ran his hand through his hair. "Okay, so I take it Georgette just got out of prison?"

Billy laughed and buried her head in her hands. So far this night bordered on the absurd. "How are you holding up?" she asked, grinning, and touching his arm.

"Jesus, she was all *over* me," he said, and not as though he was bragging about it, but as if he were disoriented and mildly concerned. "Anyway, I didn't find out too much—the music was too loud. I kept trying to ask her about the jubilee, and she kept having to lean in closer to hear me. At one point my lips almost touched her ear—a little too intimate for me."

"I'm sorry," Billy said, "but let's give it a little longer. Try again when she comes back." She ignored Seth's grimace. "Also, I was thinking about the tomatoes smeared on my window. It makes sense. Georgette must've heard me telling Melissa about my feud with my neighbor, and that's how she got that idea."

Just then Georgette came bounding back. "Move over, hot stuff," she said, winking at Seth. When she slid into the booth, she blatantly hip-checked him. He winced with slight annoyance, but she didn't seem to notice. Then Georgette drunkenly took out her wallet and dumped its contents on the table. As she was sorting through dollar bills, presumably to pay for her three tequilas, Billy noticed some wallet-size photos strewn across the table. She nudged Seth, who picked them up.

"Oh, who's this?" he asked, sounding interested—solicitous.

"That's Gary, the asshole," Georgette replied, grimacing like she were just barely holding down the puke.

"And what about this guy?" Seth asked, now holding up a photo of a black man, around thirty.

"That was Leroy," Georgette said, her mouth drooping into a lopsided frown. "My ex-husband."

What?

"This is your ex-husband?" Billy asked, shocked. Just then she spotted a worn-looking social security card on the table. Almost savagely Billy snatched it up and read the name printed across it: *Georgette Walters.*

Grabbing Leroy's photo out of Seth's hand, Georgette tried to spit on it, but her spittle missed its target. "Damn bastard, I loved you," she said, and then she started bawling. And Billy sat there, absorbing the fact that her whole brilliant, airtight theory had just crumbled.

"Now what?" Seth asked as he and Billy sat in his car with the heat running. "Does that scrap the whole Bella Donna theory?"

Billy had been mulling exactly that since they'd dismissed Georgette as a suspect, and then she suddenly remembered something Des had said. A thought occurred to her; it was a crazy thought. Turning to Seth, she pushed her scarf down to uncover her mouth and said, "What about Melissa?"

"You don't think . . . *Melissa?* But you know her; you went to school with her. She's your friend."

"Well, I went to school with her, but to be honest, I don't think I'd really call her my friend." It was the truth. Melissa was good to chat with at work, and for some occasional laughs, but they really didn't spend time together outside of work. Billy supposed it was because, at the heart of it, besides a degree from Boston College, they had very little in common. Melissa was stylish, a little snobby, and sometimes passive-aggressive—while Billy wore a battered old coat and wasn't particularly passive *or* aggressive. Unless she really wanted something, and then, she supposed, she was aggressive-aggressive. Like now.

"Let's go," she said, suddenly realizing what they had to do.

"Where are we going?" Seth asked, revving up the engine, poising his hand on the gearshift.

"Law school," she replied. He shot her a skeptical look but she urged him on, and he pulled out of the parking lot and headed back onto Lansdowne Street. "I want to talk to Melissa. I just remembered she has a seminar tonight." Billy glanced at the clock in Seth's car. "Oh, my God, it gets out at ten, and it's already nine forty-five!"

They sped down Comm. Ave., and Seth asked, "So you really think Melissa killed Ted?"

"I don't know, but I'd forgotten that Melissa had left the jubilee early. Said she had a headache. But what if she didn't leave Churchill at all?"

"Where are you getting that?" he asked curiously. She explained about Melissa's car being wet from the rain, and the possibility that Melissa had only pretended to leave the jubilee early so she would have an alibi in case anyone suspected foul play in Ted Schneider's death. "But what was her motive?" Seth said.

Billy related what Des had said about Melissa's finally locating her long-lost father. "Her real dad was a drifter—just like Ted Schneider was. If Ted *was* Melissa's father, maybe she killed him to get back at him for abandoning her and never being a part of her life."

She looked at the clock again. *Damn it!* Nine fifty-five.

"Seth, can't you go any faster?" Billy asked frantically.

"Yeah, I could go a lot faster if there weren't cars on the road," he said.

"Okay, okay," she said, anxiously twisting her hands in her lap as she watched the city lights blitz past her window, feeling that they were on the verge of a major confrontation. If only they could make it to Melissa on time.

Chapter Twenty-seven

"She has to be coming out anytime now," Billy whispered to Seth as they hunkered down behind a thick cloud of bushes outside the law building. There was a stone quad with a fountain in the middle, and students were drifting out the double doors. They were waiting to see Melissa—looking for telltale signs in the darkness: her long, curly hair, her stick-skinny body, her trademark cup of coffee in hand.

"There she is!" Billy said.

"Come on; let's go," Seth said, starting to come out of the bushes.

"No, wait!" she said, tugging on the arm of his coat to pull him back. "You stay here."

"Why?"

"Trust me; she'll never open up if you're there. The best chance I have of getting her to admit anything is if I talk to her myself."

"New twist," Seth said dryly—obviously still somewhat traumatized by Georgette's advances. "But what's your plan?"

"To bluff," was all she said. Brushing some leaves off the front of her sweater, she whispered, "But wait here in case I need you."

"Billy, I don't like this. I want to be there to make sure nothing happens to you."

"Please, just do it my way," she said, squeezing his arm with affection, and he relented with a frustrated sigh. Good enough.

Bursting onto the quad, Billy scurried over to Melissa just as she was tossing her coffee cup into a nearby trash bin.

"Melissa!" she called, coming closer.

Melissa's eyes shot wide open. "Billy? What are you doing here?"

"I'm here to talk to you about some threats I've received."

"What, more from your neighbor?"

"No, more from you," Billy replied. Her tone was deliberately calm—confident—as pulse-pounding adrenaline rattled through her. *Bluff.*

"What are you talking about?" Melissa said waspishly.

"It took me a while to figure it out," Billy said, walking right up to her. "The way I'd tell you about the threats, and you'd always convince me not to go to the police, not to confront my neighbor. Because it was *you*."

Melissa scoffed. "You're crazy. I'm out of here."

"If you go now, I *will* go to the police," Billy called after her.

Melissa turned around, her mass of curly hair flying. "And tell them *what*? You have no proof of anything."

"No? What if I could prove that you didn't really leave early the night of the jubilee? That you were in Churchill the whole time?" Whipping around, Melissa bit her lip, looking anxious, almost tremulous. She was panicking! "You never went home," Billy continued, deliberately sounding overconfident. "You were in Churchill. I know what you did."

"Oh, why don't you just go back to your perfect life and leave me alone!" Melissa snapped, clutching her forehead as though she were literally browbeaten. Meanwhile, Billy wondered, Perfect life? Where had that come from?

"Is that what you were hoping for?" Billy asked. "That by threatening me with phone messages and creepy notes and the tomatoes that I'd just stop asking questions about Ted Schneider's murder?"

Melissa shut her eyes, obviously not fully listening, but willing Billy to disappear. "Why did you have to come work at Bella Donna?" she muttered. "Everything was so much better before you came."

"You mean better before I started asking questions about Ted Schneider?" Billy challenged.

"Huh?" Melissa said, looking genuinely baffled. "Who's that?"

"Nice try. Ted Schneider—as in the man who died at the jubilee. As in the man you killed. As in your *father*!"

"*What?*" Melissa yelled, and manically shook her head. "What the hell are you talking about?"

"I . . . um . . . wait—what are *you* talking about?" Billy said. "I mean, Ted Schneider was your father—"

"No, he wasn't. I didn't even know the guy!"

"But . . . Des said you found your father."

"I did; he was a truck driver from Belmont, left-handed like me. What does that have to do with anything?"

"But if you didn't kill Ted, why did you do all those things? The notes, the calls? The tomatoes, for chrissake?"

Melissa sighed, looking drained and tired. Sinking down onto a bench, she buried her face in her hands.

"Melissa?" Billy pressed. "You did do those things, didn't you?"

Finally she mumbled, "I'm sorry." Billy waited for her to elaborate—forgetting for a moment that Seth was in the bushes watching all of this unfold. "I did those things because I just wanted you to go away," Melissa explained. Well, Billy had to admit, the phone messages and notes that said, quote, "Go away," definitely made the point. "I also threw out Des's manifesto so he'd see it and think that you'd done it—so he'd hate you."

"But why?" Billy asked, confused. If this wasn't about Ted Schneider, then what? Melissa was the one who'd gotten Billy the job at Bella Donna in the first place. Now all of a sudden she hated her?

"I was jealous," Melissa said. "Damn, I need coffee. I knew the tomatoes would be a good idea because I remembered what you'd told me once about your neighbor being pissed about her tomatoes. I thought I'd mess with your head, make you feel paranoid in your own home. Hopefully even get you to make a fool of yourself by accusing your neighbor." *Mission accomplished,* Billy thought, remembering her now-ludicrous confrontation with Lady McAvit.

Billy sat down next to her on the bench. "You said you were jealous. But, Melissa, jealous of *what*?" Futilely, she tried to keep the incredulity out of her voice, the disbelief that someone would be so jealous of *her*.

"Of Mark," Melissa replied, looking up at Billy. "I liked him before you ever worked at the bakery. He used to come in, and I really, really liked him. And then you showed up and he immediately falls for *you*. I couldn't believe it! It wasn't fair," she went on. "I'm skinny, I wear nice clothes, I'm in law school—I'm the one he should've gone for." The implication was clear: Billy was dumpy, frumpy, and headed nowhere. Way to add insult to injury.

But when tears welled in Melissa's eyes, Billy felt an irrational stab of pity. "Melissa, I had no idea you liked Mark," she said. "I never would've gone out with him if I'd known." As immature as it was, it was true. She would've backed off if Melissa had called dibs.

"Mark was bad enough," Melissa went on, starting to sob, "but then when your hot-as-hell ex-boyfriend shows up, and *he's* all into you, too, I just couldn't take it anymore! I don't get it—how do these guys all like you? You're not even *thin*." True, but she still hoped Seth hadn't heard that part. In fact, she'd hoped that Seth and Mark hadn't noticed the soft, gushy conglomeration of curves and jiggles she liked to call her body.

"I couldn't believe it," Melissa said again. "It's like everything just comes so easily to you. You start working at the bakery, and boom, after two months you're Donna's favorite with all your stupid little cake designs," Melissa said snidely. And suddenly Billy remembered. . . .

"My original cakes for the jubilee—you ruined them?" she asked, just guessing.

With a dry laugh, Melissa barked, "A lot of good it did me! You just made even *better* ones. Life is so unfair!" Her sobs became heavier, louder, until her shoulders shook and her face completely crumpled. Then, burying her head in her hands, Melissa began to howl.

Billy looked around to see if anyone was looking, but the quad was deserted. She shrugged at Seth in the bushes, whom she couldn't see, but knew was there. What was this, nervous breakdown night? First Georgette, now Melissa. Two people who seemed the most in control of their own destinies. "Seemed" being the key word. (But then, wasn't it always?)

Billy let the howling go on for a couple moments before patting Melissa's shoulder. "Melissa? Um . . . are you okay?" Brilliant question. Obviously "okay" was the last thing she was. Melissa sniffled a response, but it was unintelligible, so Billy went on, "Look, don't worry about what's happened, all right?" She couldn't believe she was saying that, but she was just trying to pacify Melissa, who was obviously a closet mess. "I mean, as long as you don't do it again, maybe we can just forget the whole thing."

"Aaaahhhh!"

Okay, did that mean she was in favor of forgetting? Had she even heard anything Billy had just said?

"Calm down, calm down," Billy said trying to coax her ex-friend off the proverbial ledge. Jeez, did Melissa really like Mark Warner *that* much? How could Billy not have seen it?

"The last thing I need is for you to be n-nice about it," she choked out through heavy sobs. "One time I even watched you and Mark outside your building. I know it was wrong, but I just felt obsessed with it." Suddenly Billy remembered the night she'd heard sounds coming from the bushes outside her brownstone. Melissa had been lurking—spying on her.

"I'm so lonely," Melissa said now, followed by another burst of *aaaahhhh*.

"Lonely? You? But you've got such a busy, full life." Of course, taking out the stalker part might leave a slight void.

"But I want a b-boyfriend," she said as she wiped her nose on her sleeve. Well, sure, who didn't? Providing the boyfriend was sweet, caring, sexy, and perfect.

"Hey, I'm sure you'll find one; it just takes time," Billy said soothingly, and in the back of her mind she knew it was vaguely ridiculous that after everything that'd happened, she was trying to comfort this girl.

Also, she felt a pang of guilt that Seth was still crouched down in the bushes, but she knew bringing him out of hiding now would only make things worse.

Finally Melissa's internal well ran dry. She quieted her racking sobs, sniffled up all her mucus, and turned to face Billy. "Can you keep a secret?" she asked, eyes wide and reddened.

"Uh, sure . . . of course," Billy said, feeling more uncomfortable by the second. Oh, come on, she didn't want to know Melissa Aggerdeen's secrets. Or anyone else's that didn't pertain to Ted Schneider's murder. She just wanted an uncomplicated existence, a paycheck, her health, and some nonrisky excitement. "But, um, don't feel pressured to tell me," she added.

Melissa seemed terribly anxious to unburden herself, though. Inhaling a deep, shuddering breath, she said, "The truth is, for the past few months I've been kind of addicted to Match-dot-com— you know, the computer dating service?"

"Why would *I* know it?" Billy said, immediately defensive, then came to her senses. "I mean, uh, sure, I've heard of it. So what's wrong with that?"

"I can't seem to stop. That's why I sneaked out of the jubilee. I went to the library to use the Internet. And I'm late to work all the time because I lose all track of time. Every day it's the same thing. I wake up at around four, go online, and before I know it it's twelve in the afternoon and I'm still in my pajamas!"

Billy didn't know whether to drop her jaw in shock or burst out laughing. So *that* was Melissa Aggerdeen's "secret." Interesting. Lame. And she supposed only mildly deviant. Suddenly she remembered what Claudia Dibbs had said about a girl using the computers the night of the jubilee. It had been Melissa.

"Only one time did I actually get the courage to meet one of the men in person," she went on. "That night at the Rack, remember?" So that *had* been Melissa—Melissa on a cyberdate! "I shouldn't have just run off," she said, sniffling again. "But I knew you saw me, and I panicked. I just felt so self-conscious about the whole thing. Why can't my life just come together like yours? Why don't men like me? I can't even meet a guy in cyberspace who really likes me— nobody likes me!"

That incited another bout of blubbering, but Billy figured Melissa needed a good cry. Anyway, she was tapped out of sympathy. If anyone came looking for Melissa, they could just follow the sound of unbridled wailing. (And it was times like these Billy wondered: Was everyone in her life crazy—including her?)

"Listen, Melissa, we'll talk another time," Billy said rising off the bench and inching away. "And by the way, I meant what I said. If you ever do anything even *remotely* harassing to me again, I *will* go to the police, and keep in mind that I've taped this whole conversation." She patted her coat pocket then, to indicate the digital recorder that didn't exist, but could've if she'd thought of it in time.

On her way off the quad, Melissa called to her: "Billy, I really am sorry for what I did. You're so lucky to have a guy like Mark— you guys are *perfect* together."

When Billy went to fetch Seth behind the bushes, he wasn't

where she'd left him. Now he was standing by a tree, a few feet away. "Holy shit, how *weird* was that!" she said, almost bursting with laughter because they'd found her stalker, who'd turned out to be more pathetic than threatening. Elation washed over her, and she reached out to touch his arm. "Seth?"

"Yeah, it was crazy," he said, stiff-jawed and stepping back a little from her touch. "Let's go."

They talked briefly about what had happened with Melissa on the ride to Billy's place, but for the most part Seth was quiet. When he pulled up in front of her brownstone, Billy said, "Seth, is anything wrong?"

"Nope," he said curtly, staring blankly through his windshield. Billy sat there waiting for him to expand on that nonanswer, and finally he added, "I'm just thinking about what Melissa said to you."

"Which part?"

"How you're lucky to have that guy Mark." *Oh,* that *part.* "I guess that's how you feel, huh?" It was somewhere between a statement and a question.

"I don't know how to answer that," she said, feeling her defenses go up. Why did she have to apologize for having someone in her life before Seth waltzed back into town? What the hell did he want from her, anyway? "Mark is a sweet guy, but—"

"And, what, you're in love with him all of a sudden?" he asked, sounding unnerved by the mere possibility.

"I never said that."

"So you're *not* in love with him."

"Well, not yet." That came out wrong, but he was flustering her.

"Oh, so you're sleeping with both of us until you fall in love with him?"

"No, I'm not sleeping with *either* of you, remember?"

"Look, Billy—"

"No, you look," she snapped, her chest constricting with anger. "Who are you to say anything to me about who I date? You come back to town and think I'm gonna fall all over you, and then you can go back to Seattle with a giant ego boost. Billy and Seth—part two."

"What? I did not—"

"I thought we could be friends after what happened between us, but forget about it," Billy said as tears blurred her vision. She needed to break this off now, before she got hurt even more. "As far as I'm concerned we're not even friends anymore."

"Billy, get back here!" he called to her as she got out of the car and slammed the door. She hurried up the steps to her brownstone.

"Just go back to Seattle," she said. "Go back to Seattle and forget all about me." She stopped herself from adding, *Again.*

Seconds later Seth peeled away from the curb and out of her life. Once he was gone Billy's street felt eerily lonely and deserted. Could life get any more annoyingly symbolic?

Damn it, Seth cursed as he sped down Beacon Street. He didn't know why he'd gone off the deep end like that. He supposed the sexual and emotional frustration had been building ever since Billy told him they should just be friends, ever since he heard that message from Mark on her machine. He was really pissed at himself. Why did he still hang around her so much? Why had he helped her with her investigation—just so she could go off and be with some other guy? Was he that desperate to spend time with her, that fucking *needy*?

Embarrassment mingled with anger and coursed through him

like hot lava rushing through his veins. *I don't need the aggravation,* he told himself. Billy blew hot and cold; she was an emotional time bomb, a drama queen, a loose cannon.

Of course, all of that would be a lot more relevant if he hadn't already fallen in love with her.

Chapter Twenty-eight

The following morning Corryn heard footsteps on the stairs, and her heart kicked up. Oh, God, he was here; she was really doing this. She remembered what Joe had said about being tired of his place, so she'd left him a message about showing him a vacant apartment on Beacon Hill. She hoped he realized it was merely a ploy to get him alone . . . or maybe she hoped he didn't. Which scenario would make her feel more relaxed?

Tapping her foot nervously, she waited as she heard his steps get louder and closer. She'd been waiting in the apartment for fifteen minutes so far, and she could smell her own perfume, which she hadn't worn in years, so she wasn't sure what was too much. Was it too much if she could smell it?

Anxiously she laced her fingers, then tapped her joined hands on her abdomen as she waited. God, she was so damn attracted to this man. Besides being sexy, Joe seemed like a sweet guy, too, but . . . Well, all in time. Right now she just wanted to see him.

Unbeknownst to Adrienne, she'd actually played a big role in what was happening today. After her pushy antics in cooking class, after shamelessly throwing Corryn at Roynald, she'd made Corryn see the light: She wasn't taking control of her own life. Yes, she was resisting her mother, but she was also standing still. Now Corryn vowed to stop wallowing and go after what she wanted, and what she wanted was Joe.

Ever since Kane had left her she'd been a mass of negativity; she knew it, but could never seem to snap out of it, so she'd tried to embrace it. Now it was just a burden—a weight on her chest. Damn it, she wanted to be happy; she wanted to enjoy life; she wanted to be in love. And she wanted *sex*.

She was going to take more risks, embrace excitement, stop fearing the hunks of the world, and put her antipenis campaign on hiatus. (She'd also toyed with the idea of quitting smoking, but she could only do so much self-improvement at once.)

Now the apartment door opened. "Hello?" she heard Joe say, his voice thick and masculine; it frittered up her nerves, sending little shocks of excitement through her body.

"Hi," Corryn called, feeling her voice catch a little. She smoothed out her navy skirt and white blouse; both were soft and formfitting, and she'd always liked the way they flattered her very subtle curves.

When he finally came into view, Corryn's heart was in her throat. God, he was handsome. "Hi," he said, smiling, coming right up to her, invading her space, making that space special. So he *did* realize that she was trying to seduce him.

With him so close to her, suddenly it was hard to breathe, to focus . . . well, to *speak*. Abruptly she turned around. "So . . . what do you think of the apartment?" she asked, cursing her own cowardice. Her breath stalled as she felt Joe come up right behind her. "I could give you the tour . . ." she stammered. His hands slid over her stomach then, and she swallowed hard. "Um . . . there are two bedrooms. . . ."

"Mmm . . ." he murmured, nuzzling his mouth against the soft, sensitive spot below her ear. His breath fanned the back of her neck, and Corryn grappled with the intense arousal stirring in her body. She broke into a sweat as her mouth ran dry and her knees wobbled, suddenly feeling weak.

"And a large storage space . . ." she mumbled as Joe dragged his mouth down lower, nudging her collar over to trail hot, wet kisses on her skin. He tightened his arms' hold around her, and, unwittingly and so aroused, she tipped her hips back and rubbed against him.

With a growl Joe pushed back, pressing his hard erection into her bottom. Corryn gasped as he slid his hands over her breasts, and Joe said, "Let's forget the tour." The heat from his palms seeped through the flimsy material of her clingy white blouse, and she moaned.

When was the last time she'd moaned? she wondered dizzily. Her mind raced with thoughts like that, and where this could go, and maybe she should turn around and put some space between them, or at least stop grinding her butt against his dick. . . .

She moaned again as Joe massaged her breasts and sucked the curve of her neck.

Forcefully Corryn pushed back, ramming his rock-hard cock against her. "Jesus," he growled, and spun her around. There was something gentle about him, even in his strength. In spite of his size he was a big, erotic teddy bear, and she wanted to strip him, to lick him. He was also the first man she'd fantasized about going down on since Kane—fantasized about taking his cock into her mouth, and actually *not* biting it like a hot dog till he screamed in pain. Talk about progress.

Now Joe was kissing her, holding her to him, and she crushed her mouth against his, kissing him back with everything she had— and she loved how he tasted a little like coffee—and then he backed her up against the wall. Clutching his shoulders, she moaned and licked deep inside his mouth. Slowly Joe's hand ran up her leg and under her skirt, and Corryn broke the kiss, breathing hard. When he fingered the damp crotch of her thong, sweat broke out, not just between her legs, but on the back of her neck, at her hairline—*everywhere*—and through breathy puffs she looked drowsily into Joe's eyes.

As he ran his fingers along the edge of her panties, he smiled at her—a gentle, simple curve of his mouth—and suddenly Corryn remembered why women put up with men . . . and why they were worth it, most of the time.

"Billy, I'm just . . . stunned."

"I know," Billy said sympathetically. "You must be so upset about his death, Aunt Pen. I'm sorry, but I felt I had to tell you."

"No, I don't mean that," Pen said. "I mean, of course I'm sad to hear Ted died, but I just can't believe you were doing all this—investigating, putting yourself in danger—"

"No, I wasn't really in danger," Billy countered, which was met with a chiding look from Aunt Pen, who obviously wasn't putting much weight in that particular technicality.

Billy had asked Pen to stop in at the bakery if she had some time, because she needed to talk to her, and now they were sitting at a table near the counter. Luckily it wasn't too crowded today, though Donna seemed to be lingering up front more than usual. Des was still giving Billy the cold shoulder after what had happened at Atlas.

After making small talk over pastries and decaf, Billy had spilled the whole story of Ted Schneider's murder. She'd explained about the threats she'd gotten, and how they'd ultimately been unrelated to the case, and she apologized for not telling Aunt Pen any of this sooner.

"Please tell me you're not going to look into all this anymore," Pen said now.

"What do you mean? Of course I am. I know if I keep digging—"

"Billy, please." Aunt Pen looked at her with soft entreaty; she knew Billy had a will of her own, but she also knew she could be a pushover. "Ted Schneider is part of my past. That chapter is completely closed. Now, I know I got a little emotional when you first asked me about him, but that's part of life. It doesn't mean I carry around those feelings all the time."

"I know, but—"

Pen shook her head and continued: "I really am happy on my own." It was one of those standard, unoriginal refrains, something people often said but didn't mean, yet right now it sounded so genuine coming from Aunt Pen that Billy nodded and said, "I know."

"By the way, how are your parents? I've been meaning to have them over for dinner, but I've been swamped with two new clients," Pen said.

"Oh, they're fine," Billy said, and told her about Adrienne's designing curtains the last time they talked, which was that morning.

"Oh, that's wonderful! Your mom really had an eye for that," Pen said, smiling.

"I was thinking maybe you two could work together or something."

"That would be great! I wonder if she'd be interested in doing some embroidery on these velvet drapes I want to put in a new house I'm working on."

Billy paused, then asked, "Hey, Aunt Pen . . . how come you and Mom aren't that close?" She couldn't help being a little curious about her aunt's take on the relationship.

Pen hesitated. "Well . . . I would never want to say anything bad about your mother, because she's really a wonderful person. But you have to understand that growing up, Adrienne was always the baby. Your grandparents spoiled her like crazy."

"And then my dad took over," Billy said, half grinning.

Pen chuckled lightly. "In a way, I guess. Anyway, I think she's just used to saying what she feels, making her preferences known, having her opinions taken very seriously." Aunt Pen was apparently the master of euphemisms. "I suppose we're just different. And also . . . um . . ."

"What?"

"Well, I've always wondered if maybe she was a little envious of my interior design business." Quickly, Pen pressed her palms to her chest and qualified: "I could be wrong, of course. It's just . . . well, you probably never noticed, but your mother occasionally makes a snide remark or two."

Billy held her tongue, though she was sitting there thinking, *Occasionally?*

"Anyway, I hope she'll call me about the drapes," Pen added, and came to her feet. Billy stood, too, because her break was over.

"I think she will," she said, smiling.

"Oh, my God," Billy said two days later, stepping back and not really believing. But it was true. "I'm finished," she said to herself. "I'm *finished*!" Around her was the expansive mural she'd dedicated the last couple of weeks to, the one that had renewed her faith in art as her sanctuary. The streetscape was finished!

Frustration welled inside her as she looked around. Jeez, here she was actually done, and there was no one around to tell! Greg Dappaport was on a yachting trip, and she and Seth weren't friends anymore—compliments of Billy's tantrum a few days ago.

Now a hollow ache settled in the pit of her stomach. She'd thought about him a thousand times since their argument—since she'd stormed out of his car and watched him drive away. She hadn't wanted him to go, so why had she said that she did?

How could he have become so unbelievably important to her in such a short time? But he had. And how could she blame him for not pushing for a future together, when she hadn't, either? Instead of simply telling Seth the truth—that she loved him, that she didn't want things to end when he went back to Seattle—she'd rationalized that once Seth was gone, she could maybe fall in love with Mark. Out of sight, out of mind. Maybe with some things, but *Seth*?

Never gonna happen.

Okay—that was it, she'd been a petty-Betty long enough. Now she was going to Seth's to tell him she loved him.

Securing the ventilated tarp in place, Billy put her supplies back in the gallery and headed toward the center of town. On her way she saw a familiar-looking string bean of a woman sitting on a bench, reading *In Touch* magazine.

"Pam?"

Pam looked up. "Oh, hi," she said glumly, and went back to her magazine. She looked so down, like a wilted, extremely tall plant.

"Is everything okay?" Billy asked.

"Yeah, it's just . . . Oh, forget it; it's stupid."

Nodding, Billy started to turn, when Pam said, "It's just that I really want to move out west." Creeping jealousy stopped Billy in her tracks, even though it was a free country, and Pam had every right to move near Seth and put the moves on him. All Billy could control was herself; she was going to tell Seth how she felt about him, and she had no idea what, if anything, would happen next.

"To Seattle, right?" Billy said, sitting next to her.

"No. To L.A. Look, don't say anything, all right?" Pam said. "I know you're friends with that guy Seth, and I don't want to hurt his feelings or anything, but . . . well, Aunt Sally said she'd give me the money to move out west and find an apartment, but the problem is, she seems to have it in her head that me and Seth would be a match made in heaven. Meanwhile he's not my type at *all*. I haven't told Sally, though, because she assumes that if I move out there, I'll get together with Seth and start applying to medical schools."

"Why would she assume that?"

"Because I kind of told her I would. The medical school part, anyway. I just know she's always hoped I'd be a doctor, and now I'm afraid that if I 'fess up about my real dream, she won't approve—won't give me the money." Sighing, Pam leaned back along the bench; there was a wobbly kind of longness about her even when she sat.

"What's your real dream?" Billy asked curiously.

"I want to be an actress."

Whoa—she did not see that coming.

"Really? Well, Pam, if that's what you want to do, you should go for it." She was just giving the advice she was following, as Billy had made up her mind to work full-time as an artist, or struggle to until she couldn't make it anymore.

"I'm just feeling frustrated," Pam said, obviously eager to vent. "I feel like I have to keep up this ruse of being interested in Seth just to please Sally, but how long do I have to keep this going? What's my obligation here? I'm sure Seth's a nice guy and all, but he just does nothing for me."

Billy almost laughed—she'd been so dead wrong about Pam's intentions, she'd been as blind as Sally, but Sally had no excuse because she was family. Which brought her to her next point. "What about your parents? Would they want to help get you set up out there?"

"Oh, no, they're on safari for the next few months."

"Look, Pam, why don't you just tell Sally the truth?" Billy suggested. "And even if she won't give you the money, then *you* come up with a plan of your own—save up for a little while, take an extra job to pay the rent if you have to, just get proactive and make it happen."

"You're right," Pam said, sitting up straighter with a new burst of energy. "I'm just going to come clean. Hey, I know I don't really know you, but thanks." As she stood and started to walk away, her iridescent leisure suit swooshed, and then, abruptly, Pam stopped. "Oh, and remember, please don't say anything about this to Seth, okay?"

"No, of course not," Billy promised.

"I just don't want to hurt his feelings," Pam said before she left. Billy sat there thinking, *No, that was my job . . . but now I'm going to fix it.*

There was a knock at Seth's door while he was packing up his stuff. "Fucking annoying bullshit," he was grumbling. "Fucking had it with this goddamn annoying bullshit."

Another knock, harder, more insistent.

"Yeah, coming," he barked, tossing his suitcase on the bed and running down the stairs. He was going to catch the first flight tomorrow back to Seattle, and he still had a shitload of packing to do. Ever since last night he was in the worst mood, and if this was Sally, she'd better not be bearing more single relatives looking for companions "out west."

When he swung the door open, his mouth dropped. *Billy.* It had been three days since their fight, and seeing her here in front of him filled him with powerful emotions. Relief . . . euphoria . . . *frustration.*

Goddamn it. Why couldn't he just take her in his arms? Why couldn't it be that easy?

"Hi," she said a little cautiously. "I came to tell you something." Seth just stood there, his face blank and unyielding, so she pushed past him into his house. She paused before she turned to face him. "Seth, I wanted to say that I'm sorry." He didn't look opposed to her continuing, so she did. "I'm sorry about all the stuff I said the other night. I didn't mean . . . I was just upset. Because of what you said about Mark—I mean, it just reminded me that you're leaving again and I don't want you to go."

"I'm staying."

She blinked at him. "What?"

"I'm staying," he said again.

"You *are*?"

"Well, I'm going back to Seattle to take care of some things, but then I'm moving back." He'd made Lucas a good offer for the firm, and Lucas had practically jumped through the phone. It was no wonder; the company was in good shape, with the loyal, thriving clientele that Seth had built up. But he couldn't help that he just didn't give a damn anymore. Of course he cared about his career and his future—a lot—but he supposed the shift now was in equating his career with his future, making it the center. There was something hollow and unsatisfying about that. He wanted *more*. He wanted serene nights in Churchill, the maple trees, the glowing autumn sunlight, the stormy blue-black nights. He wanted a woman like Billy to love and to sleep with and to share his life with.

"Why?" Billy asked now, swallowing a lump of emotion clogged in her throat. "I mean, when did you decide this?"

Seth said, "It's been on my mind ever since I got back. Things just feel better around here. To be honest, I don't even like Seattle. It's gray, it's dismal, and . . . I'm lonely as hell. So I'm selling the firm to my VP and buying the house from my mom."

She just stood there, looking stupidly confused and shell-shocked, and Seth came to her, put his hands on her face, touched her cheeks, her heart, and said, "I love you, Billy."

Tears rose quickly, choking her, stinging her eyes, blurring everything, even Seth's beautiful face, and breathing new life into her. "That's what I was gonna say," she murmured, and pulled him down to kiss her. With a short laugh Seth pulled her body up against his, hugging her so tight she could barely breathe, and Billy clung even tighter. "I love you," she said. Her voice was a soft whisper of breath against his shoulder, which was dampening with her tears. "I love you so much."

"I love *you*," he said, and slanted his mouth over hers, capturing it in a slow, deep kiss. It was gentle and warm and lingering, but Billy's urgent mouth coaxed for more.

When their lips parted Seth pressed his forehead to hers, and then he kissed her again—with more intensity, with complete possession— and Billy made a small, strangled sound in the back of her throat and wrapped her arms around his neck, gripping him to her and possessing him back.

"Ohh," she moaned when the kiss broke momentarily, "Seth . . ." His mouth devoured hers again, and he swept her off her feet into his arms and headed up the stairs.

She yelped in surprise. "You're gonna hurt yourself!"

"No, I'm not," he said hurriedly—breathlessly—dragging sucking kisses along her neck as he maneuvered up the stairs and down the hall. Hazily, Billy noted the strength of his arms, the strained curve of muscles as he held her, the way she felt so protected and insulated, and when they got to his room they both fell on the bed. "Let's start in bed this time," Seth said, grinning and tipping her face up so her parted mouth was less than an inch from his.

But he didn't kiss her.

Instead, in a blatantly sexual gesture, he slicked his tongue along her bottom lip . . . and when her mouth dropped open, he licked her tongue. She moaned and rocked her hips on the bed, and Seth climbed on top of her. "I love you so much," he muttered, his voice low and urgent. His words filled her up, drugged her, as his head descended between her breasts and his hands descended on her jeans.

Lightly he bit her nipple through her shirt, just enough to make

her yelp, then yanked her jeans and panties down in one quick motion. He looked down at her half-naked body and groaned, a thick,
guttural sound that reminded Billy how hungry and feral Seth was
in bed—*yum*—and the next thing she knew he had a bared nipple
in his mouth and two fingers inside her, and she was vibrating off
the bed in sharp, jerky movements, begging him not to stop. And
she was so wet she could hear the sluicing sounds of his fingers
fucking her.

"Ohhh," Billy moaned as Seth kissed down her stomach, then
licked her clitoris, sucked on it. "Oh . . . *God.*"

Pushing his fingers deeper, harder, as he licked her, Seth drove
her to the brink of orgasm. Blood rang in her ears, and her heart-
beat sped up, her cheeks burned, and her crotch flamed. Seth rose
up on his knees, whipped off his shirt, tossed it somewhere, then
unbuckled his belt.

She tried to stretch up, to reach for him, but she was too weak,
too spent already, and her body ached . . . and craved *more.* Once
Seth got the front of his pants undone, he shoved them and his
boxers down enough to free his penis, then grabbed a condom from
the drawer in the nightstand. He didn't have to do anything to get
her ready for sex, but he did it anyway, working his hand inside her
again, withdrawing, then thrusting again.

"Oh . . . yes . . . yes," she whispered, begged almost. But instead
of listening to her, Seth withdrew his fingers and stopped touching her altogether, except for the hands on her knees spreading her
legs wide. He paused, just letting her lie there hot, trembling, wet,
needy, and the moments ticked by brutally.

Billy twisted on the bed, arching her back, squirming under
Seth's strength, and finally lost her patience. "Come *on.* . . ."

Seth positioned himself, then thrust inside her. "Goddamn," he
said, his voice tight with strain.

Together they found a rhythm, rocking back and forth, up and down. Seth's hips jerked as Billy rose to meet each thrust, and then, just when the friction got too hot, too unbearable, Seth pulled out.

Why was he stopping? *Why, why, why . . . ?*

They both panted hard as Seth rose up on his knees and just waited.

Waited for *what*?

"Oh!"

He drove inside her again, lifting her legs up to bring him even deeper than before. With her head pressed back into the pillows, Billy moaned, almost silently, because she could barely speak. "Jesus," Seth muttered thickly, and launched into a succession of hard, powerful thrusts, each one driving Billy's hips off the bed until she started to come. Then he growled, dropped his head back, and shook as he came.

Seth gathered her up in his arms and rolled over so they were lying side by side, facing each other. He kissed her forehead, and she could feel the dampness of his skin when she stroked his neck and shoulder. Still vibrating from what had just happened, she felt like she wanted to lie there forever, exhausted, drained, and satisfied.

"I love you," he said. "I think I always have."

Suddenly Billy's nose burned—the acute stinging of impending tears. She mumbled something into the warmth of Seth's chest. It was strong but had a comforting softness, as if it were cushioning her head, making everything feel safe and warm and insulated. And she could hear the strong thumping of his heart, which gave her an inexplicable rush of euphoria. Seth was real, he was really there with her, and he was *hers*. "Billy?" Seth said gently, and snuggled her closer. "Are you okay?" Now she started to cry—again. It would almost be funny if it didn't all mean so much. "What is it, sweetheart? Are those tears of joy?" he asked hopefully.

"I just . . . I just love you so much!" she said, and cried some more. Somehow every emotion she'd struggled to keep in check since she first laid eyes on Seth again was brimming on the surface now, bursting out with very little provocation.

Seth smiled against her sweaty temple, and kissed her there. "You're too much woman for me," he whispered teasingly. Then, smiling, he added, "But you're still all mine."

Chapter Twenty-nine

They'd been lying there for she didn't know how long, talking about the future—and talking about the past. "I wish you'd come with me when I moved," Seth said.

"You never asked," Billy blurted.

"You're right. But I didn't feel I *could* ask. We'd only been dating a few months. I couldn't ask you to pick up everything and move."

"And I couldn't ask you to stay," Billy said, which was obvious.

"Anyway, we're together now," Seth said softly, and kissed her cheek. "Now what about that guy, Mark?"

"Oh," Billy said, waving her hand through the air. "It was never serious with him. I'll tell him it's totally over."

"Okay, good," Seth said, sounding relieved.

Suddenly Billy shot up in bed, just realizing. "Wait, what time is it?"

"Uh . . ." Seth rolled onto his back and checked the alarm clock on the side table. "Almost three o'clock."

"What!" she yelped, hopping up, not even thinking about her nakedness as she scrambled around for her clothes. "I've gotta get back to the city. I'm supposed to work at Bella Donna at three-thirty!"

Seth sat up, running his hand through his rumpled hair. "Wait, I'll drive you," he said, and got out of bed to put his clothes on. Biting her lip, Billy looked lustfully at his body, sleek and muscled, but soft and smooth, and his rounded, perfect butt . . . Okay, this wasn't getting her to work on time.

"No, I don't have time. There's a big detour on the way to my apartment, and I have to stop there first to check on Pike. It'll be faster if I take the train right to Brookline."

"Are you sure?" She nodded. "Okay, but I'll pick you up when you close tonight." Billy smiled at him then—tenderly, euphorically—so filled with emotion she knew the high couldn't last. Or could it? "By the way, is it gonna be weird seeing Melissa tonight?" Seth asked, tossing his shirt over his head.

"No, she's not working." As fate would have it—thank God—she hadn't worked the same shift with Melissa since their confrontation. "So what are you going to do while I'm at work?" Billy added, smiling almost coyly as she wrapped her arms around Seth's waist, pressing her body to his. She rubbed her pelvis against him and felt his dick stir with arousal.

"Don't tease me," Seth said, grinning, firmly putting his hands on her hips to stop the rocking.

"Sorry," Billy replied, smiling.

"Uh-huh. Anyway, I don't know what I'll do. Now that I know you're not in danger anymore, and that what happened with Melissa wasn't related to Ted Schneider's death, I'm feeling a lot more relaxed."

"I still say he was murdered," Billy said.

Seth nodded. "I know it's a possibility, but at this point maybe we should just give up the quest. We seem to have hit a dead end."

"True. And it's not like I have anything great to tell my aunt Pen about him anyway. I'd hoped I'd have some heroic truth to make her feel better about his leaving her, but when I talked to her the other day, I realized that she honestly doesn't *need* any cheering up. Her life is so full and . . ." With a sigh, Billy said simply, "She's perfect as far as I'm concerned."

Grinning down at her, Seth pulled her close and pressed a warm, gentle kiss to her mouth. "I love you," he said softly.

I love you, too, Billy thought, and made a concerted effort not to cry.

After checking on Pike, Billy hopped down the stairs to the lobby of her brownstone, pausing at her mailbox on the wall. She wasn't expecting anything good, just bills and ads, but very disturbingly, she'd set her hopes too high.

Among the bills and ads was a plain white envelope. It had Billy's name and address printed neatly on it, in blue ink and all caps, and there was no return address.

It lay mysteriously in her pile of mail, setting her on edge. Until she reminded herself that the threatening notes she'd gotten before had been from Melissa, who hadn't bothered her since their confrontation, and who ultimately seemed to be harmless. Twisted but harmless.

Running her finger under the seam of the sealed envelope, Billy tore it open. She pulled out the slip of paper inside and unfolded it. "Oh, no," she whispered as she read, feeling her heart slam hard against her ribs and hearing it pound fiercely in her ears.

Her stomach clenched nervously as she pressed a hand to her chest and swallowed a full, solid lump of near terror in her throat. "Oh, no, what's happening?"

She flipped over the torn envelope to check the postmark.

Churchill, Massachusetts.

Swallowing hard, Billy pressed a hand to her racing heart and another to her forehead. She shut her eyes and tried not to panic, but it was too late.

Someone in Churchill had sent her a note that said, *You'd better stop what you're doing—before you die.*

* * *

That evening while Billy was at work, Seth surfed the Net, anxiously trying to find any information he could about Ted Schneider, Greg Dappaport, and a dozen random people in Churchill he could think of. He had been so shocked by Billy's frantic call earlier, telling him about the letter she'd received. He couldn't believe it! He'd thought the threats were over; he'd thought she was completely safe.

Cursing out loud when his computer froze, he banged hard on the keyboard. The mouse kicked back in, which undoubtedly had nothing to do with Seth.

He couldn't even look at the pizza that had gone cold, or the can of Coke he'd popped open right before Billy had called. *Goddamn it.* He hated feeling so powerless to protect her. If it had been up to him he would've insisted that Billy skip work tonight and go straight to the police with him, but she'd called him from the Copley Mall, telling him that she wanted to go, that at least she felt safe there, and that they would go to the police when he picked her up.

He'd left a message for Joe, but was still waiting to hear back, and in the meantime he was a desperate man scouring the Internet for any scrap of useful information. Who the hell could be behind this? Was it someone he *knew*, for chrissake?

When he reached across his desk for a pen and pad, he accidentally knocked his mouse, causing it to click the translation bar on his browser. He hit "back" without even thinking, but then registered something he'd just seen.

Quickly, Seth hit "forward," pressed "reload," and reread a link that came up on his screen: *English Translations of German Surnames.* He zeroed in on one name in particular, and when he clicked on the link, it took him only a few seconds to find the answer.

* * *

Work had gone by pretty uneventfully that night. Donna had been in the back for the past few hours, keeping to herself. Apparently Des was still holding a grudge against Billy, because he'd been giving her the semi–silent treatment all night; finally she'd given up on him, and whenever she'd had a question she'd covertly asked Katie's grandmother to ask *for* her. It was all very ridiculous, and Billy might even laugh if she weren't so preoccupied thinking about the note she'd gotten a few hours earlier.

She'd called Melissa's cell phone to ask her if she knew anything about it—i.e., did it—but predictably Melissa hadn't called her back. But Billy didn't believe it was Melissa. Not this time. She might be bitter, but she wasn't certifiable, and she definitely didn't want to get in trouble with the law. But, God, *who?*

It had occurred to her that maybe Joe had been right. He'd made a comment at Uno's that maybe someone didn't like the idea of Billy and Seth spending so much time together. Billy had blown it off at the time. But now . . .

Pam kept popping into her mind. Not that Pam wanted Seth, but there was no question that her aunt Sally wanted Seth *for* Pam. The question was: How *much* did she want it?

The bakery had been closed for about ten minutes now. The light was shut off in the front, and everyone was working in the back when, all of a sudden, Billy went to shut down the register and heard someone calling her name. She looked up. Seth was standing outside the metal gate that locked the store. Instinctively she checked the clock on the wall, because she wasn't expecting Seth until after cleanup, which wouldn't be for about another half hour.

"Sweetheart, I need to talk to you," Seth whispered, motioning with his hand for her to come closer.

Eyes wide with surprise, Billy darted to the side door, unlocked it, and let him inside. "Seth, what's up? You're early—is everything okay?"

"Yeah, but I couldn't wait till later to tell you this."

"What?"

"I figured out who killed Ted."

"You *did*?" she said, shocked. "Omigod, who? And how did you figure it out?"

"It was an accident. And you're not even going to believe it." After he explained about stumbling onto the wrong Web site, he said, "See, Schneider is a German name."

"Yeah . . ."

"And *'schneider'* in English means 'tailor.' "

"I knew I should've changed my name."

Billy and Seth whipped their heads around. Mrs. Tailor, who must've overheard Seth say that he'd solved Ted's murder, had come quietly out of the back . . . and was dragging Des along with her, holding a knife to his throat.

"All right, now just do what I say and I won't have to splatter Des's guts on the floor," Mrs. Tailor said, her voice holding a steely calm. The image was ridiculous; she was a little wizened woman and Des was a young, quasi-virile man, but she must've caught him at a vulnerable moment, and now the knifepoint was digging so far into his neck, Billy couldn't believe he wasn't bleeding yet.

"Oh, my God, Mrs. Tailor," Billy stammered. "I don't understand this." She looked to Seth for clarification, and he took her hand and squeezed it for comfort. Then it clicked. "Wait a minute—*you're* Gertrude Swain?"

"Ding, ding, ding!" she said mockingly. "That's right. *Formerly* Gertrude Swain—now I'm Gertrude Tailor. Divorced women can keep their married names, can't they?"

Jeez, how stupid did Billy feel? She'd never even known Katie's grandmother's first name. That could've saved her a lot of trouble.

"Please," Des begged, croaking out the words, "please don't hurt me."

"What do you want?" Billy said, panicked. "Please let Des go. He didn't do anything."

"Yeah—we'll just all forget all about this," Seth said, taking Billy's hand in his and squeezing it with fierce affection. Billy gripped it back, praying that God would get her out of this. *God, please, I don't ask for much.*

Okay, I do—but this time I mean it.

"Oh, I'll be happy to let him go," Mrs. Tailor said, "after *I'm* safely gone." She motioned with her head for Seth and Billy to go into the back. "C'mon, move or I slit his throat right here, right now."

They followed her orders for Des's sake. Des was whimpering a little in pain from the knife point, and hunched over sideways, while Mrs. Tailor practically hung on him to keep her knife pressed to his neck. "You two, get in the freezer," she ordered Billy and Seth.

Billy held her hands up and started moving backward to the walk-in freezer. "But I don't understand this," she stammered. " I mean, what happened? Have you been after Ted all this time?"

"I haven't been after him at all. I moved on—left my conniving family behind and started over. Of course, that's not to say my view of the world wasn't tainted. But when I saw Ted at the jubilee . . . what can I say? I couldn't resist the opportunity to give him what he had coming," Mrs. Tailor said, then muttered, "No-good fortune-hunting bastard."

"But he must've recognized you at the jubilee," Seth asked, backing up slowly alongside Billy. "Why didn't he say anything?"

Mrs. Tailor barked a harsh, hateful laugh. "You'd think he would've recognized me, wouldn't you? My heart almost stopped when I saw him at the jubilee. I couldn't decide if I should confront him or just leave before he had a chance to see me. But when he came up to me, I knew he'd seen me. I thought he was going to try to apologize, and I was going to tell him what I really thought of him. Only he *didn't* recognize me. He didn't want to apologize. He wanted a *drink*. And you know what he said to me?"

"No, what?" Billy said, because no one else did. She and Seth were poised at the door to the walk-in freezer, while Des had terror imprinted on his face as Mrs. Tailor pressed the blade harder against his neck.

"He said, 'Hey, Grandma, go make yourself useful.' I almost died. Here I was his *wife*, that motherfucking *asshole*!"

"Oh, man, that's messed up," Des agreed, even though he was still at knife point. But he was right—it *was* messed up. Ted Schneider had been a class-A jackass!

Mrs. Tailor nodded and bitterly continued, "I was furious—livid—so I'd been a few years older than him. But to not even *recognize* me? Well, what can I say? I snapped. The next time he came around, asking me about the nuts, I remembered how severe his allergy was. And I knew chocolate was his weakness, so after he talked to Georgette I fixed a paper plate of double-fudge brownies and took it to him. He never saw it coming."

"But wait," Billy said, confused. "Georgette's fudge brownies don't have nuts in them."

"They do when you crush up nuts, mix them with caramel, and drizzle it on top." *Oh.* "I thought the whole matter was closed, but when I heard you talking to your aunt about how you'd been digging into Ted's death, the threats you'd gotten—and how you were going to *keep* digging—"

"So *you* sent me the note," Billy said as she put it all together. Mrs. Tailor had been working the day that Aunt Pen had come into the bakery, but Billy hadn't paid her any mind. She never did; she was just a sweet, harmless old lady. Or not. "But the letter was from Churchill."

"I mailed it from Churchill to throw you off. It wasn't exactly brain surgery," Mrs. Tailor remarked. "Now get in the freezer!"

"Please, Mrs. Tailor, you don't want to—"

"I'm warning you, Billy," she said, "I like you, but if you don't cooperate, Des here is going to end up with a hole in his throat the size of a muffin." Des groaned at the disturbingly graphic, yet timely metaphor, and Billy and Seth obliged, quickly darting inside the icy-cold, pitch-dark freezer. "And shut the door behind you," Mrs. Tailor snapped.

"Please, Mrs. Tailor, you'll never get away with this. Donna's just upstairs," Billy cried as Seth swung the freezer door shut.

"Actually, Donna left early," Mrs. Tailor called out. "I told her I'd lock up for her. What a fortunate coincidence, huh?"

In the icy darkness Billy shook and shivered, and Seth pulled her close for heat. Running his hands over her body, he tried like crazy to warm her up. "I'm so sorry," he whispered. "I had no idea she was working tonight." They could hear Des pleading on the other side, and Seth felt fucking awful for him. Christ, he'd never meant for this to happen when he'd come to tell Billy what he'd learned. It never even occurred to him that Mrs. Tailor would be working at the bakery tonight. *Goddamn it!* He was solely responsible for what was happening; if Billy or Des got hurt, it would be all his fault.

God, Billy . . . He couldn't let anything happen to her.

"I can't believe this is happening," Billy whispered, still trying to process everything that was happening. Mrs. Tailor—Katie's grandma—a *killer*? And that begged the question . . .

"What about Katie?" she called out, not knowing whether Mrs. Tailor had heard. Teeth chattering, she tightened her arms around Seth, trying to absorb his strength, needing him to settle the fear still skittering along her nerves. With a little less vigor, she called again, "What about *Katie*?" Did she have any idea about all of this?

No, she couldn't; Katie was too sweet and bubbly for the darkness of murder.

"I'll get in touch with Katie in good time," Mrs. Tailor called through the freezer door. "And when I tell her everything, believe me, she'll understand. Sorry it turned out this way, everyone. I really did like you all, but life's tough all over. Believe me, I should know."

There was a loud bang and then silence.

"What's happening?" Billy whispered frantically, not sure if she and Seth should come out. What would Mrs. Tailor do to Des if they did? Or maybe she'd already done it.

"Let's go," Seth said, taking her hand and tentatively leading her out of the freezer.

Mrs. Tailor was gone.

"Oh, my God, Des!" Billy cried when she saw her coworker lying on the floor.

"She must've knocked him out with that," Seth said, pointing to the big metal pan that had rolled under the sink. While Billy raced over and crouched down beside Des, Seth grabbed the phone on the wall and called 911.

"He's still alive," Billy said on a breath. "Oh, thank God."

After practically throwing the phone back on its hook, Seth pulled Billy into his arms, trying to take the cold from her, trying to take away her shiver. "It's all right," he said gently, rocking her quivering body tightly in his arms. "It's over, sweetheart."

Chapter Thirty

Later, when they were lying together in her bed, with Pike Bishop lounging at the foot, they talked about everything that had happened. Pressing her head against Seth's chest, Billy murmured, "Poor Katie. She'll be devastated if her grandmother goes to prison."

"If they catch her," Seth said, remembering that the last they'd heard, the cops were sending out an APB on a little old lady with white hair. Something told him that Mrs. Tailor would slip away—disappear—just as she'd done thirty years before.

"So does this mean that Katie was related to Ted?" Seth asked now.

"No, no. After leaving her family, Mrs. Tailor—Gertrude—met Jeff Spiegal. She married him, but never took his name. He had a thirteen-year-old son when they got married."

"Katie's dad," Seth supplied with a nod.

"Right. Katie mentioned once that her grandfather, Jeff, died several years ago. I guess Gertrude won't be collecting his pension now that she's on the lam . . . but somehow she'll probably manage."

"Man," Seth said on a sigh, "what a night." After he ducked his head down to kiss her neck, he said, "Sorry, I need to shave."

"I like it," she said, smiling at the feel of his roughened cheek against the underside of her jaw. "You know, I still don't understand why Ted left Aunt Pen before he'd gotten any money off her. Do you think maybe he had an attack of conscience? Like maybe he saw how sweet and caring she was, and he couldn't go through with it?"

"Yeah, that's definitely possible," Seth said.

"And so he gave her his 'someone's after me' getaway line early?"

"Maybe," Seth said, looking into her eyes, smiling at her sweetness, her warmth, and how much she wanted to believe that. And hell, maybe it was the truth, but they'd never know now, and some wounds were best unopened. Most, in fact.

"I guess I should just let all this go," Billy said, as though realizing what Seth knew, too. The past was the past—the future was now. Cuddling closer, she tightened her arm around his stomach and sighed into his chest. "I love you so much," she whispered.

"I love you, too, baby," he said, and drifted off to sleep.

When Billy got to Mark's apartment she didn't expect to find it vacant. She'd come here to tell him it was over, and in a bizarre way he'd stolen her thunder. "Hello?" she said, walking in slowly. Her voice echoed and boomeranged back to her. What the hell was going on? Did she have the wrong address? She'd been there only a couple of times, when they first started dating, but she was sure this was the place.

"Can I help you, miss?" She spun around and saw a short, balding man standing in the doorway. "I'm the landlord."

"Oh, yes. Do you know where the guy who lives here is? Mark Warner?"

"Right, Warner. Decent tenant. But he moved out over a month ago."

"He *did*?"

"Broke the lease, said he had insufficient funds."

What? That was crazy. "Well . . . where did he go?" she asked.

"He left a forwarding address," he said. "Not sure what it is, offhand."

"Oh, please, it's really an emergency. I'm his girlfriend, sort of."

His eyebrow quirked up at that. A girlfriend who didn't know he moved. That smacked of psycho-ex syndrome. Still, she smiled sweetly at him. "Please?"

"Follow me," he said, and led her to his apartment on the first floor.

"I'll wait out here," Billy said, when he went inside, leaving the door open.

After rifling through some papers on his desk, he said, "Oh, here it is," and handed her a slip with an address in Natick.

The suburbs?

An hour later Billy sat parked in her parents' car in front of a pink house with a picket fence. A sickening feeling roiled in her stomach. Dear God—Mark was married.

Now she understood why he could hardly ever get together on weeknights. Why he never wanted her to come to his apartment—or the love nest that he'd had for show in the beginning of their relationship. She wasn't sure why he'd gotten rid of it, because obviously he couldn't really have had insufficient funds. Not with the fast-paced, lucrative position he always said he loved so much.

Just then a horrible thought popped into her mind. That time his cell wasn't working, and she'd called him at another number, another woman had answered. Oh, God, that had been his wife! She felt dirty, nauseous—fuming—but she pulled herself together, stormed out of the car, and charged up to the front door.

She rang the doorbell. It was Sunday, so Mark wouldn't be working. *Come on, open up, you bastard!*

"Billy?" he said, obviously shocked when he swung open the front door. "W-what are you doing here?"

"Mark, what in the hell is going on here? I went to your apartment and found out you *moved*? A *month* ago? That *this* is where you live?"

"I can explain," he said quickly.

"Yeah, so can I. You're married."

That stopped him short. "No, I'm not," he said, furrowing his eyebrows.

"You're not? But then—"

"Mark, I'm not going to tell you again!" a woman's voice called from inside the house. "Pick up your clothes!"

"Okay, Mom!" he called back to her, his smile faltering as he braved a slow glance back at Billy. "I moved back in with my parents," he said.

"You did? But Mark, why would you keep that a secret from me? I don't understand this."

"I lost my job," he explained with a hapless shrug. "I ran out of money."

"When did you lose your job?"

"About a week after our first date."

Her eyes shot up. "But whenever I ask you about work, you say it's going great."

"Well, I like to stay positive." So he was a liar.

"But you always said work was the reason you could never do stuff on the weeknights, or sleep over at my place."

"Well, my curfew's eleven, but my mom really doesn't like me out on school nights." So he was a mama's boy, to boot. In fact, now she realized it had been his *mom* who'd answered the phone that night. "Billy, I'm sorry I lied. I just didn't want you to know that I lost my job and that I had to move back home. I didn't want *anyone* to know."

"But Mark, you could've told me. And you have so many friends—couldn't anyone help you out? Let you crash with them till you got back on your feet?"

He looked a little perplexed at that. And then Billy grasped the obvious: Just because he knew a thousand people didn't mean he was *close* to a thousand people. In fact, it almost guaranteed that he wasn't. Now it made sense why Mark had been so thrifty lately—especially the night he'd made them split fries and a soda from Burger King, then horded the free ketchup packets.

Shaking her head, she said, "Oh, wow . . . I never saw any of this coming."

"So I guess we're done, huh?" he asked plaintively. But he clearly saw the writing on the wall. There wasn't that much between them in the first place, and their relationship had been full of lies, anyway.

"Yeah, we're done," she agreed. "But I hope things work out for you."

"Thanks. You, too."

Before she turned to go, she reached into her wallet and pulled out Kip Belding's card. "Here, maybe this guy can help."

"Oh, thanks," he said, and took the card.

"Sure."

On the way down the steps, she paused, then angled her head back. "By the way . . . how do you feel about hospitals?"

"Did you ever get the feeling that you've been going through life without paying attention?"

"What do you mean?" Seth asked, rubbing her shoulders, sitting behind her in his tub. They had a bottle of Shiraz and candlelight. Billy sank happily against him, feeling his erection pressed against her bottom, turning her on already.

She sighed. "I just mean, in just a couple weeks, I found out that half the people I know have been living a lie of some kind or another. Melissa, Mrs. Tailor, Mark. What's next? If I find out you are, I'll die," she threw in quickly, flashing him a small but hopeful smile.

Smiling back, he kissed her shoulder, then leaned his cheek against it. "I'm not. What you see is what you get, I swear." A thrilling anticipation bubbled inside her, because what she saw was already too much to hope for.

Epilogue

One year later

"Exactly how many times can we 'christen' one desk?"

Seth laughed into her neck, kissed her gently there, then mumbled something into her naked shoulder.

"What?" Billy said, giggling and pushing him up so she could hear. She was lying on top of the desk with her robe open, and Seth was lying on top of her with his jeans undone.

"I said, it's your fault for being all over me," he replied, grinning.

She let out a laugh. "I just came in to kiss you good morning!"

"Well, there you go."

"Seriously . . ." she said, pushing out from under him. "We've gotta get ready." Seth had gotten up early to work on putting Billy's studio together, as he had every morning for the last month. They'd transformed the guest room in the Churchill house into a studio for Billy, which had meant ripping up the carpet and carving out a larger window for more light. Seth had built her a large tilted desk for her to draw on, and bought her an easel for her to paint on.

Her business was still brand-new, but it was growing quickly in Churchill, especially with Greg Dappaport's connections. She'd done portraits for the polo club, and afterward members of the yacht club had wanted to commission her, too. Apparently they all had the same self-aggrandizing flair for interior design—but hey, it worked for her.

Seth had helped her lease an empty shop on Main Street, where she sold landscape paintings she'd done, framed in all sizes, and painted portraits upon arrangement. The local junior high had called her last week and asked if she'd come in and do a painting workshop for the kids. Things were definitely coming along. Plus, Seth had assured her that come summertime, the tourist trade would give her shop a jolt into the black.

And she trusted his judgment, of course, because he was still a savvy business consultant, even though he'd sold his Seattle firm to come back to Churchill. In fact, right now he was laying the groundwork for a new company based in Massachusetts. Honestly, Billy didn't know how he did it all . . . or how she'd gotten so lucky.

Sometimes she missed her job at Bella Donna, but she still stopped in. In fact, she'd ordered her wedding cake last week. While she was there, she'd chatted with Katie—who still claimed that she didn't know where her grandma was. (Nobody truly believed that.)

"Come on; let's hurry," she said, smacking his butt now, and looking ultrainnocent when he glanced back at her. They were meeting Corryn and Joe at the Churchill Art Gallery, where Dappaport was unveiling Billy's newest mural, on the side of the building that faced the water. Her first one had gotten such great reception that she couldn't pass up the chance to work for Dappaport again. She always remembered how Dappaport saw something in her— believed in her—before he really had any reason to, and she couldn't help thinking that underneath his silk neckerchiefs and fake accents, he was actually one of the most genuine people she'd ever met.

"Okay, I'm almost ready," Seth said, and he zipped up his jeans and tossed his shirt back on. "Let me just finish sanding the drawing table."

Billy knew it was futile to argue, so she came up behind him, wrapped her arms around his waist, and pressed a kiss to his back, feeling the heat through his T-shirt. "I love you," she whispered. But he didn't hear her over the rasping of the sander, and anyway, it was just as well, because if he looked at her now, she might start to cry—and for no other reason except she was happy.

Loving Seth was better the second time around. And to think it all began with just a little crush.

Jill Winters discovered her love for writing fiction while she was procrastinating on her master's thesis at Boston's many bookstores and coffee shops. A Phi Beta Kappa, summa cum laude graduate of Boston College, she has taught women's studies and is the author of two previous novels, *Plum Girl* and *Blushing Pink*.

Visit her online at: www.jillwinters.com.